Praise for *Blowout*

"David Hagberg is a proven master of the thriller genre, and Senator Byron Dorgan brings a unique insider's view on politics and the world. Together they've woven a complicated tale, told deceptively simple, that will leave you wanting more. Plenty of sizzle in this page-turner."
—Steve Berry, *New York Times* bestselling author of *The Jefferson Key*

"A unique, thought-provoking, and, above all, ceaselessly exciting novel about today's hidden security threat: our willingness to overlook evil in our addiction to foreign energy supplies. The pace will make you sweat, the plot will make you think, and the peril is very real."
—Ralph Peters, *New York Times* bestselling author of *The War After Armageddon*

"An edge-of-the-seat thriller about energy that will stretch your imagination and keep you guessing until the very last page."
—Former U.S. Senate majority leader Tom Daschle

"This book hits the bull's-eye on our energy challenge. How to end our addiction to foreign oil by finding new ways to produce energy here at home while at the same time protecting our environment? *Blowout* combines a healthy imagination about an energy future with fast-paced action."
—Former governor of New Mexico and U.S. energy secretary Bill Richardson

"The authors smoothly blend near-constant action and cutting-edge science." —*Publishers Weekly*

"Plenty of action and narrow escapes . . . An enjoyable and fast-moving tale that will leave readers eagerly awaiting the next one." —*Kirkus Reviews*

BLOWOUT

BYRON L. DORGAN

AND

DAVID HAGBERG

A TOM DOHERTY ASSOCIATES BOOK
NEW YORK

This is a work of fiction. All of the characters, organizations, and events portrayed in this novel are either products of the authors' imaginations or are used fictitiously.

BLOWOUT

Copyright © 2012 by Byron L. Dorgan and David Hagberg

All rights reserved.

Map by Rhys Davies

A Forge Book
Published by Tom Doherty Associates, LLC
175 Fifth Avenue
New York, NY 10010

www.tor-forge.com

Forge® is a registered trademark of Tom Doherty Associates, LLC.

ISBN 978-0-7653-6587-3

Forge books may be purchased for educational, business, or promotional use. For information on bulk purchases, please contact Macmillan Corporate and Premium Sales Department at 1-800-221-7945 extension 5442 or write specialmarkets©macmillan.com.

First Edition: March 2012
First Mass Market Edition: March 2013

Printed in the United States of America

0 9 8 7 6 5 4 3 2 1

*To Kim, for thirty years
and many, many more* . . .
—BYRON L. DORGAN

For Laurie, as always

—DAVID HAGBERG

ACKNOWLEDGMENTS

My heartfelt thanks to Mel Berger at William Morris Endeavor (WME) for his role in helping make this project a reality. No author could have a better or more knowledgeable advocate in the book business than I have had with Mel Berger. He's the best!

This book owes its existence to an idea from Tom Doherty at Tor Books, who has an abiding interest in a clean and renewable energy future. Tom believes that new and interesting ideas can awaken the public consciousness through books of fiction. I agree!

The ideas and guidance by Bob Gleason at Tor Books have also played a major role in the completion of this book. Thanks to both of them for the inspiration and encouragement. And a special thanks to Katharine Critchlow at Tor Books for keeping us on schedule and handling the myriad of details needed to get a book ready for publication.

And finally my admiration and gratitude go to my co-author, David Hagberg. Pairing me to work with an unbelievably talented fiction writer like David has been a burden for him, I'm sure. When the two of us conspired on a plot that would represent a leap ahead in thinking about energy policy in the future, I learned about David's facile mind and creative imagination. It's clear why he has been such a successful fiction writer over so many years. It has been a treat to work with him on this book and to brainstorm with him about our energy future. Thanks, David!

AUTHORS' NOTE

We may have already reached the carbon dioxide tipping point, which in effect means that even if the planet reduced its carbon emission to zero, it may take a thousand years for Earth to heal itself. As dramatic as this might sound, the situation is closer to reality than even Al Gore's *An Inconvenient Truth* was.

Of course, doing nothing is not an option. We have to act now, to at least mitigate the effects of the poisons we are pumping into the air.

One possibility is a proposal called the Dakota District Initiative, which is to our environment what the Manhattan District Project (to develop the atomic bomb) was to ending World War II.

Carbon dioxide emissions into our atmosphere will kill us. Like the nuclear clock of the sixties, the carbon dioxide death zone clock is at one minute before midnight. Added to that is the threat to our survival as a nation from the dependence on foreign oil.

Our entire planet is being held hostage, and there is no guarantee unless something is done soon—something drastic—that the ransom will be paid and the victim rescued.

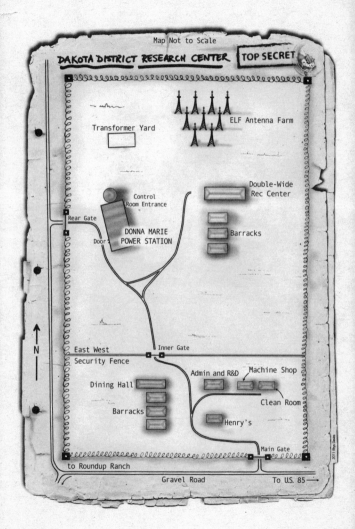

BLOWOUT

Baytown, Texas
ExxonMobil Baytown Oil Refinery

THE PROBLEM IS that once you teach a man how to fight, and then place him in harm's way on the battlefield, he just might get a taste for killing that's so deeply embedded in his soul that he can't simply walk away. It happens to one extent or another in every conflict, but escalated after the first Iraqi war, which saw an increase in post-traumatic stress syndrome casualties and the start of a serious number of GIs committing suicide. It was crazy.

They were volunteers, actually financial conscripts with nowhere else to turn for jobs, from the poorer sections of Chicago and New York, the barrios of Los Angeles, and places like Michigan City, Philly, Duluth, and Waterloo, and remote spots in Montana, Wyoming, and Idaho, and sometimes from the Yoopers, as they are called in the backwoods of Upper Peninsula Michigan. Lots of them drifting toward fringe and radical groups like the Posse Comitatus, Armed Forces of National Liberation, Aryan Nations, the Covenant, the Christian Patriots Defense League, the United Underground, and a host of others.

Warren Kowalski, about to turn fifty-five tomorrow and under five-five with narrow features and the small man's chip on his shoulder, lay on his belly in a ditch twenty feet from the back maintenance gate of the ExxonMobil fuel refinery—the sixth-largest port in the world—sprawling across thirty-four-hundred acres along the Houston Ship Channel, the air stinking of gasoline and a dozen other chemicals. Employing four thousand people, the facility was vital not only to Southeast Texas, but to the entire U.S. economy. Without its six hundred thousand barrels of oil per day the engines of the entire nation would be seriously hurt; gasoline prices at the pump would spike.

But Baytown was more than a facility to refine oil into diesel fuel and gasoline, it was also the largest petrochemical facility in the world, producing olefins used for making a wide variety of plastics; aromatics used for solvents and mostly as additives to gasoline to raise its octane rating; synthetic rubber for tires; polyethylene, the most widely used plastic in the world; and polypropylene, used for everything from medical equipment, clothing, and even the plastic tops on soda and water bottles; along with a host of other oil-based compounds absolutely vital to modern life and commerce.

And Kowalski and his assault force of five men—all of them veterans from the Iraq-Kuwait wars, all of them highly decorated, all of them Posse Comitatus, men with deep-seated hatreds and angers—were here to destroy the place.

It was late, after two in the morning, the sky overcast, no moon, a very light drizzle—all factors, except for the rain, that Kowalski, the sarge, had planned for.

"Hit them when they least expect it," he'd told his people; Higgins and Marachek who'd come over from

Montana out of the Brotherhood, Laffin and Ziegler from the Upper Peninsula, and Dick Webber, who had connections at Fort Hood, which got them the M-16s and Colt 1911A1 .45 pistols.

Good men all of them, Kowalski, thought, preparing to give the signal.

He'd been born and raised in Michigan City, his father, brothers, uncle, and several cousins all working at the steel mills, from which he had escaped by joining the army two years before Iraq started to go bad.

He'd just been a grunt, corporal a couple of times, but then got busted because he couldn't take orders, and he liked his beer and pot combo a little too much, yet the guys had taken to calling him "Sarge" from the beginning because this was his plan, and he saw no need to correct them, as long as they followed orders. Nor had he known any of them before three weeks ago, when he'd posted a notice on the Posse Comitatus news board on the Net and on-site in Billings and Sault Sainte Marie for an op to, in his words: "Gain payback for the bastards who kept extending us no matter what it did to our gourds." It was the fat cats who made obscene profits off the backs of the grunts with their noses in the mud and shit, who back in the world owned steel plants, coal mines, oil wells, and power stations. Millionaires with their noses up the Pentagon's ass.

"And just like in Kuwait and Iraq during the first dustup with the burning wells spewing black shit into the air which fucked us up royally, they're doing the same thing with their refineries—fucking up the air so we can't even breathe it."

The guys either didn't give a shit about his message or didn't understand—or both; they were just interested in getting back into it. They wanted to shoot someone, blow up some shit. The air pollution thing didn't matter, most of them were heavy smokers, especially Kowalski with his two and a half packs of Camel unfiltereds.

But for Kowalski the message was everything—or at least that's what he'd convinced himself was the truth—though if he was being honest with himself in a rare moment, too rare his ex-wife would have said, he was really just like the others. A disaffected grunt who hadn't gotten enough; he wanted more, message or not. Knock the entire bastard country back to the horse-and-buggy days. Simpler times, when men were men and no one fucked with them.

They had comms units with earbuds and vox-operated mikes attached to the lapels of their night fighter black camos that they'd each paid for out of their own pockets. Kowalski keyed his: "Go in ten," he whispered. The units were low power, so there was little chance their traffic would be intercepted even if anyone was listening, which was doubtful. Attacks like this had hardly ever happened since the antiwar riots of the late sixties and early seventies.

"Roger one," Higgins came back. Followed by the other four.

"This is a supercritical refinery," Kowalski had explained at one of their initial briefings in Kalispell before they'd begun field training prior to moving south.

"Who gives a damn, Sarge," Marachek had asked. He was angrier than the others. His twin brother had died in his arms in the middle of a firefight across the border with Pakistan. Officially his death had been listed as an accidental self-inflicted gunshot wound. Thirteen of them.

"You all need to give a damn, because what I'm trying

to tell you is that just about everything inside the plant is sensitive to gunfire and especially to C4."

"So we take out the gate guard, go in, blow up some shit, waste a few dudes, and get the fuck out," Laffin—JP to the squad—had said. He wasn't angry, he was simply the craziest of the lot. He lived with his wife and their two daughters in a dilapidated mobile home parked in the woods outside of Bergland in the Upper Peninsula's Ottawa National Forest.

"Do that and you just might get all of us killed," Kowalski had answered, tamping down his own anger. He wanted to tell them about the point he was trying to make, but he gave it up as a lost cause because sometimes even he didn't know exactly what his point was.

"All right, we're listening, Sarge," Ziegler had said.

"We're after shutting them down for a long time. Make 'em think about the shit they're doing. About the crap they're doing to us. So we're going to maximize our strike, by setting so many fires that nobody will be able to put them out for a very long time. First off we set C4 charges at the base of each cracking tower, and then we take over the computer center from where we can open every fuel-routing valve in the entire complex so that when the C4 blows, the entire place will go up in a wall of flames. With any luck the fire will spread to the two main chemical plants, plus the polymers center and the olefins plant. All that shit will go up like Roman candles on the Fourth of July."

"Let's get it on," Ziegler had said. He was a small kid from somewhere in Southern California who thought he was good-looking enough to be in movies. No one else thought the same, and he was in a permanent state of surprise.

"Pop any of this stuff at the wrong time, and we're all broiled meat. Happen so goddamn fast you wouldn't know what hit you. One second you're a swinging dick, the next you're on the menu."

"We're listening," Webber had said. He was the steadiest of them all. In Iraq he'd been in a bomb disposal unit. Called for steady nerves and zero day-before shakes.

"Soon as we hit the back gate the clock starts, and the cops will come a runnin'. We need to get in, set our charges, get out, and beat feat."

Houston was only twenty miles to the west where Kowalski had a born-again sister who'd agreed to put them up. She thought she could help her brother and save a few souls in the bargain.

"What about the plant personnel?" Webber had asked, even though he and the others already knew the answer.

And Kowalski didn't even have to think about it. Payback time. "We waste them."

He looked at his wristwatch. "Now, now, now," he said into his lapel mike, and he got to his feet, scrambled up onto the blacktop, and zigzagged through the darkness into the lights over the gate.

He was point man, peripherally aware that his people were on his tail right and left, his main concentration on the gatehouse where a lone guard was supposed to be stationed. But the gatehouse was empty, and that struck him as more than odd, unless the guy was taking a nap on the floor, or had gone somewhere to take a piss.

Webber passed him on the right, molded two small lumps of C4 on the gate's hinges, and tied them together with one timer. "Fire in the hole!" he shouted, and he ran a few yards to the left.

A few seconds later a pair of impressive bangs cut the night air and the gate fell to the ground with a clatter.

Kowalski hesitated for just a moment. No sirens. And the silence bothered him. He'd been told that the gates were wired to alarms. Open one without the proper procedure and all hell would break loose. But nothing. And stepping over the downed gate he glanced inside the guard shack—the muzzle of his M16 moving left to right—but no one was inside, taking a nap or otherwise. No one.

They'd come from Lake Charles, Louisiana, on I-10 through Beaumont across the Texas border, past Baytown itself then down State Road 146 to La Porte just across the ship canal from the refinery where a friend of the Posse had a shrimp boat waiting for them; disenfranchised men, wanting to strike out at some unknown force that was holding them back from what they felt was rightfully theirs even though none of them, Kowalski included, could say what that might be.

Shit or get off the pot, his daddy who'd come through 'Nam and who used to beat him regularly was fond of saying. It worked.

The off-loading docks where the oil tankers dropped their cargoes were just below the main atmospheric distillation towers, from which gas and light naphtha was released from the top end, followed below by heavy naphtha, jet fuel, kerosene, and diesel oil—and it was to this five-story-tall complex that Kowalski directed his fighters.

Friends, actually, because in the manner of most military units the men you slept and ate with, the ones you trained beside, and the ones who went into battle with you to possibly die, became friends practically the instant you all came together. And Kowalski felt damned good. He—they—were on a mission.

Thirty yards from the tower from which a maze of pipes carrying highly volatile fuels and gases spread in every direction, strong lights suddenly illuminated the entire refinery complex, and Kowalski pulled up short as a pair of APCs came around from both sides of the massive distillation unit, and at least fifty armed men he immediately recognized as Texas Army National Guard showed up in flanking positions.

"Lay your weapons on the ground." An amplified voice rose above the noise from the complex.

They had the fatigues and the weapons, but in Kowalski's estimation most of them were probably nothing more than weekend warriors who'd never seen combat.

"Do it now," the voice, probably some rat-ass lieutenant, ordered.

"Pussies," Kowalski muttered.

But the sons of bitches had the firepower, and the position.

Kowalski would have liked to see his ex-wife's son Barry come back from Afghanistan—the kid was supposed to be tough. He was twenty or thirty or something like that—Kowalski tended to forget that kind of shit—and he'd been hard on the boy and his mother, but it was a tough old world out there. And getting tougher by the day. So maybe he'd done them a favor.

"Lay down your weapons!"

Kowalski glanced over at Marachek who was grinning like a madman.

"Fuck it, Sarge," Marachek said, and Kowalski agreed.

And he raised his M-16 and started running toward the tower as he began firing, his men right behind him, firing as they ran.

He never felt the shot that killed him. One moment he was alive and the next he was dead. But he'd always figured that sooner or later he'd end up in a better place.

The Baytown attack, as it came to be known in places

like Montana and the Upper Peninsula, rose to a cult-level status among ecoterrorists. Brave men who'd been willing to give their lives in a fight to save the planet!

And so the struggle began.

Des Moines, Iowa
The Trent Building
Three Years Later

THE TROUBLE WITH making a lot of money is that after a while many people can't stop. So after the usual real estate and stock market investments, which can be reduced to a sort of science, and after the IPOs for innovative start-up companies, and even for some bright, ears-to-the-ground entrepreneurs who invested hundreds of millions in micro-loans mostly in the Far East, some kind of an end comes in sight. All too soon.

So the exotics were invented; flash trading in which computers bought and sold stocks in microseconds, making profits in the tenths and hundredths of points that over a period, say a year, amounted to a billion or so.

Or naked credit default swaps that was a type of insurance—though it was never called that lest it be regulated—in which the investor bet that the company he was backing would fail so he could collect a payout. Insure your neighbor's house for two hundred thousand, pay the premiums, and if it burned down you collected on the policy. More of a high-stakes wager than anything else.

And that had come from the brain of Robert B. Muskett, the boy genius over at U.S. National Trust.

Or derivatives, which was another sort of insurance policy, or hedge funds, in which you bet on futures you didn't own. It got to the point that the oil derivatives alone were worth eight or ten times the total amount of all the oil in the ground everywhere on the earth.

When these investments were leveraged for ten cents on the dollar, and the markets began to rumble, a lot of very rich people began to get nervous. A ten-billion-dollar position that lost only one billion was gone, bankrupt, because the owners of the exotic were left with a bill of nine billion to make up the difference; what in the old days had been termed a margin call.

Which was exactly the barrel of the gun Donald Stearns Wood, D.S. to his associates, was looking down, and he was getting more than desperate.

On an early Friday evening in the middle of a January Iowa snowstorm his salvation came to him in the form of a courier-delivered message his secretary handed to him as he was about to leave his twelfth-floor office across Walnut Avenue from the Capitol Building.

"This just came for you," she said.

It was a FedEx envelope with a security seal, warning of federal penalties for unauthorized use. The return address was simply Command Systems, and D.S.'s hand wanted to shake, but he smiled pleasantly. "You'd best be leaving now, Mrs. Cordell, lest you get stuck here for the weekend."

"I was on my way out the door when this came in," he said. She'd been his secretary for fifteen years, including two bust times when Trent Holdings was in serious trouble. And during that time the sixty-year-old woman, who was dignified in looks and deeds, had learned when not to question her boss too closely about things she did not understand. Like a message with no clear return address.

"Take care now," he told her. She lived out in Windsor Heights, and one of her perks was a company car and driver who picked her up for work and dropped her off at home. On a night like this it was just as well, because the buses had almost stopped running, but one of the company's Hummers would get through.

D.S. went back into his office, laid the envelope on the desk, and went to the floor-to-ceiling windows to watch the slanting flow of windblown snow and the flashing lights of the snowplows below on the streets, long enough for him to catch his breath.

At forty-eight, D.S. had all of his hair though it was snow white, but his face had sagged over the years so that he now looked, and sometimes acted, more like a bulldog with old-fashioned white muttonchops than the director of Trent Holdings, one of the wealthiest hedge funds anywhere on the planet, which invested in derivatives and credit default swaps with total on-paper assets approaching one trillion dollars. Almost all of it leveraged, of course. So leveraged that the company was cash poor. Except for a pension fund spin-off the firm was privately owned. It had never sold stocks; the public had no stake nor was it a corporation so the government regulators did not have access to its books. Its cash-poor position—cash poor almost to the point of insolvency—was a secret so far.

Staring out the window he remembered a *Wall Street Journal* senior editor right here in this room eight or ten years ago, who was writing an article on D.S's remarkable success story, and who called him the most savvy investor ever—his results were even more reliable and spectacular than Warren Buffet's.

"Warren is good at playing the trends, and Bill Gates is even better at inventing things and cornering the market," D.S. had told the editor. "But I make my money the old-fashioned way; by convincing people, by whatever means, to do things my way."

"You've been accused of stretching ethical boundaries."

D.S. clearly remembered the sly accusation, and he'd laughed in the man's face. "Profits have never been about ethics. It's the American way."

"But federal regulations—"

"Have never done a single thing to stop or even soften the boom-to-bust natural order of the markets."

"What you're saying, in effect, is for the government to do whatever it wants to appease the voters, while you do whatever you think is necessary."

"Exactly. What you've just stated, in a nutshell, is Harvard MBA one-oh-one."

"That's cold," the senior editor had said, who over a twenty-five-year career had reported on the titans of finance and industry in the U.S. and abroad.

And D.S. had smiled. "Haven't you learned by now that there's nothing cold about making money?" And before the editor could say anything else, D.S. added: "Ask the holders of the pension funds I manage if they think my method of making money is cold."

And the editor had politely said his thanks. A week later a story appeared in the *Wall Street Journal*, the upshot of which was: hate him or love him, D. S. Wood knows how to make money at least as well as the robber barons at the turn of the century—the century before last, that is. The article had tweaked his vanity.

Tonight he and his wife were hosting a dinner party for Iowa Senator Justin Holmes, who was beginning to put out campaign feelers for a run at the presidency in four years, and depending on what the man had to say, D.S. would support him at least for the short term.

"Keep your options open," he told his people. It was the golden rule at Trent, and let everyone else figure it out themselves at their own peril.

God, he loved this. Or had until the last couple of years. If it all went bust he would be facing a lot of years in a federal penitentiary somewhere—the rest of his life, actually. Because he'd cut a lot of corners making Russian and Chinese deals for oil fields in Iran and Iraq and mineral deposits in Afghanistan, most of them strictly against U.S. law. He'd possibly end up as roommates with guys like Bernie Madoff. But he wouldn't allow it to happen to him. No power on earth would make him submit to something like that.

He poured a small snifter of a respectable Napoleon brandy at the sideboard and sat down at his desk, opened the envelope, and read the one-line memo.

After a moment he telephoned his wife. "I'll be a little late, please give the senator my apologies."

"A problem, Donnie?" she asked. They'd been married for twenty-three years, and she was the only one who called him by that name.

"Nothing earth-shattering, sweetheart, but it's just something I have to deal with tonight."

"I understand," she said. "Take care."

"You, too," he said tenderly, and he hung up and read the memo a second time.

When he was finished he shredded the thing, and sat back with his brandy to think things out before he called Bob Kast, president of Command Systems, which was a shell company for the contractor service Venture Plus, headquartered in South Carolina. Bob had made his chops in Iraq, getting his foot in the door after Blackwater's stumble from grace. He was a man who got things done.

"Basically you can't keep doing business as usual, is that what you're telling me?" Bob had asked at their first meeting at Venture's sprawling training base in the Blue Ridge Mountains outside Greenville.

"Not if it pits me against Washington," D.S. had said, still not in full panic mode.

"And you think that's a possibility. One that you want me to find out for you. Pitting me against Washington."

"Exactly what I want."

"It'll cost."

"Money is no object, Bob," D.S. had promised. "Time is important to me, so don't dawdle."

The problem was carbon dioxide and other global warming gases being spewed into the atmosphere. It was not the fact that our increasing dependence on foreign oil was bankrupting us, but that the financial problem was only secondary to the fact that most scientists were coming to the consensus that the U.S. was on the verge of reaching some tipping point where no matter what it did to save itself it would be too late.

Carbon dioxide was putting the entire planet into a death zone of unbreathable air, with drastically rising temperatures and sea levels and no place for people to run. No place to hide.

The burning of fossil fuel was the culprit, and the majority of Trent Holdings' derivative stake was in oil. They had gotten hold of a dinosaur's tail and were being dragged to death, but they couldn't let go lest the beast turn around and devour them on the spot. And the issue had become one of the major security problems facing the U.S. Not only was the civilian population being held hostage by OPEC, but except for nuclear-powered naval vessels and a few green-fueled ships, our military was totally dependent upon fossil fuels. Interrupt the supply and our ability to defend the country would suffer.

It had taken Kast's people only two months to come up with the answers, and D.S. had flown in secret down to South Carolina last November where over a credible filet and a very good red, he'd been told for sure something that he'd been guessing at for nearly three years.

In the forties when the outcome of the war in Europe and the Pacific was anything but certain for the U.S., and when military intelligence uncovered evidence that the Nazis were feverishly working on a new wonder weapon—a bomb so powerful that it could wipe out an entire city—Albert Einstein wrote a letter to F.D.R. urging that the U.S. develop such a weapon first to ensure the survival of the free world.

The top secret Manhattan District Project was created, its main research and development facility located in a remote mountain location north of Albuquerque called Los Alamos. Working with the brightest minds in universities and industrial corporations across the country, the charter was to design, develop, and test an atomic bomb. Despite war shortages, the project was given top priority; it got whatever money and materials—no matter how restricted—it needed. The goal was to drop bombs on Germany and Japan to end the war.

"We're in the same situation now," Kast had reported. "It's called the Dakota District Initiative, and just like Los Alamos, the main research-and-development center is in a really remote part of the country. In this case the North Dakota Badlands not too far from the Montana border."

"It's because of the Baytown near miss," D.S. said, amazed at how simple—and dangerous to him personally—this might be. "Tell me."

"You're exactly right. If that had succeeded and the refinery destroyed it would have driven gasoline to twenty, and some experts thought fifty dollars per gallon. Two months later the president put together a bipartisan coalition of congressmen, plus high-ranking representatives from Homeland Security, NOAA, the CIA, and the National Security Agency, a few cabinet members including Treasury and Interior, the FBI, and the Pentagon—mostly for site security—plus representatives from the Energy Security Leadership Council and the organization SAFE—Securing America's Future Energy—along with the top minds at a dozen universities and as many corporations, including Microsoft, IBM, Westinghouse, and GE. Their preliminary black budget was five hundred billion dollars that was buried in the Iraq and Afghanistan wars and then supplemented in the bank and mortgage bailout package. It was either that or bankrupt the nation. No choice, really. It was sink or swim on the largest scale possible since the Second World War."

D.S. remembered that the entire concept had come crashing down around his head and shoulders like some Mount Rushmore that had fallen to pieces. The initiative had something to do with coal, which was the most abundant fuel source the U.S. had within its borders—enough by most conservative estimates to easily take care of all our projected energy needs for at least the next five hundred years. Half a millennium.

The problem was, of course, that burning coal to produce steam from water to drive turbines that in turn drove generators to produce electricity was just about the dirtiest way to do it. Wind power engineering was coming along, and so was solar. And while the country would get more energy in the future from both sources it would not solve the energy supply problem. Nuclear power stations produced material that would be dangerously radioactive for tens of thousands of years, and the plants were prohibitively expensive.

Hydroelectric was projected to begin to fail in the near term because global warming was not only reducing snowfall and glaciers from which the rivers to produce the power were fed, but rainfall patterns were changing, and not beneficially. Along with the dozens of other devices and schemes for producing power, coal, and to a much lesser extent natural gas and oil, were the only reliable means. But coal was dirty. It would kill the environment.

It had always been his goal to fight the nukes replacing them with oil—but just for the short term.

The fact was he probably had thirty years or so left to live, and he meant to live those years in comfort, making money until the day he died.

"Coal," D.S. had said again, aware that Kast was looking at him like a biologist looking through a microscope at a bug he wasn't familiar with. "Are you telling me that they've found a way to use coal to make electricity without pumping out carbon dioxide? Something cheaper than sequestration? Something usable? Something practical?"

"I don't have all the answers," Kast had admitted. "Just the location of the facility, south of Medora, and the possibility that whatever they're about to try has something to do with microbiology."

"How did you come up with that?"

"The chief scientist on the project is Dr. Whitney Lipton, who until six years ago was the leading microbiologist at the CDC when she suddenly retired. At age twenty-seven."

The idea of injecting a coal-eating bacteria into pulverized coal in a sealed environment, producing methane that could be burned instead of the coal, and with a significant drop in CO_2, had been bandied about by environmentalists over the past decade or so. But no one could make it work on a practical basis; the decrease in CO_2, though significant, wasn't worth the trouble and there was the risk of methane escaping into the atmosphere—which would cause a lot more damage to the ozone layer.

Not nearly enough information. "What else?" D.S. demanded.

"We don't have all of the details, except that the buzz on the Hill is that they're trying some big experiment in thirteen months. In mid-December next year, just before Christmas. And it's supposed to be significant. They're talking about the *'gadget.'*"

D.S. spread his hands.

"That's what they called the first atomic bomb," Kast said.

And D.S. had come up with his decision practically at the speed of light. His survival was at stake. "We need to stop it. Sabotage the thing. Derail it. Push it back for a year, maybe more."

Kast had been adamant. "I won't fire a gun on U.S. soil, I don't care how much money you're offering. And what'll a year buy you?"

"Just that," D.S. had said. "It'll buy me time."

They'd gone out to the long veranda along the south side of the main house that looked over a mountain valley, the view in the full moonlight nothing less than spectacular.

"I need help, Bob," D.S. had said.

"I know."

"There could be consequences."

Kast had looked at him like he was a madman. "Consequences indeed," he had said angrily. "Try Leavenworth."

"I meant from the experiment. We can take the position that if the experiment fails, and if enough methane is produced it could trigger a catastrophic release directly into the atmosphere that could in theory wipe out all life on the planet in less than five years."

"I did my homework," Kast had shot back. "Enrico Fermi thought it was possible that if a nuclear device were set off, it could cause a runaway ignition of all the oxygen in the atmosphere—everywhere on the earth. But it didn't happen."

"No," D.S. had admitted. "But not every long shot is a bust."

Kast had finished his wine, and then looked at his expensive crystal glass and suddenly tossed it over the railing. Both men watched it sparkling, catching the rays of the moon, as it seemed to fall forever into the valley.

"I'll find someone for you," he had said without turning to look at D.S.

And tonight the memo.

THE SOLUTION IS IN HAND. GO OR NO GO?

D.S. telephoned Kast's encrypted Nokia and the contractor answered on the first ring. "Yes?" Music played in the background, and a lot of people were talking and laughing. It sounded like a party.

"Go," D.S. said. "The down payment will be credited to your Command Systems' Cayman account within the hour."

"Very well," Kast said, and the connection was broken.

PART ONE

OPENING GAMBIT

Present Day
Early December

1

FIFTEEN MILES SOUTH of Medora in the North Dakota Badlands the panorama was nothing short of stunning, otherworldly, ancient, atavistic in a way in its appeal. The late afternoon was cold, near zero, a light wind blowing down from the Montana high plains when the forty-five-foot Newell Motorcoach, towing an open trailer with three rugged ATVs, topped a rise and pulled off to the side of the narrow gravel road.

Barry Egan stepped out, walked a few yards farther up a gentle slope, and raised a pair of Steiner mil specs binoculars to scope out the broad valley that ran roughly north and south through the middle of the Badlands' Little Missouri National Grassland. In the far distance he followed the tall, razor-wire-topped fence marked U.S. GOVERNMENT RESERVATION: VISTORS BY PERMIT ONLY to a group of buildings low on the horizon to the east.

Another man got out of the coach, dressed like Egan in an elk hunter's camouflage Carhartts, boots, and stocking cap, and took up a west flanking position down the road. For now he was armed with a .338 Winchester Magnum big game hunting rifle, with three-hundred-grain cartridges that had enough stopping power to put down a grizzly, or even a polar bear.

Egan, a man in his late twenties, was good-looking in a narrow-faced but sincere way; his dark eyes and the thin line of his mouth sometimes showed happiness, and when it happened everyone within shouting distance seemed to relax. All the conflict went out of the air, and people felt good, even confident.

But it was mostly an act, because Egan had been angry for as long as he could remember; at first because his step-father had come back from the first Iraq war a changed, angry man, who beat on his wife, and then when life seemed to be getting at least tolerable, the old bastard had gotten himself shot to death inside a refinery in Texas, leaving his wife and son to fend for themselves in what was a tough old world.

Like father like son, Egan thought as he lowered the binoculars and turned back to his outriders and grinned. "After all this trouble, doesn't look like much after all, does it?"

Craig "Moose" Swain, by far the largest of the five operators Egan had brought with him, laughed out loud. He was a former Delta Force corporal who'd gone a little overboard during what was supposed to be a preliminary recon mission in a mountain valley near Asmar on the Afghan-Pakistan border, killing a family of eight, including the father and five brothers, none of them armed. He'd been given an other-than-honorable discharge and had wandered around the Soldier of Fortune, American Firster, and Super Patriot organizations before finally winding up in Bozeman, Montana, where he'd appeared in Egan's radar, moving in and around the New Silver Shirts, Christian Identity, and Sovereign Citizen movements. A player. A soldier for God.

"Tonight?" he asked.

"Supper time," Egan said. "Eighteen hundred hours. It'll be dark by then."

Moose, who'd loved every minute he spent in Afghanistan, had been scoping a narrow plume of smoke rising in the southwest, lowered his rifle. "That it, Sarge?" he asked.

Egan turned his binoculars to where Moose, with what Egan called his Strike Force Alpha team thousand-yard stare, was pointing, and studied the dark smudge being shredded by the wind, and shook his head.

"Campfire, maybe a cabin fireplace, or something from the Badlands Roundup Lodge," he said. "Shouldn't be no smoke from Donna Marie, unless they screwed up."

"We'd go anyway?"

Like the others he liked blowing up things and killing people. He didn't know why, none of them could articulate their passion with any degree of clarity, not even Egan, who except for Gordy Widell, their seventeen-year-old computer hacker, and Dr. Kemal, their microbiologist, was the brightest of the lot. But a lot of the people Egan knew growing up in Upper Peninsula Michigan were crazies who hated the government—any government from Washington to the mayor and his cops in Marquette—and knew that it wouldn't be long before the anarchy that was coming any day would finally arrive and their only way out would be when Adolf Hitler's grandson came back to lead the resistance.

He'd fit in up there, with the groups in Wyoming and the Posse Comitatus in Montana, in his estimation all of them Jesus-crazy out of their skulls, and with his Team Alpha who he'd recruited and trained over the past ten months and eighteen days.

But the one thing the old man had taught him before

he'd gone off to Texas was to be practical. "It sure as shit ain't easy out there, kid. So if you got any talent don't give it away. Sell it. A man's gotta make his way in the world. There's no free lunch. Remember it." And he'd cuffed his stepson, already a grown man, so hard on the left ear that to this day Barry was partially deaf, so he always had to turn his good ear toward whoever was trying to tell him something. It was a nuisance, but he remembered the old bastard's words. And the Iraqis he'd guarded and sometimes tortured at Abu Ghraib thought when he cocked his head like that he was listening to some hidden earpiece, getting his orders from some general back in Washington.

"They didn't screw up," Egan said. "We're going in at nightfall."

He scanned the horizon out toward what the government called the Dakota District Initiative where supposedly the world's most secret and most powerful extremely low frequency, or ELF, radio station ever to be built had been under construction for several years. When it was finished, sometime this month, actually this week before Christmas, radio messages could be sent to anyone anywhere in the world, atop or inside mountains, in the deepest gold mines or at the bottom of any ocean where only deep-sea bathyspheres could go.

Supposedly. But Egan knew better, and he was being paid what for he and the others was a fabulous sum of money to destroy the place and everyone in it; to stop, he was told, the poisoning of the entire atmosphere. In reality, the money was only secondary to him. Blowing up shit and killing people was the game. Payback.

Nothing moved for as far as he could see. This was the end of North Dakota's special elk hunting season to cull the overpopulated herds on government lands, and in the eight days they'd been wandering around out here they'd seen almost no one else. A few other hunters, and one morning a rancher who'd come up to take a look at their license.

Egan had shown the man their permit and the rancher was not happy—he'd never much cared for out-of-staters, hunting permits had always been issued mostly to locals— but he was convinced, and he'd left, not realizing just how close he'd come to dying.

Satisfied that nothing was coming their way in the waning afternoon, Egan and his outriders went back into the motor home that had been custom-designed and outfitted for them down in South Carolina, no expense spared, and shipped to a rental agency up in Billings that sometimes did business with the Posse.

In its original C2 configuration the Newell had three major spaces starting at the front in the salon with seating and dining space for ten people just aft of the driver's position, with its state-of-the-art GPS receiver, and collision avoidance radar automatically linked to the braking system, as was the FLIR system, or Forward Looking Infrared detector. Behind that was the galley and head plus another small lounge. And at the rear what in the original model was called the Special Villa Section was a large space of pull-down bunks and a long conference table.

All of the interior was done up in marble and thick carpets and stainless steel appliances and expensive leather upholstery with Tempur-Pedic mattresses and wide-screen HD plasma TVs, everything top-shelf. And everything apparently legitimate for seven well-heeled elk hunters.

Egan, Moose, Widell, Dr. Mohammed al-Kassem Kemal, the Sudanese-born Pakistani who was on just about every terrorist watch list in the world, and the two girls, just as batshit crazy as the rest of them.

Brenda Ackerman, short, dumpy-looking, except for her

oval face with wide-open, innocent-looking brown eyes, who'd served on a small-town Mississippi police force until she was eased out when it was suspected but never proven that she had organized an old-fashioned KKK lynching of an elderly black farmer. For a time afterward she had worked as a truck driver and then a roustabout on Alaska's Prudhoe Bay oil fields, until she'd killed a man who'd called her a dyke in a bar fight and ran to Upper Peninsula Michigan to be with Ada Norman whom she'd met on the Internet.

Ada was a raging skinhead neo-Nazi who believed that Hitler's grandson was alive and ready to rise up for the cause. At forty-two she was almost eight years older than Brenda, but she'd been trained well by her militia group and could put a respectable pattern on a pistol range target at two hundred fifty inches, firing a Glock 17 at better than one round per second. She was Brenda's backup driver.

"We go at eighteen hundred," Egan told them.

The girls at the front of the rig looked up as did Widell from his computer. Dr. Kemal, who hated everything Western because the CIA had killed his parents who'd fought alongside Uncle Osama, had come from the back with a book in his hand and he blinked rapidly behind his spectacles. Like the rest of them he was a very good shot, especially with the Kalashnikov, the rifle he'd been raised with.

"Are we quite alone, Sergeant?" he asked.

"Yes," Egan said. "Everyone check your weapons and munitions, and get something to eat, could be a long night."

Widell went back into the galley and released a number of latches that moved the built-in refrigerator, range, and dishwasher aside, revealing banks of computers, radars, satellite receivers, and radio signal detectors that covered everything from high frequency to VHF, UHF, and above into the C and Ku bands used for uplinks. The compact microwave and satellite dishes were concealed in the air-conditioning units on the roof, and everything else was disguised as normal AM/FM broadcast, Sirius radio service, CB, or television dish antennas.

The equipment on board could not only detect signals to and from the Dakota District Initiative headquarters and the Donna Marie experimental coal-seam electrical-generating station, but security alerts from within that would bring help within minutes.

Standing there, Egan thought about his stepbrother Peter who'd been born eight months after the old man had been shot to death in Texas. He'd been the only one of them who'd had the possibility of a normal life. And just shy of his second birthday he'd wandered out of the trailer and had fallen into the creek at the bottom of the hill and drowned. Dead for nearly four hours before anyone realized he wasn't asleep in his bedroom.

It was a tough old world.

2

ASHLEY BORDEN HATED the runaround she figured she'd been getting ever since she was a kid and had discovered that boys and girls were different. It wasn't just the differences in how they went to the bathroom; she'd figured that out when she was five and had taken down her pants behind the garage at home in Fargo to show Harold Thompson hers, and he'd done the same, and when she'd laughed at him he'd knocked her down and ran off. But it was in school a couple of years later when kickball or baseball or football teams were called up, and only the boys were picked.

It wasn't fair, because she knew that she was just as fast and as strong as they were. Only it got worse in high school when boys were supposedly *naturally* better at math and science, and even worse in college at the University of Missouri in Columbia, which was ranked the number one school of journalism in the U.S. Girls as good-looking as Ashley were supposed to be working toward jobs as broadcast news readers and/or husbands heading to law school, not as print journalists.

Pulling up just before six at the Dakota District south

gate in her dusty Toyota Tacoma pickup after a very late start, the *Bismarck Tribune* magnetic logo on both doors, she was just about ready for a fight. At twenty-seven she was five-seven, slender, with light brown hair worn short, and wide dark eyes, still a little too tomboyish to be considered a beauty, with the cocky, sometimes even brash attitude of a service brat—the daughter of a two-star army general who'd raised her as a single father after her mother had died when she was seven. This afternoon she was dressed in jeans, a turtleneck fisherman's sweater, and a dark blue parka, hood back.

An air force cop, wearing winter BDUs, a sidearm on his hip, an M4 carbine slung over his shoulder, came out of the guardhouse and walked over as Ashley rolled down her window.

"Good afternoon, ma'am, may I help you?" he asked. He was young, in his very early twenties, built like a linebacker. His name tape read: ANDERSON.

Ashley held out her press pass. "I've come out to interview Dr. Lipton."

"No one by that name here, ma'am," the MP said.

Whitney Lipton was one of the leading minds on microbe biology and the genetic manipulation of bacteria. She'd worked at the Centers for Disease Control in Atlanta until four years ago when the president had tapped her to lead the Clean Coal Research team for the Department of Energy. And she had disappeared from view.

It was Washington politics and the name wouldn't have meant anything to Ashley who'd come to Bismarck right out of J school and had never managed to leave because she'd had a life of moving and she was sick of it, but her dad was stationed at the Pentagon and whenever she could she'd pop out to visit him. Three years ago she'd flown to D.C. without calling first, meaning to surprise him for his birthday. As she was getting out of the cab in front of her father's Fort McNair house, a fit-looking woman was just getting into the back of a plain Chevrolet Impala with government plates and their eyes met. The woman nodded and she was gone.

Her father hadn't been surprised that his daughter had shown up out of the blue; nothing about her surprised him. She gave him a peck on the cheek.

"Hi, Poppy," she had said. "Who's the lady I just met outside?"

He'd laughed. "Is that a daughter's or a reporter's question?"

Something had not quite set right with her. "Both."

"Sorry, no romance there. She's Whitney Lipton, an egghead over at the CDC. Could be doing something for us, and that's all you're going to get out of me."

"So, happy birthday."

Ashley had been curious and she'd Googled the woman, finding out that she was a hell of a lot more than a CDC egghead; in fact she was one of the leading minds on microbe biology and the genetic manipulation of bacteria, and yet there was almost nothing in any of the search engines that Ashley used that connected Dr. Lipton with the president's Clean Coal Research initiative her dad was working on, or any hint that she was doing work for the Pentagon.

And that might have been the end of it, except that Ashley had started a file on the Dakota District ELF project that she and a number of journalists had been allowed to visit three years ago, because a lot of things out there didn't make sense to her. For starters she was just about 100 percent certain that most of the people were military, yet most of them didn't wear uniforms. None of the construction crews working on the power-generating station—

which they were not allowed to tour because of the danger—thirty-six hundred yards away from the head-quarters compound were local. And they'd been asked to not concentrate their stories on what was happening out there, because the actual details were a military secret.

"We don't want to start a panic like what happened with the ELF station up in Wisconsin when people thought they were all going to die of radiation poisoning," the Army Public Information officer had told them. "But if you're going to write about us, we'd be happy to fact-check you."

"Yeah, right," one of the reporters said.

"I said fact-check, not censor."

A few stories had been published, but the project was in North Dakota—out in the boonies—and even the locals didn't much care and interest quickly died.

Except for Ashley, who by happenstance was at the Bismarck Airport three days ago to interview North Dakota's junior senator William Frey, a decorated war hero just returning from an ABC *Good Morning America* segment. But standing on the tarmac next to the senator's car and driver the first person off the plane was Dr. Lipton, who was met by her own car and driver that took off across the airport to the general aviation terminal.

A few minutes later as the senator was finally getting off the plane, Ashley watched the doctor get out of her car and board a helicopter, which immediately took off and headed to the west.

It had taken her two days to find out that no flight plan had been filed for the helicopter that had, according to the dispatcher, taken a pair of elk hunters on a tour around the Teddy Roosevelt Elkhorn Ranch. An outright lie.

So what the hell was a leading microbe biologist on assignment for the president, a woman who knew her father who was a Pentagon general working for the newly formed

ARPA-E, the Advanced Research Projects Agency-Energy, doing at the Dakota District ELF facility?

"Well, call her and tell her that I'm here," Ashley told the AP a little more sharply than she meant to. It was cold with the window down, it was late, and she would have to stay in Medora or maybe Dickinson for the night.

"Sorry—"

"She knows me, goddamnit. Just pick up your phone and tell her that I'm General Forester's daughter. We met at my dad's house a couple of years ago and I just saw her at the Bismarck Airport a few days ago."

The AP smiled tightly. "Ma'am, you need to turn around now and leave or I will have to place you under arrest."

"Good!" Ashley practically shouted. "We're making progress. Call someone and get them out here with the cuffs before I freeze my ass off."

"May I have your driver's license?"

Ashley handed it over, and the AP went back to the gatehouse. She could see him on the phone, looking at her through the window, and looking at her ID. After several minutes, he put the phone down and came out.

"Ma'am, it'll be about ten minutes. Our Public Affairs officer Lieutenant Magliano is coming out to escort you to Donna Marie."

"Who's that?"

"It's our power station. You'll be met there."

"By Dr. Lipton?"

"I'm sorry, ma'am, but no one by that name works here."

3

THE ONLY THING Gordy Widell really hated about himself was his acne, which no matter what solution or cream he tried would not disappear. His mom told him that he ate too much chocolate and his dad, before he'd hung himself in the garage after getting laid off at the GM assembly plant, told him to stop being a pussy and live with it.

But by then Gordy was already a geek who no one understood and he'd taken off when he was fifteen and came under the care of a couple of gay guys from Rockford who moved out to Bozeman where he moved in with a computer geek even smarter and crazier than he was, and so his real education had begun.

It was fully dark when he'd powered up his equipment, and began delicately sampling the electronic spectrum on just about every band—AM, FM, and microwave—he could think of, searching for every emission from the Dakota District's main research campus and especially from Donna Marie, the experimental electrical-generating facility, where within twenty-four to seventy-two hours the first test run of the gadget would take place.

"Could kill us all," Barry had told them. Not a cheery thought, but Gordy didn't really believe it. He'd been hired to make it possible for the others to stop the test.

"Piece of cake," he muttered under his breath as he studied the three main monitors.

Brenda was sitting behind him, a finger twining in the curls at the back of his neck. She did it to make her girlfriend jealous, even though it never worked. "What'd you say, sweetheart?"

"Fuck off."

She laughed loud enough for everyone in the motor home to hear. "Do it right, Gooordyyy."

The problem, as Gordy had figured it, was twofold.

First, electronic traffic coming into the facility—that included landline, cell, and satellite phones, plus computers and all the other satellite and microwave links as well as quantum-effect encrypted burst transmissions of top secret material—had to be intercepted and mined for information that was pertinent to this operation. Were Air Force security units from Rapid City en route for an unannounced exercise as happened several times each year? Were some VIPs from Washington going to show up sometime tonight? Maybe CDC or even NOAA scientists arriving for the experiment? Extra bodies that would have to be dealt with. Or had the FBI somehow gotten wind of what was about to happen, and were sending warnings: Help is on the way, batten down the hatches.

Second, and most important, was electronic traffic leaving the facility. All of it had to be intercepted and washed of any hint of trouble. The delay of a few milliseconds between the time a signal was sent and actually received at the other end—mostly in Washington—because it had been picked up by Gordy's computer, cleansed, and resent, would not be noticeable, at least not in the short run.

It especially had to include alarm signals between Donna Marie and the main campus.

All they really needed was ninety minutes—time enough for them to get in, neutralize the personnel, especially security so that Dr. Kemal could inject his cocktail of bacteria into the seam through the wellhead, and then get out.

That last part was the most problematic in Gordy's mind. But like his old man had said: stop being a pussy.

Besides the normal cell phone services just about everything coming in or leaving the facility was relayed through the WGSS, Wideband Global Satellite System communication network, or the updated Milstar, which was the Military Strategic and Tactical Relay system.

Egan came back. "How's it going?"

Gordy ignored the question for just a few seconds, then hit ENTER, and looked up. "We're in, Sarge."

"Good man," Egan said, and patted Gordy on the shoulder.

4

BOB FORESTER'S DAUGHTER showing up here was the last thing Whitney Lipton wanted or expected. Today of all days. In the morning they were injecting the bacteria-talker into the test bore, and seventy-two hours afterward, they would know if the gadget was a success. In which case everyone would probably get drunk and stay that way for a week, or a failure, in which case everyone would probably get drunk but stay that way only for a day until they got back to work to find out where the science or technology had gone wrong.

If they were still alive after the initial test.

Forester was in conference at his ARPA-E office on Independence Avenue in Washington and could not be disturbed; at any rate he once admitted that since Ashley was about thirteen he'd just about lost any realistic control over her behavior.

Whitney, Doc or the boss to her science team, and Doctor, which she'd always thought sounded a little pretentious, to just about all the government overseers on the project, was thirty-three, nearly six feet, with a pleasant face, high cheekbones, sleek black hair, and a slender, almost bony, frame that some of her friends said made her look something like the movie actor Lara Flynn Boyle. She grabbed her parka and on her way out of her office phoned Jim Cameron, chief of security at Donna Marie.

"Pete Magliano is bringing Forester's daughter out to look around," she said.

"Right now?" Cameron demanded. "You can't be serious."

"She showed up at post one and said she was here to interview me, I didn't know what the hell else to do with her. There's no way I wanted her here tonight, not in the state my people are in."

"Well, it's no better over here."

"Right," Whitney said, chuckling. Actually she and Jim Cameron had hit it off nearly four years ago. She'd had a predisposition not to like military types, especially security people with their sometimes unreasonable lockstep SOPs, and she'd been mildly surprised at first by his laid-back nature. He was reasonably good-looking, he was bright and well read and well rounded, something her ex was not, and he made her laugh. At thirty-two he was only one year younger than her.

"What do you want me to do with her?"

"Show her around the place. Looks like a power plant."

"No coal cars."

"We're going to burn methane."

"The girl's not stupid. There're a lot of storage tanks and processing equipment and piping more like you'd see at a refinery. From what I've heard she's bright, and maybe her father let something slip. Maybe she's put two and two together, which is going to bump up against our security provisions."

Whitney was a little vexed, had been from the beginning, by the supersecrecy the White House had placed on her work. But the president had explained to her that if they announced the project—which would eventually cost taxpayers upwards of $750 billion—and it failed, heads would roll. His head would roll. In a democracy the electorate ruled, whether anybody liked it or not.

The bigger problem, as it had been explained to her, was potentially very large trouble in the run-up to any revolution. The fact was that within U.S. borders there were enough coal deposits to satisfy its energy needs for four or five centuries—even adding in demands that were expected to rise exponentially if cheap electricity could be produced to run the increasingly electric economy—including all electrically heated and cooled homes, electric ships, electric trains, even electric airplanes and, of course, electric cars.

But coal was dirty. Every coal-powered electrical-generating plant pumped thousands of tons of poisonous carbon dioxide into the atmosphere each year. Even stations that sequestered stack gases by a dozen different processes, including olivine capture in which the gas would be converted to the stable magnesium iron silicate, which was one of the most benign and common materials on earth, or used the carbon dioxide to make a zinc-based aliphatic polycarbonate plastic that could be used in hundreds of applications—a plastic that was totally biodegradable—or even the more expensive chilled ammonia carbon capture in which supersonic shock waves compressed the carbon for storage deep underground, were polluters.

And the biggest problem of all, the reason the president had explained to her and the others on the original committee he had called together at the White House for the intensely secret initial briefing, was big oil and the managers of the oil derivative funds who would squeeze our economy to the breaking point if they got so much as a whiff of the

possibility that coal-produced electricity would be the motive power that drove the cars and trucks, putting them out
of business. It would be all-out war—for survival.

"Anyway I'm on my way over so you won't have to deal
with her on your own," Whitney said. "But I'll probably
be a half hour behind."

"Thank you for small favors."

"Give me a break."

"You know what I mean," Cameron said. "I can explain
to her everything we're doing here in four sentences. We're
going to inject three classes of microbes directly into the
coal seam Donna Marie is sitting atop. One breaks down
the long hydrocarbons in the deposit. The second converts
those into organic acids and alcohols. And the third—
methanogens—feed on the first two and convert them to
methane that we pump to the surface and burn as fuel to
power our turbines. The problem is what do I tell her after
that spiel? That there's a real possibility we'll have a methane blowout that would be a million times worse in terms
of atmospheric damage than a large coal-burning generating plant produces? That some of our bacteria produces a
lot of oxygen that could ignite the entire coal seam, which
would involve probably a fourth of the entire state? Suffo-
cate all the cattle? Really piss off the tourists?"

"You could quit and go back to Washington."

"And miss all this fun?" Cameron said. "Just get over
here as quickly as you can. You know this woman."

"I know her dad, and I only bumped into her once,
briefly," Whitney said. "I need to talk to my crew and I'll
be right over. In the meantime use your Irish charm. Works
on me."

She hung up before he could reply.

Her secretary Marney Morgan was gone for the evening, back in housing across the mall, where most of them

lived most of the time, or at this hour possibly in Henry's, which was a Upper West Side, Manhattan, transplant bar and a really good restaurant, or at the army dining hall—which had been dubbed Grunt City or Vomit Valley—but certainly not on her way into Medora. Everyone who was on base this evening was staying there. The gadget that contained the equipment to "talk" to the cocktail of microbes would be lowered into the deep injection borehole at six in the morning. And then what?

Whitney held up in the second-floor corridor of the main administration and research-and-development building, quiet just now because just about all of her techs and postdocs were downstairs in the main control center getting ready for the event, as the injection was being called, leaving mostly the roustabouts and power plant engineers over at Donna Marie, and gave a brief thought to how she'd gotten to this point.

It was crazy, even she could admit it to herself at the odd moment. But eight years ago she'd come up with the notion that microbes—bacteria—could communicate with each other. She'd not been the only scientist to come up with the idea, of course, Princeton's Bonnie Bassler being the most brilliant and well known of the others, but she'd figured out how to talk back to them and in an efficient, no-fail way. Train them like Pavlov did with his dogs. Ring the dinner bell and her babies would begin to eat—just about anything she engineered them to eat, coal included. That had been the tough part, the coal and what her bacterial cocktail produced—methane—and how it produced it and the speed at which it produced the gas, and the other byproducts.

But the really tough parts were understanding the exact language of each bacteria colony, the fact that in general bacteria were multilingual, and finally learning a universal language that *Smithsonian* magazine had dubbed "microbial Esperanto."

And then, of course, the design of the gadget, which when lowered into the borehole could translate her instructions into microbial Esperanto and transmit them.

It worked on a very small scale in the lab. But the real test would come first thing in the morning. And if she were being honest with herself, she would admit that she was damned scared, not only because of the possible side effects—primarily a methane runaway or a coal-seam fire—but of the effects that a failure would have on the initiative and on her career.

Or the long-term alternatives; that because of the increasing amount of carbon dioxide being relentlessly pumped into the atmosphere by cars and trucks and buses, by coal- and oil-burning electrical plants, by factories and by the deforestation of large sections of South America— trees that consumed carbon dioxide and converted it to oxygen, which was a nifty bit of natural sequestration—people were literally killing the planet. Sooner or later, unless something were done—something drastic because it was nearly at the point of no return—Earth would be unfit for human life. It could even become another Venus with runaway heating; rivers of molten lead, a world where just about all biologic life was extinct.

Scientists had been sending the message for years but no one had really listened until the near miss in Texas, and the White House had suddenly sat up and taken notice that the U.S. was vulnerable.

Too late, Whitney thought as she took the stairs down and heard the raucous party going on in the control center. She wanted to be angry with them for their levity at a time like this. But they were kids, some of them, and just as nervous as she was, just as frightened as were the scientists, techs, and engineers at Trinity in the New Mexico desert the night before the gadget—the first atomic bomb—was to be test-fired, and they were letting off steam.

Music with a very heavy bass thump, but almost no tune, some sort of country and western, fairly vibrated the corridor walls and rattled the door to the control center and when she came around the corner someone in the room burst out laughing.

She had six people at this end—Bernhardt Stein, her lab coordinator who'd come over from ARPA-E on Forester's orders; Harvard's Alex Melin, her assistant microbiologist and one of the brightest people she'd ever known; plus her postdocs, Jeff Roemer, Donald Unzen, Susan Watts (the class clown), and serious Frank Neubert from a small town somewhere in Iowa who was their prophet of doom. All of them really serious people. Really bright. Really dedicated.

And really in trouble, Whitney wanted to say when she walked in, but she couldn't and she almost burst out laughing.

As soon as she was noticed, someone cut the music, everyone stopped talking and laughing, and everyone turned toward her; like lemmings, she thought, facing the cliff.

Everyone was dressed in pajamas over which they wore lab coats and fuzzy bunny slippers, and all of them had donned gas masks.

Susan, only recognizable because she was the smallest of them and because of her blond hair, walked over and handed Whitney a glass of champagne. "Boolean algebra gone bad," she said solemnly.

"Divide by zero," someone else said.

"If you can't normalize the equation, invent a constant."

Whitney got it, and she raised her glass. "Gas masks won't save you from carbon dioxide."

Everyone raised their gas masks and glasses. "Illogic,"

Roemer said. "It's what brought us all here in the first place, right?"

And she loved them all at that moment. The camaraderie, the friendship, the trust, the good and gentle humor, and even the naïveté. She'd gotten the real beginning of her science at the Centers for Disease Control labs in Atlanta where she'd come up with the notion of not only listening to bacteria, but talking to them. Instructing whole colonies of them, through a mechanism called quorum sensing in which groups like the six hundred different bacteria that made up dental plaque, each of them speaking a different chemical language, could understand a lingua franca that allowed them to work toward a common purpose. In that case the purpose was a bad one. But she began to think of ways in which to speak to bacterial colonies, give them a quorum-sensing mechanism that would direct them to do something beneficial.

Maybe unlock the secret of curing viral disease.

"Maybe a Nobel," her boss over at the CDC had suggested.

And the White House had called, and she'd dropped everything and run here to North Dakota to be with these people, and even now, basking in their goodwill and cheery bonhomie she couldn't answer why. Except that it was good to be here. It felt right.

She toasted them, and put her glass aside. "Make it an early night, we have a big seventy-two hours starting first thing in the morning."

They all laughed, and someone put on the rap music and Susan handed her another glass of champagne and everyone else ignored her.

"Party time, Doc?" Susan asked over the noise.

"I have to get over to Donna Marie."

"Get some sleep. Oh six hundred comes awfully early."

5

BARRY EGAN, ALONE on the first of the three Honda ATVs, approached the ridge above Donna Marie at about two miles per hour. The highly muffled engine, designed for wildlife photographers who wanted to sneak up on their prey, especially polar bears in the Arctic, was scarcely more than a whisper within ten feet.

He held up his hand for them to stop, and behind him Ada and Brenda on one machine, and Dr. Kemal riding tandem on Moose's, pulled up behind him. They wore white coveralls and Bluetooth earpieces connected to encrypted sat phones with which they could communicate with one another as well as with Gordy, who was monitoring and controlling all electronic emissions from the research facility back at the motor home. But he'd cautioned them all at the beginning that anything electronic could be intercepted.

"Nothing but nothing beats a well-orchestrated plan in which everyone knows exactly what needs to be done." Barry had drummed it into their heads. "Know the mission plan, follow the mission plan. Hand signals when possible. No need to tell the sons of bitches what we're up to."

It had become their mantra, and whenever he spoke the last part out loud he would laugh, bray actually, so hard that even Brenda and Ada knew he was bugshit crazy.

He got on his hands and knees and crawled the rest of the way to the crest of the hill where he glassed the brightly lit compound through his mil specs Steiner binoculars. Except for the lights the place could have been deserted; there was no movement he could detect. A large building that housed the generating chain; starting with the borehole into the coal seam that would be tapped in the morning, the furnace that would burn the methane, the boilers that would produce the superheated steam that would turn the small three-stage turbine generating nearly one megawatt that would then be sent to the transformer and distribution yard, rose up from the prairie a couple of hundred yards away from a cluster of mobile homes housing the barracks, dining hall, and rec center—a safe enough distance if there was an accident.

The power generated led to an impressive-looking array of transmission towers that supposedly would send messages to any military unit anywhere on the planet, even to submarines a thousand or more feet beneath the surface. Donna Marie would guarantee that in case of an all-out war vital communications—especially data transfers to military units—would not be interrupted even if our satellites were knocked out.

In actuality Donna Marie was nothing more than a methane-powered electrical-generating station. No big deal in Egan's estimation. But he'd studied the blueprints, and he'd been given the list of the nine personnel—four engineers, including Tim Snow who was in overall charge here, plus five tool pushers, and each person's probable location at any given moment, and even though he didn't fully understand the importance of the mission, he did understand the fabulous money he and his people would be paid, and their need to strike back at the fat cats getting rich on the back of the working man.

Moose crawled up beside him. "How's it look, boss?"

"Nobody knows we're here," Barry said without lowering the binoculars. Someone had just come out of the main turbine building. "Base one," he spoke softly into his comms unit.

"One, base," Gordy responded.

"We're in position. Are we secure?"

"We own the place. Ninety-minute window."

Ninety minutes, it's all Barry had asked for. After an hour and a half Gordy's system would begin to deteriorate, primarily because of overload—the computers in the motor home could only hold a finite amount of data. Sooner or later information flowing to and from the facility to ARPA-E and a half-dozen other governmental facilities, including NOAA, NASA, the CIA, NSA and, of course, Homeland Security, would have to be dumped. Links would be broken. Questions would be asked.

But in ninety minutes the entire operation would be mounted and conducted, leaving a good margin for an orderly retreat when they could again become ordinary elk hunters.

So long as there were no witnesses—electronic or human.

"The clock starts now," he radioed.

"The operation is at plus one, eighty-nine remaining," Gordy said.

The man in white coveralls, who'd come out of the turbine building, drove a golf cart across to the trailers, and there was no further activity that Barry could see and he started to lower the binoculars when Moose nudged him.

"Forty-five right."

Barry scanned right along Donna Marie's west inner fence and around the corner to the front gate on the south side as two vehicles, one of them a gray Hummer with government plates, followed by a blue pickup, approached the unmanned gate as it slowly swung inward. The logo on the side of the pickup was for the *Bismarck Tribune*.

When the gate was fully opened, the two vehicles went into the power station yard and directly over to the turbine building, where a man in civilian clothes got out of the Hummer and a young woman with short hair got out of the pickup before they went inside.

"Trouble?" Moose asked.

Barry lowered his binoculars. "Two extra bodies in the turbine building," he said. "But no trouble." And his mind was suddenly abuzz. He liked the press—the power of the media. And he started spinning out scenarios of how the death of a *Bismarck Tribune* reporter—if that's what she was—could advance the cause. His cause.

"Are we a go, boss?" Moose asked.

Barry couldn't help but smile. "Yeah, we're a go," he said.

He and Moose crawled backwards from the crest of the hill until they could get to their feet and rejoin the others.

"We're good to go," Barry said.

"Know the mission plan, follow the mission plan," Brenda said.

It was the very same thing that Bob Kast had told him at the training base outside Greenville. "That comes first. Everything else is secondary. Are you with me?"

"Yes, sir," Barry had replied. They were in the middle of the Blue Ridge Mountains and from their perch at an observation post he could see the puffs of explosions in the distance, and seconds later hear the explosions. A lot of them. Some big and decisive, others short, sharp, angry.

Gunfire came from several of the shooting ranges, including one urban setting. People were jumping out of airplanes, practicing precision nighttime HALO—High Altitude Low Opening—insertions. Hand-to-hand combat instructors, one at a time, followed heavily armed men in groups of four, taking them down completely by surprise, even though the men knew they would be subjected to a simulated attack.

Barry had loved every second of it, all the more because what he was witnessing was simulated. He'd been hired to do the real thing.

"Your mission, your plan, your people, your responsibility," Kast had stressed. "Succeed and you'll be a wealthy man. Fuck it up and you'll end up dead. Because we *will* find you. I know some very good people."

"What if we're arrested: what's to stop us from copping a plea bargain?" Barry had asked, thinking how smart he was to bargain like that. In his mind, seeing the Command Systems spread, his risk ought to be worth more than he'd been offered.

Kast had given him a hard look. "The Bureau's Witness Security Program leaks like a sieve, so it wouldn't help you, and even if they stuck you someplace like Leavenworth, we'd still get to you." And the man had grinned, making him look like a wolf about to strike. "But that would never be a problem, would it, Barry? Because you and your people are nutcases, lunatics. Fringe. Certifiable. No one would believe you."

Posse Comitatus, indeed, Barry had thought then and now. But Kast had been right about the craziness.

"Saddle up," he told Brenda and the others, and on his lead, lights out, they headed northwest, not turning back toward the west fence until they were a couple of ridges over from the front gate and safe from detection by anyone inside the power plant or the trailers.

This far inside the Initiative's main reservation, and in such a remote spot, and with continuous satellite surveillance overhead and infrared sensors and motion detectors and lo-lux closed-circuit television cameras mounted just about everywhere—systems that Gordy was now in control of—everyone on the project felt safe.

They were about to be taught a lesson, Barry thought, and he stopped himself from laughing out loud.

6

THE PROJECT'S PUBLIC Affairs officer, Army Lieutenant Peter Magliano, tall, dark, and handsome, looked like an Italian movie star from the thirties, but Ashley was unimpressed. Or at least she wanted to be unimpressed, but he was smooth without being overly smarmy, reasonably bright, familiar with her bylines, and knew who her father was.

"I took my mother's last name when I turned eighteen," she'd explained though she had absolutely no idea why.

"Rebellion, maybe," he'd suggested.

"Maybe," she'd replied noncommittally, thinking he might be playing with her.

They were in the main turbine gallery of the power plant, a huge space more than two hundred feet long, fifty feet wide, and soaring more than five stories to the domed ceiling, white operating-room clean tile everywhere because dust was a turbine's worst enemy, no operating personnel in sight, and as the lieutenant had explained before they walked through the double doors, like airlocks on a spaceship, he wanted her to experience the big picture from the get-go. A maze of pipes and heavy bundles of electrical cables and other incomprehensible equipment were all attached at the front and the back of the main turbine, an immense tubular machine shaped more or less like a sausage that was dented in the middle.

"How much power are you producing right now?" she shouted.

"Actually none," Magliano told her. "We're electrically running the turbines to check balance, bearing tolerances, stuff like that. Keep the shafts from sagging out of true."

"I only noticed the one smokestack. Not much of a rig for a coal-burning plant. And where are the storage yards and pulverizing plants? I didn't see any conveyor belts or mining equipment for that matter."

In fact when she'd followed Magliano in the Hummer her first impression was that this place was some sort of a scam, some sort of a government boondoggle, what some of the contractors over in Iraq and Afghanistan had been playing at, sucking billions of dollars from the public trough while returning little or no service of any value. Like the Alaskan bridge to nowhere.

"This project is not about burning coal to produce electricity to run the communications system."

"You're on top of a coal seam."

"We've injected a series of microbes into the seam, and we think that we'll be able to produce enough methane to run the turbines."

"I've heard of that work. Still produces carbon dioxide emission into the atmosphere."

"Not the sort of methane we're going to produce."

"Methane is methane. I know my basic chemistry."

"Ours has a bacteria attached to it," Magliano said.

Ashley was startled. "Are you talking about sequestration before the smokestack?"

"In the smokestack, actually," he said. "But I'm no

scientist, so I'm at the limit of my knowledge here. Dr. Lipton can explain it better than I can."

Ashley walked over to the huge, science-fictiony turbine supported by four concrete cradles that raised the bottom of the thick steel cover six feet off the tiled floor and reached up and brushed the case with her fingertips.

The thing was alive, incredibly smooth, nearly vibrationless, and yet she could feel its heartbeat, or actually the currents or something along its nerves, almost as if the machine were communicating with her. Almost ESP.

She turned and looked at Magliano who was smiling patiently, and she wanted to think that he was an ass, but she decided on the spot that his smile was anything but disingenuous. "How many people are here right now?"

"Here in the turbine building, just Tim Snow, who's our chief project engineer, and Mike Ridder, who runs the control board upstairs. Plus you and I, and I think Jim Cameron our chief of security, might be running around here someplace, unless he went back to the party. We're conducting our first test in the morning. And the others are probably over at the rec center, too."

"What about Dr. Lipton?"

"She's on her way, but usually she and her techs and scientists spend most of their time over at the R and D Center. No need for them to be here, just about everything is mostly controlled by computers."

None of this was really adding up for her. Like Magliano she was no scientist, but she knew enough basic science from high school and from college where Chemistry 101 was the lesser of two evils when matched against Physics 101 that took a lot more math.

"Why the secrecy about the power plant?" she asked.

"I don't know what you mean."

"The AP at the gate said there was no one by the name

of Dr. Lipton working here. This place has all but been off-limits to the press—and when we were out here a couple of years ago you gave us a lot of stuff about a long-range communications system, almost none of which made much sense. I can tell a snow job when I see one because my father's had to lie all of his career with military intel and I'm used to it."

"Then you know when not to push," the lieutenant said, his smile a little forced. "You're your father's daughter and all, but you wouldn't have been let through the front gate if we'd been able to reach him. You're here because I was ordered to try to calm you down, maybe put a lid on whatever you think you know, and whatever else it is that you want to find out. What we're doing here, how we're doing, and why we're doing it, is top secret. A matter of national security."

"Come off it, Lieutenant," Ashley said. "You're converting coal to methane to make electricity to supposedly power another ELF system like over in Wisconsin. What's so earth-shattering about that?"

"I'll leave that one up to Dr. Lipton. She's the boss lady. I was just told to bring you out here and hold your hand."

Which also made no sense to Ashley. Why put a CDC microbiologist, practically a Nobel Prize laureate, in charge of a power plant to supply a communications center?

She turned and walked beneath the turbine, trailing her fingers on the case, the vibration going completely through her body. Melodrama, she thought, and she looked back at Magliano to tell him just that, when the side of his head erupted in a geyser of blood and he was flung backwards off his feet.

7

B ARRY, CARRYING A Knight PDW 6x35mm compact automatic carbine, appeared at the doorway to the power plant primary control room three stories above the turbine floor as one man was grabbing for a telephone and the other, a look of fear and anger on his face, was turning away from the large plate glass window.

"What do you want?" the man at the window, who Barry identified as Mike Ridder, the system's board operator, shouted.

"You know," Barry said, and he shot the man, driving him against the window, then switched aim and fired a two-round burst at Tim Snow, whom he also recognized from photographs he'd studied, one of the rounds catching the chief engineer in the side of the head, driving him to the floor.

"The male down by the turbine," Moose's voice came over Barry's earpiece.

"Two down up here. What about the woman?" Barry radioed.

"No sign."

"Take her alive if possible. And get the doctor started. I'm on my way to beta."

"Roger."

"Team two, copy?" Barry radioed as he turned and raced down the corridor and took the stairs to the main floor.

Brenda came back. "They're all in the rec center. North double-wide. Looks like party time."

"Give me a head count."

"Six."

"One missing," Barry radioed. "Stand by, I'm en route."

"Wilco."

Two loose ends, Barry thought as he reached the back door on the main floor, went outside, and took his Honda across to the cluster of mobile homes all lit up. Even from a quarter of a mile he could hear the music from the party in the main trailer. The first was the head count at the rec center, and the other was the newspaper reporter somewhere inside the power station. It wasn't likely that she was armed, so she wouldn't interfere with Dr. Kemal's work— the primary reason for this operation—but he'd thought of a number of interesting possibilities for her. Maybe as a bargaining chip with Kast for even more money.

Mission one was securing the power plant. Which had been accomplished. Mission two was taking down the remainder of the personnel, which was going to happen within the next four or five minutes—except for the one missing warm body. Mission three was introducing Dr. Kemal's counterbacterial strain into the borehole. And mission four was setting enough charges to take out the furnace and boiler, the turbine and generator, and the wellhead that was secured top and bottom by a series of blowout preventers, just like on an oil rig. Only these preventers were controllable. They could be opened and closed in any sequence. Presumably to allow the introduction of Dr. Lipton's coal-eating bacteria.

Mission five—the bonus—was to take out the good doctor if she was on site. They were not to take a chance of trying to reach the main research center two miles away, so Dr. Lipton's presence here would have to be a piece of good luck.

Brenda and Ada were hunched up flat against the back of the double-wide trailer when Barry pulled up, dismounted, and joined them. Even over the loud country and western music they could hear people laughing and singing at the tops of their lungs. The stupid bastards were having a party instead of taking care of business as they should have been.

"Base, one," he radioed.

"One, base," Gordy came back. "Plus fifteen, seventy-five remaining."

"Are we clear?"

"Roger."

"Do it now," Barry told the women. "I'll check the other trailers," he said, and he got to his feet and headed in a dead run to the first of the three single-wides.

The two women stepped around the corner of the double-wide and began firing, walking the rounds about chest height from left to right, the bullets easily slicing through the thin aluminum skin, insulation, and inside wall board.

The techs and roustabouts inside screamed in pain and desperation, someone shouted someone's name, and the music abruptly stopped.

Reloading, the two women fired another sixty rounds into the side of the double-wide and the screaming stopped.

Barry turned back for just a moment to see the girls

jumping up and down. Didn't matter who they killed as long as they got to kill someone. He'd chosen well. "Team two, I want a body count in three."

"Wilco," Brenda radioed. She and Ada would enter the double-wide to search for and deal with survivors.

"Rendezvous at alpha."

"Roger."

Barry burst into the side door of one of the trailers, which served as living quarters for the crew, and swept through the four bedroom layout. But no one was at home, as he expected would be the case. It was the night before the experiment and everyone was partying.

Except for the one missing man.

Trailers two and three were also empty, and when he emerged Brenda and Ada had mounted their machines and were headed back to the turbine building.

"Team two, what's your count?"

"Six down."

"Are you sure?"

"Roger, we made a sweep of the trailer. Nowhere to hide."

"Roger, understood," Barry radioed. "Base, one."

"One, base."

"Clear?"

"Roger. Plus nineteen, seventy-one remaining."

Moose's job was to secure the floor of the turbine building, which would allow Dr. Kemal a full fifteen minutes to introduce one gallon of his bacterial strain into the primary check valve for the main methane line coming off the wellhead. The soupy liquid would remain aboveground until the morning when the well was opened and methane was allowed to flow up from the coal seam, at which time it would begin to mix with the gas. Within minutes, the scientist had promised, possibly sooner, the new bacteria would interact with what was coming out of the well to produce oxygen. A lot of it, creating a highly explosive mix.

They'd been seated across the conference table in the cabin at their training ranch outside of Kalispell, Montana, when the doctor had explained what was likely to happen.

"Certainly an initial explosion that will destroy that end of the operation," he'd said. "And then most likely the coal seam will catch fire, perhaps even it, too, will explode. Should be quite spectacular."

"Better than nine-eleven?" Gordy had asked, and Dr. Kemal, who'd helped with the initial planning for the al-Qaeda attack, had nodded vigorously.

It had been Kemal who'd predicted that when the towers came down the dust and smoke sent roiling through the streets would contain a toxic concentration of bacteria from the human remains. A lot of the first responders would develop horrible health problems over the coming years. And he'd been right.

Barry reached the power plant two minutes behind the women. Brenda was already molding lumps of plastique explosive on the turbine case and Ada was right behind her, inserting fuses and stringing wire to the detonator box. They had fifteen minutes allotted to wire the turbine, the generator, the cooling water and boiler feed-water pumps, the surface condenser, and the base of the furnace itself.

They didn't look up as Barry passed them and ran through the length of the building to where Moose and Dr. Kemal were at the wellhead, Moose using an electric nut driver to remove the twelve bolts holding the access port to the check valve chamber.

"How long until you're operational here?" Barry asked.

"Five minutes, plus or minus two, if my battery holds out," Moose said. "The son of a bitch bolts are stiff."

Dr. Kemal looked owlish behind his wire-rimmed glasses. But he was calm. Know the plan, follow the plan.

"Base, one."

"One, base," Gordy came back. "Still clear, though I'm starting to get a data pileup. Nothing my mainframe can't handle for now. Plus twenty-eight, sixty-two remaining."

"Roger," Barry said, and he went looking for the newspaper reporter who had to be somewhere in the building.

8

WHEN ASHLEY WAS nineteen she'd dated a Special Forces second lieutenant, who in an effort to make an impression, snuck her onto the nearly two hundred square mile survival training wilderness of Fort Bragg with only a KA-BAR knife, flint, compass, and fifty meters of light nylon cord. It had been absolute freezing hell for three days until, totally lost, they were finally picked up by the MPs. At this moment she wished she were·back there.

She'd managed to make her way along the base of the turbine to a cubbyhole halfway back within a towering structure of complex machinery, pipelines, gauges, and other things incomprehensible to her, except that she thought she was somewhere under the furnace where the methane would be burned. The space was barely three feet on one side and perhaps eighteen inches deep, about ten feet above the main floor, and pulling her legs up beneath her she tried to make herself invisible.

Two men in white coveralls were down on the floor to the left, about fifty feet away. Their backs were to her so she couldn't see their faces, but one of them was large with a mane of black hair, while the other was small, and she got the impression he was a much older man.

A third man, also dressed in white coveralls, passed just below her hiding place and the pit of her stomach went hollow. He was armed with some sort of a short, wicked-looking rifle that he held as if he were ready to fire at anything or anyone who got in his way. She got a brief glimpse of his face, and he seemed angry to her. Driven, she decided. He had a purpose and nothing was going to get in his way.

He stopped for a second a few feet to her right, barely ten feet away from her and she held her breath. All he had to do was turn his head to the left and look over his shoulder and he would see her.

It looked to her as if he was talking to someone, the noise of the spinning turbines too loud for her to hear anything, but a second later a woman, also dressed in white, came into view and she said something to him, and then reached into a canvas bag slung over her broad shoulder and pulled out a piece of what looked like Play-Doh about the size of several slices of bread rolled up into a fat tube.

The man said something else then hurried off as the woman molded what Ashley realized was Semtex or C4 plastic explosive around the flange of a big pipe and seconds later moved out of view. A second, much smaller woman with a narrow face and very short cropped hair appeared in view. She plugged a fuse into the lump of plastique and, trailing a bundle of thin wires, disappeared.

They had killed Magliano and they were here to destroy this place. Only by the grace of God had she been out of sight under the turbine when the lieutenant had been shot to death, otherwise she knew damned well that she'd be lying in a pool of her own blood next to him.

Which gave her two problems to solve, the first being

how to stay alive long enough for the three men and two women to finish their work and leave so she could get the hell out, or for the cavalry to show up. The second was to get the hell out before the plastique popped off, because it was going to get real unhealthy around here when it did.

But another part of her, the reporter part, was fascinated by what was going on. She was in the middle of a terrorist attack, though the five people she'd watched didn't seem to be Middle Eastern. More homegrown, or maybe European. It was like being on the sidelines of a 9/11, and she wanted to see everything, hear everything, smell everything, and commit it all to memory, because if she got out of here alive she would have one hell of a story.

A clatter of metal down on the floor startled her so badly she almost cried out and she turned in time to see the older man take what looked like a plastic gallon of something out of his shoulder bag, open it, and pour it into a waist-high opening in a big pipe that ran down into a circular grate about the size of a manhole cover in the floor.

The woman with the plastique appeared when he was finished and the three of them had a conversation as the black-haired man placed a thick metal plate over the opening and used a tool to screw on bolts or nuts to hold it in place.

None of this made any sense to Ashley. The terrorists were here to sabotage the facility, but if the Initiative was really all about worldwide ELF communications she would have thought destroying the antennas would have been more important than destroying the electrical-generating station.

From where she was hiding she couldn't see Magliano's body but in her mind's eye she could play back in slow motion and living color his head jerking to the left, a spray of blood and something else, something chunky, flying out of his skull as he was flung backwards, his hands flying outward as if he were raising them in a cheer. It was an image she knew that she would never forget.

She turned to the right and hunched down a little lower to get a better angle, but the man with the gun was gone, and all she could see was tile, and the maze of pipes and wire conduits.

Something made her turn back and when she looked down the man with the thick mane of black hair was directly below, staring up at her.

9

J IM CAMERON, THE director of project security, raced
up the metal stairs to the second-level access door
that led directly into the power station control room and
held up for just a moment. At thirty-two he didn't have
the wind he'd had when he'd played quarterback for the
Navy, and he was dripping blood from bullet wounds in
his right thigh and left arm just above the elbow, but he
was seriously motivated.

He was a career SEAL lieutenant commander conning
a desk who'd happily come over from the Pentagon to
take on the role of chief of security for the Initiative. Like
most SEALs he was slightly built, a little under six feet,
with short-cropped hair and an even, sometimes bland
demeanor. But anyone who'd ever met him immediately
saw something in his eyes, the way he carried himself, the
quietness of his voice, that was somehow impressive, even
comforting in a way. When Jim Cameron walked into a
room, heads turned and just about everybody breathed a
sigh of relief; he's here, everything will be okay now.

But everyone back in the rec center was dead, and the
vision of their shot-to-hell bodies would never leave him.

He'd been crawling around beneath the double-wide, chipping away ice from a frozen toilet discharge pipe when the shooting had begun, two of the shots from what he figured were light caliber automatic weapons hitting him from an oblique angle. The two shooters had been somewhere outside the rec room, but close. And the hell of it was that he'd left his weapon in the office at the rear of the trailer. His people were having a party, not preparing for an invasion.

By the time he had scrambled out from under the double-wide the gunmen had already left, and he'd gone inside knowing exactly what he'd find, and knowing exactly why the shooters were here.

He'd retrieved his Glock 33 that fired hollow point .357 SIG ammunition, hesitated for just a second back in the rec room—they had become his friends—before he'd checked to make sure one of the killers hadn't stayed behind and then had raced on foot over to the power station as he tried to call out on his cell phone.

He stopped and looked at it now. The battery was up but there were no signal bars. They had their own cell phone tower atop the power plant's one-hundred-and-fifty-foot chimney, and from where he stood the thing seemed intact to him.

Which made no sense.

He'd wanted to reach the Air Force's Special Forces Rapid Response team from Ellsworth down in Rapid City, which was on call 24/7, or at the very least Whitney to warn her to stay away. But he was getting nothing.

Easing the heavy arctic door open Cameron stepped into the narrow confines of the cold room designed to keep the below-zero winter winds from following someone inside the control room, and hesitated again to listen. In the far distance, below, he could hear the low-pitched hum of the turbine spinning on maintenance power to keep the shaft from sagging, but nothing else. No shooting, no one crying for help. The normalcy was ominous, and he got the terrible feeling that he was too late, that just like in the rec room everyone here was already dead.

He opened the inner door and rolled inside, keeping low and moving fast to the left, his pistol in both hands out front and low, and he stopped before he got five feet. Tim Snow was crumpled in a bloody heap at the side of his desk, the telephone still in his hand, and Mike Ridder was slumped on his knees, his head on the floor as if he were praying like a Muslim, his blood splattered all over the plate-glass window that looked down on the turbine floor.

This was a military-style operation. Cut the communications and then eliminate the personnel. Problem was that Pete Magliano was here with General Forester's daughter who had stormed the gates.

Still keeping low, Cameron made his way around the control console to where the window ended, flattened himself against the wall, and took a quick look down at the floor.

Pete was nowhere to be seen, but a slightly built man in white coveralls scurried from around the air preheater and disappeared beneath the economizer mechanism at the base of the furnace, as another much larger man, also dressed in white, pointing a short carbine weapon at something or someone above him, made a "come here" gesture.

A slightly built woman in jeans and a dark blue windbreaker crawled out of a narrow space beneath the furnace about ten feet off the floor, and made her way slowly down the ladder from what was probably a maintenance point.

It was Ashley Borden, the newspaper reporter Whitney had warned was coming their way. Pete might have hidden her there, but he was a PR flack, not combat trained, and he wouldn't have had a chance against whoever these people were.

Which was beside the point.

Cameron sprinted to the door and out into the short corridor that ran back to the control center auxiliary electrical room, which held racks of repeaters for all the monitoring and operating panels, and directly to the right to another door that led out to the balcony from which stairs led down ninety feet to the turbine floor.

The man with the carbine had moved to the left and was apparently talking into a lapel mike, while keeping his weapon pointed at Ashley.

The distance was impossible for a pistol, but the noise was loud enough to more than easily cover the sounds of someone coming down the stairs, which Cameron took two at a time.

The big man made a gesture with the weapon for Ashley to head in the same direction the other man had taken, but spotting Cameron, who'd nearly reached the bottom, she stepped back and suddenly dropped to her knees.

Cameron fired four shots, center mass, as he moved in a dead run across the turbine floor, the first and second of them going wild, but the third and fourth hitting the big man in the right shoulder, and low in his back. He went down, the carbine skittering across the floor.

"You okay?" Cameron shouted to Ashley, his voice barely carrying over the turbine noise.

"There're at least four others!" she shouted. She was white-faced, but she didn't look frightened.

The large man was struggling to reach inside his coveralls for something when Cameron pointed the Glock at his forehead from a distance of less than three feet.

"Not worth dying for today."

Moose said something into his lapel mike, as he pulled out a standard U.S. Army–issue Beretta 92F semiauto pistol and started to raise it, a wild look in his dark eyes.

Cameron fired one shot, the man's head crashing back on the tile floor, a large pool of blood spreading from the back of his skull.

Ashley got to her feet and stepped back. "They've planted explosives all over the place!" she shouted. "Plastique, I think. Wires leading from the detonator caps."

"Can you show me?"

She nodded.

"What about Pete Magliano, the guy who brought you over here?"

"He's dead, back by the front of the turbine."

Cameron bent over Moose's body and pulled the bud from the man's left ear, and held it up to his ear.

"Team two, one, sitrep?" a man demanded.

"Team two, good to go in three," a woman replied. "What delay do you want?"

"Stand by," the man identified as one replied. "Base, one, clear?"

"We're degrading, but still clear. Plus thirty-six, fifty-four remaining."

"Moose, one, I have Kemal. What's the holdup?"

Cameron bent close enough to Moose's body so that he could speak into the lapel mike. "One, Moose. I have the reporter."

"Good, we're out of here in three. Hustle," Egan radioed. "Two, one. Fifteen-minute initial delay, coordinated over eight."

"Roger, setting it now," the woman came back. She sounded excited.

"Rendezvous now," Egan radioed and he sounded just as excited as the woman.

Cameron pocketed the earbud. "Now show me where they planted the Semtex."

10

OUTSIDE, BETWEEN THE south wall of the turbine building and the transformer yard where they'd parked the three ATVs, Barry waited with Dr. Kemal for the others. The wind had come up and Barry felt a deep chill, as if something or someone had just walked over his grave.

He was about to speak into his lapel mike when Ada Norman came out of the door, a wild look in her eyes.

"It's set," she said breathlessly. In the overhead lights atop the building her face was shiny with sweat. She pushed up a sleeve of her white coveralls to look at her watch. "The first charge goes in thirteen, and the last eight minutes later."

"Where's Brenda?"

"She was setting the last plastique under the preheater," Ada said. She spoke into her lapel mike. "Brenda, where the hell are you? We're waiting."

There was no answer but all of them could hear the high-pitched sound in their earbuds like an electrical motor or something running. Someone's voice-operated transmit relay was being triggered by the noise.

"Ackerman, get your ass out of there. We're running out of time!" Ada shouted, and she looked fearfully at Barry.

"Moose, copy?" he radioed.

But there was no answer.

"Something's gone wrong," Ada told him. She started back to the door, but Barry grabbed her.

"It's too late!" he shouted. "Someone else got to them. The guy we missed at the double-wide. We're outa here now."

"We can't leave her, goddamnit. If they take her alive she'll talk."

"They won't take her alive, and you know it," Barry said. He'd planned for this contingency. In fact he'd expected it. The only one he couldn't leave behind was Dr. Kemal. He was coming out dead or alive. Just the presence of his dead body would be enough to tip off the Initiative people—especially Whitney Lipton—what the real mission had been tonight.

"Fuck you, I'm going after her!" Ada screamed.

She pulled away and started for the door, when Barry fired two shots, both of them hitting her high in the back, and she went down hard, her head bouncing off the gravel, her body skidding a few feet under her momentum.

Dr. Kemal stepped back a pace.

"Start one of the machines, you're coming with me," Barry ordered, and he went to where Ada lay facedown and put a round point-blank into the back of her head. "It's a tough old world," he muttered.

Dr. Kemal started one of the ATVs and he stood flat-footed like a deer caught in headlights on a country highway.

"Moose, Brenda, copy?" Barry radioed, but there was no answer. They were down. He went back to the ATV and climbed aboard, motioning for Dr. Kemal to ride pillion, the same as he had with Moose.

Gordy had been monitoring all the radio traffic. "One, base. Trouble?" he radioed.

"Nothing we can't handle," Barry said, hitting the throttle and pulling away, Dr. Kemal clutching at him. "Are we still clear?"

"Roger. Plus forty, five-zero remaining. What about Moose and Brenda?"

It came to Barry that the son of a bitch kid was a sentimentalist after all his bullshit talk about technology being the only real form of truth and honesty. "Computers don't lie to you, man," he'd said once. "If they fuck up it's always your fault. Garbage in, garbage out."

"They're down," Barry radioed. "So is Ada."

"Shit, oh, shit."

"Stand by to move out. We're incoming."

"You can't leave them."

"Base, one!" Barry shouted. "You copy my orders? We're incoming, get prepped to move out."

He angled to the west, keeping the bulk of the generator station between him and the south and west exits. It would take some time for anyone to respond to the emergency because no signals were getting out of the station. Except for the one guy they had missed and presumably the newspaper reporter. But in a few minutes they were going to have their hands full when the Semtex the girls had planted started popping off.

Fire in the hole, indeed, he thought, and he began braying like a madman.

11

BILLINGS COUNTY SHERIFF Nathan Osborne leaned
his six-four frame against the front left fender of his
mud-spattered Saturn SUV radio car, his elbows on the
hood to steady his binoculars as he glassed the rugged
countryside to the northeast. It was late, well after dark,
the light wind raw, and he should have been home with
his family eating dinner.

But all he had was an ex and an eight-year-old daughter living now in Orlando, near Disneyworld. No one in
Medora. Sometimes no reason to go home. Maybe to
Fred's for a beer and a steak and fries, but not the ranch
he'd inherited from his parents five miles out of town
near Fryburg.

At thirty-four he was just about in the same shape he'd
been in as a Marine Force Recon lieutenant running
around doing black ops in the Afghan mountains until his
left leg below the knee had been shot off by a Taliban
sharpshooter who'd gotten lucky with a Barrett A2 .50
caliber U.S. sniper rifle at three hundred meters, just clip-
ping the base of his knee. His next conscious memory was
at the Landstuhl Hospital outside Ramstein in Germany

when a White House representative was at his bedside congratulating him and his wife. Soon as he got well enough to travel to Washington, the president was going to drape the Medal of Honor around his neck.

It was only a week or so later until he'd understood that he hadn't screwed up by getting shot, in fact he'd saved the entire forward fire team by crawling wounded for nearly one hundred meters, through withering fire, to a position where he took out the sniper with his M-16 and then eight other Taliban who'd had the high ground waiting to launch their attack after the sniper had taken out the officer and platoon sergeant.

Failure to maintain a proper lookout, he'd told himself over and over, just about every day since then. Failure to maintain a situational awareness. Failure, as his Annapolis friends used to say, to keep his head fully withdrawn from his rectum at all times.

Afterwards he'd been promoted to captain and had been given a desk job in public affairs at the Pentagon, where he'd seriously chafed at the bit for two years until he'd been promoted to major and reassigned to the 2nd Recon Battalion at Lejeune, North Carolina, as a black ops and high risk personnel instructor.

There were only three hundred and fifty officers and enlisted men in all of FORECON so they were a tight-knit group, and having a grizzled veteran—an "old man," even though at that time he was only twenty-nine—and a Medal of Honor winner to boot, was impressive, and the kids actually did listen to him. But he'd kept track of the ones he'd trained who came back in body bags. They were good, but they weren't supermen, and neither was he, so he had quit and came home to western North Dakota.

His wife Carolyn had managed Washington and even Lejeune, but not North Dakota, even though her husband had been elected Billings County sheriff in a virtual land-slide because no one ran against him. She'd only lasted six months before she'd filed for divorce and headed to warmer climes. The fact that he was an amputee hadn't helped, but as he had told her at the time: "Can't promise you I'll be any good at dancing."

"You never were," she'd told him, smiling. They were still friends.

But it wasn't what he had expected after Afghanistan. Wasn't what he'd hoped for, because he'd lived the RECON creed in and out of the service, and he'd figured that was enough to see him through.

R for Realizing it's my choice to be a Recon Marine I accept all challenges.

E for Exceeding beyond the limitations set down by others shall be my goal.

C for Conquering all obstacles, I shall never quit.

O for On the battlefield as in all areas of life I shall stand tall above the competition.

And N for Never shall I forget the Recon Marine's principles of honor, perseverance, spirit, and heart.

A Recon Marine can speak without saying a word and achieve what others can only imagine. Hoo-rah!

The sheriff's office was only open in the winter from eight to four Monday through Friday, but 911 worked for emergencies and the 1-800 State Radio number was even better.

Sally at State had called him an hour ago that Ashley Borden, the *Bismarck Tribune* reporter, had been nosing around Medora all day trying to find someone who would admit to working at the ELF project, and when she'd gotten nowhere she'd disappeared.

"Tom Campbell was on Ninety-four coming back from Patterson Lake when he saw the girl's pickup truck heading south on Eighty-five," she'd said. "Could be she's going to storm the gates. What do you think?"

Osborne had chuckled. "I think that you're in the perfect job for an old busybody, but thanks for the info. I'll head down there and take a look."

Nothing much had been happening in the main administrative compound, so he'd driven down to the power station and ELF antenna farm, and through the glasses he had spotted the reporter's pickup truck parked next to a gray Hummer, one of the project vehicles. But just peeking out around the far corner of the main generating building, beyond which was the transformer yard, was the tail end of what looked to Osborne to be an ATV. It was hard to make out any details in the harsh light from atop the building, but he'd never seen anything like that out here, and a little alarm bell began tinkling at the back of his head.

Because of his former Recon position in the Pentagon, and his present position as sheriff, he'd been among a handful of state representatives who'd been partially briefed four years ago at the start—and the emphasis that day at the Department of Homeland Security in Washington had been on *partially*—on the Initiative, which had absolutely nothing to do with a new communications system. It was a top secret project to generate clean energy that didn't use natural gas or oil or nuclear power. No carbon dioxide emissions, the undersecretary who'd briefed them promised.

"Coal," someone had suggested. "We have plenty of that in the state. But cleaning it up in any way that makes economic sense isn't possible."

"ARPA-E is in charge," the man had said; the Advanced Research Projects Agency-Energy under the Department of Energy that was modeled after the Pentagon's DARPA that had developed everything from the precursor of the Internet to predatory drones, passive radar systems, and advanced computer and artificial intelligence programs and devices. And everyone except for the briefer fell silent. "Unfortunately energy independence for the U.S. has become a matter of national security."

What Osborne hadn't known until about a year ago when Jim Cameron, chief of security out here, had let it slip over a beer in town was that Ashley Borden was the daughter of retired Army Major General Bob Forester who was the Initiative's director.

"She's pushy as hell," Cameron had warned. "Sticks her nose wherever she can. Only be a matter of time before she shows up out here in earnest. And when that happens we're going to have to deal with her."

"Can we shoot her?" Osborne had asked.

"No, but it's a pleasant thought."

And she was apparently here now and it was dark and Osborne had a gut feeling that he'd stumbled into the middle of something. It was the same sort of feeling he'd had in Afghanistan every time something went to hell, and he'd learned to listen to his instincts.

He'd met her twice in the past few years; once at the initial open house and briefing for the ELF project, and again about nine months ago when a tourist in the Roosevelt Park South Unit had gone berserk and chopped his wife and two children to pieces with a hatchet and then had slit his wrists with a hunting knife, and the initial investigation and media briefing was a Billings County job even though the crime had taken place on federal land. He remembered her as an attractive woman who asked some good questions, among them what had driven the ad executive from Minneapolis to suddenly go nuts? But she'd been too pushy. And Carolyn's leaving him still grated. And he'd shut out of his mind any thoughts about seeing any woman as anything more than a criminal or a plain no one.

Osborne used his cell phone to call Cameron's number, but he couldn't get through, so he called State radio and had Sally call the number on a landline.

"No service," she said. "Want me to call the phone company?"

"That's okay, I'll take care of it."

"Problems?"

"Yeah, someone probably forgot to pay the phone bill," Osborne said. His phone had service to State, but not to the Initiative, which at this point made no sense. Alarm bells were jangling all along his nerves. It was like the battlefield all over again.

"What do you want me to do, Nate?"

"I think there might be some sort of a problem out here. Look up the emergency number at Ellsworth—it's on your contact list—and give them the heads-up."

"What sort of a problem, they'll want to know."

"Sally, just make the call, please."

12

WHITNEY LIPTON PULLED up in front of the rec center double-wide at Donna Marie and slowly got out of her Mercedes station wagon, her heart in her throat.

The trailer was pockmarked with dozens, if not hundreds, of holes, the windows all shattered, the blinds hanging in tatters, only a few lights on inside, and no sound; no music, no laughter or talking. And it took her a full minute to realize that what she was seeing and not hearing were the results of some sort of a military attack. The holes had been made by bullets, and she knew that everyone inside was dead.

She stepped back, the movement reflexive, then turned and grabbed her cell phone from her purse. But she had no signal bars, which was impossible. The Initiative had its own cell phone antenna.

"Christ," she said, and she turned toward the power station.

Nothing seemed out of the ordinary. The red light atop the smokestack, on which the cell phone antenna was attached, was flashing and even from this distance she could hear the thrum of the turbine spinning at its maintenance revolutions. Magliano's Hummer was parked alongside a pickup truck at the rear entrance. And maybe two other smaller vehicles, something that looked like ATVs, were pulled up nearby, but she'd never seen them before.

It came to her that whoever had attacked the rec center, had probably driven here on the ATVs and were probably still inside the power station, and she was torn between checking to see if anyone was alive and using a landline to call for help or driving back to the R & D Center to call for help. But that was two miles away, and she had a feeling there was no time.

She pocketed her phone, hurried across to the rec center, and yanked open the door where she was rocked back before she could step across the threshold. Bodies and blood were everywhere, the stench of blood and human entrails so overpowering it made her weak in the knees and she nearly vomited.

She knew these people, she had worked with them for the last four years, and for several long seconds she simply couldn't wrap her mind around what she was seeing. She couldn't grasp the enormity of it.

They had been shot to death, their horribly mutilated bodies lying at all angles, the expressions on their faces pure panic and intense pain.

Their killers had stood outside the double-wide and fired into the rec center through the thin aluminum skin.

But she didn't see Jim among them. After just a half minute she was sure of it and she almost felt guilty for being relieved.

Girding herself to move, she went inside, stepping with extreme care to avoid the blood and gore, went to a wall telephone, and picked it up at the same moment there was an explosion over at the power plant.

13

CAMERON HAD DROPPED to his knees a few feet away from Magliano's body in front of a small electronic device from which nearly a dozen wires snaked back into the station when a short, sharp explosion went off somewhere at the other end of the plant. He turned to look when a second, much larger explosion rocked the concrete floor.

Ashley, knocked off balance, sprawled half on top of him. "We're too late!" she shouted.

"Not yet," Cameron said, and he turned back to the detonator. An LED counter was passing the eight-minute mark, and another smaller number in the lower right-hand corner of the display blinked nine.

Nine what? he asked himself as he frantically studied the device. His first instinct was to yank the wires that had to lead back to the plastique explosive Ashley had seen the terrorists plant, but he stopped. The device was vaguely familiar to him, but different from anything he'd remembered from his BUDs (Basic Underwater Demolitions) evolution. In the end his expertise had been mostly as an intel officer, but he'd taken the basic course as everyone else in SEALs had. And this thing looked like something he'd seen before. Fail-safe. Pull the wires and a disconnect signal was sent to the detonators, which sparked, blowing the explosives.

But there was a way to disarm the thing. A code, a shut-off switch, a safety. Something simple if you knew it. But studying the thing he knew that he didn't, and he was going to have to start taking chances if there was any hope of saving the station.

"Get the hell out of here!" he shouted without looking over his shoulder.

"Where to?"

"I don't care! Anywhere. Just get out."

"No!" Ashely shouted. "Tell me what to do to help!"

The LED counter passed the 7:45 mark, and for a long second or two he felt completely lost, helpless. He didn't know what to do. Acrid smoke poured from somewhere in the vicinity of the methane furnace five hundred feet away. But no fuel was coming up from the seam; this was at least one break in their favor. Whoever had planned this had come twenty-four hours early. By this time tomorrow any explosion back there would have cascaded into an all-out conflagration that would have obliterated the entire plant.

"I don't know how to disarm this thing," he admitted. He looked up. "I need to pull the wires out of the plastique, and you'll have to tell me where they are. It'll be faster."

Ashley could see the LED counter. "I'll show you!" she shouted over the turbine noise. "I'll show you!"

Cameron wanted to argue, but she was right. He got to his feet. "We're running out of time."

The detonator control box was positioned just below the generator less than twenty feet from the rear door. Ashley turned and sprinted to the front of the unit where a ten-

inch-in-diameter shaft protected by a reinforced and tem-
pered steel case was connected to the turbine and pulled
up short, searching for something.

She ducked beneath the generator and scrambled to a
spot between it and the boiler feedwater pump directly
ahead of the turbine.

"Here!" she cried, and she moved aside to let Cameron
squeeze into the small space.

A wire led up to a gray lump of Semtex smelling faintly
of vinegar and looking something like ordinary plumber's
putty that had been molded on to the shaft case. There was
a lot of it, probably three or four kilos. Enough, Cameron
knew, to not only destroy the shaft case and the shaft itself, but to just about vaporize anyone within ten feet of it
when it blew.

"Get back," he told Ashley.

"I'll find the next one," she said in his ear and she was
gone.

Semtex plastic explosive was extremely stable. It would
not explode if it were dropped on the floor or hit with a
hammer or even if it were shot with a bullet or tossed in a
fire. Only an acid fuse or in this case an electrical charge
could set it off. The problem was the electronic detonator
unit back by the door. Disturbing any part of the circuit,
including the wire coming out of the plastique, might initi-
ate a momentary current surge enough to set it off.

Cameron smiled. In for a penny in for a pound, his prag-
matic grandmother who'd raised him used to say. She'd
emigrated from Ireland with her husband, who'd died of
cancer three months after he'd been sworn in as a U.S.
citizen. Six months later her unmarried daughter, eight
months pregnant, had committed suicide by slitting her
wrists. The premature baby—Jim Cameron—had been
taken by paramedics, and never once had his grandmother

burdened him with any sort of sadness, or some dour Irish philosophy of life's travails. In for a penny in for a pound had been the worst of it.

He reached up and eased the wire out. And for just an instant he was back in SEAL Hell Week, the toughest training evolution in any special ops service in any military anywhere in the world ever—even tougher than the old Soviet Spetsnaz regimen. The unknown was as common as the unexpected. Pain was constant. If an operation was going well you were probably running into a trap. Murphy's Law. That and incoming rounds had the right of way, something he'd been reminded of at the rec center.

"Over here!" Ashely shouted as Cameron scrambled out from beneath the shaft.

The shock from the impact of the bullet in his right thigh was wearing off, and he was limping as he reached where she was crouched beneath the forward end of the feedwater pump, above which was the turbine case, where another lump of Semtex had been molded.

She started to move aside. "You've been shot," she said.

"I'll live," Cameron said. "Let me in there."

"No, I'll do it," Ashley said, and she reached up for the wire and started to pull, but Cameron grabbed her wrist and held it in place.

"Easy," he said. "No sparks."

Their faces were inches apart, and when she realized exactly what he was telling her, she blanched and released the wire.

"You do it," she said. "I'll go find the next one."

At that moment another massive explosion rocked the power plant, this one much closer, but higher up toward the top of the furnace nearer to the forward end of the wellhead, and debris was falling back there, twisting metal and what sounded like piping.

Cameron steadied himself against the feedwater pump case and gently eased the wire out of the explosive.

"We need to get out of here," he said, turning, but Ashley was already gone, and as he ducked out from beneath the pump he saw her disappear beneath the steam control valve assemblies, as even more debris rained down from the towering furnace structure less than one hundred feet away.

He leaned up against the pump, which was about the size of an SUV, his head swirling. He'd lost a fair amount of blood, and although his wounds were only seeping now, he was having trouble keeping on track. But help wasn't coming. It was just him and the boss's daughter, a brassy woman with more balls than just about every civilian he'd ever met.

Pushing away from the case he limped twenty feet farther along the power chain to where Ashley had crawled up beneath a series of large diameter steel pipes coated in a carbon fiber heat jacket. He could only see her feet and her legs from the hips down about fifteen feet up.

"Wait!" he shouted.

A second later she ducked out from beneath the maze, a seriously nervous look on her face, but then she smiled. "I did it!" she shouted, climbing back down.

A third explosion came, this one near the base of the furnace and practically on top of them, so close that the air danced in front of Cameron's eyes and he was thrown to the floor, his ears ringing, the hum of the turbine blotted out.

Ashley had fallen to her knees and she was just scrambling to her feet when Whitney was suddenly there, a stricken look on her face, and she was saying something, shouting it seemed to Cameron, but he could barely make out her words.

The two women helped him to his feet, and he managed to get his voice.

"Too late. We have to get out of here right now. The ceiling is about to cave in."

"They're all dead in the rec room, Jim. What's going on? Who's doing this?"

Cameron grabbed her arm. "I don't know, but Mike and Tim are dead up in the control room, and we have to go right now!"

Ashley suddenly spun around as if she'd been hit in the leg or hip, and blood suddenly erupted from a long gash just below the waistband of her jeans.

Cameron hadn't heard the shot but he knew damn well that they were taking incoming fire from at least one of the terrorists left behind. He pulled Whitney to the right and slammed into Ashley, knocking her off her feet, the three of them dropping to the floor behind a steel beam supporting the deaerator casing as two more bullets ricocheted off the concrete floor, just missing them.

14

A S FAR AS Egan was concerned stealth was no longer an issue nor were comms with his team, because the explosions had already started and all that was left were Dr. Kemal riding pillion and Gordy manning the electronics in the motor home. There was just about zero chance that anyone was coming to the rescue and no one inside the power plant was going to survive.

They topped the last rise and raced down to the Newell parked in a shallow bowl as Gordy appeared at the open door, and started to hop from foot to foot, the same thing he said that a computer genius he'd heard of did whenever he was excited.

"You son of a bitch, you did it!" he shouted as Egan pulled up, shut the ATV down, and dismounted.

"Time?"

"Fifty-nine, thirty-one."

"Start up, we're getting out of here."

Gordy looked back up toward the rise. "Where're Moose and the girls?"

"Dead," Egan said. "Now, start up."

"He shot Ada!" Kemal screamed.

Egan looked at the scientist, nothing more than a rag-head in his estimation. "It was necessary," he said. He turned back to Gordy. "I'm going to disconnect the trailer and then we're going to drive away, unless you want to wait around for the cops or somebody to show up and arrest us all."

Widell stopped hopping. "Right," he said. "Loud and clear. We got miles to make." And he went back inside the motor home.

Dr. Kemal was shaking with rage and fear. "They were our team. Our friends."

"Get inside, I'll be right behind," Egan said. He was beginning to lose his patience, but Kemal was the one person he could not leave behind. If his body was found and identified too soon, the eggheads across at the operations center might put it together and take a little extra care sifting through the debris once things cooled down. If that were to happen before the bacteria at the wellhead was released into the coal seam everything they'd done would have been for nothing. Repairs would be made, and Donna Marie would be back up and running within a month or two. Not part of his contract.

"There's still time."

"No."

"We can't leave them! For the sake of Allah and our prophet we must go back!"

The motor home's diesel rumbled into life.

"Go inside!" Egan shouted.

Kemal turned back to the ATV and climbed aboard, but the key was gone, and when he realized it he jumped off and pulled a pistol out from a pocket in his coveralls.

"Do you want to spend the rest of your life in jail, you stupid bastard?" Egan shouted. He pointed back toward the rise. "Moose is dead, you saw his body. And no one inside the power plant will survive."

"You shot Ada."

"The bitch would have died trying to find her friend. They were dykes. What does your religion say about that?"

Kemal shook his head in despair. "They were ready to convert. I gave them a Quran."

"Go back and get them, if that's what you want," Eagan said, and he tossed the key over. "But you'll die trying, and we won't wait for you."

"Give me ten minutes," Kemal said, and pocketing his pistol he turned to get back aboard the ATV.

Egan unslung his carbine and fired a short burst, catching Kemal low in the back, knocking him forward, the second and third shots taking the back of his skull off.

"It's a tough old world," Egan mumbled.

Gordy came back to the door, his eyes wide. "Holy shit, you wasted the doc."

"He was getting stupid on me."

The two of them carried Kemal's body into the motor home and dumped it on the floor in the rear compartment. Egan went back outside and disconnected the ATV trailer from the hitch, undid the chains, and let the tongue drop to the ground.

He checked his wristwatch and looked up toward the crest of the rise. The next explosion, this one just behind the wellhead would occur within the next five minutes, and as much as he wanted to wait around to hear it, he wanted to be well away before the cavalry arrived—which would happen at some point this evening.

If the final phase of the operation went as he'd planned it, he would be drinking a cold beer he'd left in the mini-fridge in his room at the Radisson in Rapid City sometime before midnight. Tomorrow morning he would fly to Chicago aboard United 6190 at six o'clock. Just another business-man trading in coal futures. Which he thought was actu-ally a good joke.

From Chicago he would lay low in Michigan's Upper Peninsula until the dust settled and he found out about his payment from Kast.

Gordy was behind the wheel when Egan climbed back aboard. "South," he said. "Twelve miles to White Butte where we'll ditch the rig and pick up our Chevy. Remem-ber the way?"

"Just the two of us now," Gordy said nervously.

Egan grinned. "Yup, it's a tough old world out there, son, but look on the bright side. Now we just have to split the money two ways, not six."

Gordy suddenly grabbed for something inside his white coveralls, but before he could turn in his seat, a pistol in his hand, Egan flipped his PDW off his shoulder and pulled off one shot at point-blank range to the side of the kid's head, slamming his body against the side window.

It took a couple of minutes to manhandle the kid out of the driver's seat and clean up the blood splatter before Egan got behind the wheel and headed south on the dirt road, twenty minutes or more before any communica-tions to or from the Initiative would be possible.

And in the following confusion it might take an hour or more before the Air Force Rapid Reponse team made it up from Ellsworth in Rapid City.

15

ASHLEY FELT NO pain in her right hip, which she didn't think was right. Jim Cameron was lying half on and half off her and Dr. Lipton, the woman who wasn't supposed to be here, was sprawled on her side under some piping, their faces inches apart.

"I think we need to get out of here before the place comes down around our heads," she said, but she was whispering and Whitney shook her head.

Cameron rolled away, his pistol in hand and he fired off two shots toward a section of the upper part of the furnace that was still intact.

The turbine was still running and the high pitched whine louder at this end made any conversation all but impossible. Ashley was sick to her stomach, her head spinning, and it took her a moment to realize that she might be in shock.

"Can you move?" Cameron shouted. "Can you at least crawl?"

"Yes!" Ashley shouted and nodded.

Whitney scrambled on all fours over to where Cameron was crouched behind a piece of machinery that looked something like an oversized water heater, and started shouting something, but Cameron shoved her back a split second before a bullet pinged off the side of the machinery.

Cameron reached around the feedwater heater and fired back once, then he dropped his pistol, which skittered out across the floor, and fell backwards, his head bouncing off the concrete floor, a crease in his right shoulder.

Ashley had once listened to her father describe a firefight he'd been involved with in Bosnia. He'd been a lieutenant colonel at the time, a UN observer outside of Sarajevo, when his group of five men, two of them Canadian, one Australian, and two South Africans, had come under intense fire from what turned out to be a Serbian ethnic cleansing squad. The gun battle had gone on for only four minutes before the Serbs had withdrawn.

"Longest and shortest four minutes of my life," her father had admitted.

That was in the late nineties after everything was over, and she'd listened to his story not just as a daughter, but as a budding journalist, and she'd read between the lines that he'd been frightened. It was then that she'd come to respect him as a man and not just love him as an iron man father. He'd become a vulnerable human being to her.

Capable of the same fear she was feeling now, and admitting it.

"There was no place to dig in, so we had to stay two steps ahead of them, firing over our shoulders as we bugged out," he'd explained.

In her mind it was just like that now. They needed to get the hell out of here.

Ashley crawled over to where Whitney was dragging Cameron back behind the machinery and lent a hand as two more shots ricocheted off the floor.

But there was nowhere to go now without exposing

themselves to the shooter. And there would be more explosions because they could no longer reach the plastique.

"Go!" Cameron shouted at them. His complexion was pale. He was obviously in a lot of pain but he wasn't out of it. "This shit's going to start coming down around your heads."

"We're pulling you out," Whitney said.

"No."

"Yes!" Ashley shouted, getting her voice. But she honestly didn't know if she could move ten feet on her own, let alone drag Cameron out even with Dr. Lipton's help.

"Jesus!" Cameron shouted, rearing back.

Ashley looked over her shoulder as a large figure suddenly loomed out of the smoke and dust. He was wearing a dark brown jacket, some kind of a billed cap on his head, a big pistol in his right hand, and he was limping but moving fast. Her first impression was that the shooter had somehow gotten around behind them and right now they were just seconds way from being blown away.

Whitney started to scramble toward Cameron's pistol, which lay about ten feet way completely exposed, when the figure shouted something like, get back, and Ashley suddenly knew who he was and she grabbed Whitney's leg and held her back.

"It's okay!" she shouted.

"About time you civilians got off your butts!" Cameron shouted. "How'd you get in?"

"Your visitors left the back gate open," Osborne said, dropping down beside Cameron. "You okay?"

"I'll live. We've got one shooter somewhere about fifty feet away, high, damned good. And we still have one or more C4 or Semtex charges set on a timer. Should go off any moment now."

"Just the one detonator by the turbine?"

"So far as I know."

"I shut it down," Osborne said. "Dr. Lipton, you okay?"

"Everybody at the rec center is dead."

"Have you been injured?"

"No."

"Ms. Borden?"

"I feel like I've been kicked in the butt."

"Looks like you're going to get a good story this time," Osborne said. He eased over to the edge of the feedwater heater and took a quick peek.

The shooter fired once, the bullet grazing the side of the pump inches away from Osborne's head and he ducked back. "Determined," he said. "What's back there that can hurt us, other than the one using us for target practice?"

"Only one?" Whitney asked.

"Yes."

She shrugged. "The furnace, but there's no gas feed to it until morning. Nothing's pressurized, no steam. If they blow up anything else, a lot of steel girders, pipes, and some serious machinery could come down on our heads. Lubricating oil reservoirs could catch fire, but most of the microbes have already been injected into the seam. All that's left is the gadget in the morning."

Osborne had a general idea what she was talking about, and so far as he knew it was all strictly classified, on a need to know basis, and someone would have to have to talk to Ashley Borden before she got out of here. The details weren't ready for the media. The attack would be reported as against the ELF project.

A lot of black smoke was roiling out from the far end of the generating hall, some of it extremely noxious, and it was starting to make breathing difficult.

"We're going to have to get out of here before we choke to death," Ashley said.

"Not without help," Whitney said. "The bastard has us pinned down."

"I tried to call for backup, but all of our communications are down," Cameron said.

"I figured as much," Osborne said. "I had State Radio call Ellsworth about ten minutes ago, so help should be on its way."

"I don't know where the hell you got the protocol, but I'm sure glad you did," Whitney said. "So how do we get out of here?"

"Create a diversion," Ashley said. "I'll go for the Glock."

She started to move out from behind the feedwater heater but Osborne grabbed her arm and pulled her back. "You'll get yourself killed that way. Whoever is doing the shooting has the high ground and they're damned good. Anyway you need to come out of this in one piece, your father would never forgive me otherwise. And I can't go out for dinner and drinks with a corpse or a cripple. Deal?"

Ashley looked up at him, and after a moment she managed a tight smile. "Deal," she said. "What's your plan?"

"You and Dr. Lipton are going to help Jim out of here," he said. He handed his 9mm SIG-Sauer and spare magazine of ammunition to Cameron. "Do you have a spare?"

"No," Cameron said, seeing what Osborne had in mind. "But I've only fired three times, and I loaded a fifteen-round mag."

"Then we're about even for now," Osborne said. His SIG was also loaded with a fifteen-round magazine. "Ready?"

Cameron checked the pistol and nodded. "I owe you one."

"What?" Whitney demanded.

"We don't have time, Doc," Cameron said as he managed to get to his knees, steadying himself with one hand.

Whitney, realizing what was about to happen, started

to protest, but Cameron reached around the feedwater heater and pulled off two shots that were immediately returned as Osborne dove out from behind the machinery, rolling as he moved, snatching the Glock with one hand while levering himself to the right with his other, and pulling off four shots in rapid succession toward where he figured the lone shooter was hiding about fifty feet above the floor.

A half-dozen shots ricocheted off the concrete floor following just behind him as he made it to the relative safety of a broad steel beam supporting the ceiling.

Ashley and Whitney helped Cameron to his feet. They looked across to where Osborne was holed up and Cameron nodded.

Osborne reached around the beam and fired two shots high and to the right. Almost instantly the shooter fired back, the bullets plinking against the beam, and Cameron reached around the feedwater heater and fired two shots.

There was no immediate return fire and Cameron and the two women stepped out from around the machinery and hobbled as quickly as they could go toward the back door.

Osborne's attention was focused on the upper portions of the boiler steam drum atop the aft sections of the furnace when he caught a slight movement and he fired three shots before ducking back.

The shooter returned fire on his position, but then realizing the mistake switched aim toward Cameron and the women but it was too late, they'd already reached the safety of the towering deaerator device.

Something about the sound of the weapon was slightly bothersome to Osborne. He was sure he knew it from somewhere. More than a semiautomatic as it had been fired to this point, because the rounds had been pulled off too easily. But it was just a feeling.

A moment later something metallic clattered down from above. Osborne heard the characteristic snap of a magazine being slapped home, and he instinctively hunched back behind the steel beam, making himself as invisible as he possibly could.

It came to him all of a sudden that the gun was a Knight Personal Defense Weapon. He'd learned about it in Afghanistan during an intensive briefing on American, British, and Australian contractors hired to act as guards for VIPS in the entire theater, including Iraq. Almost to a man their automatic weapon of preference was the Knight. It fired a 6x35mm round that was considerably larger and more powerful than either the standard 9mm Para or .45 ACP with twice the muzzle velocity and a theoretical cyclic rate of seven hundred rounds per minute. Plus it was extremely compact with a length of less than eighteen inches when the stock was retracted and an empty weight of only four and a half pounds.

An instant after the shooter reloaded they fired a full thirty rounds on full auto, the bullets slamming into the steel beam, off the concrete floor, and into the wall behind Osborne, sending chips and bullet fragments everywhere, one of them nicking the side of his neck just below his right ear.

Osborne waited for the sound of another magazine being ejected and discarded, but for several long seconds there was nothing except for the whine of the turbine, until a tremendous explosion somewhere behind and below the shooter's position blotted out all sounds and sights, and it seemed as if the entire installation were caving in on top of him and he started to run.

16

OSBORNE FIGURED THAT the shooter had managed to manually fire one of the remaining blocks of Semtex as a last-ditch suicide mission, which made them crazy, most likely some Islamic militant. But that didn't make a lot of sense. Why hit a research facility?

Something was on fire at the front end of the generating hall, and the noises of machinery and metal beams collapsing, concrete breaking up, and the roof coming down blotted out just about everything except for the high-pitched whine of the turbine still spinning.

A tall, slender man in white coveralls, a bullet hole in the side of his head, lay on the floor, his arms flung out as if he were trying to give up. Osborne had seen him on the way in, and now he recognized it was Pete Magliano, who was the Army Public Information officer for the project. It would have been him who escorted Ashley over here and he'd given his life for it.

Pocketing Cameron's pistol, he scooped up Magliano's body and carried it the rest of the way to the rear door and outside, the night air dry and the wind bitterly cold. He gently laid it down next to the body of a woman dressed in white coveralls and armed with a PDW. She'd been shot several times in the back.

Whitney was with Cameron, who'd managed to climb into his Hummer and was on the radio with someone, and in the distance to the south Osborne could hear several helicopters incoming. When he had them located he spotted their lights, low and fast, up from Ellsworth one hundred and fifty miles away.

Ashley was leaning against her pickup and she was pulling out her cell phone, but when she saw Osborne she came over. "You made it," she said, and looked at Magliano's body. "We had no idea what was going to happen. He had just explained to me about the turbine and I ducked under it to get a better look when they shot him. I don't think he knew what hit him."

"Probably not," Osborne said, and he held out his hand. "Give me your cell phone."

"Doesn't work in here," she said. But then she realized what he meant and she stepped back. "No way in hell, Sheriff."

"I don't want to arrest you after all of this, but unless you give me your phone I'll turn you over to the Air Force team who'll be here any minute."

"Goddamnit, this is my story."

"Not yet. Maybe never. But certainly not until we find out who's behind this mess and why."

"Terrorists."

"Probably. But there was no reason for them to hit an ELF station, there've been no protests out here like in Wisconsin."

"This is no ELF facility and you know it," Ashley said. "It's a power station all right, but the antennas out there are fake. Dr. Lipton is a microbiologist not an electronics expert and Lieutenant Magliano told me something about microbes being injected into the coal seam. Plus my dad is involved out here and he used to be DARPA. Heavy-duty shit."

The helicopters were much closer now, and Osborne counted four of them by their lights. "Tell that to the Air Force and you'll start off in the brig at Ellsworth, and then probably a federal penitentiary somewhere, and your father—if he is involved—would most likely sign the order."

"Bullshit," Ashley said. She glanced at Whitney, at Cameron, and then at the incoming choppers. "I won't give you my phone, but I promise not to use it in connection with this story."

"Or write about it when you get back to Bismarck."

"I won't, I promise you that much, too, but I'm going to lean on some people—starting with my dad—to find out what's going on. I was shot at tonight, and I don't very much like that."

"Nobody does, especially Pete Maglianao."

"Sorry," she said. "I didn't mean it that way."

"I expect you didn't," Osborne said. "But I'm going to hold you to your promise."

"Okay."

"And you have dirt on your chin."

Ashley laughed and pocketed her cell phone as Osborne walked over to Cameron and Whitney.

"How do you guys want to play this?" he asked. "I've probably seen and heard too much tonight."

"You had the briefing in Washington, and I expect after tonight you'll probably be given the whole thing. At least that's what Whitney and I are going to recommend, but it'll be up to General Forester."

"He's in charge?"

"Yeah," Cameron said. "Which makes his daughter a problem."

"She's promised to hold off until she talks to him."

"Do you trust her?" Whitney asked.

"Yes, I do."

"Fair enough, Nate," Cameron said. He had a lot of blood on his jacket and he was pale. "But for now let me do most of the talking. You were on a routine patrol cruising for illegal elk hunters, saw the back gate open, and drove down."

"Wasn't for you we'd all be dead," Whitney said, glancing toward the rec center and the other trailers.

"What about your scientists over at the control center?"

"I'll tell them we had an accident. But one thing's for sure, we sure as hell won't run the experiment in the morning. Maybe not for months, even a year."

The four helicopters, two of them MH-60 Black Hawk combat choppers, the other two heavy lifters, circled the power station then came around, flared, and touched down in a row in a field about twenty yards away. Immediately a half-dozen medics jumped out and came over on a run, some of them carrying back boards and others with medical equipment; twelve or fifteen others were armed and immediately set up a loose perimeter. A medium-height man with a dark mustache dressed in a flight suit, captain's bars sewn on his collars, and a pistol holstered across his chest, strode across to where Cameron climbed painfully out of the Hummer.

The captain, whose name tag read NETTLES, saluted even as he was eyeing Cameron and the others. "You've been hit," he said. "Medic!"

"Glad you could make it, Glenn, but the situation is contained so far as I can tell," Cameron said.

"This facility is under lockdown as of this moment. How much damage have you sustained inside the plant?"

"A lot, but there isn't much flammable if the wellhead

wasn't damaged, we'll be back up in business within a month or six weeks. But we need more on-site security here, and you know damned well we do."

But this was rural North Dakota, and the U.S. wasn't in a global war, so ARPA-E had decided on the low-key route. And tonight was a direct result of something that could have been prevented, and Cameron was bitter at the same time. As head of Initiative Security this was his fault, and yet it had been beyond his control.

"Not your fault, Jim."

"Tell that to Pete Magliano's family, and the families of the two guys up in the control center and the others over at the rec center. It was a bloodbath. They didn't have a chance."

A medic came over and made a quick examination of Cameron who leaned against the Hummer. "Looks like you got lucky," he said, swabbing the shoulder and leg wounds and placing field dressings over them. "We're setting up a MASH unit, but this should hold you for the time being."

Ashley had come over and the medic checked her out, placing another field dressing over the crease in her hip.

Four people were erecting a tent about fifty feet away, and even as it was going up others were off-loading medical equipment from the choppers.

"We have casualties over at the double-wide," Cameron said. "I think they're all dead, but check it out please."

"I'm on it," the medic said, and looked at Osborne. "You're wounded, sir," he said.

"It'll hold," Osborne said. "Did any of your people see anything on the way in?"

"We saw nothing," Nettles said. "But we weren't looking especially hard. Our mission is to secure this facility; we leave criminal apprehension to the civilian authorities. In any event, what are you doing here, sir?" Nettles demanded.

"Saving our asses," Cameron said, and he explained the situation beginning with the sudden attack on the party at the double-wide, the bodies of the engineers in the power station control, Lieutenant Magliano's body on the main floor, and the planted plastique charges, some of which he and Ashley Borden had managed to disarm, and the confrontation after Osborne had arrived through the open back gate.

"Then the project owes you a thanks, Sheriff," Nettles said. "But if you don't require any medical treatment I'd ask that you leave this facility, but make yourself available within the next twenty-four hours for debriefing. The same goes for you, Ms. Borden."

"No," Whitney said. "Sheriff Osborne saved some lives here tonight, and although the situation looks bad he probably prevented a lot more damage. This is a civilian facility and I am the principal scientist in charge. He will be briefed here and now."

"That include newspaper reporters?"

"At this moment, I'd say yes."

"You're going to have a crowd out here within the next few hours, Captain, whether you like it or not," Ashley said. "You'll need a rep who knows the requirements of the service as well as the media."

The Rapid Response Team was air force because Ellsworth was the nearest military base that could field such a C^3I plus medical mission that included Command, Control, Communications, and Intelligence, plus medics, but the Initiative was under the DoE, and even though on-site security was provided by the army, Dr. Lipton was in charge.

"On your orders, ma'am," Nettles told Whitney. "But in the meantime all the casualties will be treated here, or medivaced to Ellsworth. No one is going to a civilian hospital." He raised his right hand and snapped his fingers, and a sergeant carrying a military-hardened laptop came forward.

"Comms have been restored, Captain," the sergeant, whose name tape read IVERSON, said.

"Get me General Forester."

Iverson set up the laptop on the lowered tailgate of Ashley's pickup truck, and got online.

"This is your part of the universe, Sheriff," Nettles said. "Didn't you notice anything or anyone unusual around here?"

"Elk hunters," Osborne said. "But they knew the codes for the back gate, and apparently they did something to wipe out communications, including cell phones. Until just now. A little more sophisticated than the average hunter or Dickinson rancher could manage."

"Not my brief, sir," Nettles snapped, his dislike obvious.

"And what is your brief, Captain?"

"Securing the facility after an incursion."

"Doesn't seem to me like you're doing a very good job of it. You haven't even determined if any of the perps are still here."

"I have General Forester, sir," the communications tech announced.

"This facility, along with the control center, has been secured. And that, sir, is my only brief for the moment."

17

OSBORNE WALKED OVER to his SUV and got on the radio to State. "Sally, you still awake?"

"Nate, thank goodness. I've been trying to reach you for the past half hour. The nine-one-one lines have been going crazy. We've already had three calls. Something about an explosion and a fire down at the ELF facility. Have you seen anything?"

"Right in the middle of it. Listen, call Burt Lance over in Bismarck and tell him that I have a developing situation that involves a possible terrorist attack on the facility. Lots of damage, lots of casualties." Lance was the commandant of the North Dakota State Highway Patrol. "Then wake up the governor, I think we might have to coordinate this with the National Guard, but that part will have to be worked out with the folks in charge here. You still with me?"

"I'm on it, what else?" Sally was a retired high school math teacher and as sharp as they came.

"Call Tommy over in Bismarck, tell him I want a fly-over out here at first light." Tommy Seagram ran Bismarck Air Charters, and had been a chopper pilot in the first Iraq war. He had an old refurbished Huey and a newer

Bell Jet Ranger. Best of all he knew western North Dakota's hunting grounds, federal parklands, and scenic areas like the palm of his hand.

"What's he supposed to be looking for?"

"Have him call me ASAP, I'm riding with him."

"Just a minute, I have an incoming," Sally said.

Osborne looked over to where Nettles and Cameron and the others were gathered around the laptop on the tailgate of Ashley's pickup. Nettles was using a handset for the audio. But then he put it aside.

Sally was back. "I just talked to a Captain Nettles, says he's on-site. He's ordered a communications blackout. I'm not supposed to say anything to anybody."

"Just do as I asked, would you? He's standing ten feet away from me. I'll take care of it."

"He's from South Dakota, what does he know?" Sally said, and she was gone.

Osborne walked over to where Nettles was giving his preliminary briefing to General Forester whose image was on the screen. The general was in a tuxedo, the bow tie undone, seated behind a desk in what could have been a library with book-lined shelves or more likely the study in someone's private home.

"You say there are casualties?" Forester demanded. He was hopping mad.

"They're all dead on this side, Bob," Whitney told him. "They were having a party in the rec room when someone shot through the side of the trailer. Tom Snow and Mike Ridder were in Donna Marie's control center and Jim said both of them were shot to death."

"Jesus," Forester said softly. "What about the research center?"

"They just hit the power station and got out. My people are okay."

"How extensive is the damage?"

"I'll need a structural engineer out here as soon as possible, but I think the wellhead and turbine have come out of it okay. As far as the experiment goes we were lucky. Twenty-four hours from now it would have been a completely different story."

"Don't say anymore," Forester said. "I'll have someone from MIT on the ground within twelve hours. In the meantime who else is involved? Captain Nettles said Nate Osborne got through the fence."

Osborne stepped into camera range. "Good evening, General."

"What's the situation as you see it?"

"Looks like a military operation to me. They apparently had the proper codes for the back gate and they came down on what I'm guessing were several ATVs—two of which they left behind—split into two teams, one taking out whoever was in the trailers and the second to take out the personnel in the power plant, and set a lot of plastique to take out some serious-looking machinery."

Cameron stepped into camera range and briefed the general on what he'd seen and done. "This was sophisticated, General. They somehow took down all of our communications channels, including cell phones, landlines, and probably satellite links. They definitely knew what they were doing, and exactly what they were after."

"What are we doing to catch up with them? They couldn't have gotten that far."

"It's dark and these are the Badlands," Osborne said.

"I'll have a KeyHole satellite tasked to take a look for heart signatures."

"They'll be long gone by the time you could convince someone over at the NSA to move a bird," Osborne said. "But I'm going to do a flyover first thing in the morning.

We'll pick up something. And besides we have two of their people here. One stuck it out inside the plant, but it looks as if there was some sort of a fallout and the second one was shot to death just outside the back door."

Forester looked away for a long moment and when he came back he seemed resolved, while at first he had seemed nonplussed as if he'd received a nasty, totally unexpected shock—which in fact he had. "Priority one is getting back up and running. The experiment must be carried out as soon as possible."

"I'm going to have to explain this to my people, and we'll need to bring in replacements for Snow and Ridder, and the generator crew," Whitney said.

"I'll see to it tonight," Forester said. "The second priority is finding the bastards who did this to us, and why—though I have a fair idea as to the latter."

"Care to fill me in, sir?" Osborne asked.

"Not tonight, but I'm going to fly out first thing in the morning. We need to get some things on the table. In the meantime I'll have the FBI send people to you, but, Nate, it's your territory. You know it better than any outsider, so these guys will be working for you, not the other way around."

"I appreciate it."

"And our third priority is containing the leaks," Forester said. "No leaks. Your PA Pete Magliano will have to hold down the fort until I can get someone out there to lend a hand. But this has got to be low-key. And I mean *low*-key."

"Pete is dead," Cameron said. "But we have another problem, sir. He was shot to death by the terrorists inside the plant while escorting your daughter on a tour."

Ashley stepped into camera range. "Hi, Daddy," she said.

Forester didn't seem surprised. He just shook his head and smiled. "What are you doing in the middle of this?"

"Trying to get a story."

"Are you okay? Have you been hurt?"

"I got shot in the butt, but I've been in worse shape."

"Nothing goes in the paper or on the wire until you and I talk. I'm serious about this."

"Nate Osborne gave me the same lecture. I'm going to keep my eyes and ears open, but I won't publish anything until I get your okay."

"Good enough for me," Forester said, but Nettles was right there.

"Sir, we need to contain any and all leaks."

"I said her word was good enough for me. I want a complete sweep through Donna Marie as well as the research center and the entire perimeter fence. And I'll expect your report no later than oh eight hundred."

"Yes, sir," Nettles said. It was obvious he didn't like it, but he turned back to his people and gave his orders, and went to his chopper where he got on the radio.

"The media are going to be here soon, how do you want me to handle them?" Whitney asked.

"Use your conference room at the center, but keep them away from Donna Marie, and no mention of a terrorist incursion."

"Casualties?"

"I'll let you handle names, but for now it was nothing more than an industrial accident."

"Someone will have taken notice of the Air Force helicopters," Ashley said.

"It's an ELF experimental station," Forester said. "Military."

"I'm in the middle of this, Dad, and I sure as hell know all about military SOP and something about journalists, so I'll make you a trade. I'll hang around as a media spokesman tonight."

"In return for what?"

"Exclusivity," Ashley said. "I want to be here with Dr. Lipton and Nate Osborne for your debriefing. You tell me everything and I promise to write nothing—not one word, not even a hint—until I get the green light from you personally."

"This is more important than you can possibly guess."

"Then you need me."

"I'll think about it," Forester said.

18

NOTHING HAD BEEN put on the police radio so none of Osborne's three deputies had heard about the business at the ELF, which for now was just fine. Less complicated at least for tonight, though sitting alone in his office on the first floor of the Billings County courthouse in Medora, he didn't know if keeping his people out of the loop for now was the right thing to do.

An Air Force medic had put two stitches in his neck wound, given him a shot of antibiotic, and told him to go home and get some sleep. And definitely no alcohol for at least twenty-four hours.

It was four in the morning, his prosthetic leg popped up on the open bottom file drawer of his desk, a glass of Jack Daniel's neat, the bottle on the desk, as he tried to sort out the conflict between good police work and the need for secrecy at the ELF station. Billings was a sprawling county of two thousand square miles with a population of only a little more than eight hundred people, down more than 7 percent in the last few years, and still dropping. Medora, the county seat, was home to less than one hundred people, that number dropping as well.

"What are you running from?" his wife Carolyn had asked three days after he'd moved her and their three-year-old daughter to the ranch he'd inherited from his parents.

It was late like now, and Elizabeth Anne was asleep in bed, and they were sitting on the front porch looking up at the crystal clear sky filled with a billion stars. He pointed up.

"It's clean out here. Uncomplicated. No smog, no freeways, no drive-by shootings, no nine-elevens."

"That's because the tallest building in one hundred miles is a grain silo," Carolyn had shot back.

They were on their second bottle of Chianti and he'd had the start of a buzz, but not her. No matter how much she drank she would never allow herself to act drunk, where he, after Afghanistan, welcomed the little release from his nightmares. And he'd just wanted to go to bed and make love to his wife, but that had been another problem between them; she couldn't stand to see him without his prosthetic leg on, and the few times they'd made love after the hospital, had been almost chaste, with the lights out and her legs spread wide so that she didn't have to feel the stump against her thigh.

"I need this for just a little while," he told her. "Maybe a couple of years tops. Can you give me that much?"

"You grew up with these people. Went to school with them. Football star, homecoming king—with your queen, who's now married and has two kids."

"Not bad."

"I'm not saying it is, Nathan. But you're home, and a couple of years from now you won't want to leave. And I don't blame you. Hell, they'll probably even put up a statue to you downtown. Nathan Osborne, hometown hero who gave his leg for his country."

Osborne looked at her and smiled sadly as her face dropped.

"I'm sorry, Nathan. I didn't mean that the way it came out, and you know it."

Not darling or sweetheart or even just plain Nate. But Nathan proper. He nodded.

"I can't stand the isolation. I'm going insane."

"Maybe you should fly down to Orlando, spend a week or two with your sister and the kids. Might do you some good to get back to the world."

She'd looked away for a longish time, but then turned back a slight smile all the way up to her eyes. "My place is here with you, for however long it takes."

Which was about six months, Osborne reflected, before she just packed up one morning and asked if he could drive her and Elizabeth Anne over to the airport at Dickinson. And that was the end of that. Here today, gone tomorrow. For good, because the divorce petition came by registered mail one year later.

That was five years ago, and it still hurt, though every year she sent Elizabeth Anne up for two weeks in the summer and he could see and hear the ex-wife in their child; a little too stiff and proper, and little too much of a young lady who didn't appreciate getting dirty, and who this last summer talked a lot about Robert, "Mother's new friend from the Guggenheim in New York."

Jim Cameron in fresh jeans and a "Go Army" sweatshirt came in through the back way, limped across the small squad room, and knocked on the open door. He'd brought a bottle of Jim Beam, which he held up. "A libation for the conquering hero?"

"Screw you," Osborne said good-naturedly. He and Cameron weren't particularly close, but they'd been introduced during Osborne's briefing on the ELF facility a few years ago, and he'd seen the man around town every now and then.

"A man of few words, that's good," Cameron said. He pulled up a chair and sat across the desk. "Got an extra glass, or am I supposed to drink out of the bottle?"

Osborne handed him a coffee cup. "Best I can do for the moment."

"Dirty," Cameron said, looking at the cup, but he poured a healthy measure of whiskey and drank it down.

"How're you feeling?"

"Actually like shit. This happened on my watch, and if it hadn't been for you I don't know how it would have turned out."

"I got lucky."

"Yeah, I guess," Cameron said, and he poured another drink.

"What's next?"

"We had the media briefing at the research center around midnight, or I should say the general's daughter ran it. She was pretty good. Knew just what to say, and whenever she got in over her head she turned it over to Whitney. They put on a hell of a dog and pony show."

"The press still out there?"

"Nope. Just another industrial accident, not big enough to rate a front page even in Bismarck. They bought the story hook, line, and sinker. How about you?"

"I'm doing a fly-over first thing in the morning."

"I meant what do you think?"

"Terrorists, but I can't do much good until I find out their motive because what happened was no random strike by some pissed off local ranchers."

"Posse Comitatus," Cameron said. "We managed to get a probable ID on the woman who'd been shot in the back. Name is Ada Norman, forty-two, born in Fairbanks. She's on the bureau's persons of interest list. Skinhead, raging neo-Nazi, last known address a fire lane number outside Kalispell, Montana. The same number as another nut job named Barry Egan. Both of them disappeared about six months ago."

Osborne didn't know either name, but he was familiar with the Posse, just about everyone west of the Missouri River was. "That was fast."

"We have a watch list."

"Do you want to share it with me? Might make my job catching these people a little easier."

"Well, that's the problem until the general gets here sometime around noon. The FBI wants to handle this on their own, the Air Force thinks it has the brief to protect the Initiative, and although the White House hasn't weighed in yet, when it does things might get a bit interesting out here. Adds up to nobody wants you sticking your nose into our business."

"I know something about how the government, especially the military, operates."

"Everyone's aware of that fact," Cameron said. "But your Medal of Honor makes you way too high-profile. You can't fart on Main Street without someone sitting up and taking notice. And the question on everybody's mind is what the hell you're doing out here when you could go anywhere and do anything you want."

Osborne raised his glass and drank. "Thing is I'm where I want to be, doing what I want to do."

Cameron nodded, raised his glass, and took a drink. "Exactly what I told them," he said. "But they brought up your daughter and your ex."

Osborne held himself in check from lashing out. "Who is the *they*?"

"The DIA—Defense Intelligence Agency. Soon as

Nettles briefed his people they started looking over your shoulder. Asked me if you had abused your wife or daughter, if you were a drunk, if you were some pissed off war hero with a grudge. Shit like that."

"What'd you tell them?"

"That you were certifiable, of course," Cameron said with a straight face. "Who the hell else would want to live out here in the middle of nowhere?"

Osborne had to laugh. "Is it that bad?"

"These guys sometimes have a little problem understanding real people. But it'll be okay when Forester gets out here."

"I hope so, because a lot of people lost their lives last night. In my county. And I want to nail the bastards who did it."

"I'm with you. But your brief will be up to the general and no one else."

"It's not an ELF facility," Osborne said as a statement, not a question.

"No," Cameron said, and Osborne started to speak, but Cameron held him off. "That's as far as it goes for now."

"I was going to say that I know the Posse Comitatus. They don't believe in any government above the county level, or any higher law authority than the county sheriff. According to the common-law nutcases, if the sheriff refuses to carry out the will of the people the Posse is supposed to string him up at high noon downtown and leave his body there until sundown as an example."

"I didn't know that part."

"A lot of them are over in Montana, and some in Michigan. Crazy people, just like some of the guys I knew in Afghanistan."

Cameron was silent for a long time. Finally he poured another drink in his cup, and one for Osborne. "Do you think if you push your investigation they'll come after you?"

Osborne drank the Jim Beam and smiled. "I hope so. Like I said, this is my county."

19

A YOUNG, GOOD-LOOKING woman who'd introduced herself as Gabriela Mandina escorted Special U.S. Envoy Rupert Mann up the elevator to the executive level of the downtown Caracas headquarters of the state-owned petroleum company PDV, Petróleos de Venezuela S.A. It was well after eight in the evening, and Mann, forty-eight, with a head that seemed to be too large for his body, wide expressive eyes, and salt-and-pepper hair parted down the middle, was getting hungry. It was past his normal dinnertime, though here the evening meal was usually taken as late as eleven.

"I hope that you had a pleasant flight from Washington, Señor Mann," the girl, who could have been a runway model, said. Her English was perfect, with a British cast.

"It was, thank you. Is this a normal time for important meetings?"

"Oh, of course, we often save the very best for last."

Mann, who had been a Harvard law professor before President Robert Thompson had tapped him to become an adviser on energy, had become something of a roving ambassador whose primary missions were to smooth over difficult problems with foreign governments not exactly friendly to U.S. interests. Besides his law degree he was fluent in Spanish, French, and German, knew psychology, had a fair grasp of philosophies from the Greeks onward—especially the philosophies of government and of justice—a little mathematics, and even poetry. The president called him "the Renaissance man." And now with the pretty receptionist he recognized that he was being patronized and it irritated him, though he didn't let it show.

"You will be meeting with Rafael Araque, their minister of Energy and Oil, and with Andres Luzardo, the president of PDV," Thompson had told him in the Oval Office yesterday afternoon. "The bastards are putting the squeeze on us and I want to know why."

In the three years Mann had worked for the president he'd learned to be patient. Learned when to speak and when to listen, especially when Thompson was angry, like now.

"Chávez, on top of his cancer, is losing it financially. Worse than us, and he's starting to pull some really crazy shit. Among other things he thinks he can get away with increasing the price per barrel of sweet crude by twenty-three percent."

"That doesn't make any sense," Mann had been moved to say. More than that, it was outrageous.

"He's just raised the bus fare by fifty percent, which has caused rioting all across Caracas, the same as in the late eighties and for the same reason."

Venezuela was the fourth-largest importer of crude oil and petroleum to the U.S. just behind Canada, Mexico, and Saudi Arabia, and raising the cost per barrel would be intolerable. People couldn't afford it. Gas lines would become commonplace because most of the other importers were already operating nearly at capacity. That, as well as the increasing pressure from China and India for oil, would put an impossibly difficult strain on the U.S. economy that was just now showing feeble signs of recovery. Wars had been started for a lot less, and the president said exactly that.

"Find out what they want, but more important for all of us, what they'll accept."

"I'll do my best, Mr. President."

"I know you will."

Off the elevator the young woman led him down a plushly carpeted corridor with fabric-covered walls in beige, photographs of PDV operations around the country hung at tasteful intervals, to a well-decorated conference room. Two men were seated at the head of a long table and they both looked up with neutral smiles.

Gabriela introduced them: Araque, short, with a thick middle and balding gray hair; Luzardo, strongly built with a square face and deep-set emotionless eyes that made Mann think of a shark just before it attacked.

"Please, Señor Mann, have a seat," Araque said.

Mann sat to their left, and Gabriella sat next to him. "I'll act as an interpreter if needed," she said, her smile as dead as Luzardo's and he thought of the remora that attached themselves to sharks.

"As you wish," Mann said.

"I hope that you had no difficulty from the airport," Araque said.

"Not at all. In any event I've been in areas of civil unrest."

"Arrogant bastard," Luzardo said in Spanish half under his breath. But Mann caught it.

"Mr. Luzardo said that your reputation precedes you," Gabriela translated.

"Actually he seems to think that I'm an arrogant bastard," Mann said in Spanish.

Luzardo shrugged, and he motioned for the young woman to leave the room. She was no longer needed as an interpreter. When she was gone he came directly to the point. "Why are you here, Señor Mann?"

"President Thompson has asked that I open a dialogue so that we can reach some agreement that might be beneficial to both our countries," Mann began. He sounded pompous to his own ear, but these kinds of discussions usually followed a general pattern. Diplomacy happened when neither side knew what to say or how far to push things.

"We're raising our price per barrel to you by twenty-three percent. Do you perceive an ambiguity?"

"But you're not raising your prices for China or India."

"No," Luzardo said.

"Why?"

"Because we can."

"It will create an unnecessary hardship for our citizens."

"Yes," Luzardo said.

"There may be serious repercussions," Mann said, already knowing that his trip here had been useless. "Can there be no negotiations?"

"With the United States?" Araque demanded.

"Yes, Venezuela is still one of our major and most trusted trade partners. In the aftermath of Katrina your government held out a hand of friendship, offering help."

"Which your President Bush arrogantly refused, while at the same time planning for Operation Balboa to invade our country."

"There were never any invasion plans, but that was a different time, a different president."

"Then there was Obama, who said that we helped Colombian guerrillas. He had the same stench as Bush."

"Your President Chávez made that statement, but at the Summit of the Americas in April oh-nine he said that he wanted to become friends with President Obama."

Araque waved it off. "Can you tell me that there are no plans to assassinate our president?"

"You have my word."

Luzardo was sitting back, the same unreadable expression in his dead eyes. "You understand that sovereign nations need to protect themselves."

"As I said, sir, there are no plans to invade your country or assassinate your president."

"Perhaps or perhaps not, but you are presently busy at work trying to ruin our economy."

"That's simply not true."

"Oil is Venezuela's lifeblood. Without it our people would be driven to starvation."

"As would happen to my people without it," Mann said, no idea where this was going. But he had an ominous feeling that he was walking into a diplomatic trap.

"Do you know about the Dakota Initiative?"

And all of a sudden Mann knew that the trap had been sprung. "I have no idea what you're talking about," he said.

"That's too bad because you are lying, of course."

"No."

"Yes," Luzardo said coldly, no inflection in his baritone voice. "If Venezuela loses its U.S. oil market it would be devastating to our economy. Even as we speak we've had to raise our bus fares, and you've already seen what that small measure has done to our people."

"Your administration—every administration beginning with your first Bush—has been arrogant," Araque said angrily. "No other people matter more than yours. You rape the planet, and when you have depleted everyone's resources you move on, leaving the rest of us in your garbage heaps."

"Twenty-three percent is just the beginning, Mr. Envoy," Luzardo said. "Tell your president that if he plays with fire to be careful he does not burn himself with its unintended consequences."

"I cannot bring him that message."

"As you wish," Luzardo said. He picked up the phone. "Come."

Gabriella appeared at the door. "If you will come with me, Señor Mann," she said brightly.

"Can there be no further discussion? No negotiation?"

Neither Luzardo nor Araque answered, they simply looked at him as if he were some disagreeable object better served out of sight.

Mann got to his feet. "Craziness," he muttered, but he followed the girl to the elevator and back to the main floor.

"Have a pleasant journey home, sir," she said and walked away, her hips swaying and her heels tapping on the marble tile.

The receptionist at the front desk, another pretty girl, looked up and smiled as he passed and went outside. The chanting crowd that had all but filled the broad Avenida Bolivar had spilled out to the side streets, hundreds of them streaming by.

The government-supplied limousine that had brought him in from the airport was gone, and when he reached the curb he began to get the first glimmer that something was wrong.

A battered windowless Mercedes Sprinter van pulled up, and before Mann could react two men jumped out and hustled him into the backseat, and then a third man behind the wheel took off, easing his way through the crowd to the next corner where he turned south and accelerated.

"What's the meaning of this?" Mann sputtered, but he felt real fear, the first since a mission had gone wrong in Somalia three years ago.

"We're taking you back to the airport, señor, so that you can bring a message to your president from our president," one of the men who had grabbed him said.

Mann could only see forward out the windshield, but after a few blocks he realized that they weren't heading for the airport, and he said as much.

"That highway has been closed, we have to use an alternate route."

Mann began to panic. "Take me back to PDV."

"It's too late for that," the one man said. He had a cruel, narrow face, and his sweatshirt and jeans were dirty, stained with what might have been oil or grease.

Five minutes later they came to what looked like an industrial district of abandoned buildings, and rusted-out factories with rutted streets, a collapsed smokestack, and bricks reducing the road to a narrow lane.

"I'm an envoy from the president of the United States."

"You should have listened with respect," the narrow-faced man told him matter-of-factly.

The van turned down another lane, and pulled into the cavernous hall of a huge factory building, all the machinery gone, and stopped in front of a workbench standing alone in the middle of the space.

Mann's captors pulled him out of the van, as three men dressed in white coveralls, white booties, and gloves came out of the shadows. Two of them were almost as large as sumo wrestlers, while the third, much smaller man, carried a chain saw, and Mann's legs turned to water.

"You can't be serious!" he shouted, but his voice was lost in the large space.

The two wrestlers hauled him to the workbench and roughly slammed him facedown, bent over at the hips. A moment later the chain saw whined to life.

"No!" Mann shouted. "Please, I beg you!"

But the chain saw was right there, right on top of him. It revved up and he nearly managed to pull away when an intensely sharp pain bit into the back of his neck, blood flying everywhere in his peripheral vision, and suddenly the pain was gone and he was floating toward blackness, no last thoughts except horror for what was happening to him.

20

OSBORNE FIGURED THAT the terrorists had only two ways in or out last night. The first was north of the power station toward the Teddy Roosevelt National Park where a gravel road wound up connecting with the interstate highway nine miles west of Medora. From there they would have had clear driving into Montana. The second was to the south along the Little Missouri River, toward Amidon on U.S. 85, where a lot of out-of-state elk hunters came up from Rapid City.

It was eight in the morning, the air crisp enough to see your breath, when Tommy Seagram headed his Bell Jet Ranger south, along the river, from where he'd picked up Osborne at Chimney Park just outside of town. Far to the west the Sentinel Butte rose from the horizon while to the southeast was the Kinley Plateau.

Within a few minutes they picked up the smudge of a lingering fire at the Initiative rising into the clear sky.

"Trouble out here last night?" Seagram asked.

They wore headsets that made it possible to talk to each other without shouting. "Some," Osborne said.

"Unidentified aircraft on a course of two zero five eight

miles south-southwest of Medora, you are entering a restricted airspace. Please turn to one eight zero. Acknowledge."

Seagram banked the chopper slightly to the left so that they would pass a couple of miles to the east of the facility, and got on the guard frequency. "Roger," he said, and he gave his tail number. "We see smoke, do you require assistance?"

There was no answer and despite himself Osborne had to laugh. Seagram had been born and raised down in Rapid City and had moved up to Bismarck to, as he said, get away from the madding crowds, and "anything that smacks of authority." It was a common trait among a lot of North Dakotans, locals as well as imports.

"Goddamn bureaucrats," the chopper pilot said.

The Little Missouri River, which came down from the Missouri Creek above the Teddy Roosevelt Elkhorn Ranch, meandered all over the place like a drunken sailor. In many stretches it was just a trickle, sandbars everywhere, in some places there were grasslands and stands of ponderosa pine, in others stunted growth brush right down to the high-water mark. A million years of flow carved little canyons that were framed by rolling brown and green hills, cellular lava outflows, and in the distance like sentinels over a wasteland, rocky outcroppings and buttes and other fantastical, even alien rocky formations. These were the Badlands and Little Missouri Grasslands, home to Osborne and to Seagram and a lot of other people—not just ranchers—who loved the openness and stark beauty of it.

"Okay, so you got me out here, Nate, what do you have in mind?" Seagram asked as he glanced over. "Anything to do with the Initiative?"

"The place was attacked last night. Maybe as many as a half-dozen terrorists. Probably Posse."

"Not surprising. Any casualties?"

"Yeah. Maybe eight or nine, plus at least two, maybe three, of the bad guys."

"Holy shit. You think they might have come this way?"

"Either that or up to the Interstate, in which case they're long gone."

"Hell, put out an APB, give it to the Highway Patrol."

"An APB for what?" Osborne said. "They came up to the Initiative on ATVs, but how they got in and out is still unknown. But I think they probably posed as elk hunters."

"Well, you can get the list of out-of-state registrants, see if any of them are Posse."

"They probably used false IDs."

Seagram grinned. "That's why I herd these things, and you're the cop. So what are we doing out here? There's no way they're still hanging around."

They were a few miles past the Initiative now, two ranges of low hills between them. Osborne had Seagram drop down to fifty feet off the deck and swing back to the west toward the river and the gravel road. They were right on the Slope county line, where the road branched, one continuing south but heading away from the river toward the Badlands Roundup Lodge, which had been in existence since the 1880s, while the other jogged straight east just south of the Initiative before it swung north and connected with U.S. 85.

"Not a good idea if we get too close," Seagram said.

"No."

"What are we looking for?" Seagram asked, but then they both saw the ATV and a disconnected trailer abandoned just in the lee of a rounded hill south of the Initiative.

"Set us down about twenty yards north," Osborne said. Seagram put the Bell Ranger practically on the deck, giving the trailer and the ATV a wide berth before he set down on the road in a flurry of dust.

"Stay here," Osborne said. He jumped out of the helicopter and ducking below the still-rotating blades headed back up the road, keeping to one side as he scanned the gravel surface for any signs of a recent disturbance.

He stopped a few yards from the ATV. There was blood splashed on the seat and handlebars and a large pool of it on the gravel road that had been disturbed possibly when the victim's body collapsed. Four shell casings littered the road about ten feet from the ATV. Just beyond that he could make out the clear impression of a jumble of footprints, plus a blood trail that along with the footprints abruptly ended not far from the tire marks of something big, something with dual wheels in the rear.

Osborne walked over to the shell casings where he hunched down and picked up one with a ballpoint pen. About the same diameter as a 9mm Para, but much longer, which meant more powder, a much greater stopping power. He was just about certain it came from the Knight PDWs the terrorists had used.

Something had gone wrong that had caused one or more of them—probably their leader—to kill the woman down at the Initiative and then shoot another of them here even though they had gotten away.

A disagreement that had gotten violent. Perhaps the man or woman who'd been shot to death here and whose body had been carried into the big vehicle with dual rear wheels—a motor home, he thought—had wanted to go back and finish the job or most likely wanted to rescue their fallen comrades. The leader disagreed and shot the dissenter to death.

He dropped the shell casing into a small plastic evidence baggie that he pocketed. Then stepping carefully, he took out another baggie and a cotton swab—things he always carried with him to a crime scene—nearer to the ATV where he bent down, scooped up some blood with the swab, and sealed it in the baggie.

Cameron had pointed him toward the Posse and two names—Ada Norman, shot to death at the back door of the power plant, and Barry Egan. The names, the automatic weapons they had used, the Semtex, and the timing device made a good start. But Osborne, straightening up, wondered why this facility, and more important, why now? Why last night, of all possible dates?

They'd come in disguised as elk hunters. He glanced over at the marks the dual rear wheels had made. From a big motor home. Common for the better-heeled out-of-state hunters. Another small lead. And it had gone south, back to Rapid City maybe. Another small lead.

But it still didn't explain why last night. Why not at the beginning of the hunting season?

"We've got company coming our way, Nate!" Seagram shouted from the open door of the helicopter.

Osborne looked up as one of the MH-60 Black Hawk helicopters from last night appeared over the top of the hill to the north and hovered for several seconds before it made a tight turn and touched down on the gravel road not twenty yards away, sand and gravel flying everywhere. It was one of the two gunships equipped with 7.62mm machine guns that had shown up to provide security for the Initiative.

Captain Nettles jumped out of the side door and marched over. He didn't look happy. "You were ordered to stand down until General Forester showed up!" he shouted.

"You're contaminating my crime scene, Captain," Osborne said, standing his ground. "Back off."

Nettles pulled up short right in the middle of the road, a foot or two away from the tire tracks and the last of the blood spoor, and after a long moment he glanced at the ATV, the shell casings, and the pool of blood.

"This site is now under military jurisdiction."

Osborne nodded toward the north. "The Initiative is yours, but right now you're in my county. Leave or I'll place you under arrest."

Nettles took a step forward, but one of the men called to him from the chopper.

"Captain, I have radio traffic for you."

"Stand by!" Nettles shouted.

"It's General Forester, he's incoming from Bismarck."

Nettles looked as if he wanted to shoot somebody. "On my way," he said. "You're coming with me, Sheriff."

"I'm flying back to my office, where I'm sending one of my deputies out here to secure the scene until the FBI forensics team shows up from Minneapolis. I'll drive out to the Initiative in a couple of hours." Osborne turned and walked back to where Seagram was waiting.

"Goddamnit!" Nettles shouted.

But Osborne reached the Bell Ranger without looking back. "Get me back to town, Tommy."

"They going to shoot us?"

Osborne laughed. "I wouldn't put it past them."

21

DAVID GRAFTON, THE newest and best educated of the three deputies, was having a heated argument about the Green Bay Packers versus the Vikings with Kevin Trembley, the oldest, when Osborne walked in. They stopped immediately.

"Ms. Novak from the governor's office called and wants to talk to you right away," Grafton said, sounding impressed. Diane Novak was the Department of Commerce commissioner.

"What'd she want?" Osborne asked, walking straight back to his small office.

Their radio dispatcher was out sick today, and Stu Burghof, their other deputy, was on vacation somewhere in California for two more days, so it was just the three of them.

"Didn't say, but she sounded kinda mad," Grafton said, following him.

Osborne tossed his ball cap on the desk and went to the big wall map of Billings County and the edges of the surrounding counties. "There was some trouble down at the ELF facility last night. Could have been a Posse attack. There were a lot of casualties, and right now an Air Force

Rapid Response team from Rapid City has taken charge. They want me down there right away."

"No shit?" Grafton said. He was excited. Almost nothing ever happened in the county, except for some domestic battery and a few drunks on the weekend.

"No need for profanity," Trembley cautioned from the doorway.

"Kevin, I want you here on the radio in case something comes up. And try to find out where Stu is staying and get him back," Osborne said. He poked a blunt finger at the spot where he'd found the ATV, the shell casings, and blood spoor, and told them about his confrontation with the Air Force captain.

"That's not federal land," Grafton said. He'd gotten his degree in criminology with a minor in law from the University of Minnesota over in Duluth, but he wasn't a big shot about it.

"I'm going to try to head them off if I can, but in the meantime I want you to get down there with an evidence kit. Put police tape around the entire area and take lots of photographs. Pick up anything you find, and make tire casts; something big was out there, I'm guessing a motor home. Dual rear wheels."

"What if this Nettles comes back and tries to stop me?"

"You're a civilian, and this is your county," Osborne said. "Pull rank on him." He gave the shell casing and blood sample to Trembley. "Get someone to run this over to Bismarck and ask if the blood is a match to any known Posse member. And find out what weapon they used; most likely came from a compact submachine gun I saw out at the power plant last night, a Knight PDW, I think. But make sure. Might be able to find out who bought them and where."

"What about the ATV and trailer?" Grafton asked.

"Lots of photographs and dust them both for prints."

"I can bring them back here."

"Okay, but put them out in the county road maintenance shed. And tell Eric and his people to keep their hands off."

"I'm on it," Grafton said.

Osborne phoned Novak at her office in Bismarck and she answered on the first ring.

"What the hell is going on out there, Nate?" she demanded.

She and Osborne's mother had been school chums in Fargo. And she had once babysat him while his parents had gone on a rare vacation down to the Grand Canyon, Hoover Dam, and Vegas. "Somebody attacked the Initiative last night, some serious damage and a number of casualties. The Air Force is up from Ellsworth and they've taken charge until General Forester shows up sometime today."

"We were told it was an industrial accident."

"Looks like the Posse," Osborne said.

The Commerce commissioner was silent for a long beat. "So where do we stand here? It's your county."

Osborne explained everything that he'd been involved with including his confrontation with Captain Nettles out on the gravel road south of the facility.

"President Thompson phoned Stuart first thing this morning, asked if we'd stay out of what was going on over there as much as possible." Stuart Howard was the second-term governor, and he and his wife, Toni, were very well liked in the state. "Now you're telling me that you're right in the middle of it? Not good, Nate."

"Too late for that. Anyway, Bob Forester wants to talk to me right away. What do you and Stuart want me to tell him?"

The commissioner chuckled. "Thought you'd say something like that," she said. "You always were a brat, Nathan, and still are. But tread with care this time. Please?"

"I'll try, Miss Dottie."

A pair of armed Rapid Response Team airmen in a Hummer blocked the gravel road past the main gate to the Initiative's Administrative and Scientific Center, and Osborne had to turn around and drive to the armed guards at the entrance. He had to wait several minutes before Jim Cameron could give word to let him through.

"Everyone's at Donna Marie, sir," the young man in white camouflage BDUs told him. "Do you need an escort?"

"I know the way," Osborne said, and when he was through he took the dirt road northwest to the power plant.

This was a different place on the ground than from the air; in some ways the countryside was more barren, certainly a lot less majestic, yet open, even limitless. He'd once tried to explain to a couple of friends at Recon school what western North Dakota was all about. One of them was from the woods of rural Pennsylvania who thought that the Badlands and the prairie were too wide open and vastly lonely, to which Osborne had explained it was just the opposite of the claustrophobia of the deep forests where a man couldn't see much farther than a dozen yards in any direction. The other was from California's Big Sur who thought that the ever-changing sea was as comforting as the ever-changing flames in a fireplace on a cold evening, to which Osborne had countered that his horizons were ever *unchanging,* something comfortable that could be counted on.

Donna Marie was a beehive of activity. Three dark blue semis with USAF markings were parked along the east side of the generating building about twenty or thirty yards from where the MASH tent had been set up this morning. Three of the four helicopters were on the ground, and approaching a large tent that had been erected after he'd left, and Osborne could hear the other gunship patrolling the perimeter a mile or so out. A half-dozen Hummers and a canvas-covered troop truck, also with Air Force markings, were parked near the big tent, and a second truck was pulled up in front of the double-wide from which bodies in zippered bags were being carried out. A lot of serious-looking people in uniforms, several of them in hazmat suits, came and went from the station. Already debris was being loaded aboard one of the semis, and the light from welding torches sputtered from the open doors.

An airman with a military police armband just outside the main tent flagged Osborne down. "General Forester and the others are expecting you, sir."

Forester stood in front of a map table listening to Whitney Lipton, who towered over him, telling him something with passion. He was a slightly built man in his late fifties with thinning gray hair, mussed now, his military parka open, his bearing erect, obviously the man in charge. And Osborne could see the resemblance between him and his daughter Ashley, who stood a few feet away looking at a blueprint spread out on the table.

Jim Cameron was on the other side of the table with several men Osborne did not know. They were listening to what Dr. Lipton was saying.

Captain Nettles, who was at Forester's elbow, was the first to notice Osborne, and he turned to the general. "The sheriff is here."

Forester turned and Whitney and everyone else looked up. "Sheriff, glad you could make it," the general said. "We've been going over the situation and trying to work out something that makes sense for what happens next, and I need your input."

"My friends call me Nate. And what happens next is figuring out why the Posse wanted to put this place out of commission, and why they did it last night."

He and the general shook hands. "Posse Comitatus?" Forester asked. Nettles started to object, but the general motioned him off.

"We have an ID on the woman we found at the back door," Cameron said. "She's Posse and one of her last known associates was a guy named Barry Egan, also Posse in Montana."

Something lit off in the general's eyes. "You sure about that?" he asked Cameron.

"Reasonably."

"If Egan was a part of this it would fit," said a pleasant-looking woman in her late thirties or early forties in jeans and dark blue FBI parka. "It was his dad who tried to hit Baytown a few years ago."

It was one of the Posse's legendary stories that Osborne had read about in an e-Guardian bulletin, which was the bureau's online system to counteract possible terrorist activities. "Might help if I was briefed on what's actually going on out here, because from where I stand it seems like you and Exxon might share a common enemy, or at least enemies with a common purpose."

Forester and the woman exchanged a look.

"We're thinking the same thing," the woman said. "I'm Deb Rausch, Special Agent in Charge of the FBI's Minneapolis office. We actually met at a regional LE conference right after you got elected. Had a drink with you and your wife that evening."

Osborne remembered. "You'd just been assigned from somewhere out west as assistant SAC."

"Salt Lake City, by way of army intel at Baghdad Central Prison."

"Welcome to Billings County," Osborne said. "Assuming for the moment that this does turn out to be a Posse operation, I have to believe that something else is going on. No reason for them to hit a facility like this one. Unless you have a serious leak in security."

"We don't need to hear this," Nettles said.

"I'm listening," Forester said.

"The Posse hit Baytown to make a statement against big oil and the corporations who are screwing up the air for a profit. But this is nothing more than an ELF facility. The protests against the installation in Wisconsin never panned out. No one got brain cancer from the radio waves. So no one would be interested in attacking this place, unless they knew what was actually going on here."

"Which is?" Forester said. The tent was silent enough for them to hear the whine of the still-spinning turbine in the power station.

"It's an experiment having something to do with the coal deposit you've tapped into and microbiology, which is Dr. Lipton's specialty."

"And the purpose?"

"I'm guessing that you want to produce methane to power the generator. Use the coal we have to make electricity without the massive dump of carbon dioxide. Something like that."

Forester glanced at Whitney again, and she shrugged. "What you suggest has been tried before," he said. "Too expensive."

"Excuse me, General, but you retired from DARPA and went to work for ARPA-E, a fair sum of money has been spent here, security is tight, and your project director is a chief scientist with the CDC. So from where I sit the Posse may have attacked last night but I think it's a fair possibility that big oil might have been calling the shots."

"Why's that?"

"This place is a threat. What I don't understand is why they chose to attack last night?"

"An important experiment was to be conducted this morning," Forester said.

"Then you have a leak."

"It would seem so. But the timing was wrong, and we'll be back up and running within a week to ten days."

"In the meantime you still have a leak, and the threat still exists."

Forester took only a moment to digest what Osborne was saying. "The experiment will go as planned. The Air Force Rapid Response Team will work with Jim to heighten our security needs. And we'll look for the leak starting in Washington, because I don't think it's someone here. In the meantime I'd like it if you would agree to work with Agent Rausch in finding this Mr. Egan and whomever he works for. Would you do this?"

Osborne took just as long for his decision, which as far as he was concerned was a no-brainer, and he nodded. "I don't like bad things happening in my county."

"Oh, shit!" Ashley suddenly shouted, and everyone turned to her. "I just remembered something."

"Yes?" Forester said.

"When I was hiding I saw two of the terrorists unscrew some sort of plate near the rear of the plant, and pour in something from a gallon jug."

"Where?" Whitney demanded.

"I can show you," Ashley said.

Christmas, Michigan

BARRY EGAN WASN'T so drunk that he would make a mistake and say something incredibly stupid; screw the pooch with the big mouth of his that had gotten him into trouble plenty of times before, but he was celebrating. His share of the money—twenty-five thousand—had been paid into his Big Sky Western Bank account in Bozeman. He'd taken out five hundred from a couple of ATMs over the past twenty-four hours, didn't want to leave a serious money trail, and already he was up nearly seven fifty at the Kewadin Indian Casino working the five-dollar slots.

The unincorporated township of about four hundred people, in the Upper Peninsula, was right on Lake Superior and in the old days the primary industry was iron smelting, twenty tons of pig in a day picked up by Great Lakes steamers. These days the primary industry was tourism, and during the Christmas season covers and postmarks, plus the occasional outlaw—which was what Barry thought of himself as—on the lam.

His uncle Fred, dead three years ago, had a single-wide trailer on a gravel road in the woods a couple of miles out of town beyond the end of Evergreen Drive that in the summer he'd used it as a fish camp and during the fall as a deer-hunting base and in the winter for snowmobiling. Barry used to come up here with his dad, so he was known around town, but the Yoopers—the year-round residents—mostly minded their own business and never bothered him whenever he showed up, opened the trailer, and bought a bunch of groceries and beer from Munising four miles east.

It was a weeknight, out of the summer tourist season, the lake hadn't frozen yet, so the ice fishermen weren't here, and it had been too warm lately, so the snowmobile season hadn't begun. Goddamn environmental shit was screwing with the seasons so that nothing was dependable anymore.

The casino was mostly empty; even so it took forever to get a drink girl to bring him a Bud and he could feel the old anger building up in him. There'd been no reason for him to have to shoot Ada and Dr. Kemal, but they'd gone crazy on him, wanting to go back for nothing.

And in the end it just made sense to take the kid down: "Loose lips sink ships," his daddy used to say all the time, quoting his own daddy, a man Barry had never met. But from what his mother told him, the old man was just as bugshit as her husband had been. It was a tough old world.

The drink girl, not bad-looking, brought his beer and set it down beside the slot he was playing. "Want me to stick around for luck?" she asked.

He was about to tell her to fuck off, but instead he looked up and managed a smile. "I think I'm going to bug out while I'm still ahead. Catch up on my z's."

"I hear ya," she said, and she walked off.

Barry had come back here because he knew that he had some serious thinking to do, mainly about what was coming next for him. There'd been nothing in the papers or on television about the attack, which on the surface was not really surprising. Yet there was a niggling thought at the back of his head that something had gone wrong at the last minute. The one man missing who'd probably killed Moose and Brenda. Maybe he'd disabled some of the critical charges. Maybe Dr. Kemal's biological soup had been discovered and neutralized. Maybe the mission had been a failure.

He'd gotten the money, but nothing else. Nothing on the Posse's Web site, nothing on Twitter or Facebook, nothing in his personal mailbox that Gordy had set up for him through something called a blind remailer that was totally untraceable.

Cashing out he took his slip over to the cage and the woman crisply counted out twelve one hundred–dollar bills, two twenties, a five, and three ones. He left a twenty and the three ones for her and went out to the Ford Taurus he'd rented in Chicago using one of the three fake driver's licenses he'd bought from a Posse contact at the Department of Justice in Helena for five hundred bucks apiece.

A couple of years ago he'd began to think of himself as a fugitive on the lam who needed to muddy the trail as much as possible. James Bond had done the same thing, only he'd had help, while Barry was on his own. Wiley, he thought of himself, and he had to grin. Wiley Coyote.

It had snowed a little this afternoon while he'd been at the casino and coming to the driveway back to his trailer he glanced in his rearview mirror to make sure no one was behind him, then stopped on the paved road before he turned in. No tire tracks. No one had been here. No one had traced him yet. No reason for them to have done so, because he'd wiped down the motor home before he'd stashed it under cover back in one of the canyons a couple of miles off U.S. 85. Moose and Brenda had refitted the

Newell in South Carolina and had it shipped up to a rental agency in Billings, not picking up the others until Cheyenne, so there was no connection to him.

Eluding possible pursuit, Barry thought, and he'd always loved the sound of it, the concept.

He drove the half mile through the woods to the clearing in which the fifty-foot-long trailer was backed up to a stand of pine. The day before yesterday he'd had a load of straw bales delivered and he'd stacked them around the skirt to help prevent the waste pipe from freezing up when it got windy. The physical labor felt good to him; he was a self-sufficient man, a hell of a lot better than guys like Dillinger and Capone who'd only known one trick because he understood manual labor and they hadn't. He was a castle builder.

It was too early in the season even here to need to plug in the car, anyway the Taurus wasn't equipped with a block heater, which in another month would be necessary. But by then he would be long gone. Maybe somewhere in Mexico. Someplace warm. Which in a way was disappointing to him. He wanted more.

Even though he was sure that he was alone out here, he took the Beretta from under the driver's seat, switched the safety off, and holding the pistol out away from his right leg approached the trailer on a hair trigger, ready to shoot anything that moved.

He'd left the front door unlocked; people up here mostly did the same, because no one stole each other's shit and he really appreciated the law-abiding honesty. Pulling it open he jumped inside, moving fast, sweeping the pistol left to right as he sidestepped into the kitchen.

"Hello," he called out, pointing the gun down the narrow corridor that led past the living room to the two bedrooms and bathroom in the back.

No one was here, but he felt really good for taking all the precautions. In his opinion there were old fugitives and bold fugitives, but never old-bold fugitives. It paid to take care.

Switching the safety on, he laid the pistol on the counter, took off his jacket and laid it on the back of a chair, pulled off his boots, and in sock feet went back to the second bedroom where his laptop was plugged into the dial-up connection.

He logged on to his Gmail account and other than spam there was only one message, this one from ktech1234@ hughes.net, the same address from which Bob Kast had initially contacted him for the North Dakota assignment, and the same from which his payments originated.

The computer was slow, but just now Barry had no need for speed as he hit the box in front of the message line. North Dakota had been a failure—maybe—even though the money had been paid. But there'd been nothing in the news. Not even a mention, which he thought would have been likely had real damage been done to the project. A lot of government people had been wiped out, someone must have taken notice.

When the e-mail came up it was only one word: Come.

Greenville, South Carolina
Command Systems

P EOPLE SHOULD BE more important than things.
And sometimes even more important than mere
ideas, which was true for the so-called North Dakota District Initiative, because actually at the core of the effort
were two women of overriding importance. Dr. Whitney
Lipton, of course, because the idea of talking the language
of bacteria so that microbes could be taught to work in
concert toward a specific goal was hers. And surprisingly,
the young Ashley Borden, because her father, General
Robert Forester, was in charge of the ARPA-E project,
and like General Leslie Groves who'd ramrodded the
Manhattan District Project in the forties, so went Forester
so went the Initiative. Interfere with his family and the
project would suffer at least until a change of leadership
took place.

And upon hearing Barry Egan's report, D. S. Wood
knew what had to happen next, along with the why and
the how, because he clearly understood the real value of
people, always had ever since he'd been a kid of fourteen
working in his father's hardware store in Ames, Iowa.

In the first months his father had been determined to

teach Donald the business from the bottom up, starting with sweeping the floors, washing the plate glass windows, and dusting the shelves. It led of course to learning about their regular customers who were the self-styled handymen, who needed the most advice, and especially those to whom expensive tools could be sold. It also led to running the cash register and doing the books each evening, keeping the ledger that showed expenses on one side and receipts on the other.

By the time he was fifteen he had discovered the stock market quotes in the *Des Moines Register,* and he began to plot stocks, settling at one point on the stock of the fast-food chain McDonald's. He got a social security number, different from his own, by sending for the birth certificate of a baby who'd died at the age of one and who was buried in the Catholic cemetery. Using that, he rented a post office box down in Des Moines, getting there and back on a Greyhound bus. One week later he opened a checking account at a bank one block from the post office and began buying his first McDonald's stocks using money he embezzled from the hardware store.

The problem was that the bank in Ames held the mortgage to his parents' house as well as the revolving line of credit that kept the hardware store open.

Two years after Donald first began buying his stocks, branching out to other corporations that he felt were up and coming, the bank audited the hardware store's books and found that nearly eight thousand dollars was missing. The blame, of course, was placed squarely on Donald's father. And although the old man denied everything, he was found guilty of embezzlement and was sent to jail. The house was lost, and within three months Donald's mother accidentally overdosed on the Valium she'd been prescribed for her depression.

By then Donald was on his way to becoming, if not exactly wealthy, at least well-off for a seventeen-year-old, and without looking back he went east to get his degrees in business and finance, though he didn't think he really needed those pieces of paper. But they would look nice on his office wall, and the people who came to him with their money would be impressed.

His philosophy then as now was never to look back. Guilt and especially remorse were for weaklings. If his father had kept his eye on the ball, he would never have been robbed.

Nor was he angry that he'd been forced to make his mark the hard way. And he wasn't angry now that the attack on the Initiative had been a failure, because Egan had shown them a better, more elegant solution. All he needed was time.

"Time for what, exactly?" Bob Kast had asked this afternoon when Egan had gone inside to grab a bottle of cognac.

But it wasn't until this evening, four hours later, when Wood could come up with an idea that made any sense. Audacious, and maybe in the end impossible to achieve let alone sustain long enough to make a difference, and yet a solution.

The problem was that one hundred dollars per barrel was a sort of tipping point for oil versus alternative energy research. The more oil cost delivered to U.S. refineries, and the higher the prices rose at the gas pumps across the country, the greater the national will became to find something else. Wind farms were being constructed all over the country using huge blades and other parts built in China, but coming online in the U.S. nevertheless. Work was steaming full speed ahead on geothermal sources, hydroelectric energy from the rivers and seas, solar power in

Florida and the desert southwest, and nuclear plants. Plus coal at the Dakota Initiative.

Below eighty dollars, however, when gas prices at the pump were well under four dollars per gallon, people began to lose interest. Voters started not to care so much. The national will began to erode, people forgot.

"How does a buck ninety-five a gallon strike you?" he asked.

Kast smirked. "For regular?" he asked.

"Premium," he said, playing the other man's sarcasm back at him. "Give me one year—delay the Initiative for that long—and I can almost guarantee oil prices well below fifty dollars per barrel."

Kast laughed. "Even if you could engineer something like that, it wouldn't last. Couldn't last. And you'd be losing money by the carload."

"I make money on the way down as well as up. I'm just asking for one year."

"And then what?"

"By then the presidential election will be less than twelve months away. A new agenda, new problems because the energy issue would have been resolved. The public's focus will have changed."

"You can't be suggesting that the Initiative will be abandoned?"

"Not abandoned, exactly," Wood said. "But put on the back burner at least for a few years until the situation once again reverses itself."

And suddenly seeing what D.S. was driving at, Kast threw his head back and laughed out loud from the bottom of his heart. "Christ, you're a devious son of a bitch."

They were on the long veranda looking out over the valley. Wood poured another cognac as he gathered his thoughts. "I'm getting old, Bob."

"You're young. Not even fifty."

"If I'm lucky I have thirty years left. Maybe twenty quality years. And I'm damned if I'm going to spend all that time as a pauper, or worse yet end up sharing a cell with guys like Madoff."

Kast gave him a sharp look. "At all costs?"

"Of course," Wood answered without a moment's hesitation, because he had given the situation—his situation—a lot of thought over the past few years. Especially since some of his derivative positions had begun to seriously slip.

Kast poured a cognac for himself. "Which is why you're here, which is why you wanted Mr. Egan to join us."

"He's a perfect fit, don't you think?"

"He is if you're suggesting what I think you're going to suggest. Another attack in North Dakota. He's expendable."

"Yes, he is, but not in the way you think," Wood said.

And Kast laughed again as Egan came outside.

"What's so funny?"

"You're going back to North Dakota," Wood said.

Egan was suddenly on guard. "I don't think that's such a hot idea. Worked once, but they'll have that place sealed up tighter than a gnat's ass."

"You're not going after the power plant, not directly."

"I'm listening."

"You're going to kidnap someone. A woman."

Egan grinned. "Okay, I gotcha. What'll the ransom be?"

"The ransom won't matter," Kast said, fully understanding what Wood was proposing. "As soon as you take the woman, you're going to kill her and dispose of the body. That way you'll have freedom of movement when they come looking for you."

"All the time in the world to negotiate," Wood added before Egan could object.

After a few beats, Egan nodded. "Okay, so if I pull this off, what's in it for me?"

"Pick a number and it's yours," Wood said.

"I know some pretty big numbers," Egan said.

"I'll just bet you do," Wood said.

PART TWO

EARLY GAME

Before Christmas

22

THE MOOD IN the White House Situation Room first thing in the morning was tense to the point of being surreal, and when President Robert Thompson arrived, his advisers, including Air Force General Robert Blake, chairman of the Joint Chiefs, shot up from their chairs.

Thompson, a short, slender, undistinguished-looking man from Ohio who'd risen to the rank of four-star admiral in the navy was in the last two years of his second term, and in those six years nothing quite like this had been handed to him.

"Good morning, Mr. President," Walter Page, director of the CIA, said as Thompson took his seat. "The feed is ready."

Thompson, who looked like a man barely in control of his anger, nodded, and Page clicked a button on a remote control.

The image of Paul F. Fay, U.S. ambassador to Venezuela, came up on one of the ultra-high-definition flat-panel monitors on the far wall. He was leaning against a desk in a small, white-tiled room, and he looked up, his bulldog features drooping as if he had all the cares of the world on his shoulders and hadn't slept for several nights.

"Good morning, Mr. President. I'm sorry to have to bring you such terrible news."

"There's no mistake?" Thompson asked, his voice stiff, tightly controlled.

"I'm afraid not, sir. Mr. Mann's body was found yesterday afternoon in a packing crate in an abandoned factory just outside of the city. We'd been given an anonymous tip where to find him, but it wasn't until a couple of hours ago before we were able to make a positive identification."

"From DNA?"

"No, sir. From dental records."

"Then why the overnight delay?" Thompson demanded.

The ambassador was obviously uncomfortable. "It took us that long to find his head. The pathologist here said it had been severed, probably by a chain saw."

"Good Lord Almighty," Thompson said softly, but the microphone was sensitive enough to pick up his voice.

"Yes, sir," the ambassador said. "Rupert was a personal friend of mine from Boston. Same club."

"Has anyone claimed responsibility?"

"No, sir. He met with Rafael Araque, the Minister of Energy, and Andres Luzardo, PDV's president downtown at the oil company's headquarters, and afterwards he disappeared. Caracas police along with SEBIN conducted what appeared to be a full-scale investigation, but it wasn't until yesterday before his remains were found."

Thompson's gut was tight. "It was a message," he said. "The bastards sent us a message, and it couldn't be clearer."

"Mr. President?" the ambassador said.

The others around the table included his secretary of state, Irving Mortenson, his adviser on national security affairs, Nicholas Fenniger, and—except for the vice president—most of his National Security Council—the secretaries for Defense and Treasury, his chief of staff, and the attorney general. They were looking at him, waiting, it seemed, for the ax to fall.

"I want you to bring his body home. We'll have a state funeral. He was a good man."

"The best," the ambassador said. "I'll send Joanna." Joanna Riggles was the deputy chief of Mission.

"You personally, Paul. I want all of your nonessential personnel out of there within twenty-four hours, and then I'm officially recalling you."

The ambassador was clearly alarmed. "Mr. President, considering the reason that you sent Mann down here was to negotiate a reduction in the oil price increase, or at least gain a delay, recalling me would be nearly the same as declaring a state of war. Or it certainly could be misinterpreted that way."

The media had been on Thompson's case since the beginning of his second term about being the wishy-washy president, the chief executive who'd caved in to special interests. Hell, even his own party had begun to question his resolve after a G7 plus one meeting in Brunei when it had seemed that he was apologizing for the U.S. not signing the Kyoto Treaty. Ironically the one positive thing he had done in the first year of his presidency—create the Dakota Initiative—was of necessity so secret that nothing political could be made of it. At least not until the results were proven.

Two days ago there'd been the attack on Donna Marie and now this brutal beheading of his special envoy to an OPEC nation, at least in Thompson's mind, had the possibility of a connection. A Saudi minister of oil had warned George W. that the U.S. had to tread carefully in its quest for alternative energy sources lest it suffer some serious unintended consequences. Perhaps even a protracted energy war—the oil-producing nations against the U.S., or any other major consumer nation that wanted to break free.

In this case it amounted to a tin pot dictator attempting to intimidate the U.S.

"Not on my watch," Thompson, who was deep in thought, mumbled.

"Sir?" Ambassador Fay asked.

"I want there to be no misinterpretation."

"Yes, sir."

"I want you on a plane out of there within twenty-four hours."

"I'd like forty-eight—" the ambassador said.

"I'm sending their ambassador home no later than this time tomorrow," the president said, and he glanced at the others around the long table before he turned back to the monitor. "I'm tired of playing games with the Chávez government. It stops now."

"There will be consequences, Mr. President," Fenniger said. He was a dour-looking man with a very bad haircut that gave him a faintly draconian air of unbending opinion.

"Consequences indeed," Thompson said. "Is there anything else, Paul?"

The ambassador shook his head. "No, sir. I'm just sorry that I could not have been of greater service here."

"It wasn't you. Bring Mann's body home with you."

"Yes, Mr. President," the ambassador said, and Thompson motioned for the connection to be terminated.

"Discussion," the president said, he was the sort of president who was wide open to divergent views and actually listened to his advisers.

"Venezuela supplies between ten and fifteen percent of our crude oil imports," Nicholas Trilling, the secretary of defense, said. Energy supplies had become a matter of national defense several years ago.

"I'll ask Canada and Mexico to make up the difference. We get more than one-third of our crude oil from them."

"If they refuse?" Trilling pressed.

"Then we'll tighten our belts," Thompson shot back. He was angry. "We will not be held hostage."

"If Canada and Mexico agree, the price per barrel will rise."

"We'll deal with it."

"Your numbers will go down," his chief of staff, Mark Young, said.

But Thompson waved him off. "I'm the lamest of ducks, isn't that what FOX calls me?"

"There may be other consequences as well," Secretary of State Mortenson said. His hair was a white lion's mane that made him look like the genius he actually was. He'd come from Columbia where for years he'd taught philosophy and ethics of just governance at the graduate level. "Chief among them war."

"The Venezuelan military is not going to start shooting at us," Thompson said. "Chávez isn't that crazy."

"But we may have to shoot at them," Mortenson said, and Thompson realized that the man in the room for whom he had the most respect was not speaking rhetorically.

"You're talking about the bureau's speculation that Venezuelan intelligence might have been behind the attack on the Initiative."

Mortenson nodded. "As far-fetched as the notion may be, it's something we have to consider."

A surgical strike against Venezuela's nine air force bases, including their two forward ones at Santo Domingo and San Antonio del Tachira, had been in the planning stages for a number of years, ever since Venezuela had taken delivery of two dozen SU-30MK2 Flanker-C advanced fighter-interceptors from Russia, and announced that it intended to sell its twenty-one U.S. F-l6 fighters to Iran. More urgency had come to the planning when Chávez announced his nuclear ambitions in partnership with Brazil, Argentina, and especially with Russia and Iran.

Operation Balboa, in fact, was just this air force base contingency plan. Deny them the use of their air strike and defense capability and an invasion—at least in the near term—would not be necessary.

"This has nothing to do with their air force," Thompson said.

"No, Mr. President, but the threat of Balboa would certainly give them pause."

Thompson chose his words carefully. "Is that what you advise?"

"No, sir. I'm merely bringing it to the table."

"Discussion."

"I think we'd need concrete proof that Chávez was behind the attack," General Blake said. "Certainly more than we had for Iraq's WMDs. We don't need another expensive debacle."

"Nor do we need a would-be nuclear power willing to make attacks on our alternative energy research facilities," Thompson said. "It's unacceptable, and Chávez needs to learn that our patience has limits."

"Yes, Mr. President," Mortenson said.

"Inform Mr. Alvarez of my decision before noon," Thompson said. Juan Alvarez was the Venezuelan ambassador to the U.S.

"Of course," the secretary of state said.

"In the meantime I'll call Duncan and Molina and give them the heads-up." James Duncan was Canada's prime minister, and Ernesto Molina was Mexico's president. "If its war Chávez wants, we'll give it to him."

"I sincerely hope not, for all of our sakes," General Blake muttered half under his breath.

The president caught it, but made no reply because he agreed.

23

A SLENDER WOMAN with a narrow, pleasant face, dark eyes, and thin lips, but a little too broad of shoulder and narrow of hip, got out of a cab in front of the elegant old Hotel Saskatchewan in downtown Regina, Canada, a few minutes after four on a gloomy afternoon. She had reservations in one of the deluxe suites for ten nights, right through New Year's Eve, under the name Beatrice Effingham from San Francisco and the bellman hustled to take her three large, surprisingly heavy bags inside while she tipped the driver a fifty-dollar bill for the ten-minute ride from the airport.

She was dressed in a dark business suit with a white shirt, narrow tie, and simple silver hoop earrings with low-cut soft Italian leather boots on her feet. A classy woman, though on the mannish side, with a pleasant smile and direct manner. A ballbuster, the cabby thought, but he was glad for the biggest tip in his life.

The assistant desk manager came out and personally swiped her AmEx platinum card—the first he'd seen recently—and signed her in. "Welcome, Ms. Effingham, if there's anything I or any of the hotel's staff can personally do to make your stay more pleasant don't hesitate to ask."

"Very kind," the woman said, her voice a little harsh, though somehow charming. "Is the lounge open yet?"

"Yes, ma'am."

"Do I need a reservation for the restaurant this evening?"

"No, but may I call and have them hold a table for one?"

"For two," the woman said, and she turned away, glanced at the bellman with her bags on a trolley, and marched across the elegant lobby that had crystal chandeliers hanging from the arched ceilings.

Barry Egan was uncomfortable in the silicone breast prosthesis and the black wig that was warm, but he knew that he looked good by the attention he'd gotten at the airport in Atlanta, and here at the hotel. He'd played around with this sort of stuff a few years ago when he was in high school and wanted to see what would happen if he went into a cowboy bar down in Waco and maybe hustle a few bucks. He'd gotten the shit kicked out of him, but the old lady who ran the bar told him that his only mistake had been his five o'clock shadow. Other than that he was cute—fucked-up, but cute.

He'd shaved four times per day for the past several days, and used a dusky makeup that made him look Mediterranean.

And the other piece of advice the old lady had given him was not to swish. "Makes you look like a goddamned faggot. Just be yourself."

"I don't want to walk like John Wayne," he'd said, and the woman had laughed at him.

"Just ain't no John Wayne in you, son. Never will be."

Upstairs Egan refused the bellman's offer to unpack

the bags, but had him get some ice. When he came back he tipped him fifty dollars and sent him away.

He touched up his makeup one more time, took a deep breath, and went back downstairs to the Monarch's Lounge, patterned more or less after an English pub with dark paneling, cozy little nooks, and a standup bar. It was only a few days before Christmas and the half dozen or so patrons looked odd to Egan, maybe even a little lost, maybe lonely. It was a feeling he had been familiar with most of his life. Christmas to him was little more than another season of regret for a lot of things he'd never had, mostly family.

He spotted Don Mattson waiting in one of the booths, but crossed to the bar first where he ordered a Grey Goose martini, straight up, very cold, two olives—sorta like a modern James Bond, he thought. In a foreign hotel. Staging the next big operation. Covering all the bases.

Mattson looked up when Egan walked over, but he'd showed no signs of recognition, only a mild irritation when Egan sat down across from him.

"Piss off, luv, I'm waiting for someone," Mattson said. He was forty-seven with the florid complexion of a long-term drinker, a hawkish nose, narrow eyes, and thinning blond hair. He'd worked as a legitimate journalist for fifteen years after J school, including a four-year stint at the *L.A. Times* London bureau where he'd picked up a few British mannerisms, ending up as a political correspondent in Tallahassee for the *Orlando Sentinel* before he showed up one too many times drunk and with a too highly inflated expense account request that almost certainly included high-priced call girls and was fired.

He'd worked his way down from daily newspapers to freelance correspondent, finally ending up at the *Freedom Socialist* newspaper in San Francisco where he saw the light and became a friend of the Posse, who were in his opinion the real friends of the American people, unlike the Tea Party who were merely in it for themselves, whatever that meant.

"Don't you recognize an old friend when you see him, luv?" Egan asked.

Mattson's face was all of a sudden a study in contrasts, from fascination and interest because he'd obviously found the woman sitting across from him at least somewhat attractive, then disgust and revulsion because he began to realize that the woman was probably a man—a transvestite—and felt guilty and dirty because of his initial attraction, and finally dumbfounded when he finally recognized who it was.

"Jesus H. Christ."

A waitress came over and asked for a drink order, but Mattson shook his head and Egan held up his nearly full martini glass.

"Who'd you expect?" Egan asked when she was gone.

"Anything but this."

Mattson had come to Egan's attention about three years ago when the Posse had robbed a bank in Waterloo, Iowa, and brought the money—about eight thousand and change—back to a squadron meeting outside of Missoula. It was Mattson who'd been recommended to conduct a nationwide PR push. "The only difference between the Posse and any organization which has the people's well-being at heart—such as the Boy Scouts—is good press. Get that and everything else falls into place."

Egan had been the mastermind of the robbery, and although he'd promised a take of one hundred thousand dollars plus, no one had found any fault with his planning or courage. It was just dumb luck that they'd hit the bank the day after a cash call of one hundred fifty thousand had arrived from the fed to cover payroll for a number of businesses, including Ronan and DC Industries, plus Menards and Powers. In this part of the country, cash was sometimes still king.

"Then I surprised you?"

"One hundred percent."

Egan nodded his satisfaction and he took a delicate hit of his martini. "We have a job to do which depends on us coming across as a couple," he said. "An in and out, should be done in time to open presents under the tree."

"Why the getup?"

"Visibility. People see what they want to see, and if they're looking for strangers they won't find a tourist couple very threatening."

Mattson glanced around the barroom. "Another bank, here in Regina?"

"Down in North Dakota, but this time it's a kidnapping."

Mattson reared back, visibly disturbed. "Not my style, man. Too much shit can go wrong if we have to hold the mark more than a day or two."

"Won't have to hold her."

"What are you talking about?" Mattson demanded, but then he leaned closer. "Her?"

"A newspaper reporter, and we're going to kill her before we start our negotiations, because the ransom doesn't mean a thing."

"I don't know what the hell you're talking about. This is crazy shit. I've told you guys about the power of the press. If they get on your case you're dog meat."

"She's worth more dead than she is alive."

"I won't do it. And I mean it. I'll just leave first thing in the morning and go back to Frisco where I can do the cause a hell of a lot more service than snatching some reporter and snuffing her out. People do hard time for that kind of shit, something I'm definitely not interested in experiencing. Anyway, if you actually pull off something like that and even a whiff connects it with the Posse you're going to need some serious spin. I can't do it if I'm in the slammer."

Egan had never really considered the possibility that anyone could turn him down. He'd never asked for much, but when he asked he expected immediate acceptance. It was a matter of loose ends, he explained to Mattson. Despite all the good work the newsman had done for the Posse he was expendable. If need be he would disappear. Happened all the time. The needs of the whole were far greater than the wishes or even well-being of the one. It was a tough old world.

After a longish beat, Mattson drained his glass and raised it for the waitress to see. She came over and he ordered another Courvosier neat. "Who is the woman?"

"Her name is Ashley Borden and she works for the *Bismarck Tribune*."

"Why do we want her? Are her parents somebody?"

"Doesn't matter," Egan said. "There's twenty-five large for you."

"Seventy-five," Mattson said without hesitation.

And Egan suppressed a smile. "Fifty," he said. He had the man as he knew he would. Mattson had been in financial trouble most of his life, in part because of his drinking, and in part because of a lot of bad decisions—many of which had been brought on by his drinking. It was circular.

The waitress came with the Courvosier. "Tell me everything," Mattson said, raising the glass to his lips.

"For starts that's your last drink until the op is completed," Egan said.

Mattson hesitated for a moment, but then put the glass down. "Fair enough."

"There'll be three of us. You and I plus Toby Trela who's a rodeo cowboy. He's waiting for us right now at the Badlands Roundup Lodge south of Medora."

"Never heard of him or the ranch or the town—if that's what it is."

"Doesn't matter, I'll explain on the way down tonight," Egan said.

"I thought we were staying here through the holidays?"

"We are. But we're hanging the 'do not disturb' sign on our door. Six hours down, twelve there and six back. We leave at two in the morning, and we'll be back at two in the morning Thursday."

24

THE MOTOR HOME had been parked unnoticed about thirty yards inside a narrow box canyon a few miles to the southeast of Amidon for several days, which was an embarrassment for Slope County Sheriff Dereck Richards who owned a ranch nearby.

A couple of elk hunters from Fargo had stumbled across it and as soon as the body of a young man had been discovered near the driver's position they'd backed off and called 911.

Richards had gone out to take a look and immediately called his old friend Nate Osborne up in Medora because the Billings County Sheriff's Department had posted an all points for information about a motor home or truck with dual rear wheels that could have been involved in an incident overnight at the ELF facility just north of the Slope County line.

Osborne got out of his SUV and walked over to where Richards, an older, weathered man in his early sixties with snow white hair was leaning against his ten-year-old Ford F150 pickup, about twenty yards behind the expensive-looking Newell, and they shook hands. No one else was out here this afternoon.

"Looks like you've got yourself into something interesting," Richards said. He had an unlit cigar in his mouth. "One body, blood spatter on the driver's side window. Looks like he was behind the wheel when someone nailed him maybe from the doorway. Right angle."

"Minneapolis FBI's coming down from the ELF station. We've got maybe a half hour. How do you see it, Dee?"

"Shot to the side of the head, maybe a .45. These guys weren't elk hunters, leastways this wasn't done with a Winchester or Weatherby. I ran the plate. It's a rental from over in Billings under the name Brenda Ackerman, about a month ago, not due back until the day after Christmas. They had money."

"What else?"

Richards looked at him. "Pisses me off I didn't find it, I'm up here at least once a week this time of the year."

"I meant inside."

"I know what you meant. But I didn't want to contaminate the scene. Figured the bureau would be interested, and they can be a bit prickly when it comes to crime scenes. Especially out in the sticks. Know what I mean? So I backed off soon as I saw the mess."

"How old? A day a week a month?"

"Less than a week," Richards said. "Fits your ELF incident. How'd you figure it?"

"We found a couple of ATVs and a trailer along with some shell casings—six by thirty-fives—and blood spoor and something heavy with dual rear wheels."

"Military ammunition?"

"Be my guess," Osborne said.

Richards nodded, and he looked toward the north at the

same time Osborne heard the rotor chop of a helicopter incoming.

"Best I stay out of this, think?"

"They'll want to talk to you, and the guys who made the call."

Richards took the cigar out of his mouth, looked at it, and stuffed it in his jacket pocket. "You know where to find me," he said.

He and Osborne shook hands and the Slope County sheriff got back in his pickup and drove off. Like a lot of locals with long family histories out here, Richards simply didn't want to get too involved with the outside world. Some drunk shooting up a transformer on a power pole, or once in a blue moon some cowboy whacking his wife and then turning the gun on himself, was about as far as he wanted to take it. Billings County was up north, and the FBI was just about from a different planet. And whatever was going on at the ELF facility just across his county line, was from a different universe. If they needed him, Nate knew where to find him.

The chopper was still a half mile out when Osborne put on his latex gloves and entered the motor coach. The copper smell of blood instantly hit the back of his throat. A youngish-looking man—maybe in his late teens early twenties at the most—was lying in a heap just behind the driver's seat. Blood had spattered on the side window, but most of it had been wiped up, leaving the majority of the mess on the fabric-covered wall.

The kid had been at the wheel when someone shot him in the side of the head, pulled his body out of the driver's seat, then cleaned up some of the mess, and drove off. Down here. Barry Egan. Apparently not a particularly easy man to work with. So far the body count was seven at the power station and more at the trailers—at least three of which were probably Egan's work. The woman just outside the station, the blood spoor at the ATV where the motor home had been parked—if the tire prints matched, which he thought they would—and this one.

The helicopter was coming in for a noisy landing as Osborne stepped around the body, avoiding the blood, and slowly made his way to the back of the coach. Lots of money, the thought came to him, but they weren't elk hunters. Guys like that were out for a good time—cards, booze, supper out of cans, or the freezer, no one cleaning up. Shit lying everywhere. He'd seen it before. But except for the body and the blood, this place was too neat.

And there was another smell that he couldn't place. He stopped about halfway back and cocked his head. Something warm, something that had been heated up, but not food. And it came to him that it was a smell he remembered from the FORECON days. But it wasn't from the field. Somewhere at a headquarters position.

He took another step toward the back of the coach. One of the cabinets above the dining table was ajar, and using the tip of a gloved finger he eased it open. The space was filled with electronic equipment, three units a little larger than DVD players stacked one on top of the other. Cables snaked from the rear of the units up toward the ceiling.

The cabinet spaces beneath the seats were filled with other electronic equipment, the purpose of which he couldn't guess. But he remembered the smell now; it was from a headquarters communications center where he'd been given a mission briefing. Electronic equipment.

It was a possible answer to the disrupted communications and computer systems at the power station. Which made these people something other than amateurs.

The helicopter had touched down outside, and someone was shouting his name. Captain Nettles, he thought.

He continued aft, past the bathroom compartment where he pulled up short. Another body lay on its side, its arms and legs splayed out as if it had been posed, its back a mass of clotted blood. The one from the ATV, he figured, where the coach had been parked south of Donna Marie.

The man was older than the one on the floor behind the driver's seat. He had a short, scruffy beard, gray like his hair, and he looked as if he had been in a great deal of pain when he'd died.

"Sheriff!" Nettles shouted from just outside the door. He sounded angry.

Something about the body seemed odd to Osborne and he stepped a little closer, avoiding the blood smears from where it had been dragged. The man's complexion was dark, his nose large and hooked, his eyes hooded; profiling, maybe, but he was just about certain that the man was Middle Eastern—Iraqi, Afghani, maybe Pakistani. Which raised the question in Osborne's mind about al-Qaeda forming some sort of an alliance with the Posse Comitatus, and it was not a very pleasant assumption.

He squatted down, his left prosthesis splayed out awkwardly so he could get a better angle on the face. Maybe something was there, something he was missing. He'd built something of a reputation in FORECON as a pretty good poker player. The guys thought he memorized the deck, like a card counter, which meant he had a better handle on the odds. But the plain fact was that he could read faces. He could pretty well tell when someone was nervous or anxious, or excited, or lying. And he'd always been surprised that everyone else didn't have the same ability. Worked in a poker game, but it was one of Carolyn's pet peeves; it just wasn't fair that he could tell when she was telling a lie. A girl had to have some secrets. But he'd always bit off the first thing that came to the tip of the tongue: "If you don't want to be caught in a lie, don't tell a lie."

The Afghani, or whoever he was, wasn't a terrorist. Osborne had seen the look on some of the really dedicated guys who were willing to give their lives for the cause. This one seemed more like a cleric, maybe a philosopher or a scientist. And he thought about the milky liquid Ashley had seen one of the attackers pour into one of the well-head ports. Whitney—Dr. Lipton—had cordoned off the area, and the material and been pumped out by two of her people who understood biohazards, and it was right now being analyzed. A sample of it had been sent to the CDC in Atlanta, and another—a control sample—had been frozen in liquid nitrogen.

And for no real reason, or maybe a dozen mostly instinctual ones, Osborne was fairly certain that this was the man who'd not only poured the stuff into the wellhead port, but the scientist who'd created it. A biological scientist, which if that were true, meant he and Egan and the team who'd attacked Donna Marie knew a hell of a lot more about the Dakota Initiative than they were supposed to know.

"Nate, what the hell are you doing?" Deb Rausch asked from behind him.

He held his stare on the dead man's face for a beat before he looked over his shoulder at the FBI SAC from Minneapolis. "I think the stuff from the wellhead that Dr. Lipton's people are working with was created by this guy. He's either an Iranian or a Pakistani scientist and whatever he cooked up is just as important as why he was shot by his own team. By Barry Egan. If we can figure out those two things we might be able to find out where General Forester's leak is."

"Get the fuck out of here, and that's an order," Nettles said. "This isn't your county."

"Shut up, Captain," Rausch said, almost offhandedly. "Have you seen this guy before?" she asked Osborne.

Osborne turned back to the dead man and shook his head. "No, but I think I recognize the type. Outside Peshawar."

"I thought you were stationed in Afghanistan," Rausch said. "Peshawar is across the border in Pakistan."

"Yeah, so is Karachi," Osborne said absently. A few beats later he got to his feet with some difficulty because of his peg leg. "Did you bring a forensics team with you?"

"They're on their way."

"Be my guess that the tire prints will match the ones we lifted south of Donna Marie, and I suspect that the guy in front and this one, were shot with the same six-by-thirty-fives, the Knight PDWs I encountered in the station. Ought to be able to trace who purchased them."

"We're waiting for the results of your forensics report from Bismarck. What else?"

"Some of the cabinets forward are loaded with electronic equipment—none of which I recognized—but I smelled it. Might answer why communications for the entire facility went down, and maybe this stuff'll be easier to trace than the PDWs."

"I'll have a full team from Washington within twelve hours," Rausch said. She turned to Nettles. "Do you have the manpower to secure this site as well as the power station?"

"Yes," Nettles said.

Rausch turned back to Osborne. "Well, Nate, I guess you're right in the middle of it now."

"Yeah. And I guess this isn't the last of it."

Nettles started to say something, but Rausch held him off. "How do you see that?"

"Too much money, too much inside intel. The Posse may have supplied some of the personnel, but the rest came from someone well-heeled. Someone high up on the food chain. Someone with a purpose."

25

STANDING OUTSIDE THE door to the main control center on the first floor of the Administration and Research-and-Development Center at three in the afternoon, Whitney Lipton was taken by the silence here and over at Vomit Valley and even Henry's, which had been all but deserted at noon. She'd e-mailed everyone to show up for a LF briefing at three sharp. Her Looking Forward staff meetings had always been free-for-alls; by Whitney's dictums, no subject, no matter how fringe, was off the table. There was no order of speakers. Nor was there any control over volume, though it was usually the one with the best idea rather than the loudest voice who won the floor. But she wasn't sure just now how it would go this time.

She loved the staff at this moment more than ever before, because she felt responsible for their well-being—both physical and mental. She wanted with everything in her power for them to feel safe, to trust her and the science, and to trust in themselves and their own abilities, including the facility to spring back in the face of a horrible adversity.

In the rush to put things together over the past week Whitney had not had the time to sit her people down and properly explain what had happened and what they were facing. Nor had she been able to give them a choice— considering the personal danger—of stay or go. She was going to do that this afternoon; and she would be disappointed, but wouldn't be surprised, if all of them quit on the spot.

Especially Susan, who'd seen the gore in the control room over at Donna Marie before the FBI people had allowed the cleanup to begin. She'd been weepy, unable to concentrate on working out what the delay in introducing the gadget to the coal seam already infected with the bacteria might have for the outcome. Only a few of the models she'd come up with made any sense, in a large part because she'd been so distracted that she'd entered a lot of objective-oriented predictive points that made no real sense, or in some cases were superfluous.

No one else on the team had been able to help her, because they, too, were distracted by the presence of the armed Air Force personnel who seemed to be everywhere and kept streaming in along with FBI agents.

Forester had refused to take the time to speak with them because they were *her* people, and it was she who could speak their language, and it was she whom they trusted. And, as he explained to her, he had a lot of what he called "fires" to put out in Washington and a leak to plug before it sunk them all.

She glanced at her watch and at three sharp she opened the door and went inside. Dominating the room were four large flat-screen monitors, blank now, mounted along one wall in front of which were a dozen workstations with their own computer monitors and keyboards. A pair of electronic document tables flanked the room on either side, and normally some kind of music played from someone's iPod attached to a speaker system—country and western or classical mostly—but this afternoon the center was silent. Nor were her six people busy at their various workstations as usual. They were clustered, as if for comfort, seated facing one another in a circle, a shabby Charlie Brown Christmas tree behind them. They looked up when she came in and pulled a chair over to join them. No lectures this time, no discussions at first, only some unvarnished past, present, and future truths.

Bernhardt Stein, her lab coordinator, and Alex Melin, her assistant microbiologist, both started to speak at the same time, but Whitney motioned them off. No free-for-alls this time.

"Some really bad things happened to us," Whitney began. "And I can't guarantee that whoever did this won't try again."

"But who?" Susan Watts asked. She was a Harvard Med School Ph.D. in microbial genetics, who was as naïve as she was funny. She was deadly serious now.

"Someone who doesn't want us to succeed."

Susan didn't look away. "Why?"

And Whitney had asked herself that question a dozen times since last night and she gave the only answer that made any sense to her. "Money. Coal provides almost fifty percent of all the electrical power generated in this country. That's a lot of money."

"But we're not changing anything, except we won't have to dig the coal out of the ground, and we'll produce almost zero carbon dioxide."

"That's the point. There's big money in mining the coal, processing it, transporting it to the stations, and processing it again. Lots of people, and not just the fat cats, depend on the process to earn a living."

"But don't they know about the Keeling curve?" Susan asked earnestly. "We're on the way to becoming another Venus. Runaway greenhouse heating. Rivers of molten lead. Nobody will survive, and making a living won't make a fucking bit of difference."

She had never used the F-word, and she was exaggerating, of course, but not by much. Dr. Charles David Keeling, an environmental scientist from San Diego, began to worry about carbon dioxide levels in the Earth's atmosphere in the late forties and early fifties and he designed a machine to measure carbon dioxide concentrations. The nearest cleanest place he could think of to install the machine was the top of Mauna Loa more than eleven thousand feet above sea level in Hawaii.

The first readings showed 310 parts per million of the gas, which meant that every million liters of air contained more than three hundred liters of carbon dioxide. It was a base level, not really significant in itself at the time. But, as he suspected, most of that gas was caused by human activities. By 2005 when he died, the concentrations of carbon dioxide had risen to 380 parts per million. Some of the rise could be explained by natural causes—such as erupting volcanoes—but a great deal of it had to do with the burning of fossil fuels, especially coal.

The ppm were expected to top 400 soon, and reach 560 by the end of the century, which was nowhere near the atmosphere of Venus, which was 96 percent carbon dioxide, but high enough that almost every reputable scientist agreed that a great deal of harm would be done to our planet, including but not limited to massive changes of weather patterns—more intense crop and animal life extinctions caused by heat waves and more intense tropical storms and tornadoes.

The Keeling curve, which graphed the ominous rise,

was considered so important it was inscribed on a plaque at the Mauna Loa observatory and on a wall in the National Academy of Sciences building in Washington, D.C., which also showed Darwin's finches and James Watson's double helix.

"The science doesn't matter to them. Only money does."

It was as if Susan and the others were hearing a foreign, even heretical language; their faces went blank and the room fell silent.

"They failed," Whitney said.

"What are you talking about?" Stein shouted, unable finally to contain himself. "Failed? Donna Marie is a morgue!"

"They didn't shut us down."

"All but."

"They'll try again," Whitney said. And this time the silence was so profound it almost made a noise of its own. A ringing in the ears, she thought. "So you—we—all of us have to make a choice. Do you want to continue with the project, or would you rather leave now?"

"You mean get out of the damage path?" Frank Neubert, one of her postdocs who was the project's prophet of doom, asked.

And Whitney cringed. "Under the circumstances, that's exactly what I'm saying."

Neubert looked around at the others. He was a tall, impossibly skinny man with an Ichabod Crane Adam's apple. "What about you, Doc? Are you quitting?"

"I'm the project director."

"I'm sorry, that's not what I asked," he said, and he sounded more angry than frightened.

She shook her head and was about to say she would *have* to stay, but suddenly changed her mind. These were her people, after all. And they needed the unvarnished truth.

"Hell no," she said. "The bastards aren't going to beat me!"

Neubert smiled, and all of a sudden everyone was talking at once, some of them shouting, laughing like little kids at a birthday party.

Whitney wanted to quiet them down in part because she wasn't sure that they really understood what they were facing, because sooner or later the Air Force and FBI would have to leave if any science were to get done, and in part because if their decision was to stay, a lot of work had to take place before they were up and running again.

In the end, however, she let them have their blowout. It was, she thought, better than champagne for them.

26

PRESIDENT THOMPSON WAS working at his desk in shirtsleeves, a thick file perched on his knee, when National Security Adviser Nicholas Fenniger brought General Forester and FBI Director Edwin Rogers back to the Oval Office.

He put the file down and got to his feet. "I hoped the peace would last a bit longer," he said, coming around the desk.

"So did I, Mr. President," Forester said, and the two men shook hands.

"How's the cleanup proceeding?"

"We should be back up and running in a week, maybe ten days."

"The gadget wasn't damaged?"

"No, and Dr. Lipton tells me that we caught a bit of luck. Her microbes in the coal seam haven't splintered as she thought they might. So it looks as if we won't have to start from scratch."

Thompson turned to Rogers. "Any progress on finding who did this to us and why?"

"This is almost certainly the work of the Posse

Comitatus, but they had help not only in terms of direction but of money," the FBI director said. He'd been a first-string starting quarterback at Northwestern beginning in his freshman year, and at fifty-two he still had the combination of broad, muscular shoulders and narrow hips, as well as keen attention for detail.

"Save the details for now, I'll read your report, but how do you see the money? Who's likely behind this and why?"

"Well, it wasn't a normal Posse shoestring operation. The motor coach they used was top-shelf—well over two hundred thousand. There was another quarter of a million in sophisticated electronic equipment aboard, plus the weapons they used were expensive and the Semtex plastic explosives and detonator mechanisms were U.S. military grade, possibly from a Saudi Arabian supplier—we're still working on that aspect. Which brings up a number of interesting and delicate possibilities."

"You're talking about motive?"

"Yes, Mr. President. Oil futures traders. Derivative players. Credit default swap folks. People with more than a vested interest in stopping or at least seriously delaying any sort of a viable approach to big-scale alternative energy sources."

"Foreign or domestic?"

"At this point I'd guess domestic. Organizations like Venezuela's SEBIN don't have the contacts with our homegrown groups such as the Posse."

Thompson was angry. "They're willing to sabotage our efforts simply for short-term profits?"

"Yes, sir. In the billions, maybe even trillions. These kinds of attacks are something we considered from the beginning of the Initiative. There're people out there who don't want us to succeed and they're willing to do whatever it takes to stop us."

"Do we have names?"

"The list is short, but finding the proof won't be easy," Rogers said. "And we have two other considerations. One of the bodies found in the abandoned motor home was that of Dr. Mohammed al-Kassem Kemal. His primary education was at the National University of Science and Technology in Rawalpindi, but he did his postdoc work in microbiology in Hungary at the University of Szeged under Laszlo Kredics."

"The Pakistani school mostly serves the military."

"Yes, sir, though not exclusively."

"And the second consideration?"

"We have a leak." Forester answered the president's question. "Probably someone on the scientific side."

"Because of Dr. Kemal?"

"We don't have all the analysis finished, but it looks as if he created a microbial cocktail and poured it into an intake port on the wellhead that would have been released when the gadget was lowered into the seam. Dr. Lipton thinks the bacteria could have been designed to counteract our efforts, and produce a catastrophic amount of oxygen and methane."

"An explosive mixture."

"Worse, Mr. President. A blowout that would have rendered the entire coal seam totally unfit for production, and probably created a dangerous release of massive amounts of methane and carbon dioxide. But he would have needed the biological makeup—the blueprints if you will—of the bacteria we designed to produce the methane."

"He couldn't have come up with the formula on his own?"

"Not according to Dr. Lipton. She tells me that there's nothing in the literature that ties everything together like she has. And that's not hubris."

"I wouldn't think so," the president said. "How is she holding up?"

"Better than I would have thought possible. She's a bright, dedicated woman. And right now she's transferred her fear and the fears of her staff into anger and determination."

President Thompson sat back for just a moment. The situation in Venezuela was threatening to ramp up because of his recall of the U.S. ambassador and his expulsion of the Venezuelan ambassador over the still unpublicized beheading of Rupert Mann. The Chinese stubbornly refused to devalue their currency, pushing the balance of trade inequality to the breaking point. The Russians had started to play a dangerous game of hide-and-seek in the Atlantic with their nuclear missile submarines close aboard our Atlantic coast. Iran continued working on weaponizing its nuclear program, and both it and North Korea had nearly completed their development of three stage intercontinental ballistic missiles that could reach the U.S. mainland as far as Denver. And the European Economic Union was still on the verge of imploding.

And those were just the high points. Now this.

"We're not taking money out of anyone's pockets," Thompson said angrily. "If the shortsighted bastards bet their money on the future they would not only make a fortune but they would possibly save the planet."

It was the campaign rhetoric that some in the media had lambasted him for as impossibly naïve. "No one thinks that way any longer," a talk show host had told him six months before the election, which he had won by a narrow margin.

"Maybe they should," he'd replied, for which he'd been branded the "Boy Candidate."

The embarrassed silence lasted only a moment or two before Thompson came back. "What's next?" he asked.

"Well, we certainly won't back down," Forester said. "We're beefing up security, of course, but we'll continue with the project while at the same time we look for the leak."

"And prepare for another attack?"

"Yes, Mr. President, we have to consider that possibility."

Thompson turned to his FBI director. "Ed?"

"We're following the Posse back to the sources, including looking for who picked up the motor coach and where they acquired the electronics, the explosives, and the weapons. But our cybercrimes division is working on re-creating just how the Initiative's communications systems were taken over. And I've appointed a special action squad to figure out who would have the most to benefit from sabotaging the Initiative."

"Don't you need to uncover the money trail first?" the president asked.

"Sorry, sir, but that's too broad. First we identify who might benefit, then look at their ledgers."

Thompson's heart hardened. The Initiative was *his* vision and his alone, like F.D.R.'s Social Security system. "Whatever you want, you will get. No questions asked. Do you understand?"

"Yes, Mr. President," a somewhat subdued Rogers replied uncertainly.

"Wiretaps, arrest without habeas corpus, whatever," Thompson said. He took a sealed envelope from his desk and handed it to the FBI director. "In writing, Ed. My signature. No equivocation."

"Yes, sir."

"Get the bastards, no matter what it takes."

27

THE ROUGH RIDERS Hotel—the best accommodations in Medora—was a couple of blocks up from Osborne's office in the Billings County Courthouse. He'd changed into civvies because he wanted to shed his LE presence and walked up just before six because he figured he needed the exercise and might need to clear his head afterwards.

The late afternoon was cold, and the fireplace in Theodore's dining room adjacent to the bar was pulling full strength. The comfortable warm, smoky atmosphere, Christmas tree in the lobby, something he'd always equated with peace and security, permeated the adjacent cocktail lounge where Ashley Borden was sitting at the bar sipping a red wine when he walked in. Only a few other couples were seated at tables, but she was alone at the bar.

He hung up his jacket, then hesitated for just a moment, her back to him, and watched her fiddle with her glass. She was dressed in a light yellow sweater over jeans and the way she sat, the set of her head, long neck and narrow shoulders, the curve of her back and narrow waist was in his estimation very attractive. But he didn't know if he should or even could take the next step.

She turned as he walked across the dining room, and he smiled at her.

"You were snooping on me, shame on you," she said, nodding at the mirror over the bar, her smile warm.

"Guilty as charged," Osborne said. "I just wanted to make sure that I wasn't being stood up. You might have been waiting for a boyfriend."

She laughed. "My dad says I'm too much of a spoiled brat to ever have a serious relationship unless I change."

"Are you a brat?"

"Certifiable."

The bartender came over with a Michelob Ultra tap. "How's it going, Nate?" she asked.

"Not bad, Tina. You?"

She nodded. "So, we heard there might have been some trouble down at the ELF station last night."

"Somebody threw a wrong switch and blew something up. No big deal."

"Anyone hurt?"

"A few bruised egos from what I was told."

"You two having dinner?"

"Thought we might."

The bartender nodded. "I'll put your names in," she said and moved off.

Ashley laughed. "I wonder if there's a waiting list." She had stayed the night, and when Osborne had called to ask her to dinner, she'd told him to get over to the hotel as soon as possible. The place was practically empty and she was getting spooked.

Osborne shrugged and took a pull of his beer. "I heard the Air Force kicked you out after the news conference."

"Nothing much to see or do except hang around and

watch the cleanup. A bunch of construction types came up by air through Ellsworth, and it's getting a little dangerous, stuff being pulled apart and hauled out to trucks. And nobody's leaning on their shovels. They're really working hard. Lipton wants the place back up and running by the end of next week. So here I sit."

"Did she say that you'd be kept in the loop?"

"Yes, but she's not really in charge. My dad is. And for now I promised to keep my mouth shut."

"You keep your promises?" Osborne asked, and she looked at his reflection in the bar mirror.

"When they make sense," she said. "Anyway I'm going to go back to Bismarck tomorrow or Friday and put in an appearance at the paper before I lose my job. Christmas is Saturday but I'll be back if anything interesting turns up."

"I thought you'd be going to Washington to be with your dad."

She shook her head. "He's pretty busy right now."

"No one in Bismarck?"

"No one special. How about you?"

"Divorced, she lives down in Orlando with our daughter."

"Couldn't stand the North Dakota wilds?"

"She grew up in a big city. It's quiet out here."

"That it is," Ashley said. "Find anything new about the Posse connection?"

"We're still digging."

"What about the Newell down by Amidon? Were either of the two bodies Posse guys?"

Osborne was surprised, although he knew he shouldn't be. She was a good reporter and she had some decent sources not only here in the state but as far away as Washington. After the murder suicide in the park, she'd found out that the father had lost his ad agency job in the Twin

Cities, had gone bankrupt, and was in the process of losing his house. All in the few months leading up to the event. He'd been despondent; deeply troubled, she'd been told by neighbors who knew the family. And the first Osborne had known about those details was when he'd read about them in her article.

"Where'd you hear about that?" he asked nonchalantly.

"Around. One was just a kid, shot in the side of the head while he was behind the wheel. But the guy in the back was older and foreign. Maybe al-Qaeda?"

"Even if I knew yet, I wouldn't say; you know how it goes."

"Your county, your investigation, isn't that what you told Captain Ranger Rick? Or has the Air Force put you on a leash, too?"

"You're going to keep the Newell out of the paper as well. If need be I'll call your dad and let him cinch up *your* leash."

Ashley stiffened. "Just doing my job same as you, Sheriff," she said sharply, a little color coming to her cheeks.

Osborne decided that he liked her even though she was a self-centered and aggressive woman with a quick temper, and he smiled. "Do you ever stop being a reporter?"

"No."

"In that case we're not going to have a hell of a lot to talk about over dinner."

She let her eyes widen. "You mean like this is supposed to be a real date or something?"

"Or something."

She nodded. "Okay, let's call it a truce. But first one more thing. What'd you do with the Newell, or did the Bureau grab it?"

"Their forensics people are taking a look."

"Is it still down in Slope County, or did they bring it up to the Initiative? Because I want to see it."

"Not until we're done," Osborne said. "The truce starts right now," he added before she could press him.

He took their drinks and they went into the dining room to a table near the fireplace.

Tina was doing double duty as a waitress and she brought them menus. "Refills?"

"Sure," Osborne said. Only one other couple was in the dining room: a slender, mildly attractive woman with surprisingly broad shoulders and a man with a sagging face. He figured that the woman probably worked out and the man had the look of a longtime boozer.

When Tina came back with their drinks, Osborne asked about them.

"I think he said San Francisco. Guy talks like a Brit. Something's wrong with the gal."

"Staying here?"

"Haven't checked the register yet, but I got the biggest tip in my life at the bar."

28

WHEN OSBORNE AND Ashley walked into the dining room, Egan had stiffened slightly and it had been enough for Mattson sitting across from him to notice. But he waited until they had their drink orders, a ginger ale on the rocks with a twist for him and a house Merlot for Barry, before he said anything.

"You know those two?" he asked.

"Yeah, Nate Osborne, he's the local sheriff, and unless I miss my guess the broad is Ashley Borden."

"The newspaper reporter?"

"I think so, but I'm not sure."

"Hell of a coincidence them being here like this."

"Not at all," Egan said, sipping his wine. "It's why I picked Medora before Bismarck, 'cause I figured that she would be right here in the middle of it."

"I don't understand."

"Her daddums is Bob Forester—General Forester, of ARPA-E—who runs what they call the Initiative."

Mattson shrugged a little irritably. "Would you mind filling me in now that I've come this far with you? Because

I don't know what the hell you're talking about. What Initiative? And what the hell is ARPA-E?"

Egan explained just about everything, including his failed attack on Donna Marie, but not who hired him, or the names of Dr. Kemal and the others, or that they were all dead. None of it had been on television or in the newspapers, not even in the Posse's blogosphere, and Mattson was stunned speechless for a long moment or two.

"And you came back, and dragged me into it?" he said at length, careful to keep his voice low and as much as possible a neutral expression on his face. "Are you fucking out of your mind?"

"No one knows my name, and sure as hell even if they did they never would expect that I'd come back as a woman."

"We're supposed to be down at the Roundup Lodge with Toby, or have you changed your plans and just forgot to tell me?" Mattson demanded, his voice rising.

"Keep a lid on it, goddamnit, or I just might scrag your ass and leave you out in the bush," Egan said, smiling for the benefit of Osborne and Borden. "I told you that we were looking for her, and unless I miss my guess we just found her."

"We came all this way and you didn't have a picture of her? Jesus."

"Yeah, from the newspaper, but it was lousy."

"Well, what the hell do we do now?" Mattson asked. His agitation was increasing.

Egan gave him a hard look to try to calm him down. Sure as hell Mattson would never go out on any field operation again, and if the conditions were right his body would stay out in the Badlands right next to the broad's. It was a tough old world sometimes.

"Stay here and keep your mouth shut," he said at last, and he got up and walked over to Osborne and Borden.

They looked up, Osborne out of curiosity, but Borden watching closely, as if she were looking through a microscope.

"Good evening," Egan said. "Hope I'm not being too much of a bother."

"Not at all," Osborne said.

"I'm Beatrice Effingham. And my significant other thought we should stay the night here, and we were just wondering if this was a decent place." Egan held out his hand, and Osborne shook it.

"Nate Osborne, I'm the Billings County sheriff."

"Then you're not staying in the hotel," Egan said, and he extended his hand to Ashley who took it, though with a little reluctance. "That's okay, sweetie, I don't bite."

Ashley smiled slightly. "Ashley Borden, *Bismarck Tribune*. You coming from or heading back to San Francisco?"

Egan's stomach flopped, but he covered himself immediately. The bartender must have told them. "Back home, actually. Can't stand all this cold weather."

"You'll have to hustle some to make it by Christmas," she said, her eyes never leaving his.

"We're thinking about spending the holidays with friends in Vegas."

"Well, there's nothing much west of here," Ashley said. "So if you don't mind a little cowboy kitsch the beds here are clean and the food is passable. But it's not Vegas or San Francisco."

"It's quaint, but it's refreshing for a change," Egan said. "Are you staying here then?"

Ashley nodded. "I was thinking about spending Christmas."

"Good enough for me then," Egan said, and he started to turn away to go back to his table, but Osborne stopped him.

"Where'd you say you folks were coming from?"

"I don't believe I did. But we spent a week in Minneapolis with some friends, and I'm telling you it's almost as cold there as it is here."

29

AFTER TINA CAME and they'd ordered steaks, baked potatoes, onion rings, and green salads, Ashley took a sip of her wine. "That thing is not a woman."

"What are you talking about?" Osborne asked, though he'd thought that something hadn't been quite right.

"Dear Beatrice with her significant other is either a man in drag, or it's had a sex change operation, and not so long ago. Did you see the makeup? Didn't quite hide the five o'clock shadow."

"I'd guess the sex change operation. It didn't seem to me as if she were trying to act like a woman."

"You've had experience with drag queens?"

Osborne had to smile. "Yes, I have," he said. "My wife took me to a show in Miami's South Beach when I was on leave."

Ashley laughed. "Why?"

Osborne shrugged. "She thought it was sophisticated."

"How about you? What'd you think?"

"It was sort of sad, actually," he said, and glanced over at the couple who were engaged in conversation. "Different strokes for different folks, I guess." The woman was odd, but to him she didn't look like the drag queens in Miami. In the first place she was a lot smaller, not so obviously garish, and actually attractive in a way.

When he looked back Ashley was studying him, something of a contemplative expression in her pretty eyes.

"So tell me, Nate, what are you doing here?"

"Having dinner with you."

"No, I mean North Dakota, Medora. You could write just about any ticket you wanted. I'm sure the bureau would take you in a New York minute."

"I wouldn't do well as a wounded vet poster boy."

Ashley was stung. "I didn't mean that, and you know it. You're bright and well-trained; with the right motivation you could be anything, go anywhere."

Osborne smiled a little sadly. He was getting a little tired of answering the same question. "I am where I want to be, doing what I want to do."

"Kinda empty out here."

"Not right now it isn't. Because whoever hit the Initiative won't stop. And I think there are probably some larger issues going on that your father hasn't shared with me."

"At the very least a leak somewhere."

"Yeah, but a leak of what? And to what end?"

"Somebody wants to destroy the place."

"Why?" Osborne asked, and his cell phone chirped.

"The sixty-four-million-dollar question, what I think you and I are going to figure out."

"A small-town newspaper reporter and an even smaller town cop," Osborne said, and his phone chirped again. It was Jim Cameron at the Initiative.

"Hope I wasn't interrupting anything important."

"Just dinner with a pretty woman," Osborne said, his slight irritation covered with interest. "What's up?"

"Some interesting developments. Can you get out here tonight?"

"Anything you can tell me on the phone?"

"Not unless you're talking on an encrypted Nokia, or something like it."

"Will it hold until after dinner?"

"Don't have dessert," Cameron said. "But we'd just as soon not have Ms. Borden out here right now, and that comes from Deb Rausch."

"Fair enough, but she's kept her promise."

"Your call, Nate, but Whitney will get the general's take first."

"I'll see you in a bit," Osborne said. "Alone." He broke the connection and pocketed his phone.

Ashley had watched him closely, the corners of her mouth turned up. "Thanks for the try," she said. "And for the compliment, if you meant it."

"You're welcome, and I did."

"Well, shucks, Sheriff, are you making a pass at me?"

Osborne frowned. "You don't take compliments very well. Is there a problem, or is it me?"

Ashley was stung again and it showed on her face. "No, I guess I don't, because it's not you. Low self-esteem, I guess. And I sometimes catch myself ashamed by liking what I'm doing and where I'm doing it." She looked away momentarily. "Goddamned backwards ice box of a place. But it grows on you. It's become home. Sappy?"

"I don't think so," Osborne said.

Tina came with their steaks and salads, along with another beer for Osborne and the bottle of Merlot to refill Ashley's glass. "Anything else?"

"See if you can overhear what they're talking about over there," Ashley said.

"I've tried but soon as I show up, they stop. But I can tell you this much, they're not happy campers."

"What about us?" Osborne asked, and Tina grinned.

"If you want my opinion, for what it's worth, you oughta ask Ms. Borden to stay for Christmas. You've got no one here, and to hear her tell she's got no one in Bismarck."

Osborne laughed. "Busybody."

"Shouldn't have moved back home if you wanted your privacy," Tina said and walked off.

Ashley was grinning. "Ball's in your court, big guy."

"I'll go out to the Initiative to see what Jim wants, and when I get back we can figure out what we should do."

This time Ashley laughed out loud. "You're not getting off the hook that easy. Do you want me to stay for Christmas or not?"

Osborne thought her smile was the nicest he'd ever seen on a woman, and he nodded. "I wish you would."

"Glad you asked, Sheriff—Nate."

"Soon as I get back we can decide about presents."

"Tomorrow," Ashley said. "I'm going to drive over to Bismarck tonight, pack a couple of things, and stop by the paper first thing in the morning. Should be back here in time for lunch."

"Careful on the road, we've got snow coming maybe tonight, for sure tomorrow sometime."

30

AFTER DINNER EGAN and Mattson lingered over their coffees until Osborne and Ashley Borden finished theirs and got up to leave. Osborne gave the woman a hug, and when she left he came over.

"Just a suggestion, folks. If you're planning on leaving tonight, I'd head south to Rapid City. But you might want to think about staying here at least for tonight, maybe for a day or two. We have a fair bit of snow coming in from the west. Could get mean out there."

"Good suggestion, Sheriff," Egan said. "I'll think we'll take you up on it. In San Francisco, we don't know from snow."

Osborne nodded. "Have a good evening then," he said, and he turned to go.

"Perhaps we could buy you and Ms. Borden an after-dinner drink?" Egan said. "We know nothing about North Dakota."

"Thanks, but it'll have to be tomorrow. I'm busy tonight. But if you stay you won't make Vegas."

Egan shrugged. "They're friends, they'll understand."

"You work out?"

"Absolute fanatic."

"Gym membership, I suppose."

"I'm too lazy for something like that. I have a few machines at our apartment. Go at my own pace, you know."

Osborne nodded again then left the dining room.

"The son of a bitch is suspicious," Mattson said. "We need to get out of here right now. Go back to Regina before we get stuck."

"We're not going anywhere until we get what we came for," Egan said.

Two couples came in from the bar and sat at a table across the room. They were dressed in jeans, boots, and cowboy shirts with bolo ties. Egan nodded pleasantly, and one of them said something and they all laughed.

Someday they'd find out that it was a tough old world, Egan thought.

"Goddamnit, I didn't sign up for this shit."

"Well, you're here now. Go get us a room, for tonight at least, but tell them that if the snow hits tomorrow we'll need it for as long as we have to stay."

"You're fucking out of your gourd."

"And you're a fucking dead man walking unless you get your head out of your ass," Egan said, his voice low but menacing. "We'll grab her tonight. The good sheriff won't suspect a thing until morning."

"What if they're together tonight?"

"Obviously not. She left first and he got a phone call while they were at the table. Be my guess that he's got work to do. You gotta really learn to open your eyes if you're going to survive for long."

"So we grab her and head back up to Regina. Dump her body on the way."

Egan shook his head. "It has to be here. Right out of this hotel."

"Why, for Christ's sake? Are you completely nuts?"

"We're sending a message that no one's safe here, no matter how much security they put in place. Even the sheriff's girlfriend isn't safe."

Mattson started to object, but Egan held him off.

"You gotta take chances in our world. It's the price of admission. But they sure as hell aren't lovers. Not yet leastways. They're still sleeping in separate beds, I'd take even money on it."

Mattson got up and walked out to the front desk, as Egan called Toby Trela, who was waiting for them down at the Roundup Lodge about twenty-five miles southwest. The kid was only nineteen, six feet, less than a hundred and fifty pounds, but wiry, strong, and as mean, according to him, as Billy the Kid, his hero. He'd been a champion rodeo cowboy out of Missoula since he was fourteen, a Dodge National Circuit Finalist when he was seventeen and eighteen, his events bull riding, saddle bronc, and all around. And in those few years he'd broken just about every bone in his body, learned all about arrogance, fathered four children, squandered all of his purse money, and in the end got some good old-time religion at which time the Posse roped him in.

Toby answered his cell phone after three rings. He sounded drunk. "What the fuck y'all want?" A girl was saying something in the background.

"You're not alone," Egan said, his anger rising.

"Numb nuts, ya think?" Toby said.

At least Moose and the others were professionals, but he needed Mattson as part of his cover, and Toby's reputation as a cowboy to pull off the diversion even though both of them were loose cannons.

"Looks like we're on for tonight. I'll call and let you know when to come."

"I've been helping feed horses all afternoon. Could be shut down here by tonight."

"I don't care."

"You dumb bastard, didn't you hear me? We'll probably be snowed in."

"Let's hope so, it'll provide perfect cover."

Toby was silent for a long moment. "Horses don't get stuck in the snow."

"That's right," Egan said, and neither do all-wheel drive Cadillac Escalades. "I'll talk to you if something changes."

Mattson came back and sat down. He was flustered. "She left."

"What are you talking about?"

"I just saw her drive off. I say we follow her right now. Could be she's headed back to Bismarck."

"Could be she'll be back," Egan said. "We'll wait."

31

JIM CAMERON WAS waiting in one of the Hummers when Whitney came out of the Administration and Research-and-Development Center, hunching up her parka against the bitterly sharp wind. He reached over and popped open the passenger door. "I'll take you over," he called to her.

She hesitated for just a moment, as if she were surprised that anyone else was left alive in the complex, but then came over and climbed up into the cab, slamming the door once she was in. "And this is just December," she said, all out of breath.

Cameron studied her face in the harsh glare from the light poles and roofline security spots. She looked beat-up, as if she hadn't slept in a week and had the weight of the world on her shoulders. A sort of lady Hercules.

"Jesus wept," his grandmother used to say when she was so bone-tired from taking care of an invalid husband, a teenage son, a daughter who'd had a baby out of wed-lock, and two jobs—one of them as a cook at the steel plant cafeteria and the other as the hat check girl at the Moose Club down the block—that she couldn't walk upstairs to bed, and instead laid fully dressed on the couch to fret about how she could possibly manage until a hour or more later she finally passed out.

"How's the work coming?" he asked.

"Coming," she said. "But it was a damned close thing, Jim. The bastards knew just how to hit us. Could have been a disaster." She managed a slight smile. "Except for you."

Cameron had to turn away, the image of the carnage in the trailer burned in his head. "I wasn't quick enough, and anyway I had help."

Whitney touched his arm. "I don't know what we—I—would have done without you."

"Well, you have another issue coming your way," Cameron said, and he headed for the gravel road down to Donna Marie.

"If you're talking about the bureau, Rausch's people were all over the place this afternoon. Pulled our computers apart, actually grilled my people—scared the hell out of Susie until I put a stop to it. Now everything's on some sort of administrative hold, except for the rebuild, which the Air Force has taken over. And she wouldn't tell me what she wanted to talk about tonight."

Whitney was an egghead, but in Cameron's estimation she was a woman who didn't have her head in the clouds; she was practical, pretty understanding of the way politics worked—had to have been working at the CDC—and above all strong with a solid sense of herself and what she could and did bring to the table in the real world. But after all that, she still carried a little of the naïveté that burdened most scientists.

"They're looking for the leak."

Whitney nodded thoughtfully. "I've been going over that myself. We've got a leak, there's absolutely no doubt about it. No other way that Kemal could have tailor-made his bioweapon to do the most damage here. And it has to be on the science side. Could be back at CDC. I did a lot of my preliminary quorum-sensing work on their main-frame."

"Password protected, I'm guessing."

"Of course."

"Any idea who'd have access?"

Whitney seemed to shrink a little into her parka, her shoulders slumping. It was pitch-black outside, and the first few flakes of snow were showing up in the headlights, isolating them. "Someone could have broken into the file. But I don't personally know anyone with that skill. My password is eleven random characters that have no intrin-sic meaning."

It was about what Cameron figured, and it deepened his depressed mood. "Anyone over there with a motive?"

"Not that I can think of."

"Well, these sorts of things usually come from left field. Blindsides us."

Whitney turned to look at him. "What are you getting at?" she asked.

"Kemal got your blueprints from the science side. And the most likely candidates are on your staff."

"Impossible," Whitney said, but then she was stopped in her tracks and her eyes widened. "Or me," she said.

"That's the conclusion Deb Rausch came to last night. She's flown in her own expert to ask you a few questions."

"Fine, because the sooner we get this over with the sooner I can get back to work."

"You're temporarily off the project as of now."

"Absurd. This is my work, and no one knows it better than I do. Did this come from General Forester, or is it just politics as usual?" She was angry, all traces of her weariness gone. "Sounds like they're trying to find a scapegoat. Did they say who their expert was?"

"Dr. William Cargo, but I haven't met him yet."

Whitney reacted as if she'd been hit by a cattle prod.

"Do you know him?"

"He was my boss for about six months over at the CDC. He got his doctorate at Yale, and for a long time he was one of the top minds in the field, but then something happened and he went stale. Didn't publish, couldn't do the lab work, so they promoted him."

"Sounds dumb."

"SOP in science. When you can't do the work, they give you the responsibilities for administering the scientists who can. And like a lot of people who get to that position, Bill Cargo resented the people he supervised."

"Including you?"

"Especially me. I took this job, which because of his seniority, he figured was his."

"Will he understand what you're trying to do here?"

Whitney was even angrier, and her voice rose. "In broad strokes he will. But he pooh-poohed my work from the start, so if he can get me to take the fall for this, or at least sling a little mud my way, he won't hesitate to do it."

"Sorry to tell you this, but if you go into this meeting with that attitude he'll have an easy time of it."

"What do you suggest I do?" she demanded.

"Fight back."

"How?"

"Come on, Whitney. This is your project, your discovery. And time is on your side. If they're going to pull an Oppenheimer on you it won't be until after the experiment." Robert Oppenheimer had been the chief scientist on the World War II atomic bomb project. But he'd toyed around with the idea of communism when he was younger and according to the FBI he still had connections. But he wasn't bounced from the project until after the first test. And then he lost his clearances so that he couldn't even read the scientific papers that he himself had written.

"I'm not going to end up that way," she cried. "This test is just the first. There's a lot more to come. Christ."

They rode for the next few minutes in silence. The snow had stopped for a moment and they could see the glow of the lights on Donna Marie. Reconstruction was coming along ahead of schedule and sometime just after Christmas the operation would be up and running. An experienced fossil fuel plant crew from the Saint Clair facility in Michigan was being briefed now and would be in place, and no one from her science staff was taking off for the holidays. They were sticking with their doc, no matter what, though as a group they were pretty frightened. "Waiting for you to make the first move," Cameron had told her earlier today.

"Who hired you in the first place?" he asked, and she turned to him.

"Bob Forester."

"No," Cameron said. "Your boss is President Thompson. This is just as much his initiative as the Manhattan District Project was F.D.R.'s. You carry some weight. Don't you think it's time to start using it?"

"What am I supposed to do? Fly out to Washington and knock on his door?"

"Exactly. And General Forester is just the man to drive you over. Thompson won't say no to the pair of you."

32

IT WAS AFTER eight when Ashley pulled off the interstate at Dickinson, and stopped at the Citgo station. She didn't really need gas, she had more than half a tank in the truck, but she filled up anyway, and afterwards parked over by the restaurant and went in for a cup of coffee.

What she really needed was time to think, because ever since Nate Osborne had told someone on the phone—Cameron, she'd guessed—that he was having dinner with a pretty woman, her stomach had been doing strange things. It was just like when she'd been a kid in sixth grade at the American elementary school at Landsthul in Germany where her father had been stationed at the time, and she had developed a nearly overwhelming crush on Joseph Lieberman who sat right in front of her. Now, like then, she had no idea what to do, what to say, or how to react.

Her first urge then was to get the boy alone on the playground after school and kick the shit out of him for making her crazy. Instead she had just stared at him whenever he was around, and had wild dreams about running away with him to some village in the mountains south of Munich where a kindly old couple would adopt them and they could live happily after. Luckily she'd never said a word to him, because three weeks later she'd fallen out of love and had no earthly idea what she could ever had seen in him.

Only a half-dozen people were in the restaurant, most of them at the counter, so she took a booth by a window, and watching the occasional car or truck pass on the interstate, she got an almost overwhelming sense of loneliness. It was crunch time, as her father used to say when he had to make a tough decision. And so far as she'd known he'd always stepped up to the plate and at least took a swing. It's why he'd gone over to the new ARPA-E and why the president had tapped him to head the Initiative.

So right now it was her own personal crunch time, and she turned the thought, more like a concept, over in her head. She was an independent person, always had been. And she always guarded her personal space. Except there was no one inside with her, and she was starting to get damned tired of going home to an empty apartment and taking something out of the freezer to nuke, and watching only the television shows she wanted to watch, and going to bed alone and waking up alone. No one to pick up after, no one to nag, to cook for, to laugh with. No one to watch her back, prop her up when she was down, pass her a handkerchief when she cried, or kick her butt when it needed to be kicked.

Like now.

The waitress was there with the coffee. "You doin' okay, sweetie?"

Ashley looked up, ready to bite the woman's head off, but she shrugged instead. "Things have been better."

"The bastard dumped you?"

"No. He thinks I'm pretty."

The waitress, a woman with a horse face but a kindly smile, laughed. "Hells bells, girl, what are you so down in the dumps about? I'd just love to have your problem, if that's what it is."

Ashley started to cry despite herself, and hating herself for it; all of a sudden she was more frightened and unsure of herself than she'd ever been in her entire life. And ashamed, she turned away, trying to hide her anguish.

But the waitress didn't make a fuss, she just handed Ashley a napkin from the holder. "A good cry is worth its weight in gold, I've always said. And when you're done, fix your pretty face—he's right, you're a pretty woman—and go to wherever he is, and tell him how you feel. Makes no sense otherwise."

Ashley looked at her. "What?"

"Don't be a dope, girl. You love him, that's obvious from across the room."

"I can't go to him right now."

"Of course you can."

"You don't understand. By now he's behind a big fence with guards all over the place."

The waitress smiled again and patted Ashley on the shoulder. "Believe me, they all are," she said, and she walked off.

Ashley cupped her hands around the coffee mug, suddenly a little chilly. She'd never much cared for women as buddies. She'd never trusted them. She'd grown up in a man's world, just her and her father, and if she wanted solace or advice she always turned to a man. But the waitress made sense.

When she finished her coffee, she laid a ten-dollar bill on the table and walked out to her car. For just a brief moment she hesitated before she pulled out and got on the interstate heading west back toward Medora.

33

JIM CAMERON, DRIVING a utility golf cart, met Osborne at the heavily guarded Donna Marie gate a few minutes before eight thirty, still a lot of heavy repair work going on, big trucks moving back and forth, dumping the twisted metal debris a half mile away near the antenna farm, and the noise of cutters and grinders and drills loud, out of place in the Badlands, as were the sputtering, unnaturally bright welding torches.

"Glad you could make it out on such short notice," Cameron said. "Leave your car here, I'll drive you over."

Osborne rode with him over to the big double-wide trailer, one of three new ones that had replaced the ones that had been shot all to hell. A couple of new tents had also been set up on the north side of the power station, one of which the Bureau's forensics people were using to dissect the Newell's electronic equipment.

"What's the urgency? You sounded like there was more trouble."

"Where's Ms. Borden?"

"On her way to Bismarck. But she's coming back tomorrow."

"Good enough. We'll try to get you back here as early as possible, though I can't guarantee how long it's going to take us."

"Where am I going?"

"Washington, buddy," Cameron said. "The president wants to have a word with you. Actually with all of us, especially Whitney. And General Forester gave me a direct order that his daughter was not to get involved, or even be told a thing."

It wasn't what Osborne expected and he was taken aback for a beat. "What the hell am I supposed to say?"

"About what?"

"For starters, Ashley. She'll expect me to be around, can I at least get word to her?"

"Afraid not."

"I'll have to let my deputies know I'll be gone overnight."

Cameron gave him a hard look. "Make damn sure they keep their mouths shut. I'm serious about this, and this goes all the way to the Oval Office, because there've been hints that something big time is happening politically."

"Something to do with the attack?"

"It's a possibility."

Osborne shook his head. "I can't do anything for you people. I'm just a small-time sheriff, nothing more."

"Your Medal of Honor says otherwise. Anyway, don't you keep saying that this is *your* county?"

And it was his county, his people who he deeply cared about. Ever since Afghanistan he'd had a strong sense of family; especially so because he had only an ex-wife and a child who was growing more distant each year, parents dead, no siblings, no aunts or uncles or cousins, only the townspeople and the ranchers and park employees.

"I'll need to get back to my place to change clothes,"

he said as they pulled up to the trailer where a half-dozen cars and Hummers and a couple of golf carts were parked.

"No time," Cameron said. "Anyway they don't want you in uniform. This is an in and out to the White House, strictly no media attention."

It wasn't making any sense to Osborne and he told Cameron as much. "I'm no expert on politics. What do they want from me?"

"You're a good judge of character."

"Comes with the job."

"Well, the other problem we're facing is the leak somewhere in the system. Almost certainly on the science side because the biological soup that they were trying to inject into the well would have caused a hell of a mess. Probably a blowout and a catastrophic release of methane. Enough to do some serious damage to our atmosphere. And the only way it could have been engineered was to know exactly what we were trying to do out here."

"Have Whitney Lipton's people been vetted?"

Cameron nodded. "They came up clean. Which leaves the doc herself."

Osborne laughed despite himself. "You have to be kidding."

"The FBI isn't."

"Why the hell would she sabotage her own project? If I'm catching even half of the drift here, we're talking a possible Nobel, so it sure wouldn't be money."

"They've already ruled that out. No offshore bank accounts, no diamonds or cars or trips to Paris or anywhere for that matter. But the Bureau brought an expert over from the CDC—Whitney's old boss—who thinks that her science is way off base, and she knows it now, so she's trying to cover her own ass."

"I know even less about biophysics than I do about geopolitics."

Cameron hesitated at the door and smiled. "I just want you to meet the guy; name's William Cargo. In my estimation he's a complete ass, but I'm a little bit prejudiced here. So I want your take. In the meantime I said politics, not geopolitics."

"If it's clean coal up against oil you have at least OPEC to contend with, and probably all the financial wizards who're making money on futures."

Cameron laughed out loud. "Simple country sheriff, my ass."

Just inside the front door a bank of monitors—most of them displaying views from inside Donna Marie—was arrayed on a wall in front of a desk, at which sat a young Air Force technician. Captain Nettles along with several men in dark blue FBI sweaters were watching over the tech's shoulder at one of the monitors that showed the view inside what appeared to be a small conference room with a table for a dozen people. Whitney Lipton was seated on one side of the table facing the Bureau's Minneapolis SAC Deb Rausch and an older man with long white hair and thick muttonchops. Rausch's expression was neutral, but the man seemed tense and angry.

Nettles looked up and scowled. "Sheriff," he said.

Osborne nodded. "Captain."

"Anything new?" Cameron asked.

"No, but I think she'd like to kick his ass," Nettles said.

"Your project has been on shaky ground from the start, but you're just too pigheaded to admit that you might be wrong," the older man said. "Heaven forbid."

"Doctor Cargo," Cameron told Osborne. "They're just down the hall."

Whitney, whose right profile was to the camera, seemed

frustrated. "Are you trying to accuse me of something, Bill? Because if you are I'd like to hear it, and I'd like your *studied* scientific opinion."

"I was asked by the Bureau to consult. So here I am. Gracious me, maybe we can work this out like professionals. Fact of the matter someone got to your bugs and found a way to neutralize your quorum-sensing mechanism."

"I thought you said it couldn't work," Whitney jumped him. "Can't have it both ways. Which will it be?"

"This is a serious situation, Dr. Lipton," Rausch said.

"You bet it is," Whitney shot back. "Because my experiment will go forward in less than one week and then we'll see."

"I meant the leak."

"So did I," Whitney said, and she got to her feet. "I have an appointment, so we'll have to wait until tomorrow afternoon to continue." She turned to Dr. Cargo. "You used to be a damned fine scientist. But somewhere along the line you lost it. Couldn't keep up. Stopped publishing. And you became an embarrassment so they promoted you."

"You can't say that to me," Cargo sputtered.

"Lead, follow, or get the hell out of my way. I have work to do."

Neither Cargo nor Rausch said anything and Whitney left the room.

"What do you think?" Cameron asked.

"The man has his own agenda, and it has nothing to do with any leak in the system," Osborne said.

"Maybe he's the leak," Cameron said, but Whitney had already stormed up the corridor and she caught the remark.

"Not him," she said. "He's too goddamned ignorant."

Nettles had stepped aside to take a call. "Your jet is standing by at Dickinson and a chopper to get you there will be here in five minutes," he announced.

34

GETTING OFF THE interstate and heading south on U.S. 85 at the small town of Belfield, Ashley had no idea what reception she was going to get when she showed up uninvited again at the Initiative, but if Nate Osborne was there no power on earth was going to stop her from storming the gates.

The turnoff was about ten miles farther south, and the night was pitch-black, no stars in an overcast sky, absolutely no traffic on the highway, but as soon as she bumped onto the gravel road—which had been kept primitive to discourage snoopers and hold down speculation about what might be back here—she could see the lights along the fence line, and a hint of the red flasher atop the Donna Marie smokestack several miles farther to the southwest.

She'd done a lot of traveling as a child with her father, as a college student on road trips during semesters, spring, and summer breaks—usually alone—and then as an investigative reporter running down story leads, also usually alone. And she did a lot of her best thinking on the road, always had. Without an audience she wasn't afraid to examine her true inner feelings. One of her father's favorite expressions was something like you can lie to just about anyone and get away with it, if you're really good, but you can't lie to yourself unless you're pathological. And if truth be told now, and if she wasn't lying to herself, she thought that she might be falling in love with the sheriff. In fact she might have been falling in love with him ever since the murders in the park. She'd thought that he was attractive and decisive, qualities she'd always liked in a man.

The light snow had let up, but the storm was expected to start hitting them sometime tomorrow. No big deal, this was December in North Dakota. But she was glad she'd decided to come back. She didn't want to take a chance of getting stuck in Bismarck for Christmas.

She drove directly past the main gate and followed the gravel road the rest of the way west and then north, to the Donna Marie entrance. Almost immediately an Apache helicopter rose up from inside the Initiative and came at her, pacing her speed off her left side and just ten or fifteen feet off the deck.

"You are trespassing on government property," a voice boomed from the chopper. "Turn around at once, or you will be subject to arrest."

Ashley powered down her window and held her press pass out.

A spotlight switched on, flooding the entire truck with a light so intense that she was blinded and had to slow down to a crawl lest she was run off the road.

Her hand was freezing so she pulled it back inside.

A minute later the spotlight was switched off.

"Your visitor's pass has been temporarily suspended," the amplified voice boomed. "You will be required to show your identification at the gate, at which time you will be directed to return the way you came or you will be subject to arrest. If you understand these orders please flash your headlights."

Ashley did as she was told, then sped up as her night vision began to return. She dialed her father's private number, but after three rings his answering machine picked up with the instruction that the person was not currently available, and to leave a message at the tone.

"Daddy, it's me," she said. "If you're there, pick up. I'm at the Initiative and they don't want to let me in for some reason."

Moments later the answering machine beeped. "For further options, please press one."

She hung up, and laid the phone on the passenger seat as she came up over a low rise at the bottom of which was the Donna Marie gate, open and lit up like day. It looked as if repairs were going ahead at full speed, and a couple of new tents had been set up. Big trucks came and went, and airmen in winter camos, night vision goggles, assault rifles—muzzles down—slung over their shoulders, seemed to be everywhere. She counted at least a dozen.

Osborne's Saturn SUV was parked just inside the fence.

Two armed guards motioned for her to stop a few yards from the gate, and one of them came over as she powered her window down.

"May I see your driver's license, ma'am," he said.

Ashley pulled it out of her purse and handed it to him. "I came out to talk to Sheriff Osborne."

"Sorry, ma'am, he's not here this evening," the guard said. He looked up from the photograph on the license, then handed it back. "Turn around please, and drive back the way you came. Make no stops until you're well clear of this installation, and do not attempt to approach the fence."

"That's the sheriff's car," she said. "I need to talk to him for just one minute."

"Ma'am, please turn around."

"Goddamnit," Ashley said, and she started to open her door, but the guard unslung his assault rifle.

"Okay," she said, closing the door. "I get your point, but first I need to make a phone call, and then I'll scoot."

"Please leave now."

"I'm having car troubles, and I want to leave word with a friend. I don't want to get stuck out here," Ashley said, and she speed dialed Osborne's cell phone.

The guard said something into a lapel mike, and then he backed down and lowered his weapon.

Osborne picked up on the second ring. "Yes!" he shouted, a terrific noise of some machinery in the background.

"Nate, it's Ashley, where are you?"

"None of your business. Are you in Bismarck already?"

"I'm at the Donna Marie back gate, about fifteen feet from your car. Can you get me in? I just want to talk for a minute."

"No," Osborne said. "I want you to turn around and get the hell out of there. Jim says that they'll arrest you if you don't. And after what's happened they're serious."

"I just want to tell you something."

"Not now. Go home and do your thing, I'll be back by tomorrow afternoon."

"Back from where?" Ashley shouted, but Osborne had broken the connection, and she closed her phone.

The guard was close enough to have heard her side of the conversation. "Ma'am," he prompted.

"Yeah," Ashley said absently. She tossed the phone on the passenger seat, closed her window, turned around, and drove off, the helicopter rising up again and trailing her just a few yards until she was back up on U.S. 85 and heading north to the interstate.

Despite what the guard said, Nate was there at the

power station. She'd seen his car with her own eyes. And on the phone she'd heard the machinery noise. But he'd said that he would be back by tomorrow afternoon. But back from where? She turned that thought over and it dawned on her that the background noise wasn't the same as the turbine whine, it was more like that of a helicopter.

She got on her phone again and phoned the Bismarck airport control tower, and got a supervisor named Lawson.

"Ashley Borden, *Bismarck Tribune*. Have you had any incoming VIP flights from Washington this evening? I'm trying to run down a lead."

"No, ma'am, but one's standing by at Dickinson."

"Spending the night?"

"I don't believe so. Hold on."

She knew damned well the aircraft would be heading to Washington tonight, before the storm hit, and that Nate and probably Dr. Lipton would be aboard. It was the call Nate had taken at dinner. Something big was going down, and her father had probably given the order to keep her away.

Lawson came back. "No, ma'am. In fact she's already in the air, IFR Andrews Air Force Base."

"Thanks, you've been a big help," Ashley said, and she broke the connection.

At Belfield, the streets lit up for Christmas, shoppers downtown for the last-minute sales, Ashley was suddenly more depressed than she'd ever remembered. She felt excluded, as if she had no family who loved her, and mostly she didn't want to be alone tonight in a strange hotel room.

At the entrance to the interstate she took the west ramp. The sign reading: MEDORA 10.

35

OSBORNE HAD BEEN to the White House, under a different president, to receive his Medal of Honor, but not at three in the morning local, and as he was ushered into the Situation Room down the hall from the Oval Office along with Whitney and Jim Cameron, it felt as if he were back in Afghanistan on the front line. This was the big leagues, the biggest of all. The president had called them here at this hour to discuss who was coming after the Initiative and why.

General Forester, in civilian clothes, had met them at Joint Base Andrews with a navy helicopter and had brought them over. He introduced them to the four men seated around the long conference table: Nicholas Fenniger, the president's adviser on national security affairs; Edwin Rogers, director of the FBI; Walter Page, director of the CIA; and Air Force Major General Hollis Reed, director of the National Security Agency.

"The president will be with us momentarily," Fenniger said as Osborne and the others sat across the table.

On the way over, Forester had briefed both Osborne and Cameron. "The president will ask some tough questions, and he'll expect some tough answers. If you don't know, don't guess. And if he doesn't like your answers—and he'll let you know—don't back down if what you're telling him is your best opinion."

"That's all well and good, General, but what the hell am I doing here?" Osborne asked.

"Because he asked for you by name," Forester said. "I understand that my daughter called you from outside the Donna Marie gate while you were in the helicopter on the way over to Dickinson."

"She did," Osborne said. He had a feeling what was coming next.

"What did she want?"

"To talk to me."

"About what?"

"She didn't say."

Forester had nodded. "She's a willful girl, always has been. What's your interest in her, Sheriff?"

"The name is Nate, sir. And that is none of your business at the moment."

Forester bridled, but Osborne went on.

"Mostly because I don't know the answer myself. But I'll let you know when I have it figured out. Right now we have a bigger problem to deal with."

"That we do," Forester said.

Everyone suddenly got to their feet, and Osborne stood up as President Thompson, tie loose, shirtsleeves rolled up, no jacket, strode in and sat down directly across from Osborne.

"Glad you could join us on such short notice, Sheriff," the president said as everyone else sat down.

"Thank you, Mr. President, but I don't know what I'm doing here."

"I'm told that you own Billings County, you have a

steady hand, you have a proven track record under fire, and until I find someone better you're my point man on the ground out there."

"I'm just a small-town sheriff."

Thompson laughed. "Tell it to the navy, Major."

Osborne had to grin. "My line has never worked, sir."

Thompson nodded to Forester.

"How much do you know about what we're trying to do at the Initiative?" Forester asked.

"It's not an ELF station. From what I can piece together Dr. Lipton has figured out a way to convert coal to methane that can be pumped out of the seam through a wellhead and then burned to heat water to turn turbines to generate electricity."

"Almost zero carbon dioxide," Forester said. "No mercury or other pollutants, and no waste, no coal ash to contend with. All the wastes stay underground. And the seam in western North and South Dakota and eastern Wyoming should last a hundred years or more."

"Why the secrecy?"

"You can answer that one yourself, Sheriff. Clean electricity, without having to mine, process, or ship coal. No need for nuclear energy. No need for foreign oil—eventually most of our ground transportation will run electrically. We're working on electrically driven aircraft—prop jobs at first—but there are some good-looking technologies on the drawing boards that could break down water into hydrogen and oxygen in sufficient quantities to power rocket engines or ramjets. Homes heated electrically—no need for heating oil."

Osborne had heard some of the arguments before, but so far nothing was feasible at the scale Forester was talking about. "Assuming it works, a lot of people are going to be out of a job. Most of them ordinary working folks."

"It's worse than that," the president said. "The national economies of places like Saudi Arabia and some of the other OPEC countries will take a serious hit. Along with the Initiative—if it works, and there's still no guarantee that it will—I'm proposing a global realignment of priorities. In the short term, while we still have oil in the ground, I'll push for a ten-year program to develop new, non-energy uses for oil far beyond pharmaceuticals, fertilizers, plastics, carpets, clothes, sneakers, and dish soap. Did you know that aspirin is made from petrochemicals?"

"No, sir."

"Better than burning it to power a billion cars, trucks, buses, ships, and airplanes."

No response was needed. But Osborne didn't think that he'd been called to the White House to talk about making aspirin out of oil.

"How soon will you be able to resume your work?" the president asked Whitney.

"Ten days tops, if nothing else happens," she said.

"And how sure are you that it will work?"

Whitney looked as if she hadn't slept in a week, and Osborne felt sorry for her.

"If you'd asked me that question last week, Mr. President, I would have told you one hundred percent. But now I'm not sure. The models all look good, and we've run a hyperbaric test on an actual piece of coal seam cut from a mine in West Virginia. Within minutes after we'd injected a small sample of our microbial mix and introduced a miniature quorum talker, we were getting methane. We ran the experiment three times with the same results."

"Where's the problem?"

"The scale. Leaks in the seam that could allow an escape of methane directly into the atmosphere. An underground fire or explosion. Or a dozen other possibilities that we haven't thought of."

"Including another attack," the president said. He turned to his FBI director. "No possibility that your people have made a mistake? Missed something?"

"No, sir," Edwin Rogers said. He was a pleasant-looking man dressed this morning in a dark suit, white shirt, and plain tie. He could have been a banker or CEO of a corporation, not the nation's top cop. "Definitely Posse Comitatus, except for Dr. Kemal. We're working on the sixth person who presumably killed the two in the motor home then hid it in a box canyon south of the Initiative, but we're coming up with only five sets of prints, matching the five bodies left behind."

"Sheriff?" the president prompted.

"He planned it that way," Osborne said. "Nothing or no one left behind."

"He?"

"The Posse uses women for some of its operations, but almost always it's a man who gives the orders."

"Any progress tracing the money?" the president asked Rogers.

"The motor home itself was custom-built, at a cost of somewhere near half a million. The electronic gear was worth another two hundred thousand, possibly even more—most of it Chinese-made, but some Russian stuff, and at least one of the computer programs they used was based on the version of the Stuxnet worm the Israelis used to interfere with Iran's nuclear program. Sophisticated stuff. We're thinking that they had an international connection."

"A lot of it points back to SEBIN," Walter Page, the CIA director, said. "Unfortunately most of what we've come up with is circumstantial, but it's pretty tight. We're also thinking that's where the money came from, though we're shaky on that part. We haven't made any sort of a clear trace yet."

Osborne glanced at Cameron who'd apparently just had the same thought. "Excuse me, sir. You're talking about SEBIN—Venezuela's intelligence service—being involved with the attack?"

Page nodded. "At this point that's exactly what it's beginning to look like."

"The Posse is a strictly homegrown terrorist organization. They'd never take orders from outsiders, so if the Venezuelans are footing the bill they have to be doing it through someone in the U.S."

"Any ideas?" Page asked.

"A contractor company," Cameron said. "Someone with field experience."

"We had the same thought," Rogers said. "But so far we've come up with nothing solid."

"Pardon me, but Chávez can't be crazy enough to try something like this," Osborne said. "It would be an act of war."

The president nodded. "Wouldn't be the first."

"We sent a special envoy down to Caracas," Nicholas Fenniger said. He had curly gray hair and a serious demeanor reminiscent of Rahm Emanuel, who'd been President Obama's chief of staff. "Wanted to talk some sense into their ministry of oil people, try to make a deal with the bastards. They were raising the price of crude by twenty-three percent—to us and no one else."

Osborne had seen something on the news. "He was killed in some kind of an accident."

"He was beheaded with a chain saw," Fenniger said. "Chávez blamed it on terrorists."

"Message sent and received," the president said. He was suddenly very angry.

"Sorry, Mr. President, but this is way out of my league," Osborne said. "I may own Billings County, as you say, but our population is probably smaller than the number of people working for you right here."

"I understand you, Sheriff, but understand me. Because of the size of your county already far too much attention is being paid to what we're trying to do. The story that it's nothing more than an ELF facility and that it was nothing but an accident won't hold much longer unless we begin to withdraw the bulk of the armed Air Force personnel as soon as possible."

This took Osborne's breath away. "It has to be kept secret at all costs for as long as possible?"

"Something like that."

"If SEBIN knows, won't the rest of OPEC know?"

"It doesn't seem to be the case so far," the president said. "The Saudis aren't pressuring us."

Whitney was caught up in the president's idea. "In ten days we'll know if it works on the scale we're hoping for. After that we can be up and running in a super short time."

"Anything moves in your county that doesn't belong, blow the whistle and you'll get all the muscle you can use," Rogers said.

"But discreetly," the president said. "Will you do that for me?"

Osborne nodded, as he knew he would. "I'll need an extra pair of eyes immediately."

"Anybody," the president said.

"She's an investigative reporter with the Bismarck paper. She's sharp, she's local, she has connections, she already knows or has guessed most of what's really going on, and she was right in the middle of the attack."

"Who is she?" the president asked.

"I believe he's talking about my daughter," General Forester said.

"Yes," Osborne said. "And in the meantime I've been told there might be a leak of classified information, possibly at the facility."

"We're taking care of it," the president said.

"If I have to watch my back I'll need to know who it is."

"It's no one out there, Sheriff," the president said, his anger rising again. He glanced at Whitney. "And it's especially not Dr. Lipton or any of her staff."

"Yes, sir."

"Anything else?"

No one said a thing, and the president got up. "Then let's get back to work."

36

I T WAS LATE, nearly one o'clock, and Egan, wearing a light shirt, his bra off, stood by the window looking toward the post office, a bank, and beyond it a church, the snow falling heavier now than it had earlier. All Midwest, prim and proper; places to pray, to stash your money, to send a postcard to your aunt Hattie in Nebraska and just downstairs a place to have a beer and a steak. But he would never fit in here, and now and then thoughts like that made him a little sad and made him realize just how bug-shit crazy he was.

Mattson had left around eleven thirty to snoop around the hotel and find out if the broad had come back or had gone to Bismarck for whatever reason, leaving Egan to his thoughts. Just like Dr. Kemal and the kid, Don would not leave the Badlands alive. Now that his part was nearly done he'd become excess baggage, not worth a damn if it came to a stand-up fight.

Soon as Ashley Borden got back from wherever—the clerk had confirmed that she was gone when Don had booked them a room—they would grab her and head out.

Operations like that were far easier than most people suspected.

"Said the broad's staying for Christmas. Practically told me the sheriff's life story, said the two of them were meant for each other."

"Touching," Egan had told him.

"No, goddamnit, you have to listen to me. The son of a bitch is a war hero. Medal of Honor in Afghanistan, and the newspaper broad is his girlfriend."

"Then he'll get a big kick out of what happens next."

They'd brought a bottle of whiskey up to their room, and Mattson had watched with a morbid fascination as Egan took off the bra and other padding that had rounded his figure.

"She knows something's wrong with you."

Egan grinned. "Good, it'll make grabbing her all the more easy. Curiosity killed the cat."

"And then what?"

Egan told him, and the newspaper reporter had almost lost his dinner.

"You're fucking out of your mind."

"You got it."

"But why?"

"We're sending a message to her daddy. Back off."

Mattson had taken a deep pull of the whiskey, turned the television to some Christmas special, and laid down fully clothed on the bed with the bottle. "I'm leaving in the morning. I'll rent a car and tell them I have to get home, family emergency or some shit."

"You know what I said I was going to do to the reporter?" Egan had asked pleasantly.

Mattson could only nod.

"Try to leave before we're finished here, and you can join her."

"I was just saying we watch ourselves."

"And lay off the booze, I want you to keep checking to see if she comes back. Because if she does we'll go tonight, and I'll want you sober."

At one precisely, Egan's encrypted Nokia phone burred softly. He'd called Kast earlier in the evening, and the Command Systems CEO had promised to call back with the requested intel.

"Yes," Egan answered.

"Lots of activity, as we'd suspected. Didn't have to use infrared."

Kast was talking about satellite images from space. Some of the better connected contractors were able to anonymously subscribe to a Department of Defense satellite surveillance system as one of the necessary perks that came with their government contracts. But in actual fact so much data was processed through thousands of government computers that no agency, not even a supercomputer dedicated to the task, could ever keep track of all the users. With the right passwords just about any computer could be hacked without the owner knowing about it.

America was great, Egan thought, but it was a tough old world out there.

"Any holes in the perimeter?"

"Most of the action is down around the power station. The west side that parallels Highway 85 looks quiet."

"Are you watching it now?"

"On my monitor."

"Any sign that the troops are pulling out or getting ready to go?"

"No, are you expecting it?" Kast asked.

"They'll have to leave if they want to keep their little

secrets. Around here just about everybody is convinced there was some sort of an accident out there, but it won't be long before they'll begin to wonder why the hell so many armed guards are hanging out."

"How do you know about the ground troops?"

"It's what I'd do," Egan said. "They start moving out, let me know."

"When do you make the grab?"

"Maybe tonight," Egan said. "We've got a snowstorm coming our way. Just what the doctor ordered." And he almost brayed like a mule, but held it back until he could break the connection, and even then he held a hand over his mouth.

Someone came to the door, the old-fashioned lock grating, and Egan grabbed his silenced Glock 39 pistol from the light table and turned around. But it was just Mattson, who was excited and all out of breath, and he didn't even notice the gun.

"She's here."

"Keep your voice down, goddamnit," Egan said. "Borden?"

"Yeah. She came in the bar while I was sitting there, and she didn't leave until just a couple of minutes ago. But she's staying here in the hotel."

"Did you manage to find out what room she's in?"

Mattson glanced at the connecting door. "You're not going to believe this shit. But she's right next door. Right fucking next to us."

Egan speed-dialed Toby's number. The rodeo cowboy answered in the first ring as if he had been expecting the call. "Yo."

"It's tonight. How fast can you get up to the rendezvous point?"

"In this shit? Two hours, three tops."

It would be cutting it close, but Egan didn't think that they could afford to wait until tomorrow night. "Start now."

"I'm on it."

"Will you be missed? Will someone call the cops?"

"Nope."

"Are you sure?"

"Only the old man and woman, a stablehand, a cook, and one guest other than me."

"The broad you were with?"

"Yeah. But it's no sweat. They're all dead."

37

THE FBI'S GULFSTREAM VIP jet was passing to the north of Minneapolis, the weather worsening the farther west they flew. It was two thirty in the morning on the ground, one thirty in Medora, and although Cameron and Whitney were sleeping, Osborne had not been able to doze off. He kept feeling that he was missing something, had been missing something all along.

From where he sat he could see nothing outside the window except for the black night punctuated by the aircraft's running lights and strobe, absolutely no hint that they were just north of a major city.

Ashley was safe in Bismarck, or at least he hoped she was, though he'd been shook up last night when she'd called from the Donna Marie gate. He had a fair idea why she had followed him there, and what she had wanted to say to him, and he didn't know if he was ready. He had been divorced now longer than he had been married, and days, actually mostly nights, he harbored the thought that somehow the separation could be erased, and that he could have his family back.

Impossible after all this time, of course; he knew that

intellectually, yet he'd shied away from any woman he'd dated who wanted to take it to another level, make it serious. There weren't many available bachelors in all of Billings County, or in the surrounding counties for that matter, so he'd always been high on the list.

Miss Dottie had been on his case lately to get on with his life. Find someone nice and settle back down. "Just because you got your fingers burned once, doesn't mean it'll happen again."

"We'll see." Osborne had tried to hold her off, but it hadn't worked.

"Nathan, you're a war hero. Don't be such a coward."

"Afghanistan was easy by comparison."

The flight attendant, a pleasant young woman in a khaki skirt and white blouse, who'd served them on the way out from Dickinson, came back. She was still smiling and looked fresh despite the late hour. "The captain would like to have a word with you, sir," she told Osborne. "It's the weather."

Osborne unbuckled and went forward to the flight deck. The pilot, a slightly built sandy-haired man whose name was Willis, looked over his shoulder. "Sorry to wake you, Sheriff, but it looks like we're going to have to land at Fargo, in about a half hour. The weather's closing in faster than we'd anticipated. Billings has already closed and they're getting ready to shut Rapid City down."

"You don't think we can make Dickinson?"

"I think Bismarck would be calling it close, but Dickinson is definitely out."

"Bismarck it is," Osborne said.

"How important is it?"

"Very," Osborne said, his gut tight, his instincts on a high pitch.

"We'll contact Bismarck right now and make sure they

keep one of their runways open for us," Willis said. "After all we have a presidential mandate."

"Good man. Now, can I make a couple of phone calls?"

"Sure. You can use the console in the backseat, starboard side."

Whitney was still asleep when Osborne went aft but Cameron was awake. "Trouble?"

"It's the weather. We're not going to make Dickinson and even Bismarck is going to be dicey."

"Are we in a hurry? Not much for us to do until Donna Marie is back and running."

"Just a feeling," Osborne said, and the plane lurched as if it had hit a pothole, nearly throwing him off his feet.

"Strap in back there," the attendant called to them. She had taken the jump seat and was buckling in.

Osborne made it to the rear seat and buckled in as the plane hit another burst of turbulence, then another. They had just found the leading edge of the front.

Cameron made it back and strapped in across the aisle. "Talk to me."

"We ran into stuff like this in Afghanistan. When the weather shut everything down, the Taliban made their worst attacks on our positions. Their eyeballs were better than our night vision gear, and they were dedicated."

"You think that the Posse is going to hit us again? Finish what they started? Because if that's the case, and they actually get the microbes into the seam, Whitney says that we can pretty well kiss off all the work they've done for the next several years. Maybe longer."

Osborne shook his head. "It won't be the same thing. Not with all the ground troops out there. But something is coming."

"And you can feel it," Cameron said.

"In my bones. And incoming rounds usually have the right of way."

"Hoo-rah," Cameron said. "Should I give Nettles the heads-up?"

"Won't hurt," Osborne said, and he passed the wireless handset across.

Whitney had awakened and she'd turned around in her seat and looked back at them. "Are we in trouble?"

"We might be late," Osborne said. "The crew is trying to get us as far as Bismarck, but it depends on what we'll run into."

"Could we get stuck out here?"

"Maybe."

"Great," she said. "I'll have to let my people know what's going on. They're all a little shook up right now."

"Anybody quit?"

"No," she said. "Not one."

"Good people."

"The best," Whitney said.

Cameron broke the connection and handed the phone back. "The guy's a prick," he said.

"I got the same impression," Osborne told him. "We can talk to Forester, if you want, and he'd be out of there on the next transport back to Rapid City."

"I didn't say the man was incompetent, I just said he was a prick."

Osborne got a dial tone and called Ashley's number at her apartment in Bismarck, hoping that he was rousing her out of bed. But after eight or nine rings, he disconnected, and called her cell phone, which she answered on the second ring.

"Good morning," she said. "Back from Washington so soon?"

"We're still in the air, trying to make it to Bismarck. I tried your apartment."

"I didn't want to risk getting stuck for Christmas, so I went back to the hotel. It's getting to feel like the Medora Ritz. What does that say about me?"

Osborne's temper flared. He wanted her to be anywhere *but* Medora, but he kept his tone reasonably light. What was done was done. "How's the weather?"

"In town it's not so bad, but the AP says it'll be pretty awful everywhere else, and the highway patrol is issuing warnings that the interstate will be closed within the next hour or so."

"Just stay put until I get there, will you?"

"I'll be okay. How about you?"

"If we can get to Bismarck I'll try to rent a four-wheel drive, or if need be a snowcat from the DOT, but it's going to be late by the time we get there."

"Seriously, Nate, take your time. I want to go Christmas shopping with you. And I forgot to ask, do you have a tree?"

"No."

"I'll get one in the morning," Ashley said. "Who's the 'we'?"

"Jim Cameron and Dr. Lipton."

Ashley laughed. "What'd my dad have to say to you guys?"

"Among other things that you were a willful girl, but he agreed to let you help out. No holds barred. No secrets. But at a price."

"Anything I write has to be vetted first."

"Something like that."

"Sam didn't like that I was staying out here, and that I didn't have story to file, but I made him understand that this was big enough that the wait would be worth it." Sam Adams was the *Bismarck Tribune*'s executive editor.

"This is bigger than we first thought. A lot bigger and more dangerous."

"Okay, now you've really got my interest. What can you tell me?"

"Not on an open line. They were sophisticated enough to block communications at the Initiative, so I don't think hacking into our phone conversation would be too difficult."

"I didn't know that."

"Listen to me, I want you to watch your back. If something doesn't look right, make a one eighty and leave."

"I'm not going anywhere in this."

"Call Sally at State, or Nettles at the Initiative."

"Can you be a little more specific?"

"Just a hunch for now. But I have a feeling that something's coming our way. Possibly tonight, maybe tomorrow night. Sometime during the storm. So stay put."

Ashley laughed. "Orders already?"

"I'm serious," Osborne said.

"I can hear it in your voice," Ashley said. "I'm going to bed now, so drive careful, okay? And call when you get close; I'll have a Mich Ultra waiting for you at the bar."

38

EGAN MOVED AWAY from the connecting door to Ashley Borden's room, troubled. She'd been talking to the sheriff, who'd apparently gone to Washington, D.C., which was almost impossible given the time line. The sheriff had been in the dining room early in the evening.

Mattson stood by the dresser, a frightened, expectant expression on his face.

If Osborne had driven directly to the airport at Dickinson a VIP jet could have picked him up, taken him to Washington for some kind of a meeting—a very brief meeting—and brought him back. But a meeting with whom? Who would he be meeting at that hour of the night? With that urgency?

General Forester was certainly a possibility, but Kast said Forester had flown from Reagan National the day after the attack, and it was likely that he'd gone to the Initiative. So who had summoned a small nowhere county sheriff in the middle of the night?

And the answer, when it came to him, was nothing short of stunning.

He focused on Mattson. "I think we may have underestimated the sheriff."

"What are you talking about?"

"The broad was on the phone with her boyfriend, and apparently he's on his way back from Washington."

"That was fast. Maybe the military flew him out."

"Or the FBI, or maybe even the president," Egan said.

The color drained from Mattson's face. "This is way out of my league, Barry. I mean, I've helped the Posse from the get-go, and I helped get you down here and all, but this shit has got to stop. I'm a journalist for the cause, not some kind of foot soldier."

"I know what you've done for us, and I appreciate it, we all do. But I need you for the rest of the morning, and soon as we've finished with what we've set out to do, I'll drive you over to the nearest airport that's open, even if it's all the way down to Rapid City. Wherever."

"Exactly what is it that we've set out to do? You've never leveled with me."

"Snatch the broad, I told you that from the start."

"Saying that we pull it off, then what? A ransom note or something?"

"Something like that."

"In the meantime where do we stash her?"

"The Roundup Lodge. Toby's bringing the horses in case the Caddy gets stuck."

"If we leave the car behind how the hell am I supposed to get to an airport? And what about the owners and the staff down there? They'll know something is wrong, and they'll call the cops."

"For starters the phone lines are down. Toby made sure of that first off."

"But what about the staff and guests? We can't hold all of them hostage."

"No problem," Egan said. "They're all dead."

Mattson stepped back. "This is beyond crazy," he said, nearly out of breath, the words choking in his throat.

"Even if the Caddy does get stuck we'll use one of their cars or trucks. I'm sure we'll figure out something."

"I'm not a killer."

"I want you to settle down. In a few hours this'll be all over for you. You have my word on it. But I need your help."

"I meant at the camp. I'll be charged as an accessory."

"They'll have to catch you first. Right now we're going to pack and soon as the bar closes and everyone goes home, you're going to bring our stuff down to the car, and we'll snatch the broad. In an hour or two this place'll be totally dead, and Toby should have just about made the rendezvous point."

"Which is where, exactly?"

"South on Eighty-five, on the way to the lodge."

By three the hotel had been quiet for more than an hour. Egan had taken off his wig, removed his makeup, and had changed into a pair of jeans, a heavy sweater, and hiking boots. Mattson had managed to get their things down to the car without being spotted. When he got back his jacket was covered in snow.

"Just our car and the *Bismarck Trib* pickup truck," he said. "Looks like we're the only ones in the hotel tonight."

"Good," Egan said, but it was about what he'd expected in a place like this a couple of days before Christmas.

He strapped the Velcro harness to his chest, checked the load on his compact Knight PDW—the same weapon they'd used on the attack at Donna Marie—and attached

it to the harness. When he pulled on his jacket and zippered it up, the weapon was undetectable.

Mattson was shook up, but he said nothing as Egan
checked the action on his silenced Glock, stuffed the
weapon in his belt, and pulled on a dark blue baseball cap
with the logo of the Billings County sheriff's department.

"Are you good to go?" Egan asked. He'd checked the
room twice to make sure that they'd left nothing behind,
especially fingerprints or DNA evidence in the bathroom.

Mattson nodded nervously.

"Go warm up the car. I'll be down directly with the
broad."

Mattson left and Egan switched off the lights, then put
his ear against the connecting door. He could hear nothing.

The corridor was deserted, and Egan went to Ashley's
door, pulled the bill of his cap low, and knocked twice.
"Ms. Borden?" he called.

The woman didn't respond.

Egan knocked again, this time a little louder. "Ms.
Borden, I'm Officer Trembley. Are you in there?"

A light shone from under the door. And someone came
to the peephole. "What is it?" Ashley asked, her voice
sleepy.

"Sorry to bother you, ma'am, but Sheriff Osborne asked
me to come over and make sure that you were okay. Are
you okay?"

"Just dandy. Now, if you don't mind, I was in the middle of a really good dream."

"It'll just take a minute, ma'am, but the sheriff gave me
specific instructions that I was to check your room, the
window latches, telephone, all that kind of stuff."

"Go away."

"If need be I'll have to stand outside your door until he gets here. I don't want to lose my job. You know how it is. It'll just take a minute."

"What's your name again?"

"Trembley. Kevin Trembley."

"Shit," Ashley said, but she undid the safety latch and opened the door.

Egan pulled out his pistol and as she started to back away, he pushed his way in and pointed the Glock directly at her head, just inches from her face. "Make a noise, any noise, and I'll blow your fucking head off. Do you understand?"

Ashley looked beyond him to the empty corridor, but she nodded. She was dressed in gray sweatpants and a Columbia University T-shirt, her feet bare.

Egan let the door close. "This is going to be a simple kidnapping. We take a little drive, I call your father with a ransom demand, he pays it, and you're free to go."

"The Posse doesn't work that way."

"It does when we need money."

"If this is your second shot at the Initiative you've screwed up."

"We know about the attack, but we decided to cash in on the paranoia down there. Figured your father is worth a few hundred thousand, maybe a million. See what he'll pay for his baby girl. So get dressed, Ms. Borden, unless you want to freeze your ass off."

Ashley stood her ground, studying his face, and suddenly she nodded. "You're the woman from the dining room. Barry Egan, I suspect."

Egan was rocked to the core, and his finger tightened on the trigger.

39

T HE LANDING AT Bismarck was dicey, the Gulf-stream nearly sliding off the icy runway in a stiff crosswind before the pilot managed to ease it back to a straight line path and taxi to the terminal. The runway lights behind them were turned off, and the airport was officially closed until the weather cleared, which was not supposed to happen for another thirty-six hours.

The attendant came back, and despite the late hour and rough landing she still looked fresh. "You have a call from General Forester," she told Osborne.

The general sounded grim. "They've taken Ashley. I got the ransom call ten minutes ago."

Osborne had been uptight all night, but he was suddenly calm; it was the same reaction he'd had on the battlefield when the expected attack finally began and the job in front of him was clearly defined. "Who was it, and what do they want?"

"It was a man's voice, said he'd been directed to halt the Initiative, not destroy it. Said that if he had my word that Donna Marie would cease operations for sixty days, my daughter would be released unharmed."

"He won't keep his word."

"I know that. So I asked for a few hours to get clearance from the White House. He gave me two."

"Did he say where she'd been taken, or how and where she would be released once you promised to do what he wanted?"

"No. And I wasn't expecting such a call, so I wasn't set up for a trace, or even a recording. But I've notified the FBI, and I called Captain Nettles to put him on alert. But he said Jim Cameron gave him the heads-up a couple of hours ago that something might be coming our way. Do you know something about this?"

"Just a hunch," Osborne said.

"Goddamnit, Sheriff, we're talking about my daughter's life, because you know damned well I can't give the order to shut down the experiment."

"If it were me coming after the Initiative I'd pick the conditions where the weather and date were on my side."

"A snowstorm and Christmas," Forester said, a little of the hard edge softening. "Do you think Ashley might be a diversion?"

Osborne wanted to think that it was. "No," he said. "But he's given us a clue."

"What clue?"

"The sixty days. It's too specific to have no meaning."

"That's not going to help us find my daughter."

"It just might, General, because I think I know where he's taken her and why. And I think I know who it is."

"How?" Forester demanded.

"Because I met him last night," Osborne said, and he broke the connection.

Cameron and Whitney were looking at him.

"They've kidnapped the general's daughter. They want

him to shut down the project for sixty days or else they'll kill her."

"That doesn't make any sense," Whitney said.

"They'll kill her no matter what," Cameron agreed. "There's no way possible for them to hold her that long. What do you want to do, Nate?"

"Nettles has already been warned, but in the meantime we have the one asset that's even more important than the wellhead and the gadget."

Cameron glanced at Whitney. "She oughta stay right here in Bismarck."

Osborne nodded. "And I want you to stay with her. We can call the state police to give you a hand if you think you need it."

The pilot came off the flight deck. "This is as far as we can take it, folks. No way we're going to make Dickinson, and we can't even make a turn around."

"Thanks for getting us this far," Osborne said. "We'll take it from here."

"What about Ashley?" Cameron asked. "You told the general that you had an idea where they've taken her."

"I think so," Osborne said, and using his cell phone he called Tommy Seagram at his home number in town. The helicopter pilot answered on the fifth ring.

"This fucking better be a beautiful woman," Seagram said.

Osborne heard Tommy's wife say something in the background. "It's me. I need you to get to the airport and power up your Huey as fast as you can get here."

"Nate? Are you out of your mind? Have you looked out the window?"

"Just flew in aboard a Gulfstream from D.C. Made it with no problem."

"You can't see shit five feet in front of your windshield."

"Fly low, and follow the interstate," Osborne said. "This is important. We have a hostage situation, and less than two hours to do something about it. And right now you're my only bet."

"Fuck you," Seagram said. "I'll be there in fifteen."

"You do know who took her and where she is," Cameron said.

"I'll know in just a minute," Cameron told him, and he called Tina Patterson, the bartender and night clerk at the Rough Riders hotel. It took ten rings before she answered.

"We're all booked up," she mumbled groggily.

"It's me," Osborne said. "I need you to do a quick favor for me. Just take a minute."

"Is this a joke?"

"I have a situation brewing. You know the couple that checked in? They were driving a Caddy Escalade. I want you to check if it's still parked out back."

"Of course it is. Who'd want to go out on the night like this?"

"Just check, would you please?"

"I'll have to go to the back door. Give me a minute."

"Hurry," Osborne said.

"What couple?" Cameron asked.

Osborne explained about the two who said they were from San Francisco, and the oddness of the woman who'd caught Ashley's attention. "They didn't fit."

Tina was back two minutes later. "It's gone, Nate. Do you want me to check their room?"

"Did they give a tag number?"

"It's probably in the computer."

"Call Sally at State for me, and have an APB put out for

the vehicle. Approach with extreme caution, suspects are probably armed, and may be traveling with a hostage."

"Hostage? Who? What's going on for God's sake?"

"Just do it for me, would you please?"

"Right away, Nate," Tina said, and Osborne broke the connection.

"Are you armed?" he asked Cameron.

"Yes," Cameron said.

"Dr. Lipton is your top priority, your only priority for now."

"Always has been," Cameron said. "Just remember to duck."

"Will do," Osborne said. He grabbed his jacket, at the door thanked the crew again, and headed into the nearly deserted terminal to meet Tommy.

40

THEY HAD DRIVEN to Belfield, absolutely no traffic on the windblown interstate that had already started to drift over, and had taken U.S. 85 south to the dirt track that ran out to the Initiative where Barry turned the Caddy around so that it was facing east. They were less than one hundred yards from the fence.

He turned around to look at the woman who glared back at him. Her mouth was covered with duct tape, and they'd used tape to bind her wrists, ankles, and knees together.

Trussed up like a hog for slaughter, Egan thought and laughed a little.

Mattson, sitting in the backseat, had distanced himself as far from her as was possible. He stared at Egan. "We're going to get stuck here if we wait too long for Toby. We should try to make it back to Regina."

"Shouldn't be long now, Donald," Egan said dreamily. He was actually daydreaming a little about what would come next, how it would even be better than sex, and he was getting aroused.

"Don't use my name."

"Take the tape off her mouth, I want to have a little chat."

Mattson was frightened, but he reached over and gently peeled the tape off Ashley's mouth.

"Thank you for at least that," she said, her voice croaky. She had put on a pair of jeans and a sweater plus her Sorel Pac boots and parka, open in front now. "Could I have something to drink?" Her hair was disheveled, but without makeup she was still attractive.

"No," Egan said. "Tell me what you know about the Initiative."

"It's an ELF communications system for contacting our submarines when they're under water."

"Already got one in Wisconsin."

"This one's better."

"Odd, isn't it, that your dad working for ARPA-E is in charge of the project?"

Ashley said nothing, but if she was worried she didn't show it.

"Means you're lying to me, and that's not a good thing."

"You probably know more about it than I do. So what's the point, Mr. Egan? My dad won't give you anything."

"Even for his precious daughter?"

Ashley shook her head.

Egan reached over the seat and caressed her cheek with the tips of his fingers, and she reacted as if she'd been touched with a branding iron. "Even your big bad sheriff won't come to your rescue?"

Ashley looked him directly in the eye. "You'd better hope he doesn't."

Egan laughed, spittle flying all over the place.

Mattson suddenly looked up. "Toby's here."

The snow blew horizontally, making it nearly impossible to see more than a few yards. But Toby was right there leading two horses, and he dismounted and came over to the Caddy as Egan got out and braced against the rising wind.

"Any trouble getting up here?"

"No, but it's going to be a bitch getting back in this shit," Toby said. He glanced at Mattson and Ashley in the backseat. "Three horses, four riders."

"Two riders, leaves us a spare," Egan said, and he motioned for Mattson to get out of the Escalade.

"I don't know how to ride a goddamn horse!" the Posse newspaperman shouted into the wind as he got out of the SUV.

Egan pulled out his pistol and shot the man in the face, just above the bridge of his nose, and Mattson fell backward, dead before he hit the snow-covered ground.

Toby shrugged, but Ashley struggled against her bindings, wildly thrashing around in the backseat, until Egan shoved the pistol back in his pocket and hauled her out of the car, dumping her on the ground.

"You maniac!" she screamed, her voice ragged.

Egan cut the tape from around her ankles and knees and pulled her to her feet. "You have two choices, either die here and now, or take your chances with what comes next. I promise I won't shoot you if you don't give me trouble."

"We can take her back, but it'll slow us down," Toby said. He was half drunk.

"We're not taking her back," Egan said, and he hustled her into the teeth of the wind to the Initiative fence line, slipping and sliding, the footing treacherous, the hundred yards taking them nearly fifteen minutes.

Toby followed them with the horses.

Egan shoved her back against the fence. "Raise your hands over your head."

Ashley, suddenly realizing what he meant to do, pushed him away, and tried to knee him in the groin, but he deflected her blow with his hip and smashed his fist into her face, driving her head back against the fence.

She flailed her arms, trying to fight back, but he hit her again, and her nose started to bleed and her knees gave way beneath her.

She was slightly built, so it was fairly easy for Egan to tie her wrists above her head to the fence with one of the plastic wire ties he'd brought for just this purpose. Once she was secured he spread her legs, tying her ankles to the fence in the same manner.

"The bitch'll freeze to death in no time at all!" Toby shouted.

"That's the idea," Egan said, enjoying himself immensely. It wasn't in the script that Kast had given him. But what the fuck, it was a tough old world.

"I thought we were holding her for ransom. They'll find her out here soon's this shitstorm lifts, maybe sooner."

"Don't care," Egan said, and he pulled out his pistol and started toward the horses.

Suddenly understanding what was about to go down, Toby reared his horse back with one hand on the reins, let go of the horses he'd been leading, and grappled for his .44 Magnum inside his parka, but Egan was right on him, and he fired two shots, both of them catching the rodeo cowboy in the chest and knocking him off his horse, which bolted along with the others.

"Son of a bitch," Toby said, and he tried to scramble backwards and still reach for his pistol.

Egan reached him and fired one shot point-blank into the kid's head. "It's a tough old world out there," he said.

Ashley had come around and when Egan turned back to her she shook her head. "Whatever you wanted for ransom you sure as hell won't get it this way," she croaked. "Won't take long for me to freeze to death."

"Maybe it'll make him think twice about finally retiring," Egan said. "And who knows, maybe your sheriff hero will come to the rescue after all."

He started back to the Caddy to put the chains on the tires, everything to this point going exactly as he had planned; the newspaper broad screaming obscenities at him until her voice was finally carried away in the biting wind.

41

THE HUEY POUNDED west twenty-five feet above the snow-covered surface of I-94, cutting to the diagonal southwest once they'd picked up the lights of Belfield where they followed U.S. 85 to the south. Visibility was almost nil, but from what Osborne had seen nothing was moving. Only a couple of semis were stranded out on the main highway, and even the snowplows were in the barn until the weather settled down.

"What're we looking for, Nate?" Seagram asked in Osborne's headset.

"A Caddy Escalade."

"Out in this shit?"

"I think so."

"What if we find it?" Seagram asked. He never turned turn to look at his passenger, instead his eyes continually darted from the view out the windshield to the attitude indicator on the panel, which assured him that they were in straight and level flight. The snow streaming past the windshield had the tendency to make a pilot drift in the same direction.

"We're looking for two guys, or maybe a man and a woman, plus Ashley Borden," Osborne said, and he explained about the couple at the Rough Riders, and the ransom call to Ashley's father in Washington.

"Where the hell are they going to hold her for two months? Not around here. Once the weather clears they'd stick out like sore thumbs."

"They're not going to hold her."

Seagram glanced at Osborne for just an instant. "No ransom, they took her to kill her?"

"I think so."

The lights of Belfield were behind them, the night once again thick, when Seagram finally got it. "If these are the same people who hit the Initiative, what's a Bismarck reporter have to do with anything?"

"Her father runs the project. They want to slow him down."

Seagram concentrated on his flying for a minute or so. "That's more than a navy communications setup," he said.

"I'd keep that speculation to yourself," Osborne said.

"I hear you, but what's your involvement? I mean why not just call out the on-site security people? It's their problem, isn't it? Why risk your life flying around in this shit? We ice up and we're going down."

"Because I'm not one hundred percent sure that they've taken her here. It's crazy. Just what these guys *shouldn't* be doing." And in part because Ashley was involved and he didn't want to turn over searching for her to Nettles and his people who might be getting a little trigger-happy about now.

"There," Seagram suddenly said.

Osborne turned in time to spot someone standing next

to the Cadillac pull something out from inside his coat. "Hard right, now!" he shouted.

Seagram's jaw disintegrated and the back of his head exploded in a spray of blood and white matter, and the helicopter rolled over sharply to the left and the snow-covered field came up to meet the windshield.

42

EGAN'S FIRST IMPRESSION was that the military was on his case, because the chopper was definitely a Huey, and more would almost certainly be on their way. But he fired directly at the pilot out of pure instinct, and as the helicopter banked sharply left and flew out of control directly overhead he couldn't spot any military markings.

Seconds later it crashed, and although it was likely there were no survivors—'cause he'd for sure scragged the pilot—he was torn between jumping into the Caddy and driving the hell out of here, or making sure whoever had come looking for him was dead.

"Whatever you do never leave loose ends, boy," his dad had drummed into his head over and over. "It's the loose ends that'll surely rise up and bite you in the ass."

"What if it's people," Barry had asked. He was a teen-ager, and his dad wasn't really talking about football, he was talking about war.

"I don't give a shit if it's your best friend; if they get in the way, put 'em away, put 'em down, take the sons a bitches out. It's a tough old world out there, kid. Just remember what ol' Satchel Paige had to say."

Egan remembered and he was worried that something just might be gaining on him, so he headed down the gentle slope to where the helicopter had gone down, no fire, which was just fine because he didn't want anyone coming out of the Initiative to investigate just yet. But on the same token he didn't want to leave any loose ends.

It took nearly ten minutes to reach the wreckage. At the last moment the chopper had turned over on its side, saving the more fragile nose from a direct impact, but smashing the pilot's body beyond any recognition, though Egan was sure it wasn't the sheriff. The body was too small.

No one was in the passenger seat, but the right-side rear hatch was partially open. Impossible to tell if anyone had been riding back there, except there were no bodies, nor could he smell blood or anything else from ripped-apart torsos. Only the smell of hot oil and leaking fuel.

He stepped back, but in the dark he couldn't see much of anything except his own tracks. If anyone had gotten out and walked or crawled away from the wreckage it was impossible to tell.

A tremendous gust of wind shook the mangled fuselage, and already snow was beginning to drift up against the side of the chopper. Egan ducked under the tail section, and made a three-sixty visual scan, but nothing was out there that he could see, though a herd of buffalo could be standing right there ten yards out and they'd be invisible.

He turned and looked back the way he had come, but from here he couldn't see the Caddy, and could barely make out his own footprints in the snow. He began to panic a little. Sure as hell he wasn't going to get his ass lost out here in the Badlands and freeze to death. He'd made his contract, he had money coming, and this time he figured he might just go someplace warm.

But first he had to make tracks. No more screwing around.

Lowering his PDW, he walked around the front of the wreck and headed as fast as he could back to the Caddy. She was a damned big machine, four-wheel drive, chains on all four tires; it was enough he figured to get him at least to Belfield, and from there he would blend; evade and escape, change appearances, be one with his environment, let 'em see what they expected to see, and just where they expected it.

43

B LOOD OOZED FROM a gash in the side of Osborne's head, a couple of his ribs were broken, and he wanted to fade out, just lie back in the snowdrift five yards from the downed chopper where he'd scrambled in case of an explosion or fire. But the worst part was the titanium prosthesis on his left leg. It had jammed under the control panel when they'd crashed, and it was bent and his stump was damaged. He could feel blood running down the side of his leg.

The man in the dark jacket had ducked under the chopper's tail, and stopped for a moment to look directly at him, but by the time Osborne had managed to pull out his pistol the man had disappeared in the blowing snow.

Osborne raised his gun anyway and started to pull off a shot, but stopped. Ashley was out there somewhere. Or at least he hoped she was, and he didn't want to shoot blind and take the risk of hitting her.

For a full minute, what seemed like an hour while at the same time just an eyeblink, Osborne lay propped up on one elbow, his pistol cocked, his aim wavering in the general direction the man had gone.

Finally he safetied it, stuffed it in the holster on his right hip, and reached for his cell phone in his jacket pocket. But it was gone. Somewhere in the wreck, or in the snow. He tried to make his head work. If he laid here he would freeze to death, and unless the son of a bitch who'd shot them down still had Ashley in the Caddy she was out here, too. He didn't want to think that the man had already killed her, although that would have been the logical thing to do.

He got up on his good knee, and trailing his bad leg, pushed himself upright with every ounce of strength he had left. His head spun and he stood, hunched into the stiff wind, his stomach heaving, his ribs on fire each time he took even a shallow breath.

Afghanistan wasn't so far away, and he remembered just then the pain mostly blocked out by adrenaline, and he stumbled the few yards to the helicopter and looked in at Tommy's mangled body. He was going to have to face Eunice at some point. Tell her why it had been necessary to call Tommy out on a night like this. Writing letters to the families of his soldiers had been the most difficult job he'd ever had, and facing Tommy's wife was going to be worse.

He worked his way to the chopper's nose, and hesitated for just a moment before he headed out in the direction he thought they'd seen the Caddy. Each time he put weight on his left leg the pain of metal grating on bare bone was nearly impossible to bear, but he put it out of his mind. Nobody died because of a hurt stump.

The wind and fiercely blowing snow was pushing him to the left, he knew this intellectually, yet it was easier to simply go with the flow, and in about fifteen minutes he topped a small sharp rise and was on the flat surface of the gravel road.

Maybe fifty yards or more, he figured, from where the Caddy had been parked. He started to draw his pistol again as he turned to the east, the wind at his back when he heard something. A woman, shouting or crying, and he turned back, his heart soaring, his ear cocked.

But there was only the wind. Numbing, shrieking, a presence impossible to ignore as was his fading strength.

He took a step back and he heard the cry again. Impossible to pinpoint exactly where, except that it was into the wind and not very far.

About fifteen or twenty yards he stumbled across a body, its legs on the road, its head and much of its torso already half buried in the blowing snow. It wasn't the guy who'd come down to the chopper, but in any case it didn't matter now.

A woman shouted his name, off to the right, and it was Ashley, he knew it for certain, and he hobbled down the road and then off into the higher drifts until he saw her spread-eagled up against the fence, her parka open in front, her chest and face and hair covered in snow.

"Nate," she cried weakly when he got to her.

The ties that held her wrists and ankles to the fence were frozen solid. Osborne holstered his pistol and sawed through them with a pocketknife.

"I'm so cold," she cried softly, and he held her close, trying to give her some of his body warmth.

After a couple of minutes he managed to zip up her parka, scoop the snow out of the inside of the hood, and from her hair and face, and pull the hood over her head.

"What took you so long?" she asked, managing a little smile.

"A little detour," he said. "Can you walk? We have to make it to the gate, maybe two miles."

"I'll try," she said, but she was nearly out of it, and after only one stumbling step her legs collapsed from under her. "Oops," she said. "Must have been the last wine."

Carrying her that far was going to be next to impossible,

but he sure as hell wasn't going to leave her. She'd never survive.

Something nudged Osborne in the back, and he shoved Ashley to the ground to shield her as he spun around and pulled out his pistol. The bastard had come back after all.

For a long beat, he had a hard time accepting what he was seeing. But it was a horse, saddled, its reins dangling from the bit. Maybe whoever was lying dead beside the road had ridden here on the horse, but the only place he could think of was the Roundup Lodge, which was fifteen miles to the south.

Didn't matter. Osborne took up the reins, gentling the horse with a few soft words, and he picked Ashley's nearly inert form from the ground and awkwardly put her up in the saddle, his bad leg nearly giving way.

The horse was shivering, and it looked as if it were nearly on the point of collapse. The animal might carry Ashley, but not both of them. The situation was what it was. Osborne shrugged and leading the horse by the reins he limped back to the road's surface, and started to the west toward the main gate, not at all sure it was possible for him to make it that far.

Ashley said something, and he turned back to her.

"Are you okay?" he asked.

She raised her head from the horse's neck and looked at him. "You're here," she said.

"I'll always be here," Osborne told her. "Now shut up, we're going for a little ride."

"Okay, Nate," she said, and she lay forward again on the horse's mane, in and out of consciousness.

One step at a time, Osborne told himself. If he could make one step, he could make the second. Just a matter of will, and he was back in Afghanistan waiting for the attack to come.

A Ranch House
Belfield, North Dakota

B ARRY EGAN SLEPT until three in the afternoon, the fierce winds that had buffeted the farmhouse through the morning hours not letting up until early afternoon. And it was the relative silence that finally roused him from a dream in which he was a worker in a meatpacking plant. Except that the gutted carcasses hanging from their ankles on the processing line were not cattle or pigs. They were humans, and working all alone in the vast abattoir he sang and hummed some tune he couldn't recognize. He was a man happy in his job.

And waking, completely refreshed, he knew that his work was far from over; in fact he'd just begun.

The ranch was a couple of miles west of U.S. 85, and he'd stumbled on the dirt track just off Thirty-seventh Street SW, recognizing it as just the sort of a place he was looking for, the nearest neighbor a mile or so away.

Pure blind luck that came only to the righteous of heart and purpose.

He padded nude into the bathroom to relieve himself, glancing with only mild interest at the old man and woman whose throats he'd slit after he'd roused them out of bed and herded them into the shower.

This morning after he'd killed them, he'd made his way through the snowstorm twenty-five yards to the bunkhouse where two hands were asleep in their beds and shot them both in the head at point-blank range. Then he'd parked the Caddy in the barn that was empty of livestock—he figured they'd either sold off any animals they might have had, or they were old and had retired from the business—before he went back to the house and cooked himself a big breakfast: a couple slices of ham, half a pound of bacon, four eggs, four pieces of toast, and the better part of a quart of milk. Hard, satisfying work always made him hungry.

Back in the corridor to the family room and kitchen Egan realized that his hands and arms were covered in dried blood, and in the kitchen the counters, the front of the fridge and stove, and the frying pans and dishes in the sink were also bloody.

Marks of a good job well done. It's a tough old world, his daddy had drummed into his head. But the old bastard would have been proud of him last night.

"No loose ends here, by Christ," Egan told himself.

He went into the guest bathroom where he took a long, hot shower, after which he found a pair of scissors and cut his hair very short, not quite a flattop, leaving a five o'clock shadow on his chin just like the old man in the shower.

"An honest haircut for an honest man," Egan told himself.

Back in the couple's bedroom he dressed in clean underwear, white socks, a dress shirt, and a blue serge suit that was a little short in the legs and a little tight in the chest, but not impossibly so. He found a red tie, and worked out a reasonable Windsor knot. The shoes were too small, so he used the kitchen sink to clean the blood off his own boots, and when he had them on he went back to the family room where he turned on the television to KDIX, out of Dickinson.

As the set warmed up he found a beer in the fridge, and sat down at the counter to watch *Days of our Lives,* and wait for the weathercast. He figured that he had a number of options. First of course was getting out of the immediate vicinity—depending on the weather either east to the airport at Bismarck or north across the border back to Regina—he thought that he'd seen something on TV at the Rough Riders before they'd snatched the broad that the storm would be concentrated more to the south—or even west all the way to Billings.

That was the easy part, because he would either make it out of here using the old man's clothes and ID, plus the Ford 4x4 F-450 pickup truck he'd spotted in a shed next to the barn, which would go through more serious shit than even the Caddy could, or he would get himself cornered and die in a shoot-out. Sure as hell he wasn't going to give himself up and spend the rest of his life behind bars. He looked fine in drag, and he just knew what would happen once he was in the can because of his dark good looks.

During a commercial break a good-looking girl in short dark hair and an earnest small-town breathlessness came on to explain the back-to-back fronts coming down from western Canada that mixed with a rapidly rising warm, moist air mass that had moved up from the Gulf and had caused the first storm, and in another eight hours would cause the second, even larger blizzard.

"If you have to drive anywhere—which we recommend you don't—better get it done before midnight, let's make it ten this evening, because if you're caught out on the highways after that you could be in some serious trouble."

Egan had the notion that the weather girl had no clue what serious trouble was all about, because when it came it almost always bit you in the ass and left marks. And he was in some serious shit, yet he'd known all his life that it would come to this point sooner or later. But at least the weather was cooperating, and he figured that if he could make it to Minneapolis ahead of the second storm front, he'd have a chance of renting a car—if the dead rancher had a credit card—and could make it down to Louisville where the Posse had some friends who could help out.

Because listening to the weather girl talk, her words flowing around him like wind chimes up in a tree, little snatches of music now and then, he'd come up with the inkling of a plan. The last big thing.

Clyde Thompson, the dead rancher, had an American Express credit card, was a member of AARP, though he was only fifty-two, AAA, the National Cattleman's Beef Association, and the North Dakota Farmers Union. He had a pair of twenties and four ones in his wallet, and a photograph of a young man, probably himself, in an army uniform, an M-16 slung barrel down over his shoulder in what looked like a jungle. On the back he'd written: *Grenada 12/12/83.*

Too bad, Egan thought, glancing toward the bathroom door. The bastard fought for his country and had come out of it in one piece. Until now. It was indeed a tough old world.

He found the keys to the Ford along with a parka in the mudroom just off the kitchen, and went out to the shed where he started the truck and checked the gas. The tank was full and with luck he figured he'd make it all the way without filling up.

Back in the house the soap opera was on, and Egan opened another beer and sat down to wait until it got dark, and think about just how he was going to tackle his next job—his last job—never once considering the probable outcome of something so radical and especially not the why of it. Because he knew that last part; he had it down cold, had it that way for as long as he could remember.

He'd told a friend out in Kalispell once that when he died he wanted to be buried upside-down, so that the whole world could kiss his ass. He was angry for a life he figured had passed him by, all the way back to high school when he'd been called slimy. And it was only years afterwards when he'd realized they'd teased him because at his house his mother thought that bathing too often would leach the natural oils out of a person's body. Saturday night baths were plenty good enough for decent folk.

And other things had happened; with a girl in Houston, a couple of friends in Frisco, a job that went seriously south in Detroit, a Social Security disability application that had been turned down three times because not one bastard doctor had been willing to certify that he had bad back problems.

Egan had a list of grievances that he'd been adding to year after year, like saving pennies and nickels and dimes until they came up to some serious money and weighed so much they sometimes brought a man to his knees.

Time to cash 'em in, he thought.

Federal Bureau of Investigation Field Office
Christmas Eve
Minneapolis

FBI DIRECTOR EDWIN Rogers had initiated an encrypted video call with Deborah Rausch, the Minneapolis SAC. It was nine in the morning in the Midwest and Deb was sure that she looked like hell, her hair a mess, her eyes bloodshot from lack of sleep and worry. She'd always had the tendency to take things on her shoulders, most of the time unnecessarily so, but this time she was in the genuine hot seat.

"Glad to see that you're on the job, Mrs. Rausch, but sorry this had to come during the holidays," Rogers told her. He was dressed just like in his official photograph, in a dark three-piece suit, the tie snugged up and straight. The same as his attitude, formal and constant.

"Thank you, sir, but Mr. Egan hasn't taken a day off. I assume that you've seen my overnight."

"Yes, and I have to brief the president later this morning, so I wanted to know your gut feelings."

"We're going to catch this guy, if that's what you mean, Mr. Director. He can't keep hiring people and then kill them when the operation has been completed. He's going to run out of associates. These guys may be crazy but a lot of them are pretty smart."

"You think that someone will turn him in?"

"Almost certainly, or else he'll make a mistake, get himself into something from which he can't slip away."

"He's a determined man."

"Indeed he is," Deb said. And it stung deeply that the bastard had made it right here to Minneapolis, right under her nose, in a stolen truck, with a stolen ID and credit card and had flown to Louisville and disappeared before anyone had reported the murders of the rancher and his wife. It was the kind of mistake that cost SACs their jobs.

"How are Sheriff Osborne and Ms. Borden?"

"They'll be released from the hospital in Dickinson this morning. No permanent harm, but it was close."

"And work at the Initiative?"

"I'm told that they expect to have it back up and running sometime after the first of the year," Deb said. "Excuse me, Mr. Director, but you know all of this."

"Yes, but you may not know that there are some other aspects that you'll have to take into consideration."

"Sir?"

"We've uncovered some evidence that points to a possible source of Mr. Egan's funds."

"Yes, sir. We're looking for his bank accounts, most likely in Bozeman, though there are a few other possibilities, and we're checking his relatives and friends, but as you can imagine they've not been very cooperative. He's probably using fake IDs including Social Security numbers, and we're running down a few leads on that score. We know that he spent a few days in Upper Peninsula Michigan, at a mobile home an uncle owned, and the RCMP in Regina said that a couple matching Egan's and Mattson's descriptions—Egan was masquerading as a woman—paid for a room for ten days but left the first night."

"Yes, that's in your report. But we've uncovered a possible connection with Venezuelan intelligence. I can't give you all the details yet, the CIA is mostly involved, except to warn you that if Venezuelan funds are involved they'll almost certainly be funneled through an American interest. The consensus thinking at this point is a contractor service."

Deb was caught a little flat-footed, and yet she and her staff had suspected an outside source of money because the Posse never had been very well funded. Most of their money had been used to stockpile emergency rations, clean sources of water in case of a nuclear attack, bunkers and underground shelters, and small arms and ammunition in case the federal government finally made its move against the population. The transformation to a dictator state would be led by the IRS, of course, which was why the Posse's main strategy had always been a refusal to pay income tax: why finance the expected suspension of all civil liberties, including habeas corpus, the right to free speech, religion, and assembly, and most important, the right to bear arms? Which meant they never had the kind of money it had taken to mount the attack on the Initiative.

"Any leads, sir?"

"Nothing solid yet."

"Why?"

"I don't understand."

"Assuming we're right in thinking that Venezuelan intel is involved, what do they hope to gain by trying to shut down the Initiative? It's only an experiment, from what I'm told. Nothing of an industrial level is expected anytime soon. Or was it just an attempt to embarrass us?"

"It's more than that," Rogers said. "But your main concern for the moment is to look for any unusual activities in your district."

Deb resisted an impulse to laugh out loud. Her father had served in Congress from Nevada, but he'd only lasted two terms. "It's a different world out there," he'd said. "They play by different rules, different expectations, and at a different pace. And a lot of the times they get themselves into positions where they have to state the obvious as if it were something they'd just discovered. They're not bad people, just different than me."

"I'm sorry, sir, but aren't we just picking up the pieces now? Their attack on the Initiative failed, and so did kidnapping General Forester's daughter. There's nothing left for them. I suspect that Egan has gone to ground somewhere and will probably stay there for the immediate future."

"We don't think so," Rogers said.

"You're expecting another attack?"

"We're pretty sure that SEBIN is politically committed. One of our special envoys was assassinated."

"Yes, sir, Rupert Mann, and the president recalled our ambassador. The word is Mann got caught in the middle of a drug cartel war."

"The president sent him to deal with the oil ministry in Caracas. Shortly after the talks broke off, Mr. Mann was kidnapped and taken to a secure spot outside the city where he was beheaded with a chain saw."

"Good Lord."

"And it wasn't the Caracas police who investigated, it was SEBIN. It's why the president recalled our ambassador and expelled theirs."

The media had reported the recall and expulsion of ambassadors as a reaction to Chávez ordering a steep hike in the price of crude—but only for oil shipped to the U.S. But this was completely different. She sat at her desk looking at the director's unblinking image on her monitor. It had begun snowing again last night, and the entire upper Midwest was all but closed down.

"Those could be the opening moves of a war," Deb said. "And that's plain nuts."

Rogers nodded. "Right on both counts, Mrs. Rausch. Keep your people on their toes, because this is just the start."

"At least we know they won't try to hit the Initiative again. The place is too well guarded now."

"Most of those troops will be pulled out as soon as the storm abates."

"That's crazy, too."

"The orders come from the White House. Officially the Initiative has nothing to do with the dispute over oil."

"But we know better."

"Exactly," Rogers said.

PART THREE

MID-GAME

New Year's Eve

44

D. S. WOOD'S BOEING 737 with the Trent Holdings logo of three interlocking circles touched down at Havana's José Marti Airport a few minutes after two in the morning, direct from Mexico City. It trundled down the deserted taxiway to an empty maintenance hangar, and once inside the engines spooled down and the big doors rumbled closed. Two men in coveralls pushed wheeled boarding stairs to the front hatch and left.

Wood had been advised to come to Cuba alone, without his secretary or advisers, for a meeting that he could not afford to miss. And, considering the source of the request, he'd been unable to demur.

"We'll only take two hours of your time," Margaret Fischer had promised.

"This have anything to do with my oil derivative funds?" Wood had asked, something clutching at his chest. If word had begun to leak just how shaky Trent's cash position was the piranhas would begin coming to the surface. And of the carnivores Margaret was the worst. It was she who'd come up with the idea for credit default swaps about the same time Blythe Masters over at Morgan

Stanley had. And like many of the other top names on Wall Street, when the securities meltdown had swept the entire world, Maggie had come out with scarcely a bruise.

"Try coal," she'd told him.

The company's airplane was laid out in four palatial sections: the master bedroom all the way aft, a boardroom and communications center just forward, the main lounge forward of that, and the cockpit, galley, and quarters for the pilot, copilot, and one flight attendant at the front.

The hangar was in semidarkness, an SUV parked to one side. But peering out a window Wood couldn't make out if anyone was inside the car.

He got the captain on the interphone. "I'm going to need a couple of hours here. I'd like you and Kelley and Tammy to head over to the VIP lounge. I'll call when I'm ready to go home."

"Yes, sir," Bob Kellogg said. "This is the first time here for any of us, so I might have to call for directions."

"A car and driver are waiting outside to take you over," Wood said. "And, Bob, don't talk to anybody, okay? We were never here."

"Yes, sir."

Kellogg and his crew exited the plane, walked across the hangar, and left through a service door. When they were gone, Maggie, dressed in a mannish business suit and fedora, got out of the SUV with a very slightly built man, who had dark shiny hair, a mustache, and dressed in jeans, a white shirt, and a dark blue blazer. They walked across to the airplane.

Wood got to his feet as they appeared in the doorway and came aft. "Good morning," he said. He had no idea who the man was or what this meeting was all about. But with Margaret this morning's business would be anything but social.

"Good morning, D.S., glad you could come down," Margaret said. "I brought Señor Guisti along because he has a number of issues to talk over with you."

Wood shook hands with them and they all sat down facing one another.

"Something to drink?" he asked.

"No," Margaret said. "I have a busy day ahead, so let's make this short and sweet, shall we?"

"You called me."

"Two things. We know that you're not so liquid just now. In fact you're right on the edge of going down. If someone made a couple of calls on certain of your holdings, you would be hard-pressed to cover them."

Wood kept his expression neutral.

"We also know that you were behind the attack on the North Dakota Initiative, and that last week you arranged to have Ashley Borden, whose father is General Bob Forester, the director of the Initiative, kidnapped. In both cases the people you hired to do the work were unsuccessful."

Wood could see everything he'd worked for all of his life unraveling, unless he did something. Made an end run, say anything he needed to say, make any promises he needed to make in order to leave himself enough time to call Bob Kast and find out where the hell the leak was. And when he did he'd kill the bastard with his own two hands if need be.

"What the hell are you talking about?"

"Actually I want essentially the same thing as you do, only from a different direction," Margaret said.

"You're making no sense."

"Then let me be plainer. I know about your financials because it's my business to know such things. And believe me, I don't need a spy inside Trent. I can add and subtract. Simple arithmetic. And I know about your dealings with

Bob Kast from Señor Guisti who bought Venture Plus five years ago."

"Turns out to be one of our better investments," Guisti said. His English was accented though very precise, very clear, even cultured. "A foot in the door, and by chance you came along at just the correct time."

"Who exactly do you represent?" Wood asked Guisti.

"A politically motivated investor, with very deep pockets, who wants the very same thing that you want."

Wood was out of his depth, but he didn't know what choices he had. A word to the fed or the FBI and he would end up in jail. Unless he cashed out and ran somewhere. The UAE, maybe Syria, or perhaps right here in Cuba. Others had cut and run before the ax had fallen. Even guys like the movie director Roman Polanski, who was wanted in the U.S. for having sex with a minor, was a free man in Europe.

"What is it do you think I want?" he asked.

"The delay in any realistic attempt to create a viable source of clean energy that would be embraced by the public that did not involve oil," Guisti said. "Simple."

"Makes the three of us partners," Margaret said. "You want to use your derivative positions to temporarily drive the price per barrel of oil as low as possible so that alternative energy research is put on a back burner, at which time the price of oil will go through the roof, making you a fortune. But that will take time, and it's not without risk, as you've already seen with the two attacks in North Dakota. From what I've been told, the big experiment with the coal seam is back on track and will probably occur sometime within the next week or so."

Wood was at a loss for anything meaningful to say. He was being manipulated and there was little or nothing he could do about it. At least not for the moment. "I'm listening," he said.

"If you'd done your own homework you would have picked up the signals that someone was making a run against your positions. For the past three years an organization that I have a controlling interest in—let's call it the XYZ Fund for the sake of simplicity—has been buying and leasing oil storage facilities all over the world, including retired single-bottom tankers, to store as much oil as we can get our hands on. But slowly, so as not to cause any major concerns. Price of oil falls, we buy and store. Prices go up, and we sell. Simple and more immediate than your plan with a lot less risk."

"There've been pressures against my futures, we're not blind," Wood said. "But your strategy and mine amount to the same thing. If oil is allowed to rise past the one-hundred-dollar mark again alternative energy research will go ahead full steam. We'll both lose in the end."

"You want the Initiative to be delayed so that you can make your money in the short run," Guisti said.

"That's what I was attempting to do," Wood said. "But Bob hired the wrong people."

"He did not, Señor Wood. He hired exactly the right people, good and loyal Americans, all. Many *cojones* but *mucho loco*. But what if I were to say to you that instead of delaying work at the Initiative, it was to be destroyed along with its principal science team? The operation carried out by the same loyal Americans right under the noses of the authorities?"

"There's not enough time, not if the experiment is to be conducted within the week."

"Oh, but you are wrong. In fact the personnel and equipment are already very nearly in place."

"Just who the hell are you?" Wood demanded. He felt as if he'd been treading water all of his life, and now he was getting tired and at any moment he was going to sink and drown.

Guisti smiled. "Either your best new friend or your worst new enemy."

45

SITTING IN HIS empty office around noon Osborne couldn't remember the last time he'd felt so alone. Maybe for the first month or so after Carolyn had left with their daughter, when he'd begun to realize that they were never coming back. Maybe when his folks were killed in a car crash; he was the only child, no brothers or sisters, an uncle and a couple of cousins out in Washington State somewhere he had not seen since he was a kid, so there'd been no one to lean on.

And maybe especially now after Christmas Eve and Christmas Day when Ashley had been here in his life. They'd not been intimate because both of them had been pretty battered, but in Osborne's mind it had been enough that they'd been together. They'd shared a couple of days of domestic bliss, even putting up a Christmas tree and getting drunk and singing Christmas carols that neither of them knew all the words to.

She'd gone back to Bismarck the day after, and had jumped right back into work, filing a blizzard of stories about the government's ELF program in the Badlands and the accident that had claimed the lives of several of the personnel. The paper had run an editorial about the absolute necessity of these government projects, especially after 9/11 and subsequent events in the Middle East, but called for more oversight, more care: slow and steady would win the race.

And Osborne had chuckled because slow and steady had never won him any races.

He'd called her on Wednesday but her editor said that she'd gone to Washington, D.C., on assignment, and she'd left a message that she would call him as soon as she got back.

That had been two days ago and he hadn't heard from her, and he supposed he had been a little depressed, because he'd been moody and had jumped on his people, until even Trembley had asked if maybe the sheriff shouldn't take another couple days of sick leave.

"The excitement has pretty much died down," the deputy had argued. "Anyway the feds are in charge. Practically taking Belfield apart. Glad it was them and not us. Terrible, just terrible."

Trembley sometimes acted like an old woman, but he'd always meant well. Except this time he was wrong. The situation wasn't over, Osborne could feel it in his gut, almost taste it on the wind. And it had made him uneasy that no one else was seeing it the same way.

"Even Nettles has pulled out," Cameron had told him on the phone this morning.

"Just you out there?" Osborne had asked.

"He left behind a half-dozen new guys in civvies, but they're definitely military. Ex–Special Forces, though they're a little vague about who they work for. General Forester gave the approval. Said he wanted me to have some low-key help."

"You're expecting another attack?"

"It's not likely. These new hired guns are just that—low-key help just in case."

"Just keep your eyes open."

"Have you come up with something I haven't?"

"Just a hunch," Osborne had said.

"I hear you," Cameron said. "In the meantime, unless you have something planned for tonight, why don't you and Ashley come down? We're having a little celebration. Whitney's people need to blow off some steam, and the new power plant techs over at Donna Marie seem to be the right sort."

"She went to Washington, and I don't think she's back yet, but it's been a rough week, you know."

Cameron was quiet for a beat. "Yeah, I do know. Just take care of yourself, okay? Shit like this has a way of working itself out. But if Ashley gets back and you change your mind, give me a call."

And after Osborne had hung up he wondered exactly what "shit" Cameron had been talking about, because it sure wasn't about the Posse, at least not exclusively. Someone was directing them, and although the FBI had finally put Barry Egan's face and particulars up on the Net as a person of extreme interest, the media had still not gotten into the real work of the Initiative.

Repairs had been made to Donna Marie. Ashley was safe. Barry Egan had disappeared into the woodwork somewhere. The experiment would take place sometime in the next week. And tonight Cameron and Lipton along with her postdocs and techs, and presumably the power plant personnel and maybe the handful of low-key hired guns were going to have a New Year's Eve party.

Osborne phoned Gerald Kasmir, the sheriff over in Stark County, who'd with the FBI's help along with the state crime lab had worked the Belfield murder scene.

They'd talked immediately afterwards, but Kasmir had promised to call back if and when he had anything or when, if ever, the dust settled.

"Never been anything like this on my watch," Kasmir said.

He'd been sheriff for nineteen years, and like Osborne had seen his share of drunk ranchers, domestic disputes, and the occasional miscreant rodeo cowboy or tourist, but nothing like what had happened at the Thompson ranch.

"How are you doing, Kas?" Osborne said.

"I don't have anything new to tell you, if that's what you're calling about, Nate," Kasmir said. "The feds took over, so there wasn't much I could do except look over some shoulders."

"It was the same for me down at the Roundup Lodge. Looked like the rodeo cowboy I found shot to death outside the ELF facility did the work. Don't know his motive, but for sure he worked alone."

"Yeah, so'd this guy. Leaves us with nothing." Kasmir sounded bitter. Like Osborne, and just about every small-county sheriff, he felt a strong sense of ownership over his jurisdiction. These were his people, he was their shepherd.

"Anybody in town see or hear anything?"

"Three people swore they saw Clyde heading toward the interstate in his pickup just after dark. He even waved at one of them. The son of a bitch was wearing Thompson's clothes. Flew out of Minneapolis on Clyde's credit card and driver's license. Doesn't say much for the TSA."

"Don't beat yourself up," Osborne said. "This guy is either well trained or just plain lucky."

Kasmir chuckled. "When's the last time you ever heard me beating up on myself? It is what it is, can't change the facts."

"Yeah. Happy New Year."

"Is this over, Nate?"

"Don't know," Osborne said. "But I think not, so keep your eyes open."

He hung up and went to get his coat when Ashley drove up in her pickup truck and he met her at the back entrance to the courthouse, the only unlocked door.

After the snowstorm, the weather had turned bitterly cold, and Ashley's breath was white on the still air and her cheeks were red. But her smile lit up the rear hall like the high noon August sun.

He reached down so she could brush a kiss on his cheek, and he couldn't help but grin, his loneliness completely forgotten.

"You had lunch yet?" she asked.

"I was just going."

"Good, I'm starved, and I have a million things from my dad that you've got to hear." She stopped. "I've got the next couple of days off, thought I'd hang out here if that's okay, big guy."

"I was hoping you'd come back."

She laughed, the sound magical. "Don't be so easy."

"That's supposed to be my line," Osborne said. "Anyway, we've been invited to a party down at the Initiative tonight, if you want to go."

"Absolutely. There's something I want to talk over with Jim Cameron and the doc."

"Well, we've got the afternoon after lunch."

"I brought a few things this time, thought I'd drop them off at your place before we went anywhere."

46

THE DIRECTOR OF the CIA's office suite was on the seventh floor of the Old Headquarters Building with double-paned windows, the dead airspace of which was filled with white noise to defeat laser eavesdropping. In fact, the entire building, the same as every other structure on the Langley campus, was protected from any sort of mechanical or electronic surveillance. Anything discussed inside these walls was secure.

Edwin Rogers had been driven over from his office in the J. Edgar Hoover Building at three on a blustery overcast afternoon, all of Washington shut down for the holiday, and was immediately escorted upstairs where Walter Page was waiting.

"Good of you to come out on such short notice, but this couldn't wait," Page said, getting up from behind his desk and extending his hand.

"I assume you've come up with something on the Initiative investigation," Rogers said, shaking hands. The aide who'd escorted him upstairs took his overcoat and left.

"Yes, actually something quite disturbing. But first

bring me up to date with what your people have come up with. Any sign of Mr. Egan?"

"Nothing. Once he reached Louisville he disappeared. But we'll find him sooner or later, even if he has dug himself a hole and crawled in."

"I saw the APB. Clever of you not to have mentioned the attack on the Initiative, only the murders and robbery of the rancher and his wife and employees, but we think that you may be wrong about him going to ground."

"No reason for him to return to North Dakota. Even if he were to show up at the head of an armored column, the rapid response teams from Ellis could be back in a matter of an hour or two. If need be I'm told that a couple of jets could be scrambled and be on scene within minutes."

Page looked pessimistic. "That's what the president said, but I don't agree, especially in light of a couple of possibilities Dan Herbert brought up this afternoon. It's why I called you." Herbert was the CIA's deputy director of intelligence, and was considered the company's reigning intellectual.

"Tell me."

"For starters we're just about certain now that SEBIN was behind the first attack on the power station. Their chief of North American operations, Hector Guisti, was spotted in Havana the week before the attack, and again very late last night or early this morning where my people on the ground think he met with a person or persons unknown at José Marti Airport. Coincidentally a private jet belonging to Trent Holdings flew from Mexico City to Havana at about the same time, stayed only a short time, and then showed up back in Mexico City where it refueled and returned to Des Moines."

"D. S. Wood," Rogers said. "The SEC has been looking at him for the past year, something to do with irregularities with one or more of his derivative positions. We were asked to do a criminal BI, but we found nothing. But even if he did meet with a SEBIN officer, what does it have to do with Egan?"

"It's speculation on Dan's part, but SEBIN and Wood essentially want the same thing: a delay in the development of anything that would seriously impact the oil business—Venezuela because of their exports to us, and Wood because of his derivative holdings, which Dan thinks might be on shaky grounds. With oil at one hundred dollars a barrel alternative energy is getting a fair amount of attention, and investor's money. And the Initiative, so far as we understand it from Pat Sheehy, is on the verge of producing industrial quantities of clean-burning methane. Sustainable quantities that could seriously impact our need for imported oil." Sheehy was the director of ARPA-E.

Rogers was skeptical and he let it show. "That's a possibility, I'll concede that much, but it's a stretch, unless you have something else to back it up."

"There was a third person at the meeting with Guisti. But it was someone already on the ground, because they drove out to the airport. Assuming that whoever it was has an interest in maintaining oil imports from Venezuela we looked at every American currently in Cuba, especially not ordinary tourists. We came up with one intriguing name: Margaret Fischer, who is the chief investments officer for Hodding Brothers, coincidentally one of the inventors of credit default swaps, along with some other exotic financial gimmicks. And who just as coincidentally has lately steered her company away from alternative energy investments into oil futures."

Rogers saw the point Page was making. "Two American investment brokers involved with oil in Havana at the same time as the high-ranking SEBIN officer," he said. "But if they did meet, what does that have to do with the attack?"

"The Posse Comitatus never has had the kind of money it took to outfit the motor home, or to make contact with people like Dr. Kemal. So we've been operating under the assumption that someone with deep pockets who might be interested in protecting their oil interests was involved. D. S. Wood, Margaret Fischer, and SEBIN are about as good a fit as we can come up with."

"You mentioned a couple of possibilities. What's the second?"

"Egan's intel on the Initiative, especially the electronic emissions from the facility, along with the exact makeup of the biological research, has led us to suspect that there is a leak somewhere either at the Initiative itself or here in Washington, D.C., inside ARPA-E."

Rogers was familiar with this line of inquiry and he said so. "Dr. Lipton and her staff have been cleared. Absolutely nothing turned up in their deep background checks that even hints at trouble, and there'd be no benefit for any of them to see the project fail. Just the opposite. Which leaves Bob Forester, or most likely someone on his staff. But so far they have turned up clean."

"We came to the same conclusions, but you're forgetting one other person," Page said.

Rogers shrugged. "We vetted the security staff, including Jim Cameron, but even he doesn't have access to the science part of it."

"Dan thought that it could be someone not actually connected to the project, but someone close. Someone who could potentially benefit immensely from the attack, and maybe another, whether or not they succeeded."

"Someone at one of the universities working on individual concepts?"

"Somebody much closer; somebody who has the confidence not only of Forester, but of Dr. Lipton and even Jim Cameron and the sheriff out there, plus your own Special Agent in Charge at Minneapolis who's the lead investigator."

Rogers was at a loss. "I don't have a clue."

"The newspaper reporter, Ashley Borden. Forester's daughter."

It was a surprise to Rogers. "Doesn't wash, Walt. They kidnapped her and tied her to the fence to let her freeze to death, which would have happened had Osborne not shown up."

"Convenient timing, wouldn't you say?"

"You can't think that he's involved, too?"

"Of course not. But Egan could certainly have been tipped off that Osborne was coming their way and staged the kidnapping."

"Tipped off by who?"

"By Ms. Borden, of course," Page said. "Were you aware that she spent the last two days here with her father? And that as soon as she flew back to Bismarck this morning she drove immediately out to Medora?"

It made no sense to Rogers, and yet Page's argument was seductive, but for one disturbing thing. "Do you have someone on the ground out there that we know nothing about?"

Page shook his head. "No. Dan had the hunch and he made a few phone calls. Nothing more than that. But I can't find fault with his reasoning."

"Ashley Borden," Rogers said. "Amazing."

"I suggest you get a court order and monitor her phone

calls. Could be interesting to see if she makes contact with Wood, Fischer, or anyone in Venezuela."

"Wood could be the money source for the Posse," Rogers said. "I'll give you that much."

"With Ms. Borden as the conduit," Page added.

47

THE THREE EIGHTEEN-WHEELERS, marked with the oil well derrick logos of Mid-Texas Industrial Supply, that had come up I-29 from Omaha, had gotten off the interchange southwest of Fargo and swept west on I-94 about four hours ago just before six. And now the sky was still clear, filled with a billion stars, the temperature minus fifteen and the highway snow free.

Jesus Campinella, the lead driver, glanced at the Escort 9500ci radar detector on the dash that showed no threat either in front, behind, or above, and put the pedal to the metal, the Kenworth's speed ramping up to ninety. His brief had been twofold: reach the Initiative before midnight, and under no circumstances get stopped by the highway patrol.

The Escort, powered by a GPS receiver, was loaded with real-time intelligence that showed the locations of speed traps, Smokeys with radar guns, and the schedules of all traffic control over flights, plus road blocks, construction projects, and any sort of a traffic delay—even those from accidents. And it was totally undetectable not only from police equipment but from the more sensitive military radar absorption gear that they might run into when they got close to the Initiative.

The manifests for each of the trucks showed that they carried oil drilling and fracting pipes and tools, bound for the newly developing Bakken oil shale fields in Northwestern North Dakota, from Mid-Texas Industrial's international depot in Houston. Such shipments were so commonplace from the Dakotas and Wyoming west and north that they were scarcely ever noticed, except by state troopers who were mostly looking for logbook violations.

But they wouldn't be subject to another weigh station inspection, before which they would have already unloaded their real cargo, and turned around for the return trip, empty.

"Taco Bell, San Juan, come back," Campinella's CD blared on nineteen.

He keyed the mike. "San Juan, what's up?"

"How about backin' off the hammer?"

"Negatory, we have a clean shot far as I can see."

"We're on schedule."

Campinella, who was the convoy leader, considered what San Juan—Ignacio Gomez—was telling him. They were right on schedule, and their orders were to reach Highway 85 just east of Belfield no earlier than ten, which was no problem. But he wanted insurance in the bank in case of trouble.

He glanced in his big door mirror, the other two trucks at the proper intervals behind him, and then at the still-clear radar detector. Born in the slums of Bachaquero on the shores of Lake Maracaibo, Campinella had lived by his wits since he was seven when his father had been killed in a bar fight and his mother had died giving birth to her ninth baby. With all those mouths to feed, his older sister, who was fifteen at the time, had taken to prostitution in the oil workers barrio, so when Jesus slipped away one night she hadn't cared.

He'd learned his lesson early and hard, so by the time he was seventeen he'd come to the attention of a local cop who'd recommended him to the secret intelligence agency, and they'd taken him in with open arms. There always was a need for ground troops; expendables, they were called.

The other drivers on this job had about the same backgrounds, but their papers identified them as legal Mexican immigrants, who were working diligently for their U.S. citizenship. They even sent money home to fictitious families in Matamoros.

"Hold one," Campinella radioed. He adjusted the display on his Escort for road problems fifty miles out, but nothing was showing. They were well west of Bismarck and in another few miles they would be coming up on a rest stop with facilities. He'd been given several choices depending on the road conditions—which to this point were near perfect—and the presence of state cops who might or might not be looking for them.

"Could just be drunk patrols for New Year's Eve," their dispatcher, a rough son of a bitch in Houston whose name Jesus was never given, told him. "But it's your call on this run. Make it to the delivery spot, unload, and do your flip-flop right back here light."

"What if we get stopped?"

"Make goddamned sure your comic book is up to date, so they've got nothing to bitch about," the dispatcher said. The comic book was the trucker's log, which showed miles run and hours behind the wheel. DOT regulations specified that a driver could only drive a maximum of eleven hours after ten hours off duty. According to their logs they'd switched drivers in Wichita and again in Sioux

Falls. In fact his co-driver, a boozer from San Antonio whose name had never been of any consequence to anyone, had spent all of his time in his berth, knocked out with a shot of methohexital, a powerful sedative. When they reached Dallas on the return run he would be given an overdose of crack that would kill him. One of the other co-drivers high on meth would kill the third with a .38 Police Special and then commit suicide. By the time the police got involved Jesus and his two operatives would be safely on a plane back to Caracas.

It was a tough old world, the general had told them at the end of their briefing in Houston. "Just see you do your jobs and don't end up the same way."

"Let the *hijas de putas* talk all they want," Campinella and the others had been instructed before they'd left Caracas. "And talk they will. Your job is a simple one. Take them to their insertion point then turn around and leave."

Campinella keyed his mike. "San Juan, Sixteen Ton, we've got a pickle park comin' up in about ten just past the one twenty-three, and I'm needin' a ten-hundred, copy?" A pickle park was a rest area with facilities, and a ten-hundred was a bathroom break.

"Taco Bell, copy."

"Sixteen Ton, I'm with ya," the third driver, Jose Ricardo, radioed. All of them had been coached on American truckers' dialect

Which was just as well, Campinella thought, because he didn't want to argue with his people, nor did he want to admit that the closer they came to their turnaround the more spooked he became. The mission planner, Major Pedro Ramirez, had warned him just before takeoff that the Americans were *loco;* it was possible that they could do almost anything.

"So watch yourself."

"Why do this, sir, if they are such a risk?"

"Because those are your orders," the major had said. "In fact I wouldn't trust this assignment to anyone else."

Campinella knew when he was being flattered. "Because I'm an expendable?"

Major Ramirez had gotten serious all of a sudden but then he threw back his head and laughed. *"Sí,"* he said. "That, too. But you're from the barrio, which means you know how to spot an opportunity."

And when to spot a lost cause for what it was and run. All the way up from Houston Campinella had been thinking what he would do if he were in the general's shoes. First on the list would be to eliminate witnesses. Make sure that his back was clear. But it would have to be done somewhere quiet. Like U.S. 85 south of Belfield. Out in the Badlands.

He didn't have all the answers, though the assignment had been specific: deliver the load to a spot fifteen miles south of the interstate on U.S. 85, then turn around and come back. But the closer they came the more nervous he got. If it doesn't smell right, he'd learned early on, it probably isn't.

The blue "rest area two miles" sign came up and Campinella began to throttle down. Almost immediately the general came on the intercom.

"Why are we slowing down?"

Campinella had rehearsed this moment. "My truck is developing a problem."

"Which is?"

"I think we got bad fuel in Sioux Falls."

"Have you told the other drivers?"

"They're a little bit jumpy. Could be we'd get stuck on Eighty-five."

"Stand by," the general said.

The radar detector was still clear ahead and behind, when Campinella began to shift down as they passed the one-mile marker.

"Do you have spare filters?" the general asked.

"Yes, but it'll take time to drain the water, change them, and bleed the air out of the system. If you want to wait, it's fine with me. But I can't guarantee that we'll be on the road on your timetable."

The intercom was silent as Campinella shifted down through the gears, slowing the semi to under thirty miles per hour as he took the off-ramp, easing the brakes to slow them even further.

"Your call, General," he called to the trailer.

"How far yet to our turn-off?"

"Sixty-five miles," Campinella said, taking the left turn to truck parking and sliding his rig into one of the slots. The rest stop was completely empty of other cars or trucks.

"How does it look?"

The other two semis pulled in beside him.

"No one else but us," Campinella said. "And the highway is clear for at least fifty miles in either direction."

"Stand by."

Campinella popped open his door, the cab instantly filling with air colder than anything he'd ever experienced in his life, and he caught a vision of his body lying on the side of some godforsaken western American wilderness frozen solid.

He reached under the dash and pulled out a Beretta 9mm pistol and stuffed it in his belt as the general called back.

"Check your radar detector now."

Campinella did. "It is still clear in all directions."

"Very well, we're getting out here."

"As you wish," Campinella muttered, and he grabbed his jacket, climbed down from the cab, and put it on, buttoning it all the way to his neck and pulling up the collar.

Gomez and Ricardo had climbed down from their cabs and came over.

"We're unloading here," Campinella told them. "Be quick about it. We have a turnaround at one ten, and I want to be heading east *muy pronto*."

"It's cold here," Ricardo said.

Campinella opened the lock on the back, swung the doors open, and climbed inside what appeared to be a trailer loaded floor to ceiling with pipes, most of them six inches or more in diameter, leaving less than two feet of clear space in front of the doors. Undoing five hidden latches, he swung the false front open in two parts like a double door.

Four men in white arctic camos over their Army Delta Force uniforms that carried no markings, M4 carbines up and at the ready, stood on either side of a Hummer, nose out, also painted white, with no markings.

Barry Egan, also dressed in white camos, open at the collar to show his one star, came out of the shadows. "Stand down, gentlemen," he said, and the troops lowered their weapons. He was not happy. "I didn't feel any problem with the truck. In fact you sped up back there."

"You have to feel it in the pedal."

Egan came to the open doors and looked outside, his breath white in the rest stop's harsh lights.

"It's not far to Eighty-five, and by the time you get there everyone will be partying," Jesus said. The four operators had lowered their carbines, but he knew that if it came to a shoot-out, he'd be dead before he could pull out his pistol.

Egan turned back and looked at him. He nodded. "It's what I would have done," he muttered. He turned to his people. "Saddle up, gentlemen, do you want to live forever?"

"Shall we lower the ramps?"

"Yes," Egan said. "Lower the ramps, and then run home to Mama. I suspect it's way too cold up here for you."

48

SINCE HE'D TALKED to Nate Osborne earlier in the day Cameron had become increasingly spooked and standing at the bar in Henry's, nursing a beer and watching Susan Watts, who was sitting on the shoulders of Bernie Stein and stringing the last of the balloons to a sprinkler head on the ceiling, he was too preoccupied to really see her. Nor was he hearing the loud music, the Beach Boys, thankfully per Whitney's orders not more rap.

All of her crew plus the four engineers from Donna Marie and two of the three Air Force gate guards were ready to party. But they were edgy, and that much he was catching because they'd been that way since this morning when Whitney had announced that all the reconstruction was finished and that the experiment would go forward tomorrow at noon.

Everyone was waiting for the other shoe to drop; the sword of Damocles, that according to Frank Neubert, the most serious of Whitney's postdocs, was hanging over all of their heads by a single hair while they yukked it up at the banquet table.

Cameron was just raising his bottle when Whitney was at his shoulder.

"A penny," she said.

He managed a smile, though he was in something of a funk. "Take more than a penny. But I'll tell you that I'll be damned glad when we get past the experiment tomorrow. And I don't much feel like a party tonight."

She studied his face. "Should I be worried again?"

"No. That's my job, you stick to the science."

"Bob Forester wouldn't have pulled out Ranger Rick and his troopers if he expected more trouble was coming our way. Do you think we should call them back, just until tomorrow?"

Cameron had been asking himself the same thing since the civilian contractors had shown up thirty-six hours ago, leaving only the Air Force cops on one-man shifts at the main gate. But he'd put it down to nothing more than a case of nerves. The same as Nate Osborne was feeling. He shook his head. "No. I'm just a little jumpy is all."

She touched his arm and gave him a tentative smile. "Okay, so do you know how to dance, or are you the kind of a guy who gets out on the floor just to grab a girl's ass?"

"Both."

"Honesty from a man. That's refreshing."

"But you'll have to give me a half hour, I want to check with Daley to make sure Donna Marie is secure and his people haven't seen or heard anything." Wayne Daley was the security team leader, and from what little Cameron had been able to piece together he'd been a navy lieutenant j.g. But he and his people had been completely vetted by Forester's office, so Cameron hadn't tried to dig any deeper.

"Don't be long, okay? Or else I'll be forced to dance with Bernie who thinks that I work for him, not the other way around."

Cameron started to turn away but Whitney stopped him.

"You're a good man to have around," she said. "I just wanted to tell you that."

"Maybe I'll just forget the dancing bit and skip to the next part."

"Don't be long," Whitney said.

Cameron grabbed his parka and headed out the door to where he'd parked his ATV when his cell phone rang. It was Deb Rausch calling from her office in Minneapolis. "Doesn't the bureau recognize New Year's Eve?" he asked.

"Not as long as Barry Egan and his nutcase friends are still on the loose," she said. "How're things out there?"

"Quiet. Everybody's at the R and D Center getting ready to party. Tomorrow's the big day."

"Your contractors on the job?"

"Not mine. Forester's office hired them, but they seem to know what they're doing," Cameron said. "But you didn't call to talk about that."

"The director called to tell me that the leak in Forester's office might have been identified. And I don't think you're going to like it one bit, because I sure as hell don't."

"Who is it? Someone on the science staff?"

"Ashley Borden."

Cameron had just straddled the ATV and was about to start the engine, but he stopped. "You have to be kidding."

"We have a wiretap order on her phone, and I called to ask you to keep your eyes open. I'm going to give Osborne the heads-up as well."

"I'd hold off calling Nate."

"Why?"

"They're starting to have a thing for each other, and I suspect that he'll think you people are more full of shit than I do. The general's daughter?"

"My same reaction, but she's been officially designated as a person of interest, which means my hands are tied."

"Well, she and Nate are on their way down here to party with us. What do you want me to do, bar them at the gate?"

Rausch was silent for a moment. "No," she said. "If she's the leak and she's at the Initiative there probably won't be another attack, or at least not until the experiment is over with. Maybe we caught a break."

"Or maybe your boss is smoking something he shouldn't be smoking," Cameron said. "But I'm armed, so if she tries anything funny I'll shoot her, okay?"

"I didn't start this, and right now my job is the same as yours."

"I'll keep my eyes open, but you guys are way off base and I'd bet just about anything on it."

"Your life?" Rausch asked.

Cameron hesitated a beat. "Of course not," he said, deflated.

"Keep in touch," Rausch said, and she rang off.

Cameron pocketed his phone, pulled on his thermal gloves, started the ATV's engine, and headed down to Donna Marie as he tried to wrap his mind around the possibility—no matter how stupid it sounded to him—that Ashley Borden could somehow have been involved with the Posse and the attack on the Initiative. The first question was why. What was her motivation? What did she hope to gain? Maybe getting back at her father for something in the past? But even if that were the case why hadn't she simply published an in-depth article about what was going on here? Embarrass the general that way, because he couldn't picture her so cold blooded as to be part of the murders of the two guys in the power plant control room and the massacre of the others in the double-wide.

He didn't know her very well, but among the opinions

he'd formed they definitely did not include insanity of the kind Barry Egan and his type were afflicted with.

One hundred yards out from the main generating building, Cameron slowed enough to key the inner gate with a remote control and drove through as it opened. He'd argued against the second level of security as unnecessary, but Forester's planning staff had insisted that only key personnel were to be allowed inside the near perimeter of the plant, where the main pieces of top secret work was being done.

The only other access was through the back gate, which was kept locked at all times and protected by closed-circuit television monitors along with motion sensors and infrared detectors that would set off alarms inside the plant as well as up at the R&D Center.

Of course those measures had been electronically defeated the last time, so now Forester's contractors had been ordered to physically guard the generating hall as well as the rear gate. Anyone who tried to get close was to be detained until more help arrived, or shot and killed if necessary.

Yesterday two men in a Hummer had been stationed at the back gate, but this evening they weren't there. Cameron angled away from the generating hall where the Air Force had set up its medical, dining, and barracks tents, gone now, only the tamped-down snowdrifts, tire tracks, and helicopter skid marks in a jumble remaining.

Stopping at the gate, Cameron dismounted from his ATV and inspected the heavy lock and chain, which were intact. The lights on the two television cameras glowed dimly red, indicating that they were functioning, and that meant that someone knew he was here.

The gate was flooded with light from above, which made the night outside the fence all but invisible. But

Cameron could feel something, almost sense eyes watching him from the crest of the low hills less than a mile out, maybe through the scope of a sniper rifle.

He turned at the sound of a Hummer racing down the access road from the generator building, its headlights bouncing all over the place until the big vehicle skidded to a stop just a few yards away. Two men, one of them Wayne Daley, jumped out and came over. They both were armed with M4 carbines.

"Mr. Cameron, weren't expecting you down here," Daley said. He was a tall, solidly built man in his late twenties, and like all of his team he was dressed in arctic white camos.

"It's lieutenant commander," Cameron said. "And why isn't this gate manned?"

"Nothing's moving out there tonight, LC, and I decided to keep my men inside where it's warm and they can conserve their strength and stay sharp." Daley shrugged. "Unless you have different orders?"

"How about sending someone up to the R&D Center? Lots of critical personnel there tonight."

"My orders were very specific: guard the generating hall, wellhead, and control room, and interdict any attempt at penetration." Daley looked away for a moment, then spoke into his lapel mike. "Roger, understand ETA in five."

"Who was that?" Cameron demanded. Something wasn't right.

"We have help on the way," Daley said.

Cameron stepped back a pace and reached for his pistol, but the second contractor raised his M4.

"Pull your weapon and drop it to the ground," Daley said.

"Son of a bitch," Cameron muttered, but he did as he was told.

"Take him back up to the wellhead and secure him. The general might have some questions."

"General?" Cameron asked.

"You'll see soon enough," Daley said, and he motioned for his man to head back to the generating hall on foot with his prisoner.

"Who the hell do you really work for?" Cameron asked. "Can you tell me that much?"

"Command Systems," Daley said, and he produced a key and walked to the gate.

49

THE THREE HUMMERS with army markings had swept through Belfield turning off U.S. 85 and headed west a little before eleven, the night pitch-black under a thick blanket of clouds that had moved in less than an hour earlier. Egan, riding shotgun in the lead vehicle, had suppressed a laugh thinking about what he was going to do tonight, and the money he was going to make that was going to guarantee his retirement.

And the land ran red with the blood of his enemies, his wrath so terrible that even kings trembled before his name.

It was a quote from somewhere Egan couldn't remember, except he thought that his daddy had used it around the house whenever he was in one of his moods. But it was a fine sentiment, one that Egan had always seen as his exclusive property, and one to which he'd always added the notion of righteousness.

And it was the righteous who would inherit the earth, just as he had been handed his own salvation on a silver platter. Twelve men, including himself, four to a Hummer. All of them dressed in arctic white camos, all of them armed with M4 carbines, 9mm Beretta pistols, a few flash-bang grenades, and enough Semtex and remote control fuses to destroy the important structures and mechanisms in the power station five times over. And all of them dedicated to his one star and to the mission for which they had already been trained.

He had called Bob Kast from Louisville and a plane had been immediately sent for him. "One final mission and then you're off the hook."

"First I want to get paid for the newspaper broad."

"She didn't die. In fact Sheriff Osborne was in the chopper you shot down, and he rescued her after you left."

Egan was walking beside Kast along a low mountain path in the woods, just the two of them, and he'd felt a sudden stab of fear. Kast had called him here to kill him and bury his body somewhere on the Command Systems remote base. No one would ever find him, because no one knew where he was.

"But you're not going to have to worry about money ever again," Kast had told him. "Do you understand what I'm saying?"

"No," Egan had replied honestly.

"We've laid out your final mission, and when it's over you'll be paid twenty-five million dollars. Do you understand what I'm saying now?"

Egan had actually licked his lips. "I'm listening" was all he could manage to say.

"You fucked up twice, so you owe us this. But that's beside the point, because this time I've personally designed the mission: I've gathered the personnel—eleven under your command to go with you to the Initiative and six more who'll already be inside."

"Your men?"

"In a manner of speaking. But they'll be yours for the

duration. Twelve hours from the time you enter the south gate until you're aboard a Gulfstream with five million in gold headed for Havana."

Egan had pulled up. "A Gulfstream won't carry eighteen men, will it?"

"Just," Kast said. "But we're counting on losing a couple of your men. There will be at least four armed security officers in the compound, presumably well motivated. But if they fail you'll have to manage to cut the number down yourself."

They had walked in silence for another ten minutes before Egan came up with at least one fatal flaw in Kast's plan. "Twelve hours is too long. Someone will notice something is wrong and they'll come running. No way they'll let us waltz over to the nearest airport and fly away."

It was Kast's turn to stop. "They'll do exactly that," he said. "And I'll explain why."

Alessandro Rodriguez was a small, dark-skinned man whose English was without accent and whom Egan had met only a few days ago in North Carolina. He was a Command Systems special operator and had been handpicked by Kast himself to act as Egan's number one, and he was driving the lead Hummer when they crested the last hill overlooking the Initiative's back gate.

"There," he said.

"Right on schedule," Egan said. Nothing seemed out of the ordinary, only the one man standing beside the open gate, beyond which was a Hummer, exactly according to plan, and his gut clenched. Keep your options open, his daddy had taught him, and despite Kast's ingenious plan, he intended to do just that.

Daley stepped aside as Rodriguez drove through the

gate and pulled to the left to allow the other two Hummers to pass.

Egan rolled down his window as the contractor walked over.

"Mr. Daley, I presume."

"Good evening, General. Run into any trouble on the way?"

"No. How about here?"

"The head of security showed up a few minutes ago asking questions, just as you called with your ETA. He's up at the wellhead secured."

"How about everyone else?"

"Everyone's up at the R and D end, at Henry's, having a party."

"How about the cell phone antenna?"

Daley glanced over his shoulder at the red light blinking atop the smokestack. "Should be going down any minute."

"Sat phones?" Egan asked. It had been his idea to task the contractors to search for satellite phones anywhere within the Initiative and to disable them.

"Four, all missing their SIM cards."

"Good work," Egan said, and he turned to Rodriguez. "I want four men covering this gate from two defensible positions. Take the others up to the plant and get the charges in place and fused, priority one. Things are apt to get a little interesting here within the hour."

"You'll be taking this vehicle up to the R and D compound I presume?" Rodriguez asked.

"Yes, along with Mr. Daley's people," Egan said, and he turned back to Daley. "Get them rounded up."

"What about the security officer? Someone is bound to come looking for him sooner or later."

"Kill him," Egan said, but then he changed his mind. "Better yet, bring him along."

"As you wish," the contractor said. He spoke into his lapel mike giving the order as Rodriguez got out and started hustling his troops and equipment.

50

PASSING THROUGH BELFIELD, Ashley suppressed a shiver and Osborne behind the wheel of his SUV glanced over at her. "You want to go back?" he asked. The nearer they'd come to U.S. 85 the quieter and more withdrawn she'd become, and he was a little concerned for her.

She shook her head and smiled. "I'm okay," she said. "But thinking about those poor people Egan killed, and how he did it, sends a shiver up my spine. They never had a chance."

"Nothing like that ever happens out here, so most folks don't even lock their doors."

Ashley looked at him. "It's one of the reasons you came home when the war was over for you, wasn't it?"

"One, not the only," Osborne said. "How about you? Why not New York, or Washington, someplace with news?"

"I don't know. Habit, maybe. Inertia. The Bismarck job came up and I took it. Guess I was just tired of all the time practically living out of a suitcase. Never having a friend for more than three years at a stretch."

"No one ever serious?"

Ashley shrugged.

"The majority of the population on most military bases is men. You should have had your pick."

This time she laughed. "You have no idea how hard it was for me to get a date. Even in high school."

"I don't believe it."

"Come on, Nate. Who has the guts to try to make time with the general's daughter?"

"I do."

"And trust me, my dad has always been a terror."

"I do," Osborne said again, and this time Ashley heard him, and she got serious.

"These last few days since Christmas, and especially this afternoon, don't have to mean anything further than what happened," she said. "I didn't set any sort of a trap for you. I just want you to know that."

"Okay," Osborne said, watching the road, but when he turned to glance at her she was staring at him with intensity. It was something new. "What?" he asked.

"The problem is I think I'm falling in love with you. And when I told my dad he said it was about time I grew up, but I didn't really know what he meant until just this instant."

Osborne didn't know what to say.

"I can't imagine my life without you," she went on. "And for me that's a heck of an admission."

Ashley's hands were clenched in her lap, and Osborne reached over and touched them. "When I saw you tied to the fence I thought I was too late to help you, and it nearly drove me crazy."

She nodded. "I won't ever walk out on you, Nate," she said. "The only way I'll leave is if you tell me you don't love me."

Osborne's chest was swelling. "That'll never happen."

She raised his hand to her lips and kissed it, then smiled. "I always thought women who acted like this were absolute saps."

"Medora's not too much?"

Ashley laughed out loud, all the tension that had built between them on the way out here suddenly gone. "Medora will be just fine, so long as we can take a vacation back to civilization now and then," she said. "You know, maybe like Dickinson or Bismarck or even Fargo."

And it was Osborne's turn to laugh, and for the first time in a very long while he felt as if everything at least had the possibility of ending up just fine, even though he still had the jitters, which rose again to the surface as they came to the gravel road that led ten miles back to the Initiative.

He slowed for the turn and Ashley was suddenly subdued. "Bastards," she muttered.

"We don't have to go to the party," Osborne said.

Ashley shook her head. "Nothing's going to happen tonight; according to my dad there're no signs of anything coming up in the near term, but this business is a lot bigger than anyone suspected. Venezuelan intelligence is apparently working with a couple of very big Wall Street types—money managers who deal with oil derivatives— who'd like to see the bigger alternative energy programs, the ones most likely to succeed on an industrial scale, fail, and fail spectacularly."

"If it's true then it's another confirmation that there's a leak somewhere," Osborne said. "But where?"

"My dad thinks it has to be on the science staff, but the bureau's cleared everyone, which leaves his staff at ARPA-E, which he doesn't want to believe. He's worked with some of those people for a good portion of his career;

called them over to help with the Initiative when the president appointed him to run the show. They're friends from the old Bosnia peacekeeping operation."

"If the financing thing has gotten to the level we're talking about that's a lot of money. Serious money that can turn serious heads."

"I said the same thing to him. But he doesn't want to believe that foxhole buddies could do something like that to each other."

"Maybe he should step down," Osborne suggested in as gentle a tone as possible.

"He will if he thinks he can't do the job. But I know him, and God help the poor bastard if it is someone on the staff and Dad catches them. He'll skin them alive."

"What else?"

"Apparently the two Wall Street types may have met with a Venezuelan intelligence agent in Havana just a few days ago, which could mean that they're planning another attack. But it'll take some time to put it together, and by then it could be a moot point if the experiment actually works. I'm going to ask the doc what she thinks her chances are and how soon we'll know one way or the other. But my dad says that time is of the essence. We need to get it right and soon."

"If that's the thinking in Washington, why the hell was the Air Force pulled out?"

"That's just the thing. Nettles's security people along with a couple of jets down at Ellsworth are standing by twenty-four/seven. They actually want another attack. If they could catch someone with their hands in the cookie jar—someone from Venezuela—it would help solve the diplomatic problem we're in."

"And get a lot of innocent people killed in the doing."

"Exactly," Ashley said. "Which is why I needed to

come out here tonight. If they're ready to do the experiment soon, I want Dr. Lipton to not tell anyone outside of the Initiative. Especially not my dad's office. If there is a leak in Washington, and they find out that the experiment is going ahead in the next week or so, the attack could come. I want her to lie to my father."

51

THE LAST OF the contractors filed out of the generating station's side door prodding Jim Cameron, his hands tied behind his back, to where Egan, Daley, and the others waited by the two Hummers.

"Barry Egan, I recognized your stench from all the way inside," Cameron said. The side of his face was cut open and blood ran down his chin.

"Lieutenant Commander, not a very impressive man for all your SEAL training," Egan said, enjoying himself. He'd always hated officers, most of whom had no earthly idea what they were doing, giving orders that half the time made absolutely no sense. Every battle and every war had been lost not by the blood and guts of the grunts, but by the bad decisions made at the top.

"If you've cut the phone service or any of the data links like last time, Air Force jets down at Ellsworth are already scrambling. Means you have twenty minutes tops to cover your ass before the shit starts raining down on you."

"Actually I expect it to take a little longer, because we've only disrupted your cell service, and of course disabled the four satellite phones. Your data links are still streaming.

I'd give Ellsworth one hour to get its shit in one sock and show up here."

Cameron glanced over his shoulder. "Your people are wiring the place to blow, but it won't matter, you know. If you destroy the plant it'll just be rebuilt. Maybe delay us by a few months."

"You will have lost access to your coal seam."

"Not the only coal in the country, or even nearby. We'll drill another well. And another, and another, if need be. You and the Posse are out of your league."

"But you're forgetting something," Egan said. "All the coal seams and wells won't mean a thing without your chief scientist and her team. But especially her."

Cameron's facial muscles tightened. "She's not the only scientist who can do the work. Anyway her methods and her formulas have all been set down. No need to kill her because if you did someone else would just pick up where she left off."

Egan suppressed a laugh. "Romance in the Badlands between the scientist and the SEAL? Officers like you are like bags of shit, a dime a dozen. In any event you're right about us destroying this place, but we're not going to kill her. We're going to hold her as hostage."

"For money?"

"Just for a little delay," Egan said. "But you'll see for yourself if you don't cause us trouble." He stepped aside so that Cameron could be loaded in the back of the Hummer, two of Daley's men bracketing him, their drawn pistols jammed into the side of his head.

Four of his men had already relocked the rear gate and had taken up defensive positions with night vision oculars. They would easily spot anything heading their way either by ground or by air. The others were inside the plant setting the explosives this time with radio-controlled detonators. No matter what happened this place was going to come crashing down, the well permanently capped. They would rebuild, if not right here, someplace close, but it would take time, and that's all Bob Kast and the spic who'd briefed him were interested in. "Buy us the time, and you'll get your reward."

Daley got behind the wheel, his other three men climbing to the middle just behind the front seats, and Egan hesitated for just a moment at the front passenger door. "Post one, team lead," he spoke into his lapel mike.

The designated squad leader at the rear gate came back immediately. "Team lead, post one secure. No perimeter movement."

"Keep your eyes open," Egan radioed back. "Post two, team lead. Report your status."

"Team lead, post two. We're about halfway home. Ten minutes."

"Assemble at your designated fire points when you're finished, and report."

"Roger that. Post two, out."

Egan wore a standard issue Beretta 9mm semiauto loader in a holster strapped to his chest beneath his camos. He took the pistol out, checked the load, and climbed up into the Hummer and they took off, passing through the interior gate and heading up toward the compound, the big, knobby tires crunching on the hard snowpack in the below-zero temperature.

"Who else out here tonight will be armed?" Egan asked.

"Just the three Air Force cops, one of whom will be manning the main gate," Daley said.

"What about the other two?"

"Should be getting some rest, but this is New Year's Eve so they'll be at Henry's."

"Good, it'll make it easier to take them down," Egan said.

"You said you weren't going to kill anyone," Cameron protested from the back.

"If he says another word, shoot him," Egan said without turning around.

A hundred yards from the R&D control building across from which were clustered the barracks, dining hall, and Henry's, the snow-covered gravel road split off left to the compound and right to the guard shack at the main gate. Egan motioned to the right.

"How do you want to play this?" Daley asked. "The gate is equipped with a panic button direct to Ellsworth special ops."

"I'll handle it," Egan said. "I'll want one of your people to take over, just in case someone else shows up."

Daley pulled up at the guard shack, and Egan hopped out and went around the front of the Hummer as the lone guard came out. He'd left his M4 carbine inside, and when he saw Egan's face—which he did not recognize—he started to reach for the pistol at his hip. But then he caught sight of the single star and he came to attention.

"Sorry, sir, I didn't know you were here."

"Your mistake," Egan said, striding directly to where the guard stood. He raised his pistol from where it was concealed behind his right leg and fired one shot at point-blank range into the man's forehead, knocking him off his feet.

One of Daley's men got out of the Hummer and came over. "Are we expecting anyone?" he asked.

"No, but you can never tell. If someone does, let me know on your tactical radio, and I'll give you instructions."

"Yes, sir," the contractor said. "I'll hide the body and clean up the mess, just in case."

"Do that," Egan said, and he fired another round into the side of the dead guard's head. "Insurance," he said, and he laughed, holding back a full bray. But God how he loved this shit.

Back in the Hummer he glanced in the rear and Cameron glared back at him, wanting to say something, but holding his tongue. Biding his time. The chief of security was almost certainly the most dangerous man here tonight, and Egan had no real idea why he didn't just kill the bastard, except that he wanted to have a little fun first.

Daley turned around, the Hummer easily bulling its way through the snow piled up at the sides of the gravel road and headed the three hundred yards up to the compound. The two-story R&D building was flanked by the living quarters and dining hall on one side and a machine shop and a low-slung concrete block building that contained the level-five clean room where Lipton had conducted her critical on-site microbial control experiments on the other.

From what little Egan understood of the doctor's work, the bugs she had created could talk to each other, as wildass impossible as that seemed, but they were no real danger to people. They preferred to munch on coal and shit out methane. The clean room was just in case she was wrong.

Which she was, Egan thought. But probably not about her bugs, just about the people she'd pissed off because of her work.

Henry's, the transplant bar and restaurant from New York's Upper West Side, housed in a ramshackle-looking plywood-sheathed structure covered with tar paper, was directly across from the R&D building. The tall narrow windows on either side of the door were lit up and as Daley parked in front Egan could hear the thump of loud music and the sounds of laughter even over the Hummer's engine noise with the windows rolled up.

"They're supposed to run the big experiment tomorrow or Monday," Daley said. "Everybody thinks that they're home free."

"Well, they're wrong," Egan said. "Is there a back door?"

"Just the fire door," Daley said. "But even if they got out they wouldn't get far." He nodded, the movement almost imperceptible.

One of Daley's key instructions was that sixty minutes prior to the takeover the fire doors and emergency exits from every building in the compound were to be jammed from the outside. He'd just indicated that the job had been done. It meant that he, too, had a good deal of respect for Cameron.

"Then let's rock and roll," Egan said.

52

I T WAS AT times like these that Bob Forester missed his wife the most. She had died when Ashley was young and afterwards he'd never had the inclination to make himself available to try again. Somehow the dating scene seemed superfluous with all that the military had given him to deal with. But now, alone in his home at Fort Mc-Nair on New Year's Eve, he suspected that he had made a terrible mistake. Not exactly a wasted life, but a lonely one.

The television in the family room was on ABC with the crowd in Times Square waiting for the ball to drop, the sound muted; he wasn't up for noise tonight. He sat on the couch, his feet propped up on the coffee table with a snifter of very good Armagnac Cames, the bottle on the lamp table beside him.

The Initiative had survived, by a bit of luck, a bit by the Rapid Response Team up from Ellsworth, and in a good measure by the efforts of Jim Cameron and Nate Osborne. More was coming their way, of course, especially after the experiment in the next few days when the president would make a formal announcement of what they'd accomplished.

OPEC would make some move, but they'd expected as much and the president had ordered more stockpiles of oil, and had been in negotiations with Canada and Mexico to increase their outputs if the Saudis cut back deliveries to the U.S. as the Venezuelans had already done.

There'd be more trouble of geopolitical nature from Russia and just about every other oil-exporting nation that would be dampened somewhat by the president's announcement that Dr. Lipton's discoveries, including the breakthrough quorum-sensing gadget, would be made available to any nation who wanted it.

But the main threat, as Forester understood it, would be from the oil hedge fund and derivative managers who would stand to lose billions. They would fight back with the only weapon at their disposal—money. In the top secret briefings he'd attended at the start more than six years ago, the president had warned them all that the Initiative could very well send this country into an economic tailspin that would be much worse than the meltdown over the housing mortgage market and truly rival the Great Depression.

"We'll have to do more than tighten our belts," the president had told them in the White House Situation Room.

His shirtsleeves had been rolled up to indicate that he was willing to dig in and get to work. And Forester remembered thinking at the time that it had been a bit of unnecessary theatrics. But it had worked. Everyone had at least figuratively rolled up their sleeves, and agreed that if the Initiative worked, if they could come up with a means of producing cheap, relatively green energy, sharply cutting the dependence on foreign oil, the risks would be well worth the rewards.

The television zoomed in on a dozen or more couples, the women in wedding dresses, the men in tuxedoes, apparently waiting to get married as the ball dropped, looking giddy, probably already half drunk, he thought. But happy, and it made him think of Ashley back with her sheriff in North Dakota. A good match, he thought. A strong man to backstop her, and a strong woman at his side to give life meaning. In that at least he was content. It was enough, and whatever else the Initiative brought he was proud that he'd had a hand in it.

He finished his drink and poured another, his third. For a moment he sat staring at the television set, but then put down his glass and speed-dialed Ashley's cell phone. He was being maudlin, he supposed, but he had the sudden urge to connect with her. Wish her a happy new year.

A mechanical voice advised that the person being called was temporarily unavailable.

Forester sat up, the first tingling of an alarm in his stomach, and speed-dialed again with the same result. Ashley almost never turned off her cell phone. She'd once explained that as a journalist she couldn't afford to be out of contact. Never. Or almost never.

He went back to his study, powered up his iPad, and found the phone number for the night duty center at the FBI's cybercrimes unit and called it. A night duty officer answered on the first ring with only the telephone number.

"This is General Bob Forester at ARPA-E, I need a little favor this evening."

"What can we do for you, sir?" the officer asked. Because of the Initiative, Forester's name had been put on a wilco list at a number of agencies in and around the metro area, including the Pentagon. If he asked for assistance it was to be given.

"I'm trying to reach a cell phone in the Medora, North Dakota, area without luck. Check the availability of service in the vicinity, would you?"

"Give me a minute."

Forester pulled up the number for the special operations unit at Ellsworth while he waited.

The officer came back on the line. "All the towers in a hundred-mile radius of that location seem to be in working order, sir. Except for the one at the Initiative installation. Are you declaring a possible incident?"

"Not yet, thanks for your help," Forester said. He phoned Ellsworth, and the number was answered immediately.

"Special ops night duty Sergeant Crowley. May I help you, sir?"

"This is General Bob Forester, I want you to check on something for me."

"Yes, sir."

"There may be a problem with the cell phone service at the Initiative. I couldn't reach a number when I tried a minute ago."

"Stand by, sir."

For just a moment Forester could not bring up an image of his daughter's face in his mind's eye, and it frightened him and he glanced at her framed graduation photograph on his desk.

Sergeant Crowley was back. "The cell phone tower up there is definitely down, but from what I'm seeing here, all the data links are streaming."

"What about the hotline to the main gate?"

"Checking, sir," Crowley said.

Forester could hear the sergeant talking to someone for a half minute or so, before he came back.

"I got through, sir, everything seems fine up there."

But it wasn't fine. Batttlefield instincts, he told himself. Trust your inner voice, trust your gut.

"Does anyone up there have a sat phone?"

"Yes, sir. I have four numbers listed."

"Call them," Forester said. He had Whitney's sat phone number but he wanted someone at Ellsworth to make the calls, to hers as well as the others.

This time it took a full minute, and when the sergeant came back he was fully engaged, crisp. "None of them are in service."

"I'm declaring a likely incident. Get your people alerted, and have Captain Nettles call me as soon as he's airborne. But make sure he understands from the get-go that if an attack is actually in progress, it wouldn't be the same smash-and-grab as before. This time it'll be more sophisticated and the incursion force will likely be better informed, trained, and equipped."

Forester headed upstairs to get into uniform as he phoned his own special operations night duty officer and ordered an aircraft to be prepped for him at Andrews and a chopper to pick him up at his home within twenty minutes.

Next he telephoned Edwin Rogers at his home, and the FBI director answered immediately.

"I thought that you would call. I just got the heads-up from my cybercrimes unit. Said you tried to reach your daughter but couldn't get through."

"Ellsworth confirms that the cell tower at the Initiative is out of service."

"Do you think that she's at the Initiative?"

"I think that it's a good possibility. Ellsworth special ops tried to reach Dr. Lipton via sat phone but couldn't get through, so I declared an emergency. They should be airborne in less than twenty minutes. I'm going out there myself tonight."

"I want you to listen to me, Bob, and make sure that you understand exactly what I'm telling you. We know that there is a leak somewhere, and we naturally assumed that it was inside either the project itself or somewhere in your staff."

The second part was news to Forester, though he wasn't surprised. "Who is it, do you know?"

"Not for sure, but our confidence was fairly high," Rogers said. "And it's even higher now."

"I don't understand," Forester said, his gut tight. "Who is it?"

"Your daughter."

53

DALEY AND EGAN came through the door, but no one noticed them at first. Music blasted from a stereo system, and most of the techs, scientists, power plant engineers, and wellhead roustabouts were on the dance floor, only a few drinking at the bar. Balloons decorated the ceiling, and a large railroad clock above the bar showed twenty minutes before midnight.

A young man in a T-shirt with white arctic camos and boots at the bar happened to glance over and when he spotted Egan's star, hastily put down his beer and saluted.

Egan walked up to him, as several others realized that something was going on and they stopped what they were doing.

"Why aren't you in your rack getting some sleep?" Egan demanded, returning the salute.

"Already got my z's, General. I'm not on duty again until oh eight hundred."

"Where is the twenty-four hundred guard? It lacks a quarter of an hour before he's due up."

"Right here, sir," another young man also in camos said, coming over. He snapped to attention and saluted.

"Sergeant Peterson said I could relieve him a few minutes late."

"Already been taken care of, son," Egan said. He pulled his Beretta and shot both men in the head at point-blank range, driving their bodies back against the bar before they collapsed on the floor.

Several of the women screamed, and one of the men shouted something, until Daley raised his M4A1 and fired a short burst into the ceiling. And except for the loud thump of the music everyone settled down.

"Turn it off!" Daley shouted.

The bartender turned off the stereo and raised her hands.

"No one else need get hurt here tonight," Egan said. "These two were combat personnel and would have caused us some trouble."

Whitney Lipton, who'd been on the dance floor, came across. "You've made a big mistake this time, Mr. Egan, but if you'll listen to reason you'll turn around and get the hell out of here before the Ellsworth special ops team arrives. I don't think they'll be in the mood this time to take prisoners."

Egan looked at her and smiled. He spoke into his lapel mike: "Post one, team lead, what's your situation?"

"Post one, clear," the squad leader at the Donna Marie gate responded.

"Post two, team lead."

"Just about to call you, team lead. We're at our fire positions."

"Did you run into any resistance?"

"Negative. The place is ours."

"Post three, team lead. Any company?"

"Negative," the guard they'd just placed at the main gate responded.

"I believe that we'll be staying until they do arrive," Egan told Whitney. "And the sooner the better."

"You've come to try to destroy us. What makes you so sure you won't fail again? You seem to be pretty good at it."

Egan's gorge rose. He wanted to kill the bitch here and now. Put a couple of rounds into her egghead skull. Maybe take her into a back room and rape her first. Maybe rape here right here on the dance floor, then shoot her. As early as grade school he used to have the same thoughts about most of his teachers, because they were the same sort of sanctimonious bitches for whom their religion—their God—was book learning that they tried to cram down your throat every chance they got.

But before he could get any of that out, Whitney had turned on Daley.

"I wondered about you. We all did."

"Yes, I know," Daley said. His voice had a slight southern accent—maybe Texas—and was insinuating. "So did the lieutenant commander. You shouldn't have waited so long to ask questions."

Egan holstered his pistol and unslung his M4 from his shoulder. "Dr. Lipton, I would like you and your people, including the power plant workers to sit down in the middle of the dance floor."

No one moved.

"Now, if you please," Egan said.

"We're not going to cooperate with you bastards," a rough-looking man in white coveralls said, breaking away from the girl he had been dancing with.

Egan figured the man for one of the power plant engineers, and he shot him, a three-round burst catching the man full in the chest, driving him backwards into several people, drenching them with blood.

Some of the women screamed wildly, but Whitney simply stepped back a pace, a horribly stricken look on her face.

"Goddamn you," she said, and she motioned for the others to sit down on one side of the small dance floor, as far away from the blood and gore as they could get.

A waitress stood petrified at the maitre d's station to the right of the dance floor, the six tables in the dining area set but empty, and Egan motioned for her to join the others who were beginning to settle down now that they realized what would happen if they refused to cooperate.

He turned to the bartender, who still had her hands in the air. "How many in the kitchen?"

"Three. Lin, he's the cook—"

"Get them out here, please, before I shoot someone else."

"They're gone out the back door by now," Whitney said, but she didn't sound as defiant as before.

"Now, please." Egan gestured to the bartender with his carbine. He had no beef with working stiffs.

The woman disappeared through a door at the end of the bar and came back with the three frightened kitchen crew almost immediately, and Egan motioned for them to come around the bar and join the others on the dance floor.

"Is there anyone else here in this building?" Egan asked.

No one answered, and he started to point his weapon at one of the techs, but Whitney spoke up.

"No, this is it," she said.

"How about at the R and D Center or the barracks? Anyone in the dining hall? A cook, maybe?"

"Everybody's here," Whitney said.

"You're lying, of course," Egan said, and he nodded to Daley. "Time to get this show on the road."

Daley went to the door and brought in the other four

contractors and their prisoner. When Cameron walked in, Whitney let out a little cry.

It was the reaction he was looking for. "So I was right after all," he said. "Love in the Badlands between the lady egghead and the macho SEAL."

Daley shoved Cameron onto the dance floor, where he slumped down heavily beside Whitney, and lowered his head. His scalp wound was still oozing blood and he looked as if he were nearly on the verge of collapsing.

Just as well, Egan thought, the egghead would be pre-occupied trying to help her lover, and would cause them less trouble. In the end when he killed the ex-SEAL she would do exactly what she was told to do.

"Team lead, post three," the guard at the main gate radioed.

"Post three, trouble?" Egan responded.

"Two people showed up, one of them is the county sheriff."

"Official business?"

"Negative, they say they've been invited to the party."

"Let me guess; the other one is a woman. Ashley Borden."

"Yes, sir."

Egan grinned. "Send them up."

54

THE GUARD IN white camos, an M4 carbine slung over his shoulder, barrel down, opened the main gate and waved them through. Osborne pulled forward and stopped, his window down. "Are they all up at the mess hall?"

"No, sir, I think they're probably at Henry's. Lieutenant Commander Cameron said for you guys to hustle on up, it's almost midnight."

Ashley leaned forward. "Is everyone partying tonight?" she asked.

"Yes, ma'am, except for me, of course," the guard said. "But you'd best hurry."

Osborne started up to the compound, watching the guard in the rearview mirror. The contractor remained at the side of the road watching them.

"Lieutenant Commander Cameron?" Ashley said. "So far as I know no one calls him that here."

"He's one of the new ones, I think," Osborne said. "Leastways I don't remember him from before."

Something was wrong, he could taste it on the air. When they'd shown up the guard had come out to talk to them, but he'd not gone back into the gatehouse to phone for authorization to let them in; instead he'd talked into a lapel mike. But no one here used field personnel communications units so far as Osborne had seen.

"What?" Ashley asked, sensing something of his sudden change in mood.

"I don't know," Osborne said.

"If it's another one of your battlefield hunches I wish you'd lighten up. You're starting to scare me."

There was no movement in the compound, but the guard said they were all inside Henry's waiting for midnight. To the south the red light and strobe atop the Donna Marie smokestack were operating as normal.

Nothing. And that, he suddenly realized, was the problem.

"No music," he said.

His window was still open, and Ashley cocked an ear to listen. "Maybe they're watching TV, waiting for the ball to drop."

Osborne glanced at his watch; it was less than a minute to midnight. He looked in his rearview mirror, and the guard was still standing at the side of the road. This was all wrong. "Somebody should be making noise," he said. "Party horns or something."

A pair of Hummers painted in desert camouflage were parked in front of Henry's across from the R&D building, but it wasn't until Osborne approached that he could see the army markings on the doors. Army, not air force. And he pulled out his handgun and slowed down to a crawl.

"Call your dad and have him alert Ellsworth. We have a problem here."

Ashley grabbed her cell phone out of her purse. "No signal bars."

Osborne drove past the Hummers. The club was

between them and the gate guard, but if someone was waiting for them inside they would be expecting him and Ashley to show up any moment now.

Reaching the far side of the club, he rounded the corner just far enough so that the rear of his SUV would not be visible to anyone coming out the front. They were opposite the mess hall, which was next to the R&D building about thirty yards away.

He got on his police radio. No one was at the office to listen for his call; at this hour everything was done by phone to 911, but some of the ranchers had police scanners and liked to listen in.

"This is Billings County Sheriff Nate Osborne. Anyone listening please call nine-one-one and report an emergency at the Initiative."

"You have another gun?" Ashley asked.

"Shotgun in the back. Do you know how to use it?"

"You kidding?" she said, and jumped out of the SUV and ran around to the back where she popped open the rear gate.

Osborne kept his eye on the rearview mirror, as he sent the same message again to anyone listening, though he didn't think it was very likely anyone would be at this exact moment. His watch showed just seconds to midnight. The countdown had begun and there should have been a lot of noise from inside.

Ashley was back with the twelve-gauge Ithaca 37 police shotgun in the short stock-pistol grip Stakeout configuration. "No noise yet," she said. She was a little breathless but steady. "How do you want to play this?"

"I don't want to start a gun battle that we'd lose."

"What about the doc and her people? Makes them hostages, unless they're already dead."

"Yeah, I know. It also means they've probably already

wired Donna Marie to blow, and the only way we can stop them is by letting Ellsworth know."

"But that's not going to happen with the guard on the gate. He's gotta be one of theirs, and any second now someone in Henry's is going to wonder what's keeping us and come looking."

"You're right, so we're going to plan B."

"Which is?"

"I'm going to slow them down long enough for you to get over to the R and D facility and find out if the landline and Internet connections have been cut, too. If not, call for backup."

"I'm not going to leave you here," Ashley protested.

"I need you to do this for me, Ash."

She wanted to argue, but she finally nodded. "Doesn't mean I'm always going to do everything you tell me to do."

They both got out of the car, and Osborne held her back as he made a quick check of the front entrance, but no one had come out yet. He hurried to the rear of the building and peeked around the corner toward the back door. But, as in the front, nothing was moving.

"Keep your ass down, I want a lot more afternoons like today's."

"Aye, aye, sir," Ashley said. She brushed a kiss on his cheek, then headed in a dead run across the open ground.

Osborne kept watch on the rear door until she reached the dining hall where she stopped long enough to wave before she disappeared around the corner. He had no idea how this could possibly turn out well, or if he'd ever see her again. But sending her away and watching her slip out of sight was possibly the worst feeling he'd ever had in his life.

"You missed the celebration," someone said from behind him.

55

THE CRACKER SHERIFF turned around and Egan got a kick out of the man's reaction. For just an instant Osborne was surprised; it showed on his face, in the tightening of his eyes. Whatever he'd expected, Egan as a brigadier general wasn't one of them.

"Help is on the way," Osborne said.

"Not yet, but soon," Egan replied. "You wouldn't have blundered through the gate otherwise." He looked beyond Osborne. "Where's your girlfriend?"

"Gone."

Egan shrugged. "That's okay, we'll find her and when we do she's dead."

"You won't have the time. And you've got bigger problems than her."

"I'm all ears."

"You'll be taken alive, of course. The Rapid Response Team guys have been given orders that they can take you down, shoot you in the kneecaps, but not kill you. They want you to stand trial. Big, public, messy, so that you can tell everyone what a Posse Comitatus hero you are. It's going to go down great on TV when they show what you looked like in drag. Like some fairy queen. You'll be a big hit at Leavenworth."

Egan's jaw tightened. "Take his gun," he said.

"I say we just shoot him," Larry Turner, one of Daley's men, said. He'd come around from the east side of the building, and he was the type who would have no second thoughts about shooting a man in the back. Even a war hero. "He's more trouble than he's worth."

"You're right, but his girlfriend is General Forester's daughter. And the sheriff here is the bait we're going to use to get her back."

"She's probably at the R and D building telling Ellsworth we're here."

"Saves us the trouble," Egan said impatiently. He was tired of explaining everything, especially to grunts like Turner. "Take his gun."

"Their orders to take Egan alive don't apply to the rest of you," Osborne said over his shoulder. "The project is worth more than your lives."

Turner came up behind him, and Osborne held out his pistol, which looked like a SIG to Egan. Nice weapon: fifteen-round magazine of 9mm Parabellum rounds, great staying power, reasonable stopping ability. A good weapon in the right hands.

He saw Turner's mistake the instant before Osborne swiveled on his peg leg, grabbed a handful of the contractor's white tunic, and pulled the man around as a shield.

Egan fired once, hitting Turner square in the chest, and ducked down behind the SUV as Osborne fired three times in rapid succession.

"You son of a bitch, you're going nowhere!" Egan screamed, his rage spiking.

He should have shot the bastard in the first place, and

knowing that he was wrong and Turner was right didn't help.

"Osborne, you bastard, do you hear me?"

Someone came around from the front of the club.

"Get down, the bastard's armed!" Egan shouted.

"He's gone, you dumb son of a bitch!" Daley shouted, racing past the SUV and skidding to a halt at the rear corner of the club.

Egan got cautiously to his feet as Daley took a look around the edge of the building. A rapid burst of M4 fire slammed into the side of the building, causing the contractor to duck back for just a moment before he shoved his carbine around the corner and fired most of the thirty rounds and ducked back to reload.

"Go after him!" Egan screamed.

"Yeah, right, chief," Daley said. He glanced down at Turner, then back up at Egan. "I don't even want to know how you fucked up here, but Osborne is armed with Larry's weapon, in addition to whatever piece he was carrying. And presumably the newspaper broad is with him."

"They're trying for the R and D building."

Daley ducked back around the corner, then shouldered his carbine and fired off five shots on single fire before he turned back again. He was pissed off. "I'd say he's going to make it, which means we're going to have some serious company sooner than we expected."

"We'll have to dig him out."

"Get your guys up from the power plant; let them try. At least they'll cover our rear."

"He's just one man, goddamnit."

"A Medal of Honor winner."

Egan started to raise his pistol, every muscle in his body screaming to put a round right in the middle of the cocksucker's forehead. Then see who the bastard gave orders to.

Daley just stood there, his M4 pointed in Egan's general direction, his trigger finger alongside the guard, the tip on the base of the magazine receiver.

But it wouldn't do. It was a tough old world, something that Daley just might find out for himself before the night was out. But not now.

Egan laughed, not sincere even in his own ears, and lowered the pistol. "You're right," he said. "We've got a lot of work ahead of us."

"I'll stick it out here for a little while to make sure he doesn't try to double back."

Egan holstered his pistol. "The cavalry will be here before too long, I suspect."

"Then you'd best get on their tactical frequency and make it clear what they need to do."

"And the consequences," Egan said.

"Yeah," Daley. "Those, too."

Egan started to turn away, but then on impulse looked back at the contractor. "Why did you take this job?"

"Money. Isn't it always the same?"

Egan nodded, and walked back around the corner to the front of the club, not at all sure why exactly he was here. "Post three, team lead," he spoke into his lapel mike. "We're going to have company pretty quick, so soon as you hear the choppers get your ass back up here."

"Copy that. What was the shooting?"

"Just someone getting a little out of line. Look sharp."

"Copy."

"Post one, team lead," Egan radioed his people at the rear gate. "You guys copy the last?"

"We're clear down here."

"Soon as you hear the choppers incoming, get your asses up here."

"Roger," the squad leader on the rear gate radioed.

It was quiet. The wind had died and the sky was perfectly clear except for the Milky Way, which out here was a broad band of illuminated fog clear from horizon to horizon. Made a man feel small sometimes, and he didn't think he could ever settle down out here, or understand a man like Osborne who could.

"Rodriguez, Egan, copy?"

"Yes."

"Switch to two," Egan said, and he reached inside his tunic and switched his comms unit to the alternate channel. Only he and Rodriguez had the spare channel, and it had been the Mexican's suggestion.

"I thought I heard gunfire." Rodriguez was there. "Does the center hold?"

The Mexican, according to the stories he'd told on the way up, had lived a rough life in some barrio, yet he was well read. The first time he'd used the "center hold" expression Egan had no idea what the man was talking about. But when Rodriguez had explained that it was from a famous poem by a guy called Yeats—"things fall apart, the center cannot hold"—Egan had understood perfectly well what the poet had meant. And when Rodriguez told him that the poem was called "The Second Coming," it had made even more sense.

"Oh, yeah," Egan said. "The center holds, my man. But we have one small problem that you need to deal with. Send a couple of men up to the R and D Center. The sheriff and his girlfriend are holed up there, probably talking to Ellsworth by now."

"Armed?"

"Yes. I'd like to include the woman in our package, but the sheriff is definitely expendable."

"I'm on it, *comp*," Rodriguez said, and signed off.

56

"HERE'S SOMETHING WRONG with him," Whitney told the nearest contractor who stood at the edge of the dance floor, his M4 pointed in their general direction. She slowly helped Cameron to his feet. Dried blood was caked on the side of his head and still more seeped from a scalp wound.

The contractor raised his carbine and the other two over by the bar looked over. All of them were nervous because of the shooting outside. It was the county sheriff and some broad who'd shown up unexpectedly.

"Get the fuck back down on the floor," one of them ordered.

Whitney took a step forward, Cameron, his head lolling on her shoulder, stumbling and nearly collapsing.

"Slowly," he mumbled into her ear. He could see the nearest contractor out of the corner of his eye. The timing was right, he just hoped that Nate and Ashley had made it, and he felt terrible that he had talked them into coming out here tonight, right in the middle of another mess.

"I said get the fuck back." The contractor came over, his carbine pointed directly at Whitney.

"The lieutenant commander is a personal friend of mine," Whitney said. "If he dies tonight because he gets no attention, you'll have to kill me, too, because I sure as hell won't cooperate with you."

Cameron was convinced that Whitney was the one person here who Egan could not afford to lose if he were to have any chance of getting out alive. They needed her as a hostage, and the Ellsworth Rapid Response Team had been given specific orders from day one that she was even more important than the bacteria and the gadget. Those could be replaced. As the Initiative's principal scientist she was just as vital to the project as Oppenheimer had been to the creation of the atomic bomb in New Mexico. Without him the Manhattan District might have been pushed back for years. And without Whitney the Initiative would be set back for nearly as long.

Time, General Forester had explained to them all after the first incident, they simply didn't have, because of the increasing pressure by OPEC and the big oil fund and derivative managers.

"This run-up has to work," he'd said. "We've just about bet the farm on it."

But what Cameron wanted to do with Whitney's help—disarm the explosive charges at Donna Marie—was the toughest decision of his life. Chances were that some good people were going to get killed because of him if things went wrong. But, he kept reminding himself, a lot of good people would probably die tonight if he did nothing.

The other hostages sitting on the floor were looking up at them. Cameron caught the eye of Susan Watts and she was startled and started to speak, but the door banged open and Egan walked in on a blast of arctic cold air.

"What the hell in Christ is going on?" he shouted, coming across the room.

"If you let him die, you'll have to kill me, too," Whitney said defiantly.

Egan came into Cameron's field of vision, and the man had a pistol in hand, a wild, crazy look in his eyes.

"I'll kill the both of you myself!" Egan screamed.

Cameron stiffened and was about to straighten up to put an end to what was likely to get them killed right now, but Whitney stuck out her chin.

"Well, go ahead, you stupid son of a bitch!" she shouted back. "And when Captain Nettles and his men show up who will you use as hostages? Each other?"

Cameron started to raise his head, but Whitney shifted her weight and took another half step toward Egan.

After a long moment, Egan lowered his pistol. "Well, what do you want?"

"There's a first aid kit in the women's room. I want to at least bandage his head to stop the bleeding. And I want to look at his eyes in some decent light to see if his pupils are the same size. He might have a concussion."

"I didn't bring a medic."

"No. I don't suppose you did. But if he is concussed I'll need to put bandages over his eyes and lay him down where we can keep him warm."

Egan turned away for a second and shook his head. "Well, don't just stand there, somebody help her," he said.

One of the contractors slung his M4 over his shoulder, muzzle down, and took one of Cameron's arms over his other shoulder and together he and Whitney headed to the corridor off the end of the bar and back to the restrooms.

Behind them Egan ordered one of his men to go out to the Hummer and power up the portable radio; he was going to talk to the Rapid Response Team and tell them what they were faced with and what they were going to do unless they wanted to be the cause of a bloodbath here.

"What was the shooting all about?" someone asked.

"The son of a bitch sheriff," Egan said. "But he's going to cease being a pain in my ass in about ten minutes."

The woman's room was at the far end of the dimly lit corridor, and in addition to the first aid kit—actually there was one in both bathrooms, one behind the bar, and another much larger kit in the kitchen—the electrical circuit breaker panel was there. A detail, Cameron hoped, that the contractors who'd been hired just after Christmas hadn't discovered. And thinking about them made him angry with himself just now. He'd known something wasn't right, and their being here definitely pointed to someone on Forester's staff, but he'd not raised any objections.

He'd been out of the field for too long, he thought bitterly. He'd lost his edge, and it was possible he would get them all killed tonight if Nettles didn't cooperate or made a mistake. He couldn't let that thought go.

Whitney opened the door and let the contractor go inside first, and then stepped away, exactly as she'd been told to do.

As soon as she was clear Cameron lurched into the contractor, as if his legs were giving way, tightening his grip around the man's shoulders. But then he straightened up, wrapped his left arm around the man's head, and twisted sharply. The contractor's neck popped with an audible sound, and Cameron lowered his convulsing body to the floor as Whitney came inside and softly closed the door.

The man was still alive, but slowly suffocating, his eyes bulging, his mouth open, and cheeks puffed out as he desperately gasped for air, and Whitney shrank back.

Cameron took the 9mm Beretta 92F from the man's hip holster, pocketed it, as well as two spare magazines of ammunition for the carbine and an extra one for the pistol, and then stripped the carbine from the contractor's shoulder.

He jumped up, yanked open the circuit breaker door, and showed Whitney the main switch that would cut off all electricity to the building once it was thrown.

"We're going to have about thirty seconds once the lights are out, so don't hesitate," Cameron said.

She nodded nervously.

Three toilet stalls faced three sinks and on the back wall was a narrow casement window, the same as in the men's room. He'd been counting on it, otherwise what they'd started would have been nothing more than an exercise in folly.

Unlatching the locking mechanism he eased the window up, cold air instantly filling the bathroom. He looked back and Whitney nodded.

Nothing moved outside, the night dark and perfectly still. They could have been the only people on the planet.

Cameron shoved the carbine out the window and lowered it to the ground where he let it fall away from the building so as to make as little noise as possible. He pulled himself up and eased his way through the narrow opening, his hips barely clearing until he was mostly outside, and he clumsily dropped headfirst to the snow-covered ground.

Grabbing the carbine, he swept left and right, but still nothing moved, so he went back to the window. Whitney was still at the circuit breaker.

"What the fuck is going on in there!" Egan bellowed from the bar.

"Now," Cameron whispered urgently.

Whitney threw the switch, plunging the entire building, including the outside lights, into darkness, and a second later she was at the window and Cameron helped her crawl through.

Someone shouted something from inside, and either

Susan or the bartender screamed. Whitney hesitated. She wanted to go back, but Cameron grabbed her arm and they started in a dead run across the thirty yards of open ground to the R&D building.

Halfway there someone from behind opened fire, one round catching Cameron high in his back on the left side, and he stumbled and went down.

"Jim!" Whitney shouted, dropping down next to him.

Incoming rounds from at least two shooters kicked up dirt and snow all around them as Cameron rolled over, brought his M4 to bear, and emptied a thirty-round magazine into the back of the building.

"Go!" he shouted, as he ejected the spent magazine and jacked in a second.

"Not without you!" she cried.

"Goddamnit," he said. He got to his feet as he fired another eight or ten rounds into the back of the building, keeping them about window level so there was little chance of hitting any of the hostages who were sitting on the floor.

He was sick to his stomach and light-headed, but their only chance was getting out of the open area between the buildings, which had become a killing ground.

He and Whitney, keeping low, zigzagged the rest of the way across the compound, when all of a sudden someone opened fire from somewhere just south of the R&D building.

57

PRESIDENT THOMPSON WAS dead-tired and just a little discouraged. He and his wife, Ruth, had choppered up to Camp David earlier in the day, their son Donald and his fiancée, Crissy, joining them just before dinner. It was the first time they'd met the girl, and they were impressed. She seemed to have a level head and it had been obvious from the first minute that she adored their son.

But watching the televised celebrations on Times Square and from elsewhere around the world, the new year no longer seemed as bright as it had just a month ago when Thompson had been briefed on the breakthrough progress Dr. Lipton and her people had made at the Initiative. He'd planned on addressing the nation on New Year's Day, expecting the final experiment in the actual coal seam to succeed as expected.

"Day one of our independence from foreign energy resources," he was going to assure the people.

The project had been just as big a financial gamble than even the Manhattan District—possibly bigger, considering the state of the world's economy.

But instead of the expected payoff they'd been delayed by two attacks on the project, had endured the bloodbaths in a small North Dakota town and at a dude ranch—that made no sense—and were facing yet another crisis over the likelihood that the Venezuelans were somehow involved.

Wars had been started for a lot less.

And now, sitting beside his wife on the couch in the main living area, he couldn't shake the sense of impending doom he'd been feeling for several days. The problem of depending on foreign oil had become a national security issue. *The New York Times* had run a long op-ed piece by General Ben Wojiak, who'd served a one-year stint as chairman of the Joint Chiefs under a previous president before he'd retired. And in the past eighteen months he'd become a chief critic of what he termed was the "do-nothing administration."

"The president and his advisers have become a flock of ostriches, their heads buried in the sand," he had written.

It was so damned unfair, and Thompson had wanted to brief Wojiak on the Initiative, until he'd been reminded by his chief of staff that the general had served as chairman of the Joint Chiefs for only one year because he'd had a history of not being able to keep his mouth shut.

"It's finally coming together," Bob Forester had reported one week ago, and Thompson wanted to believe him; wanted to believe that the breakthrough they'd all worked for so hard and for so long was actually just around the corner. "A matter of days now, not weeks," Forester had promised.

But a day later Ed Rogers had brought up the terrible suspicion that the project's leak was possibly the general's daughter. The Bureau's confidence was high and she was the subject of a very vigorous investigation.

"Has Bob been told?"

"I don't believe so, Mr. President, nor do I think it would be wise at this point to do so."

And that, too, had contributed to Thompson's funk, which he'd hoped to alleviate at least a little by having his family around him for a New Year's Eve celebration. The new year had always meant new beginnings to him. But not tonight. Not this year.

Carson McLean, his chief of the Camp David staff, came across from the kitchen and Thompson looked up, but could read nothing from the man's bland expression.

"There is a telephone call for you, Mr. President," he said.

"I'll take it here," Thompson said, reaching for the extension phone on the table.

"Might be better if you take it in your study, sir."

His wife and the kids were looking at him, so he smiled for their benefit. "Goes with the job," he said. "Be just a minute." He walked back to his study where he closed the door and picked up the call. Like telegrams years ago, calls like this in the middle of the night were never good.

"Mr. President, this is Bob Forester, it looks as if the Initiative has come under attack again."

"Goddamnit, what's going on?" Thompson said, sitting down, his temper boiling over. All he could think of was Chávez and the Venezuelan intelligence service.

"I tried to reach my daughter earlier this evening—she's out at Medora celebrating with Nate Osborne—but when I couldn't reach her in town I thought she and Osborne might have driven down to the Initiative. But her cell phone was not working there as well, so I checked with the Bureau's cybercrimes unit who told me that the only cell tower within one hundred miles of Medora that wasn't working was the one at the Initiative. I phoned Ellsworth and declared an incident."

The connection was noisy, as if Forester was in the middle of traffic at rush hour. "Where are you calling from?"

"I'm in the air, just took off from Andrews," Forester said.

"Are you sure we're under attack again?"

"Not one hundred percent, Mr. President, but I thought that it was worth sounding the alarm. Especially considering that my daughter is probably out there, and in light of what Ed Rogers told me this evening."

"Which was?"

"That my daughter is suspected of spying on the project and passing information to somebody—possibly Venezuelan intelligence."

"The Bureau is investigating everyone with even a remote connection, on my orders," Thompson said. "That includes Dr. Lipton and her entire staff, along with your staff. You, too, and your daughter."

Forester didn't respond.

"Has any contact been made with anyone inside the Initiative?" Thompson asked.

"Not to this point, Mr. President. But unless whoever's down there are on a suicide mission, they'll probably take hostages. So we need to be sure of what our response will be."

"I will not negotiate to save the experiment," Thompson said angrily. "We can always rebuild."

"How about to save my daughter's life?"

"Don't put that kind of a spin on this."

"How about Whitney Lipton's life? Would you make an exception for her?"

Of course he would. She was the exception. Everyone and everything else was expendable. But he didn't say it, and the silence stretched.

"Once we're past this latest business, you'll have my resignation on your desk."

"I won't accept it, Bob," Thompson said. "You've taken us this far, I won't let you walk away until we're over the finish line. As winners."

"That won't be up to you, Mr. President," Forester said, and the connection was broken.

Thompson held on for several beats, willing himself to calm down, but then telephoned his adviser on national security affairs. Fenniger answered on the third ring, the sounds of a party in the background.

"I'm calling an emergency meeting of the National Security Council for this morning, as soon as you can get everyone up and running," Thompson said.

Including the president and vice president, the council consisted of nineteen people, from the secretaries of State and Defense all the way to the directors of Homeland Security and CIA, and including the attorney general and even the ambassador to the UN.

"Yes, Mr. President. Are you talking about the Venezuelan situation?"

"I may have to order Operation Balboa after all."

"My God. Don't tell me that they've hit the Initiative again?"

"Could be in progress right now," the president said. "Shake a leg, Nick."

58

OSBORNE HAD HELD up at the corner of the R&D building long enough to make sure that no one was coming after them from Henry's. Inside now on the first floor, he'd taken the wrong direction down the corridor, ending up at a series of offices. He had wanted the control center, but he'd never been there before, so he didn't know where it was.

He turned around and raced the opposite way down the corridor, past stairs leading to the second floor, when some serious shooting started from across the compound, and as he reached another intersection, someone else started shooting from the south in the direction of Donna Marie. At least two guns, and he was torn between finding Ashley and getting her out of here before they got caught in an attack coming from two directions, and going out to meet whatever was coming their way.

But the shooting stopped as he pulled up short, and the sudden silence was ominous.

First he had to find Ashley and make sure that she'd made contact with Ellsworth, and then they could get the hell out of here and keep out of everyone's way until help arrived.

He turned as Ashley came from a door halfway down the corridor, the short-barrel Ithaca shotgun in her hands, up and ready to fire.

"You bastards!" she screamed, completely hyped-up, but determined, not frightened.

Osborne stepped back and raised a hand. "It's me!" he shouted.

She just stood there, the shotgun pointed down the corridor.

"Come down now," Osborne said. "It's me. Ease up."

She lowered the shotgun, her face contorted as if she were going to cry, but she laughed a short little bark. "Someone was shooting. I didn't know who."

Another burst of firing came from the south side of the compound, but closer this time.

Osborne hurried down the corridor to her. "Did you get through?" The windowless room she'd come out of was long and narrow, and filled with electronic equipment and four desks with computers. Several plasma screen monitors were mounted on the walls.

"I did," Ashley said. "I told them that we were under attack, and someone was shooting at us."

"Are they sending help?"

Ashley looked up at him, puzzlement on her face, and she shook her head. "I don't know."

"What are you talking about?"

Someone fired two rounds, this time from the east side of the building, and very close. Answering fire came again from the south.

Ashley was distracted, and she looked down the corridor toward the front entrance. "What's going on? Who's shooting?"

Osborne grabbed her shoulder and turned her back. "Is help coming? Did they say that they understood?"

"I don't know," Ashley said. "I told them what was happening, and they wanted to know who I was and when I told them the connection was shut down. It made no sense."

It made no sense to Osborne, either, but the people at Ellsworth knew that something was going on up here. At the very least they would have to send someone up to take a look.

Whitney and Ashley would make perfect hostages, but this attack wasn't about money, it was about the same thing as the first—the destruction of Donna Marie—and hostages would only serve to give Egan and his people time to set the charges and then get out.

He figured that Whitney had already been taken and was likely down at Henry's with the others. Which left Ashley and Donna Marie.

What sounded like someone coming through a window on the north side of the building was followed by more gunfire along the front. They'd just about run out of options.

Ashley stepped back, a determined look on her face. "What do you want to do?"

Osborne winked at her. "Attack. It's the only thing we can do."

She glanced down the corridor toward where they'd heard the window breaking. "Whatever it is, big guy, I suggest we do it now."

"Right," Osborne said, and he hustled her back down to the corridor to the stairs he'd passed just a minute ago, and headed up, making as little noise as possible.

At the top they ducked around the corner and held up, Osborne's every sense listening for the sound of someone coming up the stairs after them. But if anyone was down there they were being stealthy now.

"They know we're in the building," Ashley said, close to his ear. "When they find out we're not downstairs, they'll be coming up here. Won't be long."

"Just long enough for us to get out of here," Osborne told her, and he led her down the corridor to the south end of the building where he tried three doors on the west side before he found one that was unlocked and led into a conference room with a long table around which were ten chairs and a large window that looked out across an open snow-covered field.

Slinging the M4 over his shoulder, Osborne started to drag the heavy table over to the door and Ashley helped him.

"Won't take them very long to figure this out, either," she said.

"Are you afraid of heights?" Osborne asked. He went to the window and looked out, watching for someone below, or at the corners of the building, waiting to cut off an escape from this direction. But if anyone was down there they were out of sight. In any event it was the only way out now.

"Less afraid of heights than bullets. Might there be a reception committee down there?"

"Could be. But I'm hoping they're busy downstairs looking for us."

A short burst of gunfire was immediately followed by another, and using the butt of the carbine, Osborne knocked out the window glass, and ran the barrel around the frame to make sure all the shards were gone.

Still nothing moved below, but it was very cold and just as dark. The only lights were a couple thousand yards to the south on the Donna Marie generating hall and the smokestack.

Someone shouted something on the first floor from what sounded like the foot of the stairs.

"Looks clear for now," Osborne said.

He took the shotgun from Ashley and laid it on the floor, then picked her up and eased her feetfirst out of the window. It was about a fifteen-foot drop into a bank of snow piled up against the base of the building.

"Ready?" he asked, holding her at arm's length.

"Right," she replied, and he let go.

She landed soft, and immediately rolled over away from the building, keeping as low a profile as she could. But after a moment, she looked up and waved for him.

He dropped the shotgun and then the carbine, both of them butt first into the snow, and as soon as Ashley had recovered them he levered himself out the window, a task made very difficult because of his titanium leg, and dropped to the ground. He hit hard, a sharp, nearly impossible pain hammering his stump, nearly dislocating his hip, and slamming all the way up his spine to the base of his neck as he lost his balance and fell over.

For just a few seconds his wind was gone and struggling to get up he almost lost his balance again, but Ashley was right there at his side.

Someone fired two short bursts from inside the building, somewhere upstairs, maybe in the corridor.

"Move your ass, soldier," Ashley said in his ear. "We've got incoming."

With her help Osborne managed to get to his feet, where he swayed unsteadily for several seconds before he took a step forward, nearly pitching to the ground. His leg was bent, or at least the socket and the tip of his stump had been damaged in the awkward landing.

"Can you make it?" Ashley asked. She was deeply concerned, worry all over her face.

"Piece of cake now that I've got my balance," Osborne said, taking the carbine, and hobbling straight west into the darkness, Ashley right beside him.

"Do you want to try for your car and get the hell out of here?" she asked.

"Nope," Osborne said through the pain. "We're going down to Donna Marie."

"What?"

"Egan's people mean to destroy the place, so we're going to stop them."

Ashley had to laugh, but the sound was without much humor. "Oh, I thought maybe you had something difficult in mind."

59

A T THE BAR, his back to the hostages sitting on the dance floor, Egan keyed the portable radio tuned to the Air Force Rapid Response Team's tactical frequency. "Ellsworth Rapid Response, this is the Initiative. Copy?"

No one responded. The six-foot fiberglass whip antenna was fully extended, nothing in the building would interfere with the signal and the radio was powerful enough to reach anyone in the air out to a range of at least fifty miles. If they were incoming, which he expected they were, they were hearing him.

"Ellsworth Rapid Response, this is Barry Egan at the South Dakota Initiative. I've taken over here, and unless you want me to start killing personnel, respond."

"Copy," the radio blared. They were close. "What is your situation?"

"I expect you already know what our situation is. Who am I speaking to?"

"I repeat, what is your situation?"

Besides a couple of little hiccups in the plan, Egan was enjoying himself. This was the big score he'd been looking for all of his life; not just in terms of money, though he'd been promised twenty-five million in cash, but in terms of status, prestige. No matter the outcome here, he would forever be known as a player, a serious contender.

"Identify yourself," Egan said.

The radio remained silent.

"As you wish," Egan muttered. He turned and motioned for one of the contractors to bring over a hostage. This one a young, frightened woman. Egan keyed the microphone and held it out to her. "Tell them your name, sweetheart," he said.

"Watts," the girl said. "I'm Susan Watts. Please help us."

Keeping the mike keyed, Egan pulled out his pistol and shot the girl in the head, driving her backwards off her feet. He held the mike up so that whoever was listening could hear the hostages' screams and shouts.

"Dump her body outside," Egan told a contractor, and he turned back to the mike. "That's one," he said. "Who am I talking to?"

"Captain Glenn Nettles, United States Air Force Rapid Response Team Alpha. There was no need to kill that girl."

"Unfortunately I knew of no other way to motivate you into cooperating with me, Nettles. And believe me, cooperate this night you will. What is your present position and strength?"

The radio was silent.

"I have plenty of hostages here, other than Dr. Lipton and Ashley Borden, who I'm ready to kill."

"We're forty klicks out directly to your south. Two MH-60 Black Hawks in the lead with six operators plus crew including two gunners in each."

"That it?"

"We have two squads of ground troops en route," Nettles radioed, obviously pissed off. "Means you walk out of there now, or we'll take you out in body bags."

Egan keyed the mike. "Bring me another fucking hostage," he said, and he released the push-to-talk button. All high drama, he thought. Theater. And he loved it.

"No, wait!" Nettles shouted.

One of the contractors was starting to pull a hostage to his feet, but Egan waved him off. He keyed the mike. "That's better."

"What do you want?"

"I think that you or the people who cut your orders know. But this is what you're going to do for us, Captain. And there will be no arguments, no bargaining, no delays. As I said I have plenty of hostages here. Are you ready to copy?"

"Roger."

"Good man. I do not want you or your people in the air or on the ground closer than ten miles from the south gate. So when you reach that point you will touch down. Failure to do so will result in more deaths. Copy?"

"Roger," Nettles said. "Let me talk to Dr. Lipton."

"Later."

"Now!" Nettles shouted.

Egan was about to key his mike, but Nettles beat him to it.

"Wait. We'll be setting down in about twelve minutes."

Egan waited to answer. In the opening moves it was always a good idea to let the other bastard sweat a little.

"You copy that?" Nettles came back.

"Roger. Are you recording my voice?"

"Yes."

"Good, then there's no need for you to write anything down. More accurate that way. Soon as you land, call again and I'll tell you what will come next."

"I need to talk to Dr. Lipton."

"Indeed you will, in due time," Egan said. He laid the mike on the bar counter and got off the stool. "Nobody touches the radio, no matter what the bastard has to say."

The contractors all nodded, and Egan went outside where he keyed his lapel mike.

"Post one, team lead, are you in your fallback position?"

"We're on our way," the squad leader said. The four of them would wait just inside the generating hall, where they had a good firing angle on the rear gate, and yet could protect the explosive charges until the choppers that would take them to the Dickinson airport arrived.

"Post two, team lead."

"We're on our way to you, but there's been a fair amount of gunfire from the R and D building," the squad leader said. "Do you want us to reinforce?"

"Stand by," Egan said. "Rodriguez, copy?"

"Yes," Rodriguez came back immediately.

"Switch to two," Egan said and switched. "Copy?"

"Sí," Rodriguez replied and switched to the secondary channel.

"I'm talking to the Air Force. They've agreed to stand off for now, as we knew they would."

"How many hostages did it take to convince them?"

"Only one, just as you predicted would happen. But they want to talk to Lipton."

"Let them."

"She and the lieutenant commander managed to get out and head up to the R and D center. You need to take charge and get her and the Borden woman back here ASAP. I've got my hands full."

"I'm not going to ask how you allowed that to happen," Rodriguez came back sharply. "But I'm on it."

Egan was going to call the man on his tone, but he

thought better of it. "Thanks," he said, and he switched back to channel one. "Post two, team lead. Rodriguez will be taking charge for the moment. Copy?"

"Copy," the squad leader said, and Egan was sure that he heard the son of a bitch snicker. His time would come, too.

Egan stalked back into the club, where he went behind the bar, grabbed a bottle of whisky, took a deep draft, and tossed it away. The contractors watched him but said nothing.

Nettles came back. "Egan, this is Nettles, we're down."

Egan grabbed the mike. "No screwing around now, Captain. You're going to have a Gulfstream or some other business jet capable of carrying twenty people to Colombia brought to the airport at Dickinson. Only the flight crew will be aboard. No weapons. Is that understood?"

"Yes."

"Also aboard will be five million dollars in gold at the current rate of—let's call it two thousand dollars per ounce."

"That may take some time," Nettles said.

"You have ten hours, nonnegotiable," Egan said. "Dr. Lipton and General Forester's daughter, Ms. Borden, will be coming with us aboard a Chinook CH-47 or some variant, which will set down in front of Donna Marie within that time period. No one but the unarmed crew will be aboard. Noncompliance will result first in Ms. Borden's death, and then if we find ourselves cornered, Dr. Lipton will die."

"Why?" Nettles asked, his tone a little more respectful.

By then Egan figured the captain finally understood that he was dealing with a professional. "Money, of course. And, one more thing for you to consider. We have planted explosives inside the power plant, in the control room, at the turbine, at the wellhead and furnace. All of them remotely controlled. Believe me, if I'm forced into it, I will not hesitate to push the button."

"I'll relay your demands," Nettles said.

Egan laid down the mike. "I'm hungry," he said. "Are you all hungry?" he asked everyone, including the hostages.

No one answered.

"Well good, then," he said. "Cooks, let's beat feet and rustle up some grub."

60

CAMERON AND WHITNEY made it to the second-floor corridor in the R&D building just steps in front of whoever had blown the hinges off the front door. Holding up just around the corner, Whitney half propping him up, Cameron held his breath and listened for someone on the stairs.

Two men, he thought. Maybe three, directly below at the foot of the stairs. One of them said something that Cameron couldn't make out, and he eased Whitney silently back a half step and raised the M4 carbine.

Right now a couple of flash-bang grenades would have come in handy, he thought. But so then would a Squad Automatic Weapon, maybe the M249 with a burst firing rate in excess of seven hundred rounds per minute.

Whitney started to whisper something, but Cameron put a finger to his lips and shook his head. He pointed toward the stairs and raised two and then three fingers. She was wide-eyed and out of breath, but she nodded that she understood.

He felt like hell, still light-headed from the blow to his

head and the loss of blood from the wound in his back. But he was in no real pain, and Whitney had staunched most of the blood by wadding up her scarf and stuffing it under his shirt. But he no longer had his legs and most of his stamina was gone.

The man in the hall said something else, and cocking his head Cameron was certain he heard them walk in opposite directions down the corridor—*away* from the stairs. They were going to search the entire building room by room, starting with the ground floor.

A few moments later a door crashed open downstairs, and Cameron backed up. "Your office," he whispered. "The computer connection might still be up."

They turned and headed down the corridor careful to make absolutely no noise, Cameron in the lead. But he pulled up short at the door to the conference room and again held a finger to his lips.

A lot of cold air was coming from under the door. A window was open. He put his ear to the door but so far as he could tell nothing moved from within. No sounds. Nothing but the intense cold.

He cautiously tried to open the door but it moved less than a quarter of an inch. It wasn't locked, but something heavy was jammed against it.

Osborne, the thought crystallized. He and Ashley had shown up for the party, but something had spooked them and they had taken off. It's what the shooting back at Henry's had been all about. They'd made it this far, and probably cornered, Nate had blocked the conference-room door, probably with a table, broken out a window, and he and Ashley had made their escape.

To Donna Marie to try to disarm the explosives. The magnificent son of a bitch hadn't tried to run, tried to get lost out in the hills until the Rapid Response Team showed up. Instead he and Ashley had taken the fight to Egan and the contractors.

Something crashed downstairs, sounding like a lot of breaking glass. "They're in the control room," Whitney whispered. "We don't have a lot of time."

"You're right," Cameron agreed, and the two of them went next door to Whitney's office where she powered up her computer, while he closed and locked the corridor door, and opened the connecting door to the conference room.

The big table was jammed against the door as he thought it might be, and the arctic cold air came through the window that Osborne had broken out. He went across and looked outside, but so far as he could see nothing moved in the darkness. Egan's people were overconfident, he thought, sloppy.

"I'm in," Whitney said excitedly.

Cameron came back to her office. "Get the duty officer, tell them what's going on," he said.

She pulled up the Rapid Response Team's duty officer down at Ellsworth. A second later the camera light came on, and the image of the OD came on-screen.

"I'm Dr. Lipton, do you recognize me?" Whitney said, keeping her voice low.

The sergeant was startled. "Holy shit. I mean yes, ma'am. Are you in a secure location?"

"No," Cameron said over her shoulder. "We're in the R and D building, but we're going to have to get out of here within the next minute or two. Is the team on its way?"

"Yes, sir. Captain Nettles and two Black Hawks were in the air, but they're in contact with the incursion force, and were ordered to land ten miles out. They're on the ground right now."

"Can you patch us over to them?"

"Yes, sir. Stand by."

A full half minute later Captain Nettles's image came up on the screen, and when he realized who he was looking at on his monitor he pursed his lips. "What's your situation?" he demanded.

"We're in the R and D Center but we're going to have to get out of here in about two mikes," Cameron said. "As you can see Dr. Lipton and I are not under the incursion force's control. Neither are Nate Osborne and Ashley Borden."

"Never mind about Borden, but I want you to keep your heads down, we're getting airborne right now. Whatever you do make damned sure that Dr. Lipton is not recaptured. You copy?"

"What do you mean, never mind about Borden?" Cameron demanded.

"It's not important. Just find a secure place and hang on. We'll be on top of you within about nine minutes."

"I asked you a question, Captain."

"The general's daughter has been identified as the probable leak."

"Bullshit," Cameron said. "And I'd bet my life on it."

"If you get in her way you just might lose."

"I think that she and Osborne are on their way down to Donna Marie to find and disarm the explosives. And we're going to help out."

"Goddamnit, listen to me, Jim, Dr. Lipton is your only consideration."

Someone came pounding up the stairs.

"We'll be at the power station, and we'll certainly have company, so mind what you shoot at," Cameron said.

He hit the escape button, and he and Whitney slipped into the conference room and closed the door. Whoever had come up the stairs had started down the corridor in the opposite direction.

"We're going out the window," he whispered to her. "And I can stash you in the crawl space under the building."

"My facility, my experiment, and no one's going to screw with it if I can help," Whitney said. "I'm coming with you."

Cameron helped her out the window feetfirst, and held her dangling at arm's length until she let go and dropped to the ground.

He waited and watched for several beats, sweeping the carbine left to right ready to take down anything that moved. But it didn't happen.

Dropping the M4 to Whitney below, he levered himself out the window and as he dropped to the trampled snowbank someone started hammering on the conference-room door.

61

TRYING TO MAKE as little noise as possible climbing the outside stairs on the west side of the generating hall, Osborne's left knee slipped in its titanium socket and he went down hard, blinding pain shooting up to his hip, slamming into his back.

He lost his grip on the carbine, but before it clattered away Ashley managed to grab it. Her face was marble white with the extreme cold, and her expression was tight-lipped and grim, but determined.

Using the railing he pulled himself up, and managed to grin. "Nice catch, Ash."

"You okay?"

He glanced over his shoulder toward the south gate. Nothing moved. "Good to go," he said. "Except my left foot itches like crazy."

A short burst of gunfire came from the general direction of the R&D Center, and Osborne immediately thought of the hostages they'd left behind. They were being murdered and he was suddenly very afraid that he and Ashley were not going to be in time to avert a major tragedy.

"It's not Whitney," Ashley said as if reading his thoughts. "They're dead without her."

"Let's hope you're right," Osborne said, though he had his doubts. Egan was a nutcase and there was no telling how he would react if cornered.

Putting his pain aside he managed to climb the rest of the stairs, Ashley right behind him with the Ithaca, and at the top he eased the heavy metal door open just a crack and looked inside. The short corridor that went past the control room to the right and the room with the electronic repeaters to the left was empty. No guard. Twenty feet ahead the corridor opened to a narrow balcony from which the inside stairs led down to the generating hall fifty feet below.

The noise from the turbine being electrically rotated to make sure the bearings remained lubricated and the shaft didn't sag grated on the nerves; loud enough to mask other sounds and high enough pitched to make Osborne's back teeth tingle.

They slipped inside, crossed to the control room that was also unguarded, and Osborne went immediately to the big plate glass windows, keeping to one side so he couldn't be spotted from the floor.

From this angle he couldn't see any of Egan's people, nor at first could he spot anything out of order. But they were down here, or had been, he was certain of it.

"Here," Ashley said, at the same moment he spotted something that looked like a bundle of small packages all wrapped in olive drab paper or plastic. Semtex. They had set the place to blow, just like they had the first time. Only he couldn't spot any wires trailing across the floor like before.

He turned, and went to where she was hunched over one of the control desks. "What do you have?" he asked.

She pulled a brick of plastic explosive about the size of a carton of cigarettes from the underside of the desk, and laid it beside a small plastic box from which a pair of wires were attached to a fuse that she eased out of the explosive. "It's a remote-controlled detonator, I think," she said, looking up. "Keyed either by a radio transmitter, or maybe a cell phone or sat phone from just about any distance."

"I don't see an antenna."

"Probably inside the box. But it's small."

"The cell phone tower here has been shut down, so this would have to be triggered at short range, somewhere inside the compound."

"Either that or by a transmitter of some kind, even a sat phone," Ashley said. "But I'm not an electrical engineer, so I'm not sure."

Osborne glanced back at the windows. He shook his head. "We'll have to find as many of them as we can and pull the wires."

Ashley looked at the windows. "Did you see anyone down there?"

"No, but that doesn't mean a thing. We're on the loose and they'll have to suspect this is where we'll come." He straightened up, but then another thought struck him.

He laid the carbine aside, and pulling out his pen-knife opened the small screwdriver blade and quickly undid the four screws holding the top plate on the detonator box.

"What?" Ashley asked.

Inside was a small circuit board to which were attached a number of components, one of them a computer chip, a nine volt battery, and another long narrow circuit board on which was etched a series of X patterns in gold.

Osborne pulled it out of the detonator box, ripping the single wire from the larger board. "This is no radio or sat phone antenna, too small. Unless I miss my guess it's meant to get a signal from right here inside Donna Marie."

"They're not going to stay here, it'd be suicide," Ashley protested.

"They've planted a booster antenna somewhere. They'll take Whitney as a hostage and once they're on their way they'll send a signal, which the booster antenna will pick up and relay to all the detonators."

"But why take the chance that once they're out of here Nettles's people will find the explosives and disarm them?"

Osborne stared at the circuit board. He was no electronics engineer, either, but he'd seen a lot of this sort of stuff—most of it cruder—in Afghanistan. The Taliban fighters, along with their brothers in Iraq, had practically written the book on IEDs. If something could explode they could figure out a way to make it happen at just the right moment and under any kind of circumstance.

And they knew about booby traps.

"There's some kind of a timer in the circuit," he said. "Maybe once the trigger signal is sent the countdown clock starts. Gives them enough time to get out."

Ashley was shaking her head. "Once this place goes up they'd be left with only Whitney to guarantee their safe passage to wherever they're planning to run."

"It's enough—"

"No," Ashley said. "They want to bring this place down. Maybe there's a timer here, but I think that once the trigger signal is sent these fuses will be switched into some active mode. As soon as someone tampers with one of them, they'll all blow." She looked up. "That's the way I'd do it."

"We need to find the booster antenna."

"On the roof," Ashley said.

"No," Osborne told her, and he knew for certain exactly

where the booster antenna would be and how and when it got there.

The plate glass windows shattered under a sustained round of automatic weapons fire, and Osborne dragged Ashley to the floor as bullets slammed into the opposite wall and glass flew everywhere.

62

EGAN STOOD AT the bar, snapping his carbine's safety switch on and off, the hamburger and fries the cook had sent untouched, a sour dry taste at the back of his throat. He should have killed Cameron on the spot down at Donna Marie when he had the chance. And he should have ordered the sheriff and his girlfriend eliminated at the front gate, instead of letting them come up here.

Should've beens, could've beens, would've beens . . . He'd heard that kind of shit most of his life and especially in the service when he'd been trained to become a non-commissioned officer: indecisiveness will jump up and bite you in the ass. Make a decision—the right decision—and stick with it.

"Barry, Alessandro, switch to two," Rodriguez radioed, and Egan could hear tension in the man's voice.

He looked at Daley and the other contractors who were eating what had been sent out from the kitchen, and just then the bartender and one of the kitchen workers brought out a couple of platters of sandwiches and chips and bottled water that they distributed to the hostages.

Everyone was watching him, waiting for him to do

something. There'd already been a lot more shooting than he'd planned for and at this point neither Dr. Lipton nor Forester's daughter had been captured.

The center wasn't going to hold for much longer and he was almost afraid to hear what Alessandro was going to tell him.

"On two." He spoke into his lapel mike and walked to the door.

"We're concentrating on Donna Marie. You need to move your ass and get everyone down here now."

"What the hell are you talking about? Have you got either of the broads?"

"Not yet, but I think they're somewhere in the generating hall."

"They were at the R and D Center," Egan shouted. "You let them escape?"

"Bring the radio, we're going to have to make our stand down here."

"I don't believe this."

"There's been shooting inside the building," Rodriguez radioed. "I'm on the north side just below the smokestack. I'll coordinate from inside. But, Barry, you're running out of time. Get down here with the radio and the hostages. It's our only chance."

"What—?" Egan shouted, but then he heard the helicopters from a long distance to the south, and he suddenly realized what Rodriguez was talking about. The bastards had reneged on their promise.

Everyone in Henry's was hearing the choppers, too.

"You stupid son of a bitch, you've gotten us all killed!" Daley shouted. And everyone else was clamoring at him.

"Not yet!" Egan shouted him and the others down. "Load as many of these people into the Hummers as you can, we're heading down to the power station."

"What the hell good is that going to do us?" Daley demanded. "We need Lipton, or at least the general's daughter."

"This is who we have, so saddle up," Egan ordered, and he looked at the civilians. Fear was a good thing. "If any of them resist, shoot them."

"You heard the man!" Daley screamed at what was left of the Initiative crew and he and the other contractors began hustling them to their feet and herding them out the door. "What about the cooks?"

"Leave them," Egan said. He keyed his lapel mike. "Rodriguez, we're moving out in five."

"Make it three," Rodriguez replied, a lot of machinery noise in the background.

"Will do," Egan said. He went back to the bar, grabbed the portable radio which was about the size of a six-pack of beer, and hustled to the door with the last of the hostages, leaving three of them plus the kitchen staff behind.

Just before he went out he turned back to the others; all of them were totally subdued, and he had the almost overwhelming urge to shoot them all. And they could see it, because two of them raised their hands as if they were trying to ward off the expected bullets. But he felt charitable all of a sudden, and he grinned.

"Your best bet is to stay right here and keep your heads down. Anyone who pokes his head out the door will get it shot off. *Capisce?*"

No one answered, but it didn't matter.

Outside, the choppers were not yet visible, but they were close. All the hostages were loaded in the two Hummers, and Egan climbed in the shotgun seat, Daley driving, and they took off toward Donna Marie.

He keyed the radio. "Nettles, this is Egan at the Initiative, copy?"

The radio was silent.

"I can't see them," Egan said.

Daley rolled down the window. "They're just about on top of us, but they're running without lights," he said. "You'd better do something right now."

Egan keyed the radio again. "Nettles, this is Egan, you'd best listen up unless you want to get a lot more people killed."

A spotlight sharply illuminated them, making it all but impossible for Daley to see the gravel road, and he had to skid to a stop.

"Exit the two vehicles with your hands over your head," Nettles radioed.

"We have hostages with us," Egan said. "Turn off the goddamn light and back off, or I *will* kill one of them."

Keeping the push-to-talk switch depressed, he held the mike over his shoulder toward the rear seats.

"Do as he says!" one of the technicians shouted. "The bastard means it."

The spotlight went out, and Daley headed south again.

"You have to know that you're not going anywhere," Nettles radioed.

"Just to Donna Marie where we're going to wait with the hostages for our Chinook," Egan said. "And for everyone's sake I hope that you've relayed our demands to someone with more authority than you have."

"Let me talk to Dr. Lipton."

Egan laughed. "You know damned well that we don't have her or Ms. Borden with us at the moment. But I can tell you that they've been herded to the power station and it'll just be a matter of time—a very short time—before we kill Lieutenant Commander Cameron and Sheriff Osborne and capture one or both of the women alive."

They came to the inner security fence, but Daley drove

right through it, never slowing down, the gate slamming off its hinges, the second Hummer driving over it.

Nettles did not reply.

"All this is about money," Egan said. "It would be too bad for those women to die and for us to blow the power station straight to hell. But listen to me, you son of a bitch, if we're cornered here, if we end up having no way out, I'll personally shoot the bitches and push the detonator button myself."

"I'll pass it on to General Forester. He'll want to talk to you on this frequency, so keep it open."

"Indeed I will, Captain," Egan said, and he brayed.

63

J IM CAMERON LAY prone on the concrete floor just
inside the control-room corridor, Whitney right beside him. They'd been harried for the last hundred yards
from the R&D building, but for some reason the firing
had stopped as they approached the generating hall and
clambered up the stairs.

A couple of minutes ago shots had been fired from
downstairs into the control room; they'd heard the shat-
tering glass, but then it had abruptly stopped and there
were no other sounds except for the constant whine of the
turbine.

The outside door they'd come through was open a couple of inches but so far as he could see nothing moved,
nor was anyone on the way up the stairs.

"Do you see anything?" Whitney asked.

To this point Jim Cameron had always thought that
he'd had a fairly easy life. Never any problems in high
school because of his low-key laid-back attitude. None in
college where he'd studied criminal justice, and not even
in SEAL training—that he'd actually found stimulating.
But he'd been a loner for the most part. Except for his fire

team, he'd never had to take responsibility for anyone else. Until now.

He looked over his shoulder. Whitney was frightened, but determined. "Nothing," he said.

"I don't understand. Why'd they stop shooting at us?"

"Probably because we ended up exactly where they want us," Cameron said. He glanced over to the control-room door. "Be my guess that Nate and Ashley made it this far, too, and Egan's people are just going to hold all of us right here. No way out through the generating hall, and no way back down the stairs."

"They wanted us as hostages, and now they have us. So what are we going to do?"

"First of all find out if I'm right about Nate and Ashley," Cameron said. He eased back from the door, an intense pain shooting down his left side and he grunted involuntarily.

Whitney reached out and tried to help him crawl back, and her hand came away covered with blood. "My God."

"There's a first aid kit in the control room," Cameron said when his head cleared. For a moment he was swimming in glue. "Watch the stairs. Anything moves, shoot it."

Whitney had the pistol he'd taken away from the contractor. "Okay, but I've never shot a gun in my life."

"Just point it in the general direction of whoever you see and start pulling the trigger. It'll kick a little, but don't stop until you run out of bullets."

She nodded uncertainly, but took her place at the door.

Cameron got to his feet and held a hand against the wall to steady himself for just a moment before he lurched down the corridor to the narrow balcony that opened to the generating hall and cautiously peered around the corner, making himself as small a target as possible.

Nothing moved below, and he turned and lurched back

to the control room where he put his ear to the door, but he couldn't hear a thing over the distant turbine whine.

Stepping aside out of the line of fire in case he was wrong, he knocked softly with the muzzle of the carbine. "Nate?"

He looked over at Whitney, who glanced over her shoulder at him and then turned back to watching outside.

"Nate," he called again when the door suddenly opened and the muzzle of a SIG-Sauer was jammed into his face before he had a chance to react, his reflexes shot because of his loss of blood.

"Jim," Osborne said, withdrawing the pistol and opening the door the rest of the way. "Dr. Lipton with you?"

"By the outside door, watching my back," Cameron said.

Osborne stepped out and Whitney looked over her shoulder. "Anyone behind you?" he asked.

"At first, but they backed off when we made it this far. I think they're herding us."

"They know we're up here, too, and they want to keep it that way, but we've got another, bigger problem," Osborne said. "Both of you'd better get in here, but keep low."

Whitney came down the corridor to the control room. "We need the first aid kit, Jim's been shot," she said, and keeping low and away from the shattered window went to a niche in the wall marked with a Red Cross and pulled out the big first aid kit next to which was a portable defibrillator.

Ashley rose from where she'd been crouched behind an overturned desk. "We heard shooting."

"I'm okay, but Jim was hit."

Cameron took one of the chairs from behind a desk and rolled it out into the corridor to the door, where he tipped it up on its side and propped it under the handle. If someone opened the door the chair would fall forward, making enough noise to give them an early warning that they were being attacked from the rear.

When he came back Whitney made him take off his blood-soaked jacket and shirt, pulled her scarf out, and wadded several big gauze pads together that she placed over the seeping bullet wound just below his shoulder. She held them in place as Ashley wrapped an Ace bandage around his chest to hold the pads in place.

It hurt like hell, but Osborne brought the detonator receiver over and showed it to him, taking his mind off the pain.

"Radio-controlled," Cameron said. "Where'd you find it?"

"Semtex on one of the control desks. And there's probably more just like it down on the turbine and other equipment."

"Won't do them any good. It's got too short a range. Have to be trigger signal from right here in the generating hall."

"The cell phone repeater is down, how about a signal from a sat phone?"

"Wrong kind of antenna."

"Egan's going to try to get out of here with a few hostages, but he'll use the threat of triggering the charges from somewhere."

"He's probably asked for a jet to pick him and his people up at Dickinson. It'll work, too, if he can get his hands on Whitney or Ashley. But he'll still need a way to reach the detonators."

"He'll use a sat phone signal to a booster antenna right here," Osborne said, and Cameron saw it at once.

"The son of a bitch planted it outside on top of the stack the same time his people were cutting the cell phone repeater."

"Right," Osborne said. "The problem will be getting to it if he has people watching the door you came through. No way we'd make it down the stairs and back to the stack without getting spotted."

"I hope they are keeping a close watch on the door to make sure none of us gets out of here. But we don't have to go that way."

Whitney saw it, too. "The cable run?"

"Exactly," Cameron said, and he got up and with Whitney's help pulled on his shirt and jacket. "It's right here, in the floor." He went to a fine-meshed metal grate about three feet wide that ran like a straight path across the floor and pulled up a four-foot section of it, revealing a trough about two and a half feet deep. Cables, some of them bundled in thick strands, ran along the bottom of the trough.

"Where do they lead?" Osborne asked.

"Some of them across the hall to the repeater room, but others along the entire length of the generating hall to the monitors and controls on all the gear down there."

"And the smokestack?"

"We're connected here with sensors in the stack so we can monitor the composition of the exhaust gases. Depending what it looks like we'll adjust the carbon-eating microbes we'll inject at the base," Whitney said.

Cameron laid his carbine aside, took the Beretta pistol from Whitney, and checked the load before he stuffed it in his belt.

"You're in no condition to go out there," Osborne said.

"And you are with that peg leg of yours?" Cameron countered. "I won't be long. In the meantime you can hold the fort until help arrives."

"I hope it's on the way," Ashley said.

"We heard the choppers, they're close," Cameron said. "Deal?"

Osborne nodded reluctantly.

"Come back," Whitney said. "To me."

Cameron grinned. "Count on it," he said.

He ducked down into the cable run, and crawled toward the north side of the generating hall about one hundred feet away, where the cable run finally exited right next to the smokestack, his head swimming, nausea threatening to incapacitate him.

64

EGAN'S HUMMER WAS backed up to the generating station's south exit, his door open despite the cold as the last of the eight hostages were hustled inside. The helicopters had landed somewhere out beyond the fence, he'd heard that much over the dull whine of the turbine. He couldn't see them in the darkness, but he could feel them out there. Feel eyes on him, Nettles's people watching through infrared detectors and night vision goggles.

Rodriguez came around the corner of the building and hurried over at the same moment General Forester called on the Rapid Response Team's tactical frequency.

"Mr. Egan, do you copy?"

"Yes, I do, General. So good of you to get back to me. Perhaps now we can defuse this situation to everyone's satisfaction and your staff can resume their important work here."

"Work that you and the people who have hired you aim to destroy."

"Those were the old days, General. I'm my own boss now, and I have a new plan that involves making money. Have you been told what we want?"

"A Gulfstream is en route to Dickinson right now, should be touching down in a couple of hours, before dawn I think. And two troop transport helicopters will arrive at your location just prior to that."

"I wanted a Chinook, one chopper to carry us all."

"None at Ellsworth, so you'll have to take what we can send up."

"Fair enough. What about the gold?"

"That'd have to come from the fed in New York. We can get it, but not until ten this morning, after which it would have to be trucked out to LaGuardia for the flight west. Might be sometime this afternoon before you'd have it."

Egan controlled his rage. It was something he should have thought through. Something that Rodriguez, looking at him, should have envisioned.

"We want to be done with this operation sooner than that. What do you propose?"

"I figured as much, therefore I managed to come up with five million in cash, all small bills. It's on a small plane right now heading for Dickinson from Minneapolis. Should arrive within the hour."

"That's acceptable," Egan said. The bills would be traceable, of course, but it didn't matter. The five million would go to however many of Daley's and Rodriguez's men survived, and it was small change compared to the twenty-five million Kast had promised.

"Let me talk to my daughter or to Dr. Lipton," Forester said.

"That's not possible at the moment."

"Listen up real close, you son of a bitch. Unless I talk to them there will be no helicopters, no Gulfstream, no money. You and the fanatics you've surrounded yourself with will come out of Donna Marie in body bags."

"And so will your daughter and Dr. Lipton!" Egan shouted into the mike. "At this moment they've barricaded themselves inside the control room along with Sheriff Osborne and Lieutenant Commander Cameron."

Forester didn't reply.

Egan slammed the mike into the dashboard then catching his breath keyed it again. "We've planted enough Semtex throughout the generating hall—including the control room—to bring this place down ten times over, and kill every living soul anywhere inside the walls."

Still the radio remained silent and Egan could feel his sanity slipping away. But he tried again.

"All of it, every single kilo is wired to a radio-controlled detonator. All I have to do is press the button and your precious daughter will disintegrate before she knows what's happened. How do you like them apples, General?"

The radio was silent and before Egan could key the mike again, Rodriguez reached in the Hummer and took the mike away.

Egan's rage spiked and he clawed the pistol out of the holster strapped to his chest, but Rodriguez didn't step back.

"Listen to me, *comp,* you and I have to get away from this place right now."

"What are you talking about?" Egan screamed, his finger tightening on the Beretta's trigger.

"The booster antenna is down. By the time we saw someone on top of the smokestack it was too late. One of Daley's people took him out, and when we got to where he'd fallen, he was on top of the antenna."

"Fix it. Put it back."

"It's gone. Destroyed."

"Impossible," Egan screamed. "Bring the prick to me!"

"He's dead."

Bright flashes were going off behind Egan's eyes and he was hearing the boom of a distant drum. "The center doesn't hold?" he heard himself ask.

"That's right. Everyone's inside now, except for us. The snipers will be moving into place any minute now."

Still Egan could not fully comprehend what had gone wrong. The plan was perfect. Even Kast himself had approved. Big money on the line. Prestige.

He looked at Rodriguez, really looked at him this time. No fear. Only urgency. A steadiness.

"Do you want to live, or do you want to die here this morning?"

Rodriguez was right, and Egan pulled himself back from the brink. "We can storm the control room from both directions. All we need is one of the women."

"The hostages on the floor would be enough to get us out of here. But even if they let us get to the plane and fly away, we would have failed here because we couldn't destroy the place."

"Twenty-five fucking million dollars."

"Does it mean that much to you?"

Egan nodded. "Yes."

"More than your life?" Rodriguez asked. "Think, *comp*."

"Then we'll kill them," Egan said, holstering his pistol. "what the fuck." He grabbed his carbine and got out of the Hummer.

"No time for that."

"I'll make the time."

They went to the rear of the Hummer and slipped inside the generating hall. The hostages were seated on the floor between the generator and turbine, their hands clasped at the back of their necks. Daley and the rest of his people plus Egan's had taken up defensive positions behind the machinery.

"The Chinook is on its way," Rodriguez told them. "We just have to sit tight until it gets here."

"What about the Gulfstream?" Daley asked.

"It'll be landing in Dickinson within the hour," Egan told them. "And we'll all be in Havana for sundowners on the beach. Five million goes a long way down there."

"Then what, goddamnit?" one of the others demanded. "We'll be stuck there."

"I don't give a flying shit!" Egan shouted. "You want to give it up, lay down your weapons, and walk out the door with your hands up? Well go ahead, but I goddamn well guarantee that the Air Force won't treat you as good as the Cubans will."

"We need to check on the wellhead before the helicopter gets here," Rodriguez said.

"First we're going to take care of some business," Egan said. He was calming down now that he saw what needed to be done. The money would come later, even if he had to put a bullet in Kast's brain.

"Hijo de puta," Rodriguez said.

Egan ignored it. He pointed his carbine at Daley and two of his people. "You're coming with me."

"Where?" Daley demanded.

"Osborne has barricaded himself in the control room with Dr. Lipton and the general's daughter. We're going to smoke them out. All I want is one of the broads, our surefire ticket outta here. Fuck the rest of them."

"About time we get to kick some ass," Daley said.

65

OSBORNE STOOD AT the edge of the shattered plate glass windows that looked down on the floor of the generating hall. Nothing moved, but a few moments ago he'd heard someone shouting something. He'd not been able to make out the words but the tone had been unmistakably angry.

Earlier he and Ashley had shoved one of the desks up against the door, and overturned the other so that they would have a decent firing position. It was a foregone conclusion in his mind that Egan or some of his people would be coming up here to recapture at least Whitney and most likely Ashley, too. The project's chief scientist and the daughter of the ARPA-E general in charge would be their tickets to ride.

But someone had to be coming up from Ellsworth by now. Their only hope was holding out long enough for the Rapid Response Team to get here. But it also depended on Cameron managing to reach the remote booster antenna and disabling it. Because without that, they were all at Egan's mercy. If the fanatic was backed into a corner, Osborne had no doubt the man would push the button without hesitation, bringing the entire place down on their heads.

"She's back," Ashley called from across the room.

Osborne turned as Whitney's head appeared above the level of the floor. Her face was white and tears streamed down her cheeks. She looked devastated and Osborne knew exactly what had happened and what it meant for them.

Ten minutes after Cameron had disappeared down the run, Whitney went after him, and nothing Osborne had tried to tell her did any good.

"He could have run into trouble, got tangled up in the wires," she'd argued in near hysterics.

"Make as little noise as possible," Osborne said. "They won't know it's you and if they hear something they won't hesitate to shoot."

"I know," Whitney had said, and she eased into the trough and crawled away.

Now she was back.

Ashley helped her out of the cable run and they sat on the floor hugging each other.

"He's dead," Whitney said finally. She looked over at Osborne. "I saw his body at the base of the stack, and there was a lot of blood on the snow." She lowered her head and began to cry in great racking sobs.

Osborne had hoped that Egan's people would have been more interested in keeping watch on the control room than the outside of the building. But the booster antenna was one of the main keys to the success of their operation. And at this point there was no telling if Cameron had managed to reach it before he'd been stopped.

Which put them back at square one because with what little they had they wouldn't be able to hold off a sustained assault for much more than one or two minutes. He had the carbine he'd taken from the contractor outside Henry's but less than half a magazine of ammunition, plus the carbine Cameron had brought with him and one full magazine, for a total of less than sixty rounds between the two M4s. Cameron had taken the Beretta with him, which left only Osborne's SIG-Sauer and about twenty-five rounds of ammunition, plus the Ithaca twelve bore and the handful of shells Ashley had gotten from the back of his SUV.

The only way into the control room other than the door was the cable run, which he hoped they hadn't figured out yet, or through the window opening that was fifty feet off the generating floor.

They wouldn't try to get a grenade through the window for fear of killing the women, nor did he think they would get up on the roof and blow their way inside with a half kilo of Semtex; too much could go wrong.

He'd tried to work out all their options, but the one that worried him the most was the one he hadn't thought of. The one a nutcase might come up with.

He caught a movement down on the floor out of the corner of his eye and just managed to duck out of the line of sight when at least two gunmen opened fire, spraying the room, most of the rounds slamming into the ceiling tiles and fluorescent light fixtures, but several of them hitting steel beams and ricocheting back into the room, at least one round slamming into a control panel near where the women were crouched.

Keeping low, Osborne made his way to the overturned desk in the middle of the room, and motioned for Whitney and Ashley to get into the cable run.

"Make your way back to the north side, and I'll put the grate back in place," he told them. "Should buy us a little time."

"And leave you here alone?" Ashley said, shaking her head. "Not a chance."

"Goddamnit, I'm trying to save your lives."

"I know."

"It's me they want," Whitney said. "But this is my facility and I'm staying until the Air Force gets here."

Someone pounded at the door. "Sheriff, we know that you're in there with Dr. Lipton and Ms. Borden!" Egan shouted.

Osborne grabbed Cameron's M4, and checked the load. The magazine was only half full, which left him his, plus the one full one. He switched it to single fire and handed it to Whitney. "Don't fire unless someone makes it through the door," he told her as someone pounded on the door again. "But once you start, don't stop until your weapon runs dry."

"Send the women out and you can walk away from this alive!" Egan shouted.

"I only have six rounds," Ashley said.

"You'll have to conserve them. Fire one the same time as the doc shoots, but then hold off until they get through the door. They probably don't know we have a shotgun, but once they find out they're going to get real cautious."

"Then what?" Ashley asked, and Whitney nodded.

"Keep firing. There can't be that many of them. Someone has to be guarding the other hostages and someone has to be keeping a lookout for Nettles and his people."

"Last chance," Egan shouted.

"Help is on its way!" Whitney said. "Jim talked to Captain Nettles."

"Do they know about the hostages?"

"Yes."

"Fire in the hole!" Egan shouted.

Osborne managed to shove the women down and shield

them with his body when a tremendous bang filled the room, hammering off the walls and ceiling. The metal door and the desk blocking it were ripped to shreds, the pieces flying up and out and bringing down half the ceiling, two pieces of shrapnel slicing into his back and left leg just above his prosthesis.

Whitney was dazed but Ashley squirmed away from Osborne and popped up the same moment he did.

A lot of dust obscured the opening, and for a long beat nothing moved, until someone poked a carbine around the corner and opened fire one-handed, spraying the room, one shot catching Osborne high in the shoulder, shoving him backwards.

Ashley fired once, the Ithaca's twelve-gauge spread completely filling the open doorway with pellets, giving Osborne time to roll right toward the shot-out window, before another M4 was poked around the corner and the shooter fired a short burst before pulling back.

They were professionals, taking their time, and Osborne's heart sank a little. Nettles was probably waiting them out in order not to jeopardize the hostages. And it was exactly the right thing to do.

The muzzle of the M4 came around the corner and Ashley fired off another round at the same moment Whitney popped up and fired four times in rapid succession.

Blood streaming from his wounds, Osborne got up and managed to hobble to the front of the room where he pulled up just to the left of the door opening.

"Fuck it," someone on the other side said, and two men rolled through.

Osborne fired at point-blank range, taking the first man in the base of his head just below his left ear at the same time Ashley and Whitney opened fire, taking the second man in the chest, driving him backwards.

Another shooter poked a carbine around the corner, and Osborne deflected its muzzle upwards with the barrel of his own weapon, a half-dozen shots going wild into the ceiling.

"Down!" he shouted at the women, as he swiveled to the right at the same moment he lowered his aim and emptied the magazine into the corridor.

Ashley had stood her ground, and as Osborne rolled back left, she opened fire with the Ithaca, giving him time to eject the spent magazine, slam home a fresh one, and charge the weapon.

Someone down on the main floor of the generating hall started shooting, and people began shouting, and immediately the shooting escalated into what sounded to Osborne like a pitched battle. Nettles.

"It's over, Mr. Egan. You and your people put your weapons down and show yourselves."

No one answered.

Osborne cocked an ear and he thought he might have heard boots on the metal stairs at the end of the short corridor.

"Cover the door!" he shouted to Ashley, and he turned and hobbled to the blown-out window in time to see two men racing to the north end of the building, both of them dressed in white military camos.

He emptied the magazine in rapid fire, one shot at a time, at the retreating figures, the rounds ricocheting off the tile floor, dangerously close to the feedwater heater, but missing until the two men ducked under the gas feed line from the wellhead where he was sure that he had hit one of them. But then they were gone.

Hobbling back to the doorway he poked his head around the corner for a snap look, but except for a third man down no one was there. He went out and checked for a pulse, but the man was dead, as were the two in the doorway.

The firing on the main floor suddenly stopped, and except for the constant whine of the turbine the power station was quiet.

"Up here!" Osborne shouted.

"Jim Cameron?" someone answered from the foot of the stairs.

"No, Sheriff Osborne. I have Dr. Lipton and Ashley Borden with me."

Two Rapid Response operators came up the stairs, their M4s at the ready, and when they came around the corner they pulled up short.

"Ms. Borden," one of them said. "Put your weapon down, please."

Ashley grinned, and lowered the Ithaca. "About time you guys showed up."

Near Mashhad, Iran
On the Border with Turkmenistan

D. S. WOOD WAS BONE-WEARY, the events of the last twenty-four hours totally unprecedented in his life, and crossing the border into Iran in his company jet, still a couple of hours before dawn, he couldn't begin to think what the next year, month, or even day, was going to bring him.

He wasn't going to end up in prison like Bernie Madoff and some of the other guys whose financial dealings landed them in prison for life. He knew that much. But watching the lights of Mashhad, a city of nearly three million people, rising in the distance to the south, he didn't know if he had done the right thing by transferring nearly two billion dollars out of his Trent Holdings into the Central Bank of Turkey at Ankara.

But Margaret Fischer had telephoned to warn him that the SEC had issued her a subpoena to answer questions about her business dealings with Trent and a recent trip to Havana.

"What do I tell them, D.S.?" she'd asked.

"The truth, that you and I never had business with each

other, and the closest I've ever come to Havana was a fishing trip out of Key West about twenty years ago."

"They may not buy it," she'd said, and he had heard a trace of fear in her voice.

"Maggie, you're a big girl in a man's playground, you figure it out," he had told her and had hung up. Whatever the SEC wanted with her, the bitch deserved it.

But that had been before Kast had telephoned on the encrypted Nokia with news of yet another failure at the Initiative, this time the Venezuelans screaming for blood, and to strongly suggest the meeting in Mashhad.

"If I were in your shoes I would transfer as much of my money out of the U.S. in the next few hours as I possibly could, because the feds will be knocking at your door any minute," Kast had warned.

"Not to Iran."

"No, nor Venezuela. My advisers tell me that Turkey would be a safe bet, since most of your derivative funds are tied up in the Middle East oil fields."

"A contractor giving financial advice to a fund manager?"

"Let's just say that I have a vested interest in keeping you out of jail and your wealth accessible. You owe me seventy-five million and I want to collect it."

"Why Iran? You can't be very welcome there."

"I've closed down operations in South Carolina, and moved everything to Mashhad because I was made an offer that I couldn't refuse."

"What are you talking about?"

"Sanctuary, D.S. You should think about it."

The phone at his elbow chimed and Wood answered, it was Captain Kellogg on the flight deck.

"We've been given clearance to land."

"No questions about invading their airspace?"

"No, sir. They were expecting us," Kellogg said. "But once we set down we're going to be pretty much out of touch with anyone in the West."

"Nothing to worry about, Bob. We're only going to be on the ground for a little while. Shorter than our Havana trip."

Kast had briefly explained that the Iranian government had offered him the chance, including financial support, to build a training base for Venture Plus in the mountains outside of Mashhad. Totally free of U.S. law, he would get help with the recruitment of enough men to form a force of at least battalion and possibly brigade strength who he would personally train for missions anywhere in the world that would never involve shooting at American servicemen.

"Same thing Erik Prince did with Blackwater," Kast said.

"But he set up in Abu Dhabi—not an enemy state," Wood had countered. "And one that's certainly a hell of a lot more stable than Iran."

"I couldn't be a chooser," Kast had said. "Neither can you be."

And Kast was right, of course. After Maggie's call, Wood had begun to feel the walls closing in on him, the cell door slamming shut, his assets frozen.

"We need to talk in person," Kast had said. "You can see the setup for yourself."

"What if I'm taken into custody, as a spy or something?"

"It'd be the first thing the Iranians did that Washington would actually agree with. Solve a big headache for them. So it won't happen."

Wood had always gone by the motto that if something didn't sound or smell right it probably wasn't. But he was stuck.

"Just come and take a look. If you don't like what you see, your jet will be refueled and you can be on your way. Back to Havana, if you want."

But Havana was out, of course, because Cuba was one of Venezuela's strongest allies. Still left a lot of more desirable places than Iran. He figured that with his money he could probably make a case for political asylum in Switzerland or maybe even Monaco or Lichtenstein.

Within a few hours of talking with Kast, Wood had made a two billion USD transfer to a Trent account in the Central Bank of Turkey, where it would be safe in the short term, and had ordered Kellogg to gather the crew and prep the aircraft for an immediate flight to Moscow with a refueling stop in the Azores.

Less than two hours after that they'd been airborne, but not to Moscow, rather to Ankara, then to Ashgabat, the capital of Turkmenistan, where they'd been given permission to turn southeast and enter Iranian airspace for the one hundred and forty mile hop to Mashhad.

Captain Kellogg called again. "I think you should come up to the flight deck, Mr. Wood, there's something you need to see."

"I thought we were about to land."

"We just started our downwind, but I don't think we want to land here."

"Coming," Wood said, his heart in his throat.

Tammy, the flight attendant stood in the galley, her eyes wide, obviously frightened.

Wood stepped onto the flight deck, the airport directly out the left window. "What's wrong?"

"Look to the end of thirty-two left, the main runway," Kellogg said.

Wood looked out the window, but at first he wasn't sure

what he was seeing, except that what looked like a convoy of some sort was parked about a hundred yards or so beyond the end of the runway. "What is it?"

"Three of those mobile units are Russian SA-2 SAMs."

"I don't know what you're talking about."

"Russian surface-to-air missiles," Kellogg said sharply. "Portable units that can be set up anywhere to shoot down an airplane."

It struck Wood all of a sudden what had happened; what a colossal blunder he had made purely out of fear of going to jail when there'd been other more viable options for him. He'd dropped everything on Kast's suggestion and had run like a stupid, panicked woman.

"Get us out of here, Bob," Wood said. "Right now."

"They'll be expecting us to land."

"They won't shoot us down, it'd cause too big an international incident. Turn around and get across the border by the shortest possible route."

"Fifty miles," Kellogg said. "Go back to the cabin and strap in, I'm declaring an emergency." He immediately made a hard right turn out of the downwind leg. "Squawk 7500," he told his copilot, Kelly Bragg. The transponder code was an automatic emergency signal that the aircraft had been hijacked. Every air traffic controller in the world understood it.

Tammy was already strapped in as Wood made it back to his seat in the main cabin and cinched his seat belt.

His seat was on the left side of the airplane, so all he was seeing was the star-filled sky; a foreign sky that made him realize how many regrets he had—how many regrets he should have had.

They made the turn to the north, the 737-700's two engines spooled up to maximum thrust, and for thirty seconds Wood convinced himself that they would make it across the border into Turkmenistan, when Kellogg shouted something from the flight deck.

Wood was about to pick up the phone, when the jet banked sharply to the left as it dove for the ground. Seconds later the plane banked sharply to the right, when something thumped hard into its belly. A huge fireball seemed to rise up from behind the left wing, and a few milliseconds later his world ended.

Badlands Ranch
That Same Day

THE FIRST THING that Egan became fully aware of was pain in his legs and hip, and then warmth. It seemed that he had been cold for a very long time with an angry buzzing in his head and a hard jostling, at times almost impossible to bear.

But slowly waking up now he realized that he was lying in a bed, still mostly dressed except for his boots and camos and trousers, and it was still night. He was in a very small room, no light coming through the window. And listening hard he thought that he was hearing someone talking. But no one replied. So far as he could tell it was a one-sided conversation.

It came to him suddenly that someone in the other room was talking on a radio or cell phone. In Spanish. Rodriguez.

He pushed the covers aside and sat up slowly, the grating pain making him wince. But he'd felt worse. Especially the time his daddy had come home in a drunken haze and beat him practically to a pulp, cutting up his face, breaking his nose, and cracking three or four ribs. It had hurt like hell just to take a shallow breath, and of course he'd not been taken to see any doctor lest his old man be hauled off by the cops. It was a tough old world. Always had been.

Getting to his feet, his head spun off in all directions and he fell down, slamming his shoulder into the floor.

The door opened and Egan managed to raise his head as Rodriguez, dressed now in jeans and a western shirt, came in. There was no light behind him.

"Take it easy, *comp,* or you're going to start bleeding again," he said, and helped Egan up off the floor and sat him down on the edge of the bed.

"Where are we?"

"The Badlands Ranch. But we're getting out of here within the hour."

It was nothing short of amazing to Egan. This was where Toby had killed the rancher and the guests. "No cops?"

"Long gone," Rodriguez said. "How do you feel?"

"Like shit. How the hell did we get here?"

"It was part of the mission plan. We thought it was possible that something would go wrong, and that at least you and I would have to get out of the power plant through a storm water drain at the north side of the main building. It ran all the way beneath the fence, and from there we had to walk nearly two miles to where an ATV was waiting for us. From there it was just a matter of avoiding the Ellsworth team. But they were so busy mopping up inside that they didn't think to check their perimeter. Arrogant bastards."

"Why wasn't I told?"

"No need if we'd taken Dr. Lipton or the general's daughter."

Egan lowered his head, a nearly infinite weariness coming over him. He'd failed once again, and there would be no other chances. No other missions. No payday.

"You were shot in the back and legs. Even so you managed to walk the two miles pretty much on your own."

"How'd you know about the storm drain?"

"My boss briefed me."

Egan really looked at Rodriguez. "How'd the ATV get out there?"

"One of our operators put it in place."

"Operators," Egan mumbled. "What's next?"

"The aircraft will be waiting for us in Rapid City four hours from now, and our transportation should be here in less than an hour."

Egan looked toward the open door. "You were talking to him on a radio?"

"Encrypted satellite phone."

Egan nodded. He'd never really been in charge of this operation. It had been Rodriguez from the start. "Where are you taking me?"

"Cuba."

It was not what Egan expected. "Havana?"

"Too many CIA there. We're taking you to a military hospital in Camagüey, where your injuries will be tended to. It's safer."

"You're not Mexican, you're Cuban military?"

"Actually SEBIN. Venezuelan intelligence."

Egan laughed, not a bray because it would have hurt too much, but a good laugh in any event. "Why bother stitching me up when you're just going to shoot me?" The Beretta he'd carried in a shoulder holster strapped to his chest was gone. Rodriguez had thought of everything.

"We're not done with you, Mr. Egan," Rodriguez said without smiling. "One more mission, a personal one. Think of it as a vendetta."

PART FOUR

CHECKMATE

Thirty Days Later

66

AT 4:00 P.M. sharp the president of the United States walked into the James S. Brady Press Briefing Room in the West Wing of the White House and took his place at the podium. Everyone in the packed auditorium got to their feet, and the president waved them back.

"Good afternoon," he began.

The timing was perfect for the nightly news cycle that began at six eastern, giving the network reporters plenty of time to digest the bulky handout package that would be made available to them after the planned fifteen-minute briefing and file their stories.

That fact was not lost on the press corps, reinforced by the president's press secretary, Tom Albert, who'd walked into the press corps' workroom just down the hall from his office at noon to announce that the president would have something important to say.

"Have anything to do with Venezuela?" CBS asked.

"In a manner of speaking, yes. You'll be getting backgrounders, after the president's remarks, but I'm giving you a heads-up: this is a big one."

"Lead story big?" ABC, who'd wandered in fifteen minutes earlier, asked.

"Bigger," Albert said, and he walked back to the Oval Office where the president was talking to Nick Fenniger.

"What's the early word?" Thompson asked.

"Bob Bradley mentioned Venezuela as you thought he would." Bradley had been given some one-on-one with the president just after lunch, for an update on the situation with the recalled ambassadors.

"What'd you tell him?" Fenniger asked.

"I promised them it would be big, and they'd be getting a comprehensive package. And Diane Sawyer wanted to know if this was lead story stuff. I told her bigger."

"We got their attention," Fenniger said.

"That we did," Albert said, and standing now along the wall with the other staffers he waited for the president's bombshell to come, half wondering if the bulk of the press corps, and even the nation, would immediately grasp the significance of what they were being told.

"Six years ago a group of scientists came to the White House to bring me a warning of something extremely serious that was on our immediate horizon, but one that they felt had a solution," the president said. "It concerned the emissions of carbon dioxide into the atmosphere not only by the United States, but by other industrialized nations, especially by China because of her size and increasing energy needs."

Whatever the press corps had expected, this sort of an Al Gore environmental warning was not it. The science on the global warming issue was still not 100 percent; a number of highly respected scientists, among them astronomers, argued that climate changes, just like on Earth, were taking place on Mars, Jupiter, and Saturn. And it wasn't because of carbon dioxide emissions, but because of fluctuations in the sun's energy output, which had been growing over the past half century. But the overwhelming scientific evidence still put the blame for increased CO_2 emissions at mankind's doorstep.

Many of those same scientists were now arguing that there was an unexpected decrease in sunspot activity that hadn't occurred for four hundred years, which had caused what had been called the Little Ice Age in Europe. So it was very possible that within the next few years temperatures around the Earth—and the entire solar system—would be going down.

Everyone agreed that the situation was a mess. But it wasn't what the president was going to say to them.

"But more than that, their warning concerned our increasing dependence on foreign oil. Except for our navy, the bulk of our military forces run on gasoline or diesel fuel. And the aircraft aboard our eleven carriers depend on fossil fuels. Which could under the right circumstances place us in the untenable position of scaling back operations when we most need to defend ourselves without the launching of nuclear missiles."

The press briefing room was deathly still. Thompson was speaking about the situation with Venezuela, which seemed to be at a breaking point, and the lead question hanging in the air was if the president was hinting at hostilities in our own hemisphere.

"We have enough gas and oil still in the ground in North America to supply all of our needs projected for at least a hundred years out, providing we wean ourselves from gas- and diesel-powered transportation within the next twenty-five years. Sooner if at all possible.

"Ford, Chrysler, and GM have assured me that the goal could be met though it would cost in the tens of billions of dollars with no guarantee that Americans would buy all-electric cars and trucks. And that it would depend on a nationwide network of charging stations. Which brings us to the solution presented to me six years ago."

The president paused, and Albert watched the faces of the people in the room, and he would have taken odds that most of them were holding their breath.

"The production of electricity from a reliable resource that we have in such abundance within the borders of the continental United States that our energy needs projected four centuries into the future could be met cleanly and cheaply.

"Electricity produced in such abundance that the cost per kilowatt would be far less than from any other source including solar, hydro, wind, and especially nuclear, because of the huge investments required to design, build, and then bring them online.

"The answer is coal, but used in a unique way that would require no mining, no hilltop removal, no transportation, no burning, no flue ash to contend with, and especially minimal carbon dioxide emissions into the air, and with, in fact, almost no pollutants whatsoever."

Fantasy. Albert could almost see the word written in the journalists' notebooks, on their lips as they whispered to one another. The president held up his hand for silence.

"It was why six years ago I directed that a top secret effort was to be made to solve the problem of clean coal, which would ultimately win our war on energy dependence from foreign resources, much the same as President Roosevelt directed that an atomic bomb be built to end the war in Europe and in the Pacific. His was the Manhattan District Project, with the lab and test site in New Mexico. Mine is the Dakota Initiative with its laboratory and remote test site in the Badlands of western North Dakota.

"The Second World War effort as well as ours was classified top secret—Roosevelt's because he did not want our enemies to know what we were doing for fear of spurring the efforts of their own nuclear scientists. And the Dakota Initiative because we have been warned repeatedly by members of the OPEC nations that should we make any real and concentrated effort to become a foreign oil independent state there would be consequences. We were warned to make the transition from gasoline-powered cars and trucks to hybrids, and finally to all-electric over the long haul. Fifty years. The financial imbalances, otherwise, would do a great and lasting harm to the entire world.

"I disagreed. And I am happy to announce this afternoon, that the efforts of the Initiative, and in particular of Dr. Whitney Lipton, who has been the lead scientist on the project, have paid off. A crucial, final experiment that took place twenty-four days ago has been a complete success.

"A borehole, using the same techniques as an oil-exploration project, was drilled one thousand feet into the heart of the Billings Vein. A mixture of microbes was injected into the seam, and a device smaller than a compact microwave oven, which was able to speak to those microbes in a language that directs a quorum-sensing mechanism, was also lowered into the seam where it sent out a signal for the tiny creatures to begin eating the coal, the by-product of which was pure methane gas."

Something similar had been tried in Wyoming and elsewhere with the same results: the injected microbes converted coal to methane, but the process could not be sustained, especially for any industrial capacities.

"Similar experiments have taken place elsewhere with poor results. The breakthrough came when Dr. Lipton was able to decipher the quorum-sensing language and work out a way in which to tell a very specific combination of microbes—some seven or eight hundred different types—not only to eat and digest the coal, but to continue to reproduce rather than die off.

"Electricity is being produced, cleanly and cheaply from an abundant resource. I have ordered Dr. Robert Benson, the director of the Office of Science and Technology, to offer this technology to any nation that wants it, starting with China."

The president pointed to Bob Bradley, who got to his feet.

"What effect will this have on our already strained relations with Venezuela? And as a follow-up, how soon will coal mining be shut down and what effect will that have on our already high unemployment?"

"That's actually three questions, Bob. For the first I can't give you a direct answer until I speak with Mr. Chávez on the telephone, something I'll do before the end of the week. And for the mining question, there will definitely be some disruptions, but the new technologies will bring with them new jobs."

Several of the journalists raised their hands, but Thompson went on.

"Understand that this was something that had to be done sooner rather than later, for our survival. Possibly even the survival of the planet, if you believe the half of the environmental scientists who've been warning us about carbon dioxide loads in the atmosphere. Or if you believe the 10 percent who are on the other side of the fence, supplying cheap, abundant electricity can have nothing but a positive effect on our economy in ways that may surprise us all." The president pointed at Diane Sawyer, who got to her feet.

"Thank you, Mr. President," she said. "Will Dr. Lipton be speaking here today?"

"No. She asked to remain in North Dakota to do follow-up work with the data that's been and is currently being collected. But she has agreed to conduct a press conference at the Initiative at noon tomorrow."

Other hands were raised, but the president said thanks and left the room.

Albert took his place at the podium. "There'll be no further follow-up questions at this time, but there are extensive briefing packages, which include the entire six-year history of the Initiative, as well as backgrounders on each of the principal scientists, for you in the workroom next door."

"You're talking about the ELF installation southwest of Dickinson, right?" the AP reporter asked as everyone was getting up and starting for the door.

"We wanted to keep it under wraps, for the reasons the president gave."

"There's been some trouble down there, Tom. Casualties. Anything to do with opposition to the project?"

Albert had half expected that question as well. "There were in fact two incidents, both of them unfortunate, but both nothing more than industrial accidents, which are a part of just about any innovation. There were accidents on the Manhattan District Project, and certainly with the space shuttle program."

"A reliable source in Caracas told us that Chávez had ordered his intelligence agency to do a full court press on us. Care to comment?"

"Nope," Albert said. "For that one you're going to have to talk to President Chávez himself."

67

C OMING THROUGH BELFIELD again and south on 85 toward the turnoff to the Initiative was almost surreal to Osborne, because in the super-bright cloudless morning everything seemed normal. Cars were parked on Donald Street and along Second and Third Avenues Northeast, people were out and about, life went on, but the effects on the town from what had happened here last month would last for a long time.

"I don't even have to ask what you're thinking," Ashley, seated beside him, said. "Gives me the willies, too."

"It's over," Osborne said, though he had to wonder.

"Egan's still out there, and that nutcase is capable of just about anything."

Osborne had hit him with at least one shot, and after the confusion had begun to die down they'd found blood spoor leading to a storm drain. But no body. It was likely that he had somehow made it as far as the Badlands Ranch, and almost certainly with someone's help; SEBIN's help, but from there he'd vanished. "The Bureau will track him down, he's number one on the list."

"Come on, Nate," Ashley said.

Osborne glanced at her. "What?"

"He could be in Caracas by now."

"Then he'd be out of our hair, and in any event he'd never get even close to the Initiative again. There's military all over the place."

"He was uniformed as a one star last time," Ashley said. "Didn't have any problems getting through the gate. Maybe this time he'll come back as a journalist. The doors are going to be wide open starting at noon."

Osborne had thought the same thing, and it was one of the reasons he'd agreed to drive down to the press briefing and tour with her. Whitney had also called after the president's announcement yesterday to ask if he'd be there for the event. And the Initiative was still in his county, his responsibility.

"You and I are the only ones who saw him twice," Ashley said. "We'd be the first to recognize him if he showed up. Provided you don't mind being seen associating with a suspected spy."

Osborne glanced at her again. She was grinning. "Anything yet from your dad?"

"No, apparently the idea came from some bright kid at the Bureau, but that still leaves the problem of who's ratting us to the Venezuelans, and he's pretty sure now that it's someone on his staff."

"That has to be hard for him."

"He told the president that as soon as Donna Marie was up and running, he's retiring for good."

They slowed for the turnoff around ten and after last night's light snow they could see that someone had already come this way. More than one vehicle. "Early birds," Osborne said, and Ashley was uptight again, her lips compressed.

"I just hope that they're on the ball down there. The

first time was practically an all-out bloodbath. Wasn't for you and Jim Cameron it would have been, and so would the others."

"He was a good man, but if he had any fault it was his lack of cynicism. He was too trusting."

They passed the spot where Ashley had been tied to the fence to freeze to death, the wreckage of the helicopter about fifty yards down the hill. Seagram had been another good man, and his wife had taken his death very hard. Osborne had stayed with her through an entire day.

"Such a waste," Ashley said dreamily. "And for what? It wasn't just insanity."

"Money."

"Same thing."

Tens and hundreds of billions, maybe much more, Osborne wanted to suggest. But she was right because entire countries stood to lose the major source of their income. Saudi Arabia would be hard-pressed to find another resource that would come even close to matching their oil revenue. And yet the royal family there, and the ruling elites of just about all the major oil-producing nations had come to realize in the past ten or twenty years that the end was in sight. Oil had become far too precious to waste on transportation. They would have to learn to husband what was left. But it had not even begun to happen yet. And with the explosion of cars in China the pressure on oil reserves would bring the entire structure into its endgame. Exploration, pumping, shipping, and refining were drawing down, and there was nothing anyone could do about it except switch to an all-electric economy. Electricity produced, for the near term at least, by what was left of our fossil fuels—coal—until solar and wind and ocean current generators could become practical on a commercial scale.

They came over a rise at the bottom of which was the Initiative's main gate, open now, a pair of Air Force Hummers flanking it. Two television vans were pulled off to the side of the road, and it looked as if an argument was going between the security team and cameramen. Just inside the gate a tent had been set up, to verify press credentials, Ashley explained. Several of the project's ATVs along with two gray Ford Taurus sedans were parked beside the tent. And as they got closer Osborne recognized Deb Rausch getting out of one of the cars, along with another man plus two from the second car, all of them wearing dark blue parkas, badges on lanyards around their necks.

"Looks like the Bureau has the same idea I do," Ashley said.

But Osborne didn't like it. He'd expected at least a courtesy call from Rausch if she was coming into his county, but after what she considered was a large, career-busting mistake letting Egan fly out of Minneapolis right under her nose, she had become a different person. Tougher, less amiable; a by-the-book SAC.

Osborne powered down his window as they approached the gate and an air policeman motioned for him to stop.

Deb Rausch walked over as Osborne and Ashley got out of the car.

"Morning, Nate," she said stiffly.

"Not surprised to see you here," Osborne said. His stump was aching from sitting too long in the car, and he was a little irascible. "But I thought you might have given me a heads-up if you had something going in my county."

"Actually you're on federal property now," she said.

Ashley came around from the passenger side of Osborne's SUV. "Looking for bad guys?" she asked.

"Found the one I was looking for," Rausch said. "Ms. Borden, I'm placing you under arrest at this time."

"What?" Ashley sputtered.

One of the FBI agents came over, pulled Ashley's hands behind her back, and cuffed her.

"You have the right to remain silent," Rausch said. "Anything you say can and will be used against you in a court of law. You have the right to speak to an attorney, and to have an attorney present during any questioning. If you cannot afford a lawyer, one will be provided for you at government expense."

Osborne was suddenly very cold, but he kept calm. "What is she being charged with?"

Rausch looked at him. "Espionage. And I strongly recommend you stay out of this, Nate."

"That'd be Sheriff Osborne, and the cuffs are not necessary, I'll vouch for her."

"Too late for that."

The television crews had their cameras up and were filming everything.

"Call my dad," Ashley told Osborne. "He'll straighten this crap out."

"It was General Forester who suggested the charge," Rausch said.

68

AFTER THREE NEARLY sleepless nights Forester sat at his desk in the Forrestal Wing of the Department of Energy in downtown Washington, watching a replay on his computer of the arrest of his daughter outside the Initiative's gate about four hours ago.

Gerry Soderbloom had been the first to come down the hall and burst into his office as soon as the news had hit FOX and CBS, a look of deep distress on his square-jawed face. "Turn on the television, it's your daughter," he'd said at the door.

"Who'd she scoop this time?" Forester had asked, hiding a smile. Of the three men he'd suspected as spies, Soderbloom would have been the one to hurt the most. He'd been more than a chief of staff on the Kosovo KFOR NATO operation in the summer of 1999, he'd been a good friend.

"The bureau's arrested her for espionage," Soderbloom had practically shouted. "Fucking unbelievable."

Which left only Vernon Harris, who'd covered his back during their first and only firefight before the hot zone in Kosovo's southeast corner had been totally pacified, and their driver, Master Sergeant Mike Acers, who later got his Ph.D. in nuclear energy systems design at MIT, and had been in the same firefight. A full bird colonel, a major, and a sergeant shoulder to shoulder, sharing the same foxhole.

Forester had come to the painful realization that of the two dozen people on his staff here at the DOE, only those three had total access not only to him personally but to the entire project, and only those three had his unconditional trust. If there was a spy here, and not out in North Dakota, it would have to be one of them.

He'd convinced Edwin Rogers over at the Bureau who'd agreed to set up the sting operation, and who'd offered his sympathy.

"Won't be pleasant for anyone, especially your daughter. Maybe you want to warn her."

Forester had considered doing just that, but in the end he'd decided that her arrest would have to be real enough that it would come as a complete shock to her and to everyone who knew her, except for the real spy, who would have to be relieved and might do something to reveal himself or herself.

"We can't stage-manage the situation," he'd told Rogers. "We're going to have to keep everyone in the dark, including your Minneapolis SAC Deb Rausch who I assume will be making the arrest."

"Any possibility your daughter will try to do something stupid?"

"No. She's smarter than that."

"They'll suspect that you're her source."

"I've already told the president that I would retire once Donna Marie was up and running."

"Soon as she's arrested heat will be coming your way. You'll be brought in for questioning."

"This won't last that long," Forester had told Rogers. "I

think we'll have an answer, if there is one, within an hour or two after her arrest hits the networks."

The Bureau's director was silent for a beat. "Okay, Bob, I'll go along with you for now. But I won't let it drag past the end of the workday. Fair enough?"

"Fair enough," Forester had replied.

Watching the replay of his daughter's arrest made his heart ache. Nate Osborne had been at her side, and he'd telephoned three times and e-mailed twice. Forester had not responded, and he felt sorry for the sheriff who was just trying to straighten out the mess Ashley was in. But if it worked out today, he would do whatever it took to make it up to them.

His secretary buzzed him. It was Rogers from the Bureau.

"We have your man," the director said.

"Are you sure?" Forester asked, not so certain he wanted to know even now.

"He's across the street from you sitting on a bench. He told the agents that he wanted to talk to you before we took him into custody. Said he owed it to you."

"How did you find out?"

"We bugged all your phones, but apparently we missed a satellite phone that was on one of the NSA's watch lists. It was a blind number through a remailer that they thought connected with the chief of SEBIN operations here in the States. When the call came up, it was automatically recorded, and since the caller was on our persons of interest list we were notified."

"I'll go down and talk to him right now."

"I'll order your daughter's immediate release," Rogers said.

"Thanks."

"Do you want to know who it is?"

"I'll find out soon enough, won't I," Forester said, and he hung up.

Out in the corridor he walked down to the elevator and rode it to the ground floor, crossed the lobby and outside stopped until the light changed so that he could cross Independence Avenue, busy at this hour of the day.

A couple of black SUVs with government plates were parked in front of the bus stop, several men in dark windbreakers, FBI stenciled on the back, keeping passersby away, but it wasn't until Forester got across the street and came around the back of the nearest SUV that he could see who it was sitting on the bench, and he almost pulled up short, his breath catching in his throat.

It wasn't Harris or Acers, none of the three and it came as a total surprise. The slightly built man in a sport coat that was a little too big for him, as were most of the clothes he wore to the office had been over the past six years, was Karl Weathers, the Initiative's comptroller. The man who held the purse strings, who controlled the research grants, payrolls, equipment expenditures, every penny that had been spent over the entire six years. And he had been a stickler for details the entire time. If someone needed a spectrum analyzer or electronic microscope or box of number two pencils, he needed a statement of purpose before he released a penny.

"He's the one man on the mission who the GAO is going to love once this is a done deal," Harris had said a couple of years ago. "He's a genius. He knows everything."

Forester nodded to the agents and sat down next to Weathers, who looked up. "You wanted to talk to me?"

"I wanted to apologize, you know. But I needed the money."

"So you sold our secrets to Venezuelan intelligence.

Didn't you understand what that would do to us? Lives were lost."

Weathers seemed genuinely surprised and shocked. "What are you talking about?"

"The attacks out in North Dakota."

"I had nothing to do with that sort of nonsense, General. You know me better than that. I mean, good God, what must you think of me? Heavens!"

"You were spying for the Venezuelan intelligence service."

"No," Weathers protested and Forester could almost believe the man was telling the truth.

"But you used a satellite phone to call them to let them know about my daughter's arrest."

"Not at all. But I'm very sorry about your daughter, I would never have guessed she was behind all of our trouble."

"Then why did you make the call?"

"To my broker," Weathers said. "If we needed something for the lab—say a thirty thousand G mini centrifuge from somebody like Thermo or Drucker—I'd get a couple of quotes for which I would allocate the funds, but then phone my broker who could get me the same devices at less than half the price. Between us we would pocket the difference."

"Money," Forester said.

Weathers lowered his head. "Yes, sir. I'm sorry, but I was in need. It's my wife, you see, she likes the nicer things in life. Things I couldn't afford on my salary." He looked up all of a sudden, pained. "Not that I'm complaining about my salary."

"Then what was today's call about?"

"Dr. Lipton wants a new gas chromatograph. Dynalene's

price was high, so I wanted to get a quote from my broker. In fact it was he who told me about your daughter. I'm so sorry for you."

"What is his name?"

"Alessandro, I don't know his last name."

"A new gas chromatograph," Forester said in wonder.

"You can't imagine how expensive."

69

THE LAST THIRTY days had seemed like a lifetime to Barry Egan. Two lifetimes. But sitting across the kitchen table from Rodriguez, drinking coffee two days after the arrest of the general's daughter, he felt a little fuzzy but overall pretty decent. He had a new assignment. A one-way ticket, but when it was over his name would be one for all the other Posse motherfuckers to live up to.

The money would've been nice, but in the end it was the status. That's what it was all about, had always been important. As a kid he'd been nothing, ditto in the service, and he'd never done jack since—nothing to compare with his daddy's gig down in Texas. Until now. And maybe he'd always understood there'd never be any money for him. For guys like him.

Thing was he'd never understood the kids over in places like Baghdad and Mumbai and Tel Aviv strapping on a ton of bad shit and walking into a crowded sidewalk café or bazaar or climbing on a bus packed with old ladies and pulling the trigger.

Never would be any pain, but he'd never understood the thing until Alessandro had explained it one step at a time.

These kids were just like him, nobodies who were going nowhere and never would in any ordinary sense. So they did the one decent and good thing left open to them, to make a difference, to make people sit up and take notice.

This morning, Rodriguez told him, was D-day, which stood for sobering up. No more of the good shit they'd been doing all month, and Egan felt a little clammy, his mouth so dry it was hard to make any spit. But he was steady.

He held out his right hand and didn't shake. "Steady as a rock, *comp*. Dig?"

"I'm impressed, Barry, I really am," Rodriguez said. "You've come a long way. You're going to do yourself proud."

"Fuckin' A."

Rodriguez finished his coffee and got up.

"Time to rock and roll?" Egan asked.

"Finish your coffee and come on back, I'll have everything ready," Rodriguez said, and he disappeared into the back bedroom of the small Alexandria house they'd shared since North Dakota.

Once in a while if the weather was mild, they would go out into the backyard and sit on the picnic table and share a couple of beers and a smoke. Shoot the shit about nothing much in particular. But those evenings were standouts in Egan's mind, because he'd finally found the sense of camaraderie he'd always wanted but had never achieved. A couple of guys watching each other's back hanging out. It was cool.

He finished his coffee and walked back to the bedroom where Rodriguez was laying out the ten kilos of Semtex, each block wrapped with two layers of duct tape that were imbedded with screws and nails and pieces of beer bottle glass, on a nylon vest with a lot of Velcro attachment points.

"Take off your shirt," Rodriguez said without looking up.

Egan pulled off his big sweatshirt, his skin mostly white except on his back, which was still puckered and red in a couple of spots where he'd been shot from behind. Hadn't been for his *comp* he wouldn't have made it out of the power station. He knew it and Rodriguez knew that he knew it. It could've been another tough old world out there.

Finished wiring the plastic explosive blocks in parallel so that they would all blow at once, Rodriguez helped Egan put it on, and fastened it securely in the front.

"It's heavy," Egan said.

"Twenty-two pounds plus the hardware," Rodriguez said, and he wrapped three turns of duct tape around Egan's chest and middle. "Can you breathe okay? I don't want you fainting on me."

"I'm fine."

Rodriguez helped Egan ease the sweatshirt back on, and ran the thin, flesh-toned wire attached to a Bluetooth headset through the neck hole, and hooked the receiver over Egan's left ear.

"You know how this works. Just before you get in range put your right hand in your pocket, and when it's time push the SEND button. Soon as the signal hits your earpiece the vest will go off."

Egan nodded. The cell phone was in the pocket of his light gray jacket. The weather in Washington had been cool lately, so a man walking up Constitution Avenue in front of the Senate office buildings with his hands in his pockets would attract no attention.

"The general has an eleven o'clock meeting in the Dirksen Building, so you'll have two chances. The first when he arrives and the second when he leaves."

"If I miss the first how will I know about the second?"

"A blond woman wearing a Tammy Hill Junior High School maroon and gold jacket leading a class field trip will come out, cross the street, and walk down Second behind the Supreme Court building. It'll mean the general and probably an aide are coming down the elevator."

"And the kids, too?"

"They'll be out of range before Forester shows up. And I'll be nearby, so that if anything should happen to you I can send the signal," Rodriguez said. "You good to go?"

Egan gave him the thumbs up, even though he was starting to feel a little sick in his stomach.

"Good man."

Egan managed a weak smile. "Could I have a glass of water?"

70

RIDING SHOTGUN IN the front seat of the Cadillac Escalade, Osborne still wasn't sure how he wanted to deal with the situation Ashley's father had put her in. They were in the backseat for the short drive from the DOE to the Dirksen Senate Office Building where they had an eleven o'clock appointment with Texas Senator Daniel Packard.

"He did what he had to do," Ashley told him in Minneapolis six hours after she'd been arrested.

They were gathered in Deb Rausch's office where the FBI director had phoned to explain what was going on, and the necessity of the thing.

"You'll have to keep out of sight for the next few days," Rogers had warned.

"Do you want me to keep her in protective custody for her safety?" Rausch had asked. She had been furious that Osborne had followed them from North Dakota, but she hadn't mentioned it to Rogers, nor had he apparently been surprised by the sheriff's presence.

"From what I understand she's in good hands with Sheriff Osborne."

It was a sentiment wholly shared by her father, who had called a few minutes after Rogers. "Are you okay, sweetheart?" he'd asked.

"Now I am, but it was a bit interesting there for a few hours," Ashley had told him. "Ed Rogers explained everything, and now he wants me to keep out of sight for a couple of days. That include from my newspaper?"

"Especially your paper."

"They know that I was arrested and they'll demand to talk to me."

"The Bureau will stall them. All we need are a couple of days tops."

"To do what?"

"We've already found out who was leaking information about the Initiative from my office, and he's been arrested. Now we're trying to find his contact, who probably works for Venezuelan intelligence. We don't think they're finished yet."

"Is Ashley in danger?" Osborne had asked.

"I'm told that Mr. Egan is still at large," Forester had said. "As unlikely as it might be, he might show up at some point, probably back in Medora where he figures you'll be. And wherever you are might lead him to my daughter."

"They can stay here in Minneapolis," Rausch had suggested.

"I want them here," Forester had said. "If that's agreeable to you, Sheriff."

"I'm not letting her out of my sight until this thing is completely settled," Osborne had said.

In Washington they'd been put up at the Hay-Adams Hotel across from the White House, at government expense, and that first day they'd gone shopping for a change of clothes and some toiletries because they hadn't been able to go home to pack. They'd not called Ashley's newspaper, but Osborne did call his office to say that he would be out of town for a couple of days. And no one had questioned him, because they figured that he was in Minneapolis where Ashley had been taken, and would stay there until the matter was settled.

Nor had they talked to the general until this morning when he'd sent a car to bring them over to the DOE. He wanted to prep them for what was likely to be a lively session with the senator who was the chairman of the Select Committee on Intelligence.

"He was never privy to what the Initiative was really all about," Forester had explained. "In fact he never suspected what was going on under his nose, and it was only an hour before the president made the announcement that Packard and a few other key members of Congress were told."

"What does he want with us?" Ashley had asked.

"If I know him as well as I think I do, he's going to want to hold your feet to the fire. Yours and Nate's. How was it that you two knew so much about the Initiative, while he didn't? He's taking it as a gross insult."

Osborne had bridled a little. "I'm not really a part of this," he'd argued. "And I'm definitely no good at playing politics."

"But you were very much a part of it. Hadn't been for you a lot more people would have lost their lives— including my daughter, and very probably Donna Marie would have been destroyed."

"Just doing my job."

"I can't order you to talk to the senator. You'd be perfectly within your rights to get up and walk out the door. But I'm asking you to help me keep the peace, because a lot more will be coming our way. Things even worse than the drastic cuts OPEC is threatening."

"The president knew what was coming, all of you did. You should have been better prepared."

"You're right, of course. But the Initiative was necessary, because we've become far too dependent on foreign oil, and the situation is getting steadily worse." Forester had looked out the window as they turned up First Street SE, the Library of Congress on the right, the Capitol on the left. "It's about money. In the tens of trillions over the next couple of decades," he had said. "And about displacements—especially in the coal mining and transportation sector. But the irony is that oil, including the futures and hedge fund markets and the derivative positions, will not be all that badly affected. We still need oil for everything from pharmaceuticals, to clothing and plastics, not to mention lubrication, and hopefully only for the short-term bunker fuel for big civilian ships, and kerosene for our jets. But just not for cars and trucks. Those will run on electricity, which Whitney Lipton's work proves we can generate in enough quantities and very soon. All we'll do to the oil people is to slow down their profit-taking, and spread it out for a lot of years. Two centuries plus, and I'm told that's just from known reserves."

Osborne had been all over the world, and the cachet of his Medal of Honor had for a time put him in the media's national spotlight. He understood that what the general was talking about meant nothing short of a major paradigm shift, probably as far reaching as the Industrial Revolution or the dawn of the Information Age. But at heart he was nothing more than a sheriff in a very small rural county. And it's all he wanted, all he'd ever wanted. Home, wife, kids. And Ashley told him that she wanted that same sort of life.

"Boring is pretty good most of the time," she'd said.

"Like the last couple of months?" he'd answered, and they'd laughed.

"We're just at the start-up stage," Forester was saying, and Osborne turned and looked back at him and Ashley.

"I'm going home right after this meeting," he said. "I don't belong here."

"And I'm going back to Bismarck," Ashley said. "I have a ton of catching up, and I'm thinking about a book."

"Tomorrow," Forester said. "Please. We'll have dinner tonight, and we'll put the two of you on a plane by one—two at the latest."

Osborne thought he spotted a vaguely familiar figure across the street as their FBI driver reached Constitution via Maryland Avenue right in front of the Dirksen Building, but a tour bus passed by and what the general *wasn't* saying distracted him.

"Why one more day?" he asked. "What's going to happen between now and then?"

"The president's going to address the nation tomorrow at noon."

"More about the Initiative?"

"In a manner of speaking. He's going to make public who was behind the attacks."

The tour bus had passed, and as their driver pulled up in front of the Senate office, Osborne looked over in time to see Barry Egan across the street at the curb waiting for an oncoming taxi.

"It's Egan!" Osborne shouted as he popped open the door and pulled his weapon. "Call for backup and get them out here now!"

"Nate!" Ashley cried, but as soon as Osborne was out the FBI driver took off, peeling rubber around the corner on Second.

The cab passed and Egan stepped back a pace, looking for a way out, his face screwed up in rage and disbelief that almost immediately faded to something like resignation.

Osborne stepped out into the street. "Just us now," he called out.

Someone came running out of the Dirksen Building. "Put the gun down!" a man shouted.

Osborne pulled out his badge without taking his eyes off Egan and held it up. "I'm a police officer, keep everyone inside, away from the front doors and windows. The FBI is on the way."

Egan stepped off the curb, his right hand in his jacket pocket.

Another cab came up Constitution right at them, but the driver evidently seeing the developing situation, Osborne with a pistol in his hand, turned north on First and sped away.

"Take your hand out of your pocket, but if you draw your weapon I will shoot you," Osborne said.

In the not too far distance they could hear sirens, and Egan took another step closer.

"I will shoot you," Osborne started to say, but everything became suddenly clear.

Egan's jacket was too big for him, the sleeves too long, but it was tight around his torso, the shape wrong. And the look on his face was familiar. Osborne had seen it in Kandahar and Kabul. Young men, sometimes only kids, and even girls as young as ten or twelve, with explosives strapped to their bodies, walking straight up to a checkpoint, or police station, or even a school ready to die for the cause. The looks on their faces were almost as bad as the ten-thousand-yard stare that came into the eyes of combat soldiers bone-weary after a series of fierce battles— resignation.

At that precise moment there was no nearby traffic, nor were there any pedestrians or gawkers within what Osborne figured was a probable blast radius.

He fired two shots, hitting Egan center mass as he rolled left and dove for the pavement, covering his head with his arms.

Before he was fully prone a tremendous explosion shattered the morning, a huge blast of furnace-hot air filled with tiny slivery objects passed just above his body, singeing the backs of his exposed hands, a few needles piercing his shoulders and pinging sharply off the back of his titanium prosthesis.

The sirens were gone, and slowly gathering his senses and rising up on his elbows Osborne realized that he'd lost his hearing. Across the street was a smoking crater the size of a minivan. The cars parked nearest to where Egan had been standing were nothing but burning hulks.

And then hands were on him, gently easing him down, and he had to smile that Egan was finally dead and Ashley was safe. And tomorrow they could go home, and figure out the rest of it together.

Epilogue

ASHLEY, WEARING A pretty print dress, a trench coat over her arm, breezed into Osborne's room at the National Naval Medical Center in Bethesda a few minutes before noon, just as a nurse was finished taking his vital signs. "Is he going to live?"

"Looks like it," the nurse said. "He has a mild concussion, a temporary loss of hearing, and a lot of cuts, bruises, and a dozen small puncture wounds, but nothing terribly serious."

"How do you feel?" Ashley asked him.

"I've felt worse," Osborne said, but he felt battered and stiff, almost like what he imagined it would be like when he got old. But he felt good that Ashley was safe and that the threat from Barry Egan was finally gone. And for the first time since before Christmas he could finally take a deep breath without wondering what was coming at them next.

"Your lunch will be here in about twenty minutes," the nurse said.

"Cancel it," Ashley said. "I'm going to help him get dressed and take him out to lunch. It's the least I can do."

"That'll be up to the doctor."

"Already talked to him," Ashley said, and she shooed the nurse out and closed the door, jamming a chair under the handle.

"I've never seen you in anything but jeans," Osborne said as she turned back, and she blushed a little.

"Don't start on me," she said. "This was my dad's idea and he was right. I just don't know if it's going to work in the Badlands."

"Just fine," Osborne said, smiling. "You look fabulous. And this is also the first time I've ever seen your legs in the light of day."

"You're going to see more than that," she said. She went to the television remote control and muted the sound.

Osborne had turned it to CNN in order to catch the president's talk to the nation at noon. "Thompson's supposed to be on any minute."

"I got a copy of his speech an hour and a half ago, and I've already filed three stories, but I wanted to get over here as soon as I could. We have a plane to catch at two thirty, which doesn't give us much time."

At that moment the president appeared on-screen at the podium in the press briefing room.

Ashley tossed her coat aside, stepped out of her flats, unzipped her dress, and stepped out of it. She was naked underneath.

"He's going to tell the country that we bombed the shit out of six of Venezuela's major air force bases," she said, shoving Osborne's cover off, and undoing his backless hospital gown and dropping it to the floor.

"Pull out my stitches and I'll have to stay another day," he said, and she laughed at him.

"Big, bad marine afraid of lil' old me?" She kissed him

on the lips and caressed an old chest wound, puckered and white now.

"Four of the bases were on the Caribbean side," she said. "Barcelona, some place called Barquisimeto, and two around Caracas, which must have chapped their asses, one was on Lake Maracaibo, and the sixth inland at San Antonio del Tachira."

Despite his wounds and the concussion, Osborne was more than ready, and she carefully got into bed with him.

"Are you going to talk all the time?" he asked, and as she rolled over on top of him, he entered her.

"President called it Operation Balboa," Ashley said, and she drew her breath. "Payback time."

"You're welcome, Ash."

Her eyes were wide. "I love you, marine, and I'll never let you forget it."

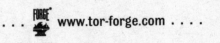